EXTREME
MEASURES

EXTREME MEASURES

MICHAEL PALMER

BANTAM BOOKS
NEW YORK • TORONTO • LONDON • SYDNEY • AUCKLAND

*Grateful acknowledgment is made for permission to reprint lyrics from "Me
and Bobby McGee" by Kris Kristofferson and Fred Foster, copyright © 1969
by Temi Combine, Inc. All rights controlled by Combine Music Corp. and
administered by Emi Blackwood Music Inc. All rights reserved. International
copyright secured. Used by permission.*

ISBN 0-553-07263-3

Published simultaneously in the United States and Canada

*Bantam Books are published by Bantam Books, a division of Bantam
Doubleday Dell Publishing Group, Inc. Its trademark, consisting of the
words "Bantam Books" and the portrayal of a rooster, is Registered in U.S.
Patent and Trademark Office and in other countries. Marca Registrada.
Bantam Books, 666 Fifth Avenue, New York, New York 10103.*

PRINTED IN THE UNITED STATES OF AMERICA

In honor of the fiftieth wedding anniversary
of May and Milton Palmer
of Longmeadow, Massachusetts,

and

In loving memory of
Mr. Fred Jewett of Barefoot Bay, Florida

ACKNOWLEDGMENTS

My deepest gratitude to Eric Radack for the spark, to Donna Prince and Susan Terry for the sounding board, to Dr. Scott Fisher for his expertise and critical reading, to Noelle for her patience, to Beverly Lewis for her editorial grace, to Jane Rotrosen Berkey for being so much more than just an agent, and to Bill W. and Dr. Bob for providing me the tools to get projects done. And a special thanks to Dr. Wade Davis. I hope we meet some day.

M.S.P.
Falmouth, Massachusetts

PROLOGUE

1

The sign, painted in uneven black letters on a two-foot length of weathered barnside, read: CHARITY, UTAH. POP. 381. It was pocked by bullet holes and wedged upside down between two dense juniper bushes.

Marilyn Colson would have missed the sign if she hadn't tripped over a root and fallen heavily onto the hard, dusty desert ground. The discovery distracted her from the newest in a growing array of bruises and scrapes, and kept her—at least momentarily—from another outburst at her husband.

Their four-year marriage was on the ropes even before they blew their vacation on this latest monument to Richard's self-centeredness. Now, as far as she was concerned, it was down for the count. The Jeep he had insisted on renting for their "four-wheel journey to nowhere and everywhere," the Jeep that Richard said he could repair with his eyes closed, had broken down God-only-knew how many miles from nowhere. And of course, the part that had gone was the only one Richard hadn't counted on. Some psychologist! The man could never see any point of view but his own.

Marilyn picked several burrs from her T-shirt. When—if, for Christ's sake—they ever made it back to L.A., she was going to call Mort Gruber and tell him to go ahead with the divorce. And that, she decided as she pushed herself angrily to her feet, was that. She pulled the sign free, blew some of the dust off it, and held it up for her husband to see.

"I give you"—she swung the barnside around in a grand gesture to the barren, rolling, shrub-covered landscape—"Charity, Utah. Home of the largest, most complete Jeep-repair center this side of—"

"Marilyn, can't you lay off just this once? I said I was sorry."

"No, you didn't."

"I did, dammit. That's all I ever do with you. Here, let me see that sign."

He studied it for a moment, then tossed it aside and pulled a frayed, sweat-stained map from his knapsack.

"It's not here," he said.

"Richard, in case you hadn't noticed, it's not *here* either."

"God, you are snide."

"No, Richard. What I am is lost. I'm lost and filthy and hurting and hungry and angry and . . . and cold." She glanced toward the hazy sun sinking into the horizon. "Dammit," she snapped suddenly, "I don't care what it takes. I'm getting the hell out of here. I work hard—as hard as you do. Harder. It's my vacation, too, and I want to eat in a French restaurant and I want to sleep between clean sheets, and take a fucking bath in a tub with a Jacuzzi."

She turned and stalked up the stony slope of one of a chain of modest hills that seemed to stretch to the horizon on either side.

"Marilyn, will you get back down here. I tell you, we're not lost. Give or take a mile, I know exactly where we are. We can camp here tonight, and then keep heading east first thing tomorrow. By noon we'll be on Highway Fifty. You'll see . . . Marilyn?"

The woman stood motionless at the crest of the hill. Then, slowly, she turned back to him.

"Richard," she called out, "maybe you'd better hike on up here. I think I may have just found Charity, Utah."

The town, half a mile or so to the south, was nestled in a valley ringed on all sides by hills. It appeared to consist of an unpaved main street, starting and ending at the desert and crossed by two or three smaller streets. To the east and north, fields of some sort stretched into the desert. The buildings lining the streets glowed eerily in the fading daylight, looking more like a Hollywood set than a functional village.

"Do you suppose it's a ghost town?" Richard asked as they dropped down the slope and into a dry arroyo, out of sight of the low brick and clapboard buildings.

"Could be, but there are people there right now. I swear I saw lights in two of the windows. God, am I going to be pissed if they don't have a place with hot water."

"You are really a princess, Marilyn. Do you know that?"

"And you are . . . well, let's forget what you are. Look, couldn't we call some kind of a truce, at least until we get out of this?"

"Sure, but you're the one who—"

"Richard, please . . ."

They followed the arid streambed for a while and then trudged up a gentle rise that ended, suddenly, in a small, well-planted field of corn—perfect rows of stalks as high as their heads, surrounded by closely strung barbed wire.

"Curiouser and curiouser," Richard mused.

Marilyn had already reached the far end of the field.

"Richard, come on," she called back.

"Where in the hell do they get the water?"

"If you'd hurry up, you could ask them," Marilyn said, gesturing toward the road where, twenty or thirty yards ahead, two men were walking casually away from them. Save for the men, the neatly swept street was deserted. No cars, no bicycles, no other people. "Excuse me," she called out. "Hey, you two up there, excuse me . . ."

The two men glanced back at her and then continued walking.

"Richard, for crying out loud, will you help me out?"

Without waiting for a response, Marilyn started after them. At that moment a bell began chiming through a series of speakers mounted on poles along the street. Almost instantly people began emerging from several of the buildings to plod after the two men. Marilyn stopped short. To her right, a woman stepped onto an open porch from beneath a sign marked simply STORE. She looked to be in her late forties, although her stoop-shouldered posture and unkempt jet hair made that only the roughest guess. She wore a short-sleeved print housedress over a pair of khaki fatigue pants. A patch with the name MARY embroidered in gold was sewn over one breast.

"Excuse me," Marilyn said.

The woman looked at her impassively.

"My name's Marilyn Colson. That's my husband, Richard. We're from Los Angeles, and we were on a camping trip, and . . ." Marilyn, studying the blank expression on the woman's face, stopped in mid-sentence. "Do you understand what I'm saying?"

"I . . . understand . . . you," the woman said.

"And can you help us out? Direct us to a hotel?"

"Hotel. . . ?"

"Yes. A place to stay."

Marilyn waited several seconds for a response, then turned to her husband.

"Dammit, Richard, will you come over here and help me out? There's something wrong with this woman."

"She's an addict," Richard said simply.

"What?"

"An addict. Look at those needle tracks on her arms. She's probably stoned to the gills—either that or totally burnt out."

"What should we do?"

"Well, for starters I think we should be a little less aggressive."

"Go to hell."

"And next, I think we should find someone else to talk to."

"You can start by talking to me," a voice behind them said.

The Colsons whirled. Marilyn gasped. Standing not ten feet from them was a man, tall and lean, wearing jeans, a plaid hunter's jacket, and a baseball cap. Strapped to his waistband was a two-way radio. The double-barreled shotgun cradled on his right arm was aimed at a spot just in front of them.

"You go on in to dinner now, Mary," the man said. "Else you'll get nothin' to eat tonight."

Without even a gesture of acknowledgment, the woman shuffled off.

"My . . . my name's Marilyn Colson," Marilyn said, clearing the fear from her throat. "This is my husband, Richard. We . . . we're lost." She smiled inwardly at her husband's likely discomfiture with the admission. "Our Jeep has broken down about half a day's walk in that direction. We were hoping someone in your town might be able to help us get it towed in and fixed."

"How'd you get here?"

"I just told you, we walked from where our—"

"No, no. I mean *here*." The man gestured to the spot where they were standing.

"We came from the north," Richard said, stepping forward. "Over those hills, then down along an arroyo, and up into your cornfield. I'm amazed at how you can get irriga—"

"What do you want?"

"Want?" Marilyn echoed with a hint of anger. "What about someone to talk to who isn't pointing a gun at us?" The man lowered the shotgun a fraction. "And then we could use a place to stay and some help with our Jeep. Isn't there anybody in this town who does cars?"

"This ain't no town," the man said, spitting through a gap between his front teeth.

"Pardon?"

"I said, this ain't no town." He spat again, then added matter-of-factly, "It's a hospital . . . a mental hospital."

"Richard?"
"Yes."
"Okay if I move my bed next to yours?"
"Sure."
"I'm sorry for the way I talked to you today. I was upset."

Marilyn Colson pushed her metal-frame bed close to Richard's and lay on her side, staring through the window of their bungalow at the infinity of stars spattered across the ebony desert sky. Slowly she slid her hand up her husband's leg and began stroking him the way he liked.

The day, one of the worst in a marriage full of such days, had taken a marked turn for the better. After a tense few minutes with the "mental health worker," as Garrett Pike, the shotgun-toting man, called himself, they had been escorted to a low cinderblock building—the clinic—and turned over to Dr. James Barber, the director of the Charity Project. Barber, a psychiatrist, was a balding, cheery man, with an open smile and manner. And although he had explained little of the project, beyond that it involved the reclamation of an old ghost town and was a federally funded experimental installation for dealing with the criminally insane, he had made them feel welcome. Further, he had promised assistance with their Jeep as soon as his maintenance man returned from a trip to "the city" with the only four-wheel-drive vehicle the project owned. His only requests were that until that time—probably by the following morning—they stay within the confines of the clinic and its fenced-in yard, and that they ask no further questions about the operation.

Now, after a hot shower, a meal of chicken-fried steak and red wine, and an after-dinner conversation in which Barber showed himself to be well-read and thoughtful in a number of areas, they were alone in the guest bungalow, just behind the clinic.

"Richard?"

"Yeah?"

"Don't you think this is sort of romantic? I mean, how many of our friends have ever done it in a mental hospital?"

Richard continued to lie on his back, hands locked behind his head, unresponsive to her touch.

"Something's wrong," he said finally.

"What are you talking about?"

"Just what I said. Something's not right here. Remember after dinner when I mentioned Stack-Sullivan's theory on maturation inversion in traumatized children?"

"Actually, I don't, no."

"Well, I described it completely backwards."

"You what?"

"Merely for the sake of discussion. And Barber just agreed with what I said. He's either an absurdly uninformed psychiatrist, or—"

"Richard, let me get this straight. Here's this man, being incredibly hospitable to us, and you're running a goddam test on him?" She pulled her hand away. "I can't believe you!"

"Yeah," he whispered. "Well, I don't think we should talk about it anymore. For all I know, this cabin is bugged."

"This is crazy, Richard. He probably just wasn't paying much attention to you. God knows I wasn't. You're not exactly riveting when you get going with that psych theory shit of yours."

Richard's response was cut short by a fit of coughing. He sat up on the side of his bed, hands on knees, until it subsided.

"What's the matter?" she asked.

"I don't know. I'm having a little trouble catching my breath. I had asthma as a kid, but nothing for years."

"Maybe there's some mold in here or something. Or maybe it's unexpressed stress."

"I'm going out into the yard for a bit."

"Should we go see the doctor?"

"I tell you, he's no—"

Once again a spasm of coughs cut him off. He pushed to his feet and stepped out of the bungalow into the cool night air.

Marilyn lay alone on her bunk, wondering how she ever could have thought the two of them were the match for a lifetime. *Well, the hell with it,* she decided. She had given it her best shot. Now it was time to move in other directions. Unable to get comfortable, she rolled over, and then rolled back. She bunched the pillow beneath her head. The air felt heavy and stale. Finally she went to the armoire and brought back a second pillow, which she bunched on top of the first.

Better, she thought as she lay back in bed. *Much better*.

One minute passed, then another. She began to feel calmer. Her eyes closed. Her breathing slowed and seemed to come more easily. The last sound she heard before the darkness of sleep drifted over her was her husband's coughing.

It was seven-thirty by her watch when the loudspeaker bell woke Marilyn from shallow, fitful sleep. She had been up for most of the night, in part from Richard's entering and leaving the bungalow several times, in part from his spasmodic racking cough, and in part from her own increasing shortness of breath—better when she sat up, more marked when she lay back.

She was alone in the cottage. Pale morning sun washed through the east window, highlighting a dense, shimmering mist of suspended dust. Marilyn found the mist reassuring. Small wonder they had had such a difficult night. She pushed herself off the bed, aware of a persistent, unsettling tightness in her chest—a band that seemed to prevent her taking in a full, deep breath.

"Richard?"

She called his name, waited a moment, then stepped into the small courtyard. He was seated, facing away from her, in a high-backed wicker chair.

"Richard, you should see all the dust in the air in there. It's no wonder—"

She crossed in front of him and stopped in mid-sentence. Her husband was awake and meeting her gaze, but she had never seen him look worse. His color was an ashen, dusky gray;

his eyes, hollow, flat, and lusterless. His breaths, drawn through cracked, pursed lips, were rapid and shallow. It was as if he had aged decades in just one night.

"I'm sick," he managed to say.

"I can see that. Richard, I'm going to get Dr. Barber."

Before he could reply she hurried off. By the time she had reached the clinic, not fifty feet away, she had to stop and catch her breath.

Barber, wearing a white lab coat over his sport clothes, listened to her account with concern.

"It's almost certainly an allergic reaction," he said. "Last year a congressman who came out to check on the program had a similar reaction. The mold, probably. I'm a psychiatrist, but I have some training in internal medicine as well. I'll have a look at your husband. Some Benadryl, and maybe a little bit of Adrenalin, and he'll be better in no time."

Within a few minutes of receiving the medication Richard did seem better, although Marilyn was not certain whether the improvement was due to Barber's treatment or the news that the mechanic had arrived back with Charity's Land Rover and was confident he could repair their Jeep. At Barber's insistence, she allowed herself to be checked over and dosed with two capsules of Benadryl and a shot of Adrenalin.

Then, after packing their knapsack and taking a supply of Benadryl from Barber, they set off in the Land Rover to retrace the trail to the Jeep indicated by Richard's careful notes and compass readings. The mechanic, a taciturn Native American who gave his name only as John, seemed to know the desert well.

"Nine mile," he said. "That is how far you walked."

"Seemed farther," Richard managed before yielding once again to a salvo of violent coughing.

"Nine mile," John said again.

Marilyn reached over and wiped a bit of pink froth from the corner of her husband's mouth. His complexion had once again begun to darken, and his fingernails were almost violet. Still, he sat forward gamely, following his notes as, one by one, they passed the landmarks he had noted. Watching him, Marilyn sensed a rebirth of the pride and caring that had long ago vanished from her feelings toward the man.

"John, will you direct us to the nearest hospital?" she asked, aware of the band once more tightening around her chest.

"St. Joe," the Indian replied. "Twenty-five, -six mile due east from where your Jeep will be."

"Half a day?"

"Maybe. Maybe more."

Struggling to ignore her own increasing shortness of breath, Marilyn wiped off the sheen of dusty sweat that covered Richard's forehead.

"Richard, maybe we should go back to the clinic."

"No . . . I'm okay," he rasped, coughing between words. "Let's just get . . . the Jeep fixed . . . and get . . . the hell . . . out of . . . here."

Marilyn washed another Benadryl down with a swig from their canteen, and then helped him do the same. Minutes later, in spite of herself, she, too, began to cough.

The nine-mile drive over roadless terrain took most of two hours. The repair of the Jeep took considerably less than one. Richard tried to help, but by the time John had finished, Richard had given up and was slumped in the passenger seat, leaning against the door, bathed in sweat.

"Okay, Mrs.," John said. "Start her up."

The engine turned over at a touch.

"Could you follow us for a ways?" she asked, fighting the sensation in her chest with all her strength.

"Ten, twelve minutes is all. Dr. Barber needs me back. There's a dirt road nine, ten mile due east. Impossible to miss. Turn south on it. Go ten mile more to Highway Fifty. Then right. I hope your husband feel better soon."

Marilyn thanked the man, attempted unsuccessfully to pay him, and then drove off as rapidly as she could manage, trying at once to keep track of the compass, Richard, and ruts in the hard desert floor. Strapped into his seat, Richard had mercifully fallen asleep. After one-half mile by her odometer, John tooted, gave her a thumbs-up sign, and then swung off to the south.

She hadn't driven another half mile when the tightness in her chest intensified. *Relax,* she urged herself. *Don't panic. . . . Don't panic.* An audible gurgling welling up from her chest began to accompany each breath. Fear, unlike any she had ever known, swept away her resolve. She stopped the Jeep.

"Richard, wake up," she gasped. "I can't breathe. I can't—"

She reached over and touched his arm. His hand dropped limply to his side.

"Richard? Richard!"

The name, though she screamed it, was barely audible. She grabbed her husband by the chin and turned his face around to her. It was puffed and gentian; his eyes were open but lifeless. Thick pink froth oozed from the corners of his mouth.

Marilyn undid his seat belt. As she staggered around the Jeep to the passenger door, she felt liquid percolate into her throat. She stumbled and fell heavily to her knees at the moment she pulled open the door. Richard's body toppled from the seat and landed heavily on her, pinning her to the ground. She struggled to push him aside, but her strength was gone. Soon, her will was gone as well. She slipped her arms around him and locked her thumbs in his belt loops.

Directly above her the sun drifted into view and passed across the sky without hurting her eyes or even causing her to blink. Over what seemed minutes, but might have been hours, she felt a strange peacefulness settle in. With that peacefulness came another feeling—a connection to Richard, a sense of closeness to him more intense than any she had ever known. And she was sure, as she felt the weight of him lessen and then vanish, that he was alive. He was alive, and he knew she was there with him.

Marilyn's breathing grew less labored. Inwardly, she smiled.

Outwardly, the sun had set. A chill evening wind rose from

the west, sweeping a film of fine desert sand over the Jeep and
the two inert figures locked in embrace on the ground beside it.

II

EIGHT MONTHS LATER

FEBRUARY 25

It was just after two o'clock in
the morning. Outside of Warehouse 18 the East Boston docks
groaned eerily beneath a crust of frozen snow. Inside, wedged
in the steel rafters thirty feet above the floor, Sandy North made
a delicate adjustment in the focus of his video transmitter and
strained to catch the conversation below. But even if he missed
part of the exchange, it was no big deal. At this distance, the
souped-up Granville pickup he had brought with him to Boston
could record a hiccup.

For nearly three months, under the deepest cover, North
had been working the docks for the Bureau of Alcohol, Tobacco,
and Firearms. He was, in essence, on loan to them through an
agency that specialized in providing such personnel. And although his agency had no official name, it was known to those
in its employ, and those who from time to time required its
services, as Plan B.

North had been sent in to pinpoint the source of a steady
trickle of weapons from Boston to Belfast, in Northern Ireland.
What he had stumbled on instead was drugs—a shipment and
sale of heroin that looked to be as big as any he had encountered
on his several assignments with the Drug Enforcement Agency.
And to boot, from what he could pull from the conversation
below, one of the two men doing the selling was almost certainly
a cop.

Frustrated by his lack of progress on the weapons shipments, and with no time to set up trustworthy backup, North had opted to video the drug sale himself. Of all the filth, all the shit his work for Plan B required him to wade through, drug dealers were the most repugnant to him, and the most rewarding to bring down. At least, he reasoned, if he was pulled off his weapons assignment, the months in Boston wouldn't have been a total loss. On the down side, if something went wrong, if by working on his own like this he blew the weapons operation, his boss at Plan B would have his nuts.

But nothing would go wrong. He had checked the rafters from every angle and had picked a spot that was absolutely hidden from view. He had taken the sort of comprehensive and imaginative precautions that had made him—even among the highly skilled operatives at his agency—something of a legend. Now, all he had to do was keep filming, and wait.

Far below him the deal was essentially complete. The cop and his partner had taken two suitcases of money and left. The buyer, who had arrived in a van with a chemist and three bodyguards, was supervising the transfer of his purchase from shipping containers to the van. He was small and wiry and nattily dressed, and he issued orders to his men with the crispness of one who was used to power.

One of the Gambone brothers, North ventured, trying to recall what he had once memorized about the powerful New England family. Possibly Ricky, the youngest. North shifted his weight a fraction to get a better look at the man, and felt something move beneath his thigh. Instinctively he reached down, but it was too late. A bolt, probably wedged on the beam since the construction of the roof, rolled off the edge and clattered to the cement floor below.

In seconds North was at the intersection of two powerful flashlight beams. Following the shouted orders of one of the men below, he dangled his revolver in two fingers and flipped it down. Then, cursing himself, he inched across the rafter and down the narrow access ladder.

It was going to be one hell of a long night.

*   *   *

Over God-only-knew how many dicey assignments, North had been taken just twice before tonight. One of those times, in Buenos Aires, he had intentionally allowed his own capture in order to free two political prisoners. The other time, in Uganda, he had endured two hours of torture before his backup arrived. Now, he silently vowed to keep the physical punishment he had to absorb to a minimum. He would have to be easy, but not too easy; frightened, but not so much that hurting him would become sport.

One of the goons took his camera, and another punched him viciously in the gut. He dropped to his knees, whimpering. They pulled him up by his jacket and threw him into a chair.

Then, as he responded haltingly to their questions, Sandy North began, one by one, to take the measure of the five men who held him.

". . . Myself. J-just myself. There's no one else. I've been w-working undercover, looking for weapons. . . ."

The chemist—frail, past middle age—*can be discounted.*

". . . It was just an accident. I . . . I stumbled on this. I swear I did. I heard two guys talking and thought I'd see if something was up. There's rewards for this kind of thing, you know. . . ."

Gambone, if in fact that's who he is, clearly likes letting others get dirty. He can be separated from his men in any number of ways.

". . . Look, seriously. I don't want to get hurt for this, and I don't want to die. I work for Tobacco and Firearms. I don't even know anyone with DEA. . . ."

Two of the three goons are young and not all that experienced. One, Mickey, actually crossed too close with his gun drawn. If the moment had been right for a move, Mickey would have been truly astounded at how quickly he and his automatic could be permanently separated.

". . . This here video transmitter's powerful, but not powerful enough to reach a satellite. I've got a receiver hidden out there. That's where the tape is. . . ."

The third goon, Donny, is the real problem. A beast. Six four or five . . . two-fifty . . . careful . . . moves well.

". . . Look, I don't care who you are or who you were dealing with. I . . . I just want to get out of this with my skin. There's got to be some kind of deal we can make. . . ."

It took most of half an hour, and several more almost gratuitous punches to his face and belly, but finally North got the promise of a deal in exchange for turning over the receiver and tape. He knew that the only deal he could realistically hope for was a painless death, but he had precious few cards to play, and what he needed most was to trim down the odds against him.

"Okay . . . okay," he said as Donny wound up for what would have been another backhand across his face. "I'm beat. The receiver's in an empty oil drum. I'll take you there."

Donny looked over at the natty buyer, who nodded.

"Fuck with us and you're dead," Donny said, jerking North to his feet.

"After you get the tape, bring him back here," the buyer ordered. He backed away from the cold as Donny opened the warehouse door.

Satisfied, North led the three bodyguards out into the raw morning.

"This better not be shit," Donny said as they passed first one warehouse, then another, " 'cause I'm getting cold and impatient."

They turned onto a broad, cluttered pier.

"The receiver's in there," North said, pointing to an oil drum, one of fifty or so stacked lengthways in a huge pyramid. The thin wire of an antenna, barely visible, protruded from a hole drilled in the top.

"Open it."

The three men moved back a step as North took a wooden mallet from between two of the drums and gingerly tapped off the cover.

"It's packed in an oilskin sack," he said, reaching inside. "It's in a—"

"Stop right there," Donny ordered. "Now, back away. That's it. You really are stupid if you think I'd let you put your hand on the weapon you have in there. Mickey, get it out."

With the third man's gun still leveled at him, North stepped away. Mickey pocketed his own revolver and reached into the drum. Almost instantly there was a loud metallic snap, followed by hideous screaming. Mickey reeled backward, pawing futilely at the jaws of a huge bear trap embedded to the hilt in his wrist.

The third bodyguard's reaction was only a momentary drift of his revolver, but for North that was enough. He kicked him sharply in the groin, and in virtually the same moment drove the heel of his hand upward into the man's nose. An expulsion of air, the snap of bone, and the man was down, not two feet from where his cohort lay screaming.

Instinctively North spun and dived away from Donny. The maneuver kept the huge man from crushing North's skull with a six-foot length of two-by-four. The blow caught North on the temple. Dazed, he stumbled to his feet just as Donny swung at him again. The board slammed him squarely in the back, dropping him to one knee. In the next instant, the giant was on him, his powerful hands working their way around North's neck, his thumbs gaining purchase against North's windpipe.

Using leverage and every bit of his remaining strength, North rolled the man over and tried clawing at his face. Donny's grip did not weaken. North felt a swirling nausea taking hold. He needed air. Again he rolled. This time his effort sent the two of them toppling over the side of the pier. Donny's death-hold lessened as they fell the twenty feet toward icy Boston Harbor. It broke entirely as, halfway down, they struck a massive support beam jutting out from beneath the pier. The beam hit North just above one ear. A fearsome pain shot through his head, followed by numbing cold as he struck the water.

Then there was only blackness.

—⊹⊹⊹—

"He's lighter, Norma. Look at the way his lids are fluttering. His random eye movements are gone too. Sir, can you hear me?

Squeeze my hand if you can hear me. . . . There, I felt it! He squeezed my hand. Sir, try and open your eyes."

Through an artillery barrage of pain, the muffled voices of two women worked their way into Sandy North's consciousness.

". . . Jean, I'm going to check on some of the other rooms. Just page if you need me."

"Thanks, Norma. You've been a big help. . . . Sir, you're in the hospital. White Memorial Hospital. Squeeze my hand if you understand that. . . . Good. My name is Dr. Goddard. I'm on the neurosurgical service. You've been unconscious, but you're going to be all right. Do you understand that?"

"I . . . I understand," North heard himself mumble.

Colors spun like a psychedelic light show as he opened his eyes and tried to focus on the concerned face looking down at him. One by one, recollections of the mayhem on the East Boston docks began floating back into place.

"That's better. Much better," the doctor said. Her reassuring smile warmed a long, angular face framed by frizzy black hair. "What happened to you?"

North looked at the IV draining into his arm, and the overhead cardiac monitor.

"You tell me," he managed.

"All we know is that someone found you unconscious, soaked, and freezing on some road in East Boston, and called the Rescue Squad. It looks like you fell and hit your head. Or else somebody hit you. It also looks like you spent some time in the water."

"I don't remember."

"That's no surprise. Amnesia's common with concussion. And you've got half a dozen bruises that could have caused one. We've done a CT scan of your head that's negative, and a bunch of other X-rays, also negative. Your temp was only eighty-nine. It's up to just about normal now. What's your name?"

"Trainor. Phillip Trainor," North said without a hitch. The lie came easily, because on other assignments he had been Phillip Trainor; on still others, any of half a dozen meticulously documented aliases. This time he had chosen to be Sandy

North. It would, he decided, be the last time. North seemed to get into more scrapes than the rest.

Subtly, he began to test his extremities. Each muscle, when called on, seemed to respond. Apparently Sandy North had dodged another bullet.

"What time is it?" he asked.

"Almost nine A.M."

"Which day?"

"Tuesday the twenty-fifth of February."

"Good. I've got to leave."

The physician patted his hand. "I'm afraid that isn't possible, Mr. Trainor."

"Why not?"

"Well, for one thing you've already been admitted," she said cheerfully. "You might as well use up one day, at least. Let us keep an eye on you." The page sounded, summoning her to another room. "Look, Mr. Trainor. I've got a man with a fractured neck I have to check on. Do me a favor and just stay put. I'll have someone come in and talk to you."

The moment she had left the room, North grabbed the siderails of the bed and pulled himself up. Just as quickly, he sank back, mortar fire barraging his temples. Seconds later he was trying again.

"Back from the dead. My God, what a recovery."

The woman behind the words, a nurse in her early fifties, entered the room and raised the back of the litter. She was a trim, officious-looking woman with carefully styled silver hair and eyes that spoke of hard times. North thanked her and leaned back against the support. The mortars were beginning to let up.

"My name is Norma Cullinet," the woman said. "I'm the nursing supervisor for this shift."

"Trainor. Phil Trainor."

"Well, welcome back, Mr. Trainor. For a while we thought we might lose you."

"I'm grateful to all of you."

"You had no wallet when you arrived. Were you assaulted? Robbed?"

"I really don't know. It sounds like I might have been. Now, if you'll pardon my abruptness, I have to leave."

"So Dr. Goddard tells me. She doesn't think that's such a good idea."

"I understand. I'll be happy to sign out against medical advice."

The nurse turned off the monitor and removed the electrodes from his chest.

"As a head injury victim, you could be kept here against your will. But neither Dr. Goddard nor I think that's appropriate. I'll tell you what. Let me get some information for our records, and then I'll pull that IV, clean off your scrapes, and you're out of here."

"Deal," North said.

"Fine." Norma Cullinet picked up a clipboard. "Name and date of birth?"

One by one North answered the nurse's questions with whatever lie he felt she would accept most readily.

"Occupation?"

"Import/export."

"Health insurance?"

"Blue Cross. I'll phone the number in as soon as I get home."

"Next of kin?"

"None."

"No one? Brothers? Sisters? Cousins?"

"None that matter."

"Aunts? Uncles? Business associates? Anyone we can call?"

"Mrs. Cullinet, please. You asked; I answered. Now how about keeping your part of the bargain. There are some things I must get out of here and do. Very important things to . . . my business. Believe me, I'll be fine."

"Sorry," the nurse said, heading for the door. "Two minutes. Just give me two minutes and I'll have you out of here. I've got to get you some clothes, anyhow. Yours are soaked."

In two minutes, as promised, Norma Cullinet was back. She gently cleansed the scrapes on his forehead and back, then gave him a set of disposable surgical scrubs.

"Tetanus okay?" she asked as she helped him off the bed.

"Up to date. Mrs. Cullinet, thanks. You've been wonderful."

"It's cold out there."

"I'll call a cab. My apartment's not far from here."

"So you said. . . ."

"Well, thanks again."

"Yes. Well, see you around."

"Pardon?"

"Nothing. Nothing. Just take care of yourself."

The nurse smiled briefly, turned and left.

North's high-cut shoes, warming by a heat register, were almost dry. He glanced around and then pulled up the inner soles and extracted three hundred-dollar bills and a twenty from beneath each shoe. His parka was sodden, but wearable. He slipped it on and then carefully made his way out of the emergency ward through a back entrance. If, as he suspected, a Boston police officer was one of the dealers, no place was safe. He had hidden the video receiver as securely as time would allow, but there was always the chance someone would stumble on it.

It was likely that two of Gambone's men had survived. By now the docks would be crawling with men looking for him or his body. Still, he had to find a way back. The weapons mission—months of planning and work—was blown to hell regardless. He would have to answer for that. But without the tape the sacrifice of his time and usefulness was absolutely futile.

He took a cab to the Salvation Army and bought a set of well-worn work clothes, gloves, an oil-stained overcoat, and a woolen cap. Next he stopped at a package store for a bottle of cheap wine. In a nearby alley he sprinkled some on his coat and placed the bottle conspicuously in his pocket. Some carefully smeared grit, a change in posture to that of a beaten man, and he was ready. The transformation, which he checked in the mirror of a gas-station restroom, was striking. He hadn't shaved in two days as it was, and the hollow fatigue around his eyes was genuine. He hoped no one would take much notice of a derelict wandering about the East Boston docks. At least not until he had his hands on that video.

Unwilling to return to his room, he checked into a seedy hotel to await the night. As he lay down on the musty mattress, he finally began to appreciate the heavy toll the events on the dock had taken on him. His headache was constant, but manageable. His legs were leaden, although that feeling, too, he could cope with. What disturbed him most, and was beginning to frighten him, was a bandlike tightness constricting his chest. He endured several fits of coughing, then sank off into a fitful sleep.

North awoke and fell back to sleep twice before he was finally able to leave the hotel and take a cab to a spot near the docks. The tightness in his chest was constant now, and every breath was an effort. He moved toward the lot where the receiver was hidden, and then he froze. There were men everywhere— two that he saw inside the fence, another across the road, not far from the receiver, and one more just cruising in a car with its headlights off. Biting almost through his lower lip to keep from coughing, North backed away and headed toward East Boston center. He would have to wait for things to cool down; a day, maybe more.

Just over a block away, he stopped and leaned against a lamppost, winded. It was crazy, he thought. During a recent screening at Plan B, he had held his breath for more than two minutes. Now he couldn't seem to get enough air. He forced himself to move on, but again had to stop. This time, without warning, he began to cough. And for several minutes, he could do nothing else.

"You all right, buddy?"

North, who was doubled over, looked up. A derelict, dressed in clothes similar to his own, was looking at him with concern.

"I . . . I'm fine, thanks. A cold. That's all."

"Could I have a hit of that?"

"Huh? Oh, sure. Here."

North handed over his bottle. The man took a long swig, wiped his mouth with the back of his hand, and headed off.

Slowly, North made his way down the street. By the time he reached the downtown area he was doubled over again, coughing mercilessly.

1

FEBRUARY 27

White Memorial, this is MedEvac helicopter. Nurse Specialist Burns speaking. We are en route to your facility from Interstate Four-nine-five with a Priority One motor vehicle accident victim. Male, age forty-four. Driver and only occupant. Multiple injuries. Definite left fractured femur. Definite right fractured forearm. No definite head or neck injuries. Hypotensive at seventy by Doppler, with no major obvious source of bleeding. EKG is sinus tach at one-fifty. Large-bore Ringer's lactate IVs times two have been established and are running wide open. MAST trousers are in place. Repeat, this is Priority One traffic. Our ETA at your helipad is twelve minutes. . . ."

Priority One—immediately life-threatening illness or injury. The words, as always, sent a surge of energy through the White Memorial Hospital emergency room.

Priority One—another chance to validate WMH's reputation as the finest trauma center in Boston, in the state, and according to many, in the world.

Before the radio report was complete, the E.R. team was in action.

Arms folded, Eric Najarian stood alone to one side of the gleaming receiving area, savoring the immense pride and confidence of the technicians, nurses, and residents as they prepared for battle that February morning.

The image of the emergency room as a feudal castle under siege had first arisen in Eric's mind during his second year of residency, and had grown in complexity and color over the two years that followed. The technicians—EKG, respiratory, and laboratory—had become the support troops and intelligence agents, gathering information and transporting arms and other gear to the militia, the nurses. The interns and junior residents were the officers—the lieutenants and captains.

And above them all, watching more than doing—waiting for the moment when the encounter with death hung on a single major decision, on one brilliant tactic—stood the lord of the castle, the trauma team leader.

Over the years of his apprenticeship at White Memorial, Eric had driven himself to the limit with thoughts of the day when he would hold that position. Now, six months into his tenure as one of the two chief residents on the emergency service, he drove himself even harder.

He had grown up in Watertown, not ten miles from the hospital, and was the first in his family even to attend college, let alone graduate school. He had started way at the back of the pack, but after eight years of schooling, every one of them as a full scholarship student, and five more years of the most grueling residency, he was finally beginning to make his mark. And Reed Marshall, the other chief resident, notwithstanding, there were those who now regarded Eric as perhaps the best that White Memorial had ever trained—the best in a hospital that had spawned 150 years of the finest physicians anywhere.

Terri Dillard, the charge nurse on the shift, finished issuing a set of orders to her staff and then spotted Eric.

"We're set for him in Four," she said, crossing to him.

"I told you we'd get one today," he responded, smiling. "I

want the crowd in there kept to a minimum, Terri, okay? Have Dierking get in a CVP line and handle the peritoneal lavage. I don't trust the other two yet, and I don't want to have to worry. June Feldman can meet the chopper and do the intubation if necessary. What did they say the guy's pressure was?"

"Seventy."

"Hmmm."

Eric stroked the moustache he had grown and shaved off half a dozen times in the past three years. He had no particular desire to have one, but there were times when he felt his authority was compromised by his looking years younger than his age, which on that day was a month shy of thirty-one.

"What are you thinking about?" Terri Dillard asked.

"Your eyes," he said absently.

"I wish."

It would be a surprise, she was thinking, if Eric Najarian ever thought about much of anything except medicine. During her nearly ten years as an E.R. nurse, she had seen all manner of residents come and go—flakes and philosophers; insecure jerks who needed to verbally abuse nurses; brilliant thinkers who came unglued at crunch time; soft-spoken young women to whom she would not hesitate to entrust her life. But this man was one of a kind. When he wasn't working killer shifts in the E.R., he was in the library or the lab. If the E.R. was backed up at the end of his shift, he would pitch in and play intern for as many hours as it took to catch up.

As a physician, Reed Marshall was good, very good; but he seldom stepped down from the pedestal of his position—seldom got "dirty." Eric was a barroom brawler. And although Terri knew nurses who had dated Eric, and even slept with him, she knew of none who had been able to compete with medicine as the love in his life.

"Why's he in shock?" Eric muttered, asking the question primarily of himself. "A spleen? A liver?"

"Aortic tear?" Terri ventured.

"Maybe . . ." His voice drifted off. "It's in his chest," he said suddenly.

"How could you know that?"

"I don't *know* it. I just feel it. God, I'd love to know what the steering wheel of that car looked like. . . ."

"The steering wh—?"

"Listen, Terri, I want you to do me a favor. Call Dave Subarsky's lab, extension four-eight-one-one, and see if you can get hold of him. Ask him to come down here right away, and tell him . . . Better still, just get him on the phone. I'll talk to him."

He raced off toward the radio. As Terri picked up the phone, she heard him raise the MedEvac helicopter and ask about the accident—particularly about seat belts and the condition of the steering wheel.

She knew from five years of watching him work, that with a Priority One just minutes away from arrival, Eric Najarian was operating in a zone few trauma specialists ever reached.

Within seconds of the MedEvac chopper's touchdown on the roof of the Richter Building, the battle was underway. June Feldman, the junior resident, began her evaluation on the way to the elevator and had her report ready for Eric by the time she and the rescue team exploded through the emergency room doors.

The prize at stake was the life of a man named Russell Cowley, the president of one of the region's larger high-tech firms. Eric's pulse had speeded up a notch at that news. This man's rescue and subsequent resurrection would be the stuff of front-page headlines.

According to the MedEvac crew, Cowley had been speeding north on the interstate, seat belt in place, when the right front tire of his Mercedes 450SL had blown. The car had careened through a snowbank and then the guardrail, sailed nearly fifty yards over an embankment, and then crashed into the base of a tree. The jaws of life had been needed to extricate him from the wreck. The steering wheel, bent almost in half, had pinned him to his seat.

"Cowley . . . Russell Cowley," one of the residents had

mused as they were awaiting the chopper. "I could swear he's a trustee of this place. In fact, I'm sure of it."

Eric had taken in the information without reaction, but the spark in his eyes grew even more intense. With Craig Worrell's abrupt dismissal and subsequent disappearance, the position of associate director of emergency services had suddenly come open. And everyone from the secretaries on up knew that only he and Reed Marshall were in the running for the job. Now, with the search committee struggling for justification to choose one or the other of them, a trustee had been dropped in his lap.

You don't know it, Mr. Russell Cowley, he was thinking, *but there is no way that you're going to die from this. Absolutely none.*

The corporate executive howled in pain as he was transferred to the hospital gurney. Crystals of windshield glass sparkled in his hair. His face, beneath the smeared blood from several lacerations, was violet. He flailed his good arm and screamed again as a nurse inadvertently jostled his left leg. Gradually he drifted off, moaning softly.

The orthopedic resident set about stabilizing the obvious fractures. Eric did a rapid exam and then stepped back. He had found nothing that argued against his notion that the impact of the steering wheel had bruised the man's heart, causing pericardial tamponade. Blood was collecting between the cardiac muscle and the pericardial membrane that surrounded it. The mounting pressure of that hemorrhage was compromising the filling and pumping power of the heart, and causing progressive shock.

If that was in fact the case, then a pericardiocentesis—drainage of the constricting blood—was in order. The standard procedure involved the insertion of an EKG-guided needle through the upper abdomen, just past the liver, then through the diaphragm, and finally through the pericardium—a tricky, potentially dangerous maneuver.

Eric had other plans. He glanced toward the doorway, wondering what was taking Dave Subarsky so damn long.

"Films first, films first," he said, forcing calm into his voice.

"I need a good lateral of his neck right away. Have them shoot a chest and pelvis as well. June, I don't think he needs a tube yet, but he might. He looks like hell. What's his pressure?"

June Feldman tried to find out with a cuff and Doppler electronic stethoscope, then shook her head.

"As soon as bloods are off to the lab, get an arterial line in him. Then a catheter," Eric ordered.

Feldman set to work cannulating the man's radial artery, while a second resident numbed a spot near his navel and thrust a tube into the abdominal cavity. A flush of saline through the tube showed no evidence of internal bleeding.

Eric nodded. The test had ruled out a ruptured spleen or liver, and had made an aortic tear less likely. The possibility of pericardial tamponade as the cause of Russell Cowley's shock had just increased severalfold.

Terri Dillard rushed into the room.

"How's he doing?" she asked breathlessly.

"No better, no worse," Eric said. "He's tamponading."

"You sure?"

"Not yet, but almost. And if it's true, hold on to your hat. You're going to get to see something no one has ever seen—not even me. That is, providing goddam Subarsky gets down here in time."

"Well, I hope whatever it is happens quickly," Terri said, "because we just got a call on the Batphone. Boston Rescue is on the way in with another Priority One—a man found in an alley in the North End. No pulse, no respiration. They're doing CPR."

"A drift diver?" Eric asked, his concentration still focused on the residents and technicians.

The term referred to the derelicts pulled from snowdrifts throughout the Boston winter. Most of the time they were well beyond salvation.

"I think so," Terri said. "The rescue people refuse to incriminate themselves over the radio, but they did say there was a nearly empty bottle of Thunderbird in the man's coat pocket."

"Is he warm?"

"I have my doubts. Rescue made it sound like they were only working on him because their protocol demands it."

"EKG?"

"Essentially straight-line, with an occasional agonal beat."

"Pupils?"

"Dilated and fixed."

"Lord. Terri, isn't there someone else around to work on him? This is big stuff going on here. This guy's the president of a company, a trustee of this hospital, and he's got treatable injuries. I don't want him shortchanged while I go through the motions with a wino who probably died hours ago."

Terri's eyes narrowed.

"You're the only senior person around," she said coolly. "If you need help, Dr. Kaiser is next door doing walk-ins."

"Well, tell him to take charge of the diver. If this guy needs his pericardium drained, I'm going to do it."

"Eric, come on," she said. "Gary Kaiser's been here a year and a half, and he still gets flustered taking care of strep throats. We all think his father must have endowed a building or something. There's no other explanation for his getting an internship here."

"Well, just tell him it's time to be a goddam doctor. That's what he came here to be. Anyhow, it sounds like this diver's going to be just another DOA. Terri, for chrissakes, don't make that face. Okay, look, I'll be over to help him as soon as— Wait, there's Subarsky. If things go the way I hope, we may be done before the diver arrives."

Dave Subarsky lumbered into the room, hauling a cart laden with complex machinery. Subarsky had a Ph.D. in biochemistry from M.I.T., but at six foot two or three, with a full beard and massive gut, he looked more like a professional wrestler. He and Eric had grown up just a few doors from each other in Watertown. And although they had entered grammar school the same year, by the time Eric graduated from high school, Subarsky was in his third year of college. It was an unexpected perk of Eric's residency appointment to find his old friend doing independent research in one of White Memorial's labs.

"Yo, David," Eric called out. "You have the right dye? Great. Run into your boss at all? No? Perfect. Okay, then, set up right there. We're going to go for it. June, is that arterial line in yet?"

"Right now," she answered. "One more second and . . . *Voila!*"

A low, rapid wave-tracing appeared on the oscilloscope beneath Russell Cowley's EKG pattern. Next to it were the numbers 50 and 0. Systolic and diastolic pressures. Cowley himself had lost consciousness, but his respiration remained steady and reasonably effective. The violet in his face, however, had deepened.

"Call the O.R. and have them mobilize the cardiac surgical team," Eric said. "If this doesn't work, we'll try a needle. But they'd best be ready to open this man's chest. Okay, David, this is it. Everybody listen up. This is Dave Subarsky. He's a biologist from M.I.T., and this is a new kind of laser he's helped develop. We're going to use it to open a window in this man's pericardium and drain the blood out from around his heart and into his chest cavity, where it will simply get absorbed."

"Is it dangerous?" one of the nurses asked.

"Not in David's hands. It was developed for vascular work, but I got the idea to adapt it for pericardiocentesis. I have total confidence in our ability to do this. We—Dave and I—have been doing animal work with it for months, mostly at three or four in the morning."

Dave Subarsky, adjusting the dials on the machine, smiled behind his beard.

As soon as it received FDA approval for general use, the combination X-ray and coaxial, flash-lamp, pumped-dye lasers would, Eric hoped, become known as the Subarsky/Najarian laser.

First, though, the technique had to work.

"I want you all to know," Eric went on, "that this procedure is virtually noninvasive—far safer and more accurate than the needle approach you're all familiar with. In that lower machine, there, we are using a dye specific for the protein in the pericardium. This upper component is an X-ray laser beam that will carry the dye laser beam through the intervening structures, right to the pericardium."

"What should we expect to see?" the same nurse asked.

"Well, for starters, a drop in his CVP, and something a little more effective than a systolic pressure of fifty," Eric replied, barely masking his growing irritation with the woman. "Now, if you'd all just move back a—"

Terri Dillard hurried into the room.

"Eric, the other Priority One is in Six. Gary Kaiser's working on him."

"What's his temp?"

"Ninety-six two."

"EKG?"

"Straight-line with a rare agonal beat."

"Tell Kaiser to pronounce the guy if that's all he's got."

"Yes, but—"

"Is the cardiac team on standby for this man?"

"Eric, we just lost his pressure," June Feldman said. "Do you want me to start CPR?"

To her right, the wave formation on the oscilloscope was a straight line. The systolic and diastolic readouts both showed zero. The heart rate began to slow. Cowley's respiration grew shallow.

"Damn," Eric whispered. "Okay, everyone, this is it. Terri, you'll just have to tell Kaiser to do his best. Then call the cardiac people and get them down here. We may have to open his chest right here. Also, get some blood. They should have him typed by now. Tell them to forget the cross-match on two units and get them over. June, keep a finger on his carotid. Ready, David?"

"Ready."

"Go for it."

Dave Subarsky hit one switch, then another. A faint blue beam shot from the upper laser, followed almost instantly by a red one from the lower. The beams intersected at a spot just above Russell Cowley's lowest left rib, and disappeared into his chest.

For five seconds, ten, there was nothing.

Eric shifted nervously and moved forward with the cardiac needle.

"More power?" he asked.

"I don't think so, Doc," Subarsky replied.

"Jesus. Okay, I'm going in," Eric said. "Someone page the cardiac people. *Stat*."

"Wait!" June Feldman was staring down at her fingertips. "Wait . . . Yes, I've got a pulse. I've got a pulse."

At virtually the same instant, the central venous pressure level began to drop. The arterial pressure monitor kicked in at 70 over 30. Seconds later, it read 90.

Subarsky, cool as snow, nodded as if the whole affair were routine, but two of the nurses began to applaud.

"I've never seen anything like that in my life," one of them exclaimed. "Never."

"Neither have I," Eric muttered, softly enough for no one to hear.

Russell Cowley's coloring improved almost as dramatically as had his blood pressure and CVP. His breathing grew strong and steady. And within two minutes, his eyes fluttered open.

No one spoke. Eric studied the faces around him. Their expressions were a wonderful mix of awe and jubilation. It was the prolonged silence of a concert audience who had just experienced the music of a master.

And Eric relished every bit of it.

Through the open doorway, he saw Terri Dillard approaching.

No, not yet, dammit, his thoughts hollered. *This is my moment. Not yet.*

"Everything okay?" Terri asked.

"Look for yourself."

He motioned toward Cowley.

"Nice going. Eric, the cardiac people are on their way down. You've really got to come in and help Kaiser."

"Lord. Any change in the diver?"

"No."

"So what's to help?"

"Eric, please."

"Okay, okay. June, have the cardiac service admit this guy to them with ortho as consult. I'll be back in a few minutes." He glanced over at Terri. "Maybe sooner."

Gary Kaiser annc yed Eric more than any resident he had ever known. He was immature, indecisive, and nervous as hell in all but the most routine situations.

It was no surprise to see him running a full Code 99 on a derelict who looked as if he had been dead for hours.

"Gary, what gives?" Eric asked.

The scene was subdued, in sharp contrast to the action and energy surrounding Russell Cowley. A nurse was doing CPR while a respiratory therapist was ventilating the man through an endotracheal tube. Nursing supervisor Norma Cullinet was assisting another nurse in keeping notes on the code and administering meds.

Kaiser, a ˋrosy-cheeked enlargement of the Pillsbury Doughboy, glanced down at the EKG machine.

"Nothing," he said.

"Nothing? Do you think this is the result of a coronary?"

"I . . . I imagine so."

The EKG pattern showed a straight line with an ineffectual electrical pulse every ten or fifteen seconds. It was the sort of complex that often persisted for hours after a patient was clinically dead.

"Who is this man?"

Reflexively, Eric motioned the nurse to stop her CPR while he checked the man's groin and neck for pulses. There were none. He motioned her to start up again.

"A John Doe," Kaiser said. "We've been working on him for almost fifteen minutes."

"Why?"

"Why?" Kaiser shifted nervously. "Well, he had those beats on his EKG."

"Those beats mean nothing more than a dead heart."

"And . . . and his temp was only ninety-six. I . . . I thought we should try to warm him up a bit before calling off the code."

As usual, Kaiser was performing mindless, cookbook medicine. It was a maxim in most hypothermic situations to warm the patient before calling off a resuscitation. But ninety-six was hardly hypothermia, and this man was clearly beyond help.

"So," Eric said, "what do you want to do?"

He checked the man's pupils, which were wide and lifeless.

"Do? Well, I . . . I was sort of hoping you'd take over here so I could get back to the walk-ins."

"Kaiser, what branch of medicine are you going into?"

"Well, I . . . I've just been accepted in a dermatology residency for next year."

"Excellent. I think that's a perfect spot for you. You're excused."

"What?"

"I said, leave. Go back to your walk-ins. I'll take over here."

"You sure it's okay?"

"It's more than okay, Gary. It's an order."

His moon face flushed with crimson, Gary Kaiser backed from the room.

"Dermatology," Eric muttered as he turned his attention to the derelict. "Thank God for dermatology."

The man, unshaven and unkempt, smelled of the alleys. He was dressed in soiled long johns, a frayed checked hunting jacket, and tattered pants, all of which had been cut away during his attempted resuscitation. He had a scar on his abdomen—possibly from an old exploratory. There was a tattoo on one hip and a bruise and healing abrasion on his forehead. Eric flashed on the corporation president lying two rooms away, and wondered what the cardiac team was saying about the remarkable save.

"Eric, do you want me to keep pumping?" the nurse asked.

"Huh? Oh, keep at it for a few moments more while I get

oriented. Thanks. You're doing a great job. Did Kaiser give him anything?" Eric asked the second nurse.

"The usual. Epinephrine, atropine. There's an Isuprel drip running now."

"Right by the ol' cookbook."

"Pardon?"

"Nothing. Norma, do we know who this man is?"

"John Doe. That's all we have."

"Well, for my money this is an exercise in futility. Any objections if I call it off, and we all go about trying to save the living? Good."

Eric studied the end-stage cardiac activity for a few more moments. With the most vigorous efforts, and a great deal of luck, they might be able to reestablish some sort of more effective heartbeat. But with no blood pressure and fixed, dilated pupils, what then? The time for battle had passed, probably well before the rescue squad had even arrived. He sighed and then reached up and flipped off the monitor.

"That's it," he said. "Thank you all. Norma, I want to get back in with that other Priority One. Can you take over and call the medical examiner about this guy?"

"No problem," the supervisor said.

"Also see what you can do about finding a next of kin. I'll talk to whoever it is, if you want."

Eric turned and hurried from the room without waiting for a reply. He wanted to be with his save for as long as possible before the cardiac team took the man away.

Norma Cullinet assisted one of the nurses in removing the derelict's IV and endotracheal tube. Then she wheeled the sheet-covered body out of the room.

You needn't worry about a next of kin, Dr. Najarian, she was thinking. *You see, I know for a fact that there isn't any.*

2

APRIL 8

Entering the crosswind leg of its landing sequence, the Delta 727 banked sharply, giving Laura Enders an expansive view of Washington, D.C. She had been there once as a ten-year-old, on the only trip she and Scott had ever taken with their parents, and had returned to their Missouri farm determined to become someone of importance. Now, she pressed her forehead against the Plexiglas window and tried to remember exactly what it was she had wanted to be.

Her flight from Little Cayman Island via Grand Cayman and Miami had been uneventful, but the few days preceding it—the phone calls, the trips to the bank on the main island, the search for someone to replace her at work—had ranged from hectic to frantic. For nearly three years she had been the scuba diving instructor and guide at the Charles Bay Club, the only resort on the tiny Caribbean paradise. It was an experience that had transformed her. But now—at least until she found Scott—it was over.

When she had first arrived at the club as a guest, she was pale, hollow-eyed, emotionally drained, and physically flabby. It took just ten days of vacation there for her to decide not to return for her fifth year of teaching special education at Montgomery High School. Now, at thirty, she was in the best shape of her life—tanned and solid. Her psyche, too, had responded to the peaceful magic of the Caribbean. And in part at Scott's urging, she had sent off a couple of inquiry letters to graduate schools in the States.

But now, all her plans were on hold. After years of nearly weekly postcards and at least once-a-month calls from her brother, more than six weeks had passed without a word from him. She had waited to act, perhaps longer than she should have; she reasoned that his globe-hopping job, setting up communications networks for a company in Virginia, could well have sent him to some inaccessible place. But now that April 3 had come and gone, and Delta had assured her that Scott had not canceled his longstanding reservation for arriving in the Caribbean on that date, there was no way she could remain passive.

Her isolation on Little Cayman had been self-imposed. But a byproduct of that exile, of her commitment to learning who Laura Enders was before allowing herself to choose another career or to fall in love again, was that Scott was all she had.

He was twenty-two and she fourteen, when a kid, high on pills and beer, had jumped a median strip and snuffed out the lives of their parents. Until that day, she and her brother had never formed any real bond or friendship. Nevertheless, Scott had refused the offer of distant cousins to have her move to Kansas City and had instead taken a hardship discharge from the Special Forces and returned home. The next eight years of his life, including Laura's four years at the university, had been focused on her.

An accident . . . a prolonged vacation in some out-of-the-way spot . . . a romance . . . a screw-up in the mails . . . For perhaps the hundredth time Laura ticked through possible explanations for Scott's failure to contact her. None of them eased her foreboding.

It had been more than five months since his last vacation on Little Cayman, and it was on the final afternoon of that visit that they had made arrangements for his April 3 return. Then they had taken the club's small skiff and motored around Southwest Point to dive the sheer coral wall at Bloody Bay. The images from that day were still as clear in Laura's mind as the water in which they dived. It was a double-tank, decompression dive to 120 feet. The day was sparkling and warm, the visibility 200 feet or more. A pair of enormous eagle rays had glided by, near enough to be stroked. Soon after, a dozen or more curious dolphins knifed past and then returned again and again, tumbling and spinning through the crystal sea. It was as close to a perfect dive as Laura ever expected to have.

The next morning Scott had flown back home to D.C. And soon after, his usual weekly postcards began arriving—this time from Boston.

". . . Ladies and gentlemen, the captain has turned on the fasten seat belt sign in preparation for our landing at Dulles International Airport. Please be sure that all carry-on baggage is securely stowed beneath your seat or in an overhead compartment, that your tray tables are locked, and that your seat-backs are in their full upright position. . . ."

The businessman who had spent the first half hour of the flight trying to impress Laura with his attainments smiled over at her from the aisle seat and winked. Laura managed a thin smile and nod in return. During three years of working at a resort, she had been forced to hone her skills at being open and friendly to men without encouraging them in the least. But this day she was far too worried to be cordial.

Despite their frequent contact, she realized now that Scott had shared surprisingly little of his life with her. He knew movies and music, played chess well enough to beat her without paying much attention, and read voraciously in a number of areas. He occasionally spoke of royalty he had dealt with in various countries, but had a self-effacing way about him that warned against being impressed by anything he said or did. He was a whiz with computers—or so he had said. And except for a brief stab at marriage, he had apparently lived a life as solitary as her own.

He had a post office box in D.C. and a phone number that invariably was picked up by an answering service. Laura would not even have known the name of the company he worked for—Communigistics International, someplace in Virginia—had he not mentioned it once in passing.

As the 727 glided over the runway, Laura felt a knot of apprehension tighten in her gut. There was so little for her to go on. Almost certainly she was overreacting. Scott had probably left Boston weeks before, and was now on the Riviera, sipping cappuccino with a beautiful model. Maybe she should just take the return flight to Cayman and wait things out for another month or so. Make some more calls.

But in truth Laura knew there would be no turning back, and no calls. As it was, she had had to beg the operator to search harder for the number of a company called Communigistics, in Virginia, before the woman finally came up with one in the town of Laurel. Laura's call was routed to the person in charge of personnel, who was far less helpful, denying that anyone named Enders had ever worked there. In fact, when Laura pressed matters the woman had actually become rude, and finally as much as hung up on her. Laura had tried a second time, and a third, but her attempts to be connected with someone other than the personnel director were stonewalled. Now, she decided, Communigistics International would find her someone else to talk with, or deal with an all-night sit-in at their offices.

The cab ride to Laurel cost sixty dollars, ten of which was spent trying to find Communigistics. After stopping twice for directions, the cabbie at last turned into an industrial park, drove past several nondescript gray marble buildings, and pulled to a stop before one that was indistinguishable from the others except for the number 300 on a small sign in front. Then he offered to wait.

"I may be a while," Laura said.

"I got a meter."

"Okay," she said. "Here's twenty. If that gets used up, it's okay for you to take off."

A week's budget just for cabfare. Laura could see that some of her perspectives were about to undergo a change. The world beyond Little Cayman clearly viewed money differently than she did.

Even though the woman in the Communigistics personnel office had denied that Scott worked there, Laura felt certain of what he had told her. It seemed strange now, entering Scott's world without his knowing—it was like looking through his closet. She crossed the sterile foyer to the directory of offices. Communigistics was on the fourth floor. She tried to imagine her brother dressed in a suit and tie, carrying a briefcase through the brass-rimmed doors and across to the bank of elevators. The image did not fit with the easygoing, independent man who dived with her on Little Cayman, and who cared so much about natural beauty and the nature of things. It was easier to imagine Scott as a professor someplace, or perhaps a foreign correspondent.

Communigistics International occupied the entire floor. A trim receptionist was typing behind a huge, solid-front desk with the name of the company emblazoned in gold across it.

"I'm looking for my brother," Laura began. "I don't know what department he works in, but his name's Enders. Scott Enders."

The woman checked her directory.

"I'm sorry," she said, "but I don't have anyone listed here by that name."

"And you don't know him?"

"No, I'm afraid I don't."

Laura fished in her purse and brought out a photograph. It was a picture the club manager had taken of Laura and her brother, dressed in wet suits, getting ready to dive the wall at Bloody Bay.

"This is Scott," she said. "It's about five months old."

The woman shrugged and smiled politely.

"How long have you worked here?" Laura asked.

"A year. Longer now."

"And you've never seen this man?"

"I'm sorry."

"This is crazy. I know he works here. He . . . he's on the road a lot. Perhaps—"

She was interrupted by the phone. The receptionist answered it, transferred the call, and then turned back to her.

"Can I help you with anything else?"

"Yes. Can I please see your personnel director? I think her name is Bullock."

"That's right. Anne Bullock. She's gone for the day."

"Well, who's here?"

"Pardon?"

The woman glanced pointedly at the work in her typewriter.

"Look," Laura said, wrestling to maintain her composure, "I want to see whoever is in charge here."

"I'm sorry, that's not—"

"Please. I've come a long way. I'm trying to be polite about all of this, but I will not leave until I've spoken to someone who might know about my brother."

"What seems to be the problem, Alicia?"

Startled, both women turned.

A man, tall and balding, perhaps in his early fifties, stood ten feet away.

"I'm looking for my brother," Laura said quickly. "His name's Scott Enders, and he works here. Only—"

"I tried telling her that no one by that name—"

"Please," Laura cut in. "Please let me finish. This is my brother." She handed over the photograph. "It was taken about six months ago at the club where I work."

"And where's that?" the man said, studying the photo.

"Little Cayman Island in the Caribbean. I'm a diving instructor at a resort there."

"I've always wanted to dive. You must love it."

"I do. Now, about my brother."

"Why don't you come on down to my office, Miss . . ."

"Enders. Same name as my brother. Laura Enders."

"Well, I'm Neil Harten," the man said. "I'm vice-president here." He extended his hand, which was large and warm. "Alicia, this woman's brother did work for us once, but I believe he left before you arrived. However," he added, looking pointedly at Laura, "he called himself Scott Shollander then, not Scott Enders. Now, if you'd like to come down to my office, I'll be happy to tell you what I know of him."

On the way to his office, Neil Harten stopped at the locked personnel office and retrieved the file on the man he had known as Scott Shollander. He poured Laura a cup of coffee, then settled in behind his desk. His office was fairly large, but not opulent. Certificates from a number of chambers of commerce, service organizations, and business bureaus were spotted on the walls, along with framed advertisements for various Communigistics programs and equipment.

Harten, who had a weariness about his eyes and deeply etched furrows across his high brow, answered Laura's queries with practiced patience. Yes, he was certain that Scott Shollander and Scott Enders were the same person. No, he had no idea why Scott would have changed his name. No, Scott hadn't been fired—he was very good at his job. He had simply walked in one day and quit. And no, he had no idea where Scott had gone or for whom he was working.

Laura reached into her purse and handed over a stack of postcards.

"Here," she said. "These are the cards I've received from Scott for the past two and a half years. There are nearly seventy of them from all over the world. He missed a week once in a while, but he's never missed two that I can remember. Now, all of a sudden, I haven't heard from him since February."

Harten flipped through the cards. Most of them contained just a line or two.

" 'Wish you were here' . . . 'Hope you're okay' . . . 'Casablanca is more mysterious now than it ever was in Bogey's day.' Your brother isn't the newsiest writer, is he?"

"There's nothing in any of them about changing jobs."

Harten shrugged. "I don't know what to say. Scott was a very private person, but I guess you know that. I can give you the address we have for him in D.C., and I can ask around. But beyond that?" He held up his hands. "Where are you staying?"

"Staying? Nowhere. I . . . I just flew in and took a cab here."

"I'll be happy to call you another cab and make reservations somewhere."

Laura wandered over to the window. Four stories below, she saw her cabbie reading a paper behind the wheel.

"That's okay. My ride's still here," she said. "But I will take that address."

"Fine. Here it is. Will you be heading back to the Caribbean from D.C.?"

"I'm not going back until I find Scott."

"Well, then, I hope you do."

"I will," Laura said. "I'll stop by this address right now."

"And then?"

"And then Boston, I guess. The last few postcards came from there."

Harten sighed and tapped his fingertips together for a time.

"Here," he said. "This is my home phone. I have business connections all over the country. Feel free to call me if there's anything you feel I can do to help."

"I appreciate that. It's very kind of you. Mr. Harten, I'm going to find him."

Neil Harten studied her face.

"I believe you will," he said.

Laura took the elevator back to the lobby and paused by the directory. Nothing made sense. Nothing at all. *Why would Scott have used a false name? Why didn't he mention leaving Communigistics?*

She thought about the years following the death of their parents—Scott's emotional and financial support during her schooling, the cards and calls, the holidays spent together, the nonjudgmental acceptance of her decisions. Throughout those years her brother had never asked a thing of her. Now he needed her. She felt that with near certainty. He was in some sort of difficulty, and he needed her. She stepped out into the graying afternoon.

"Take me to the city, please. This address," she told the cabbie, handing over the note Harten had printed for her.

"You got it," he said.

They drove out of the industrial park and onto the highway. Moments later, a dark sedan swung around the corner and followed.

3

By the time his bedside alarm
sounded to wake him at 5:45 A.M. Eric Najarian had already
completed twenty minutes of intense calisthenics and was skim-
ming through a medical journal as he wolfed down two glasses
of orange juice and a bagel. It was rare that he ever slept past
five, and he would have reset the clock to an earlier hour had he
ever thought to do so. But invariably his thoughts were otherwise
occupied—usually with medicine.

On this April morning, absorbing a significant percentage
of those thoughts was the selection of the new associate director
of the White Memorial Hospital emergency service. The position
carried with it an associate professorship at the medical school,
and it continued to be, at least according to rumor, a two-man
contest between Reed Marshall and himself.

Now, after months of interviews and speculation, the three-
person search committee was scheduled to meet at four o'clock
to announce its decision. If Eric was chosen, he would become
the youngest faculty member to be tenured in the history of
White Memorial. In over a century and a half, the youngest. For

years he had worked toward rewards and acclaim that such an honor would bring. Finally, before this day was over, he would know.

Engrossed in an article extolling the value of placing portable defibrillators in airplanes and on golf courses, he stumbled over cartons of books as he picked his way down the cluttered hallway to his bedroom. The unpacked boxes, sparse furnishings, and unhung pictures gave the impression that he had moved into the Beacon Hill apartment just that week. In reality it had been well over a year. Initially, his friends had teased him about ignoring the place. With time, they had become more concerned. Eric, however, simply didn't care.

He turned off the alarm and opened Verdi's cage. The macaw hopped out onto the bed, then swaggered over to him for a dog biscuit, which it devoured with the voraciousness of a German shepherd. The bird had been a fixture in Eric's life for nearly three years—since the day it was delivered by the uniformed chauffeur of a man whose son Eric had saved from a potentially fatal gunshot wound. It arrived with no note or instructions—no name, no age, no sex—and spent its first month in Eric's company glaring at him.

Eric initially named the bird Hippocrates after the father of medicine. But that was before it began singing opera. From what Eric could tell, it could do snatches of a dozen or more arias—all Italian. There was no way it could be induced to sing on cue; nor, once it started, was there any nonviolent way to stop it. But sing it did, sometimes for as long as ten minutes at a stretch. And although Eric had never held any great interest in opera, he had listened to enough of it now to tell that Verdi was not very good.

Eric waited until the macaw had headed down the hall before shoving the box of biscuits back under a sweater in his closet. Then he checked his calendar and confirmed that Marshall would be covering the E.R. that day. Eric had decided to pass the hours until the search committee meeting working in the lab with Dave Subarsky. The prospect was bittersweet. From all indications, Subarsky would be closing shop soon.

Over the few months since he and Eric had successfully introduced their pericardial laser, the biochemist's lab, like many others at the hospital, had fallen on hard times. Two government grants he had been counting on—grants that would have been automatic in the past—had been refused. A reordering of priorities coupled with a decrease in available funds was the explanation the NIH and National Science Foundation people kept giving. But everyone in science knew what they really meant.

Finding a cure for AIDS had become politicized, both within the scientific community and without. Pressure on the federal government had been passed on to the big government research installations, which, in turn, had responded with a demand for more authority to direct investigations, and of course for more funding. The reductions in university-centered programs such as Subarsky's had gone from cuts to hatchet jobs. A whole community of scientists were suddenly "outsiders," and for them the situation was desperate.

The professor with whom Dave originally worked had given up basic research altogether and returned to full-time clinical practice. Subarsky had begun searching for jobs in industry. But even using the laser as bait, he had been unable to attract any decent offers.

Today, unless some miracle had intervened over the few days since they had last spoken, Eric knew that he and his friend would begin dismantling and packing their work. Their laser project was, for both of them, a sideline. They had proven its applicability in one rather unusual medical situation. Unfortunately, "sideline" and "unusual medical situation" were not what the current Washington funding sources wanted to hear.

In a month or two, Dave Subarsky, perhaps the brightest man Eric had ever known, would be unemployed.

Eric sat on the edge of his bed and flipped through the classified ads in the back of the *New England Journal of Medicine*. There were a dozen or so from various hospitals for emergency physicians, but none for genius biochemists. If the committee chose Marshall, Eric would have no problem finding a job somewhere—probably a damn good one, too. Such options were a luxury Dave Subarsky did not have. Yet not once had Eric seen even a small crack in the man's quietly positive outlook.

Why, he wondered, couldn't he get his own situation into perspective? Why, for weeks, had there been a persistent knot of anxiety in his chest?

The answer to both questions, Eric knew, was the same. He would admit it to no one, and could barely admit it to himself, but he wanted this position more than he had ever wanted anything in his life: more than acceptance to college or medical school, more than the appointment to White Memorial, more than the chief residency. To his parents and much of the Armenian community in Watertown, his accomplishments and degree already made him something of a hero. But to the university people—the Ivy Leaguers who dominated most of the departments and residency slots—he was still a state school grad, good at what he did but lacking the scope, the sophistication, to make it big in their academic world.

He wandered to the window. The narrow street, three stories below, was deserted. To the north, over the tops of buildings, Cambridge was bathed in the sterile gray light of dawn. Thinking about what this day held in store was at once exciting and frightening. Of all the cities in the world, Boston was still the one most looked to in medicine. And at the epicenter of the Boston medical community was White Memorial.

Is it wrong to want to be acknowledged as the best of the best? Armenians had always been special, had always risen to the top, to positions of influence in their societies. The Turks had known and feared that uniqueness, and over a million Armenians had been massacred on the altar of that fear. Now, seventy years later, the descendants of those victims were again being persecuted, this time by the Soviets. *Is it wrong to dream?*

The phone had rung three times before the sound intruded on Eric's thoughts. He glanced at the clock radio. Six-fifteen. The call could only be trouble. His father had retired from his maintenance job after his second heart attack. His younger brother George, a dropout from high school, had already served two brief jail terms.

"Hello?"

"Please listen, and listen carefully, Dr. Najarian."

The voice, probably a man's, was monotonal and distorted. A vibration machine, Eric thought—the sort held against the neck by a patient whose larynx had been removed. On one level, he felt certain the call was a prank. On another, much more primal level, he found the bizarre, emotionless tone chilling.

"Who is this?"

"We are Caduceus, your brothers and sisters in medicine. We care about the things you care about. We care about you."

"Dammit, who are you?" The chill grew more intense. This was no prank.

"In the days soon to come, we may call on you for help."

"What kind of help?"

"Do as we ask, and the rewards will be great—for you and for the patients you care for so well."

"Rewards? Would you please—"

"Our work is of the utmost importance, and we need you. We can also help you. There is a position in your emergency service. That position can be yours."

For the first time since the phone had rung, Eric felt some lessening of his tension.

"You're full of shit," he said. "The committee has already made its choice. They're announcing it this afternoon."

"When we contact you," the voice went on, as if he had not spoken, "you may be asked to administer a certain treatment to a patient in a manner that is unfamiliar to you. Trust us, do as we ask, speak of this conversation to no one, and you will have what you wish."

"That's nonsense. I told you, the committee has already made its—"

The dial tone cut him short.

The Proctor Building, a thirty-year-old, ten-story monument to the monolithic architecture of the late fifties, held most of the research labs at White Memorial. The biochemistry unit filled the eighth and ninth floors. At one time, laboratory space—especially at WMH—had been at a premium. Now, Eric noted as he wandered off the elevator and down the dimly lit corridor, several of the labs were deserted.

It was nearly nine-thirty. Following the bizarre phone call earlier that morning, he had gone for a prolonged walk along the Charles, over the Massachusetts Avenue Bridge, and then back by the Museum of Science. Part of him still clung to the hope that the eerie call was part of some elaborate spoof. But he knew otherwise.

Caduceus. The staff and twin serpents symbolizing medicine. He had looked up the word, hoping that some aspect of its definition might give him insight. All he had learned was that in mythology, the staff was borne by Hermes, the wing-footed messenger of the gods, patron of travelers and rogues, conductor of the dead to Hades, known for his invention and cunning. How it had come to signify the healing arts, he had not yet learned.

Throughout the walk, just over four miles, he had played and replayed the brief conversation in his mind. It simply made no sense. *Administer a treatment in a manner unfamiliar . . .* What sort of treatment? To what end? How could Caduceus promise him the E.R. appointment when that decision had already been made?

He had entered the hospital through a side entrance and stopped by the speech pathology lab. The speech therapist, a bright, enthusiastic woman, was pleased to demonstrate for him the voice device, known as an artificial electrolarynx. Pressed tightly against a "sweet spot" beneath the jaw, it transmitted impulses from the mouth and worked whether its user had a functioning larynx or not. The voice it produced when Eric tried it was virtually indistinguishable from that made by the therapist. On a whim he had asked her if anyone at the hospital had borrowed such a device or shown a special interest in it. Her response had been a predictable negative.

His size-thirteen sneakers propped on his desk, Dave Subarsky was sipping coffee as he pecked with one finger at his computer keyboard.

"Greetings, Doctor," Eric said. "I've been sent here by the Nobel Prize Committee to check on what you're up to."

"I've been expecting you," Subarsky said, hitting the return key. "Convey my thanks to your committee, and tell them that I—and my trusty IBM here—are on the verge of proving, beyond a shadow of a doubt, that someone with no income, eighteen hundred dollars in monthly expenses, and three thousand dollars in the bank, cannot stay out of the poorhouse for more than two months."

"That bad, huh?"

"It's starting to look that way."

"Something will turn up."

"Maybe. But it ain't gonna be a grant from the Sackett Foundation."

"You heard?"

"Uh-huh. This morning. The cupboard is bare. I tried telling them that a mind was a terrible thing to waste, but they didn't buy it. They said my work was too theoretical."

"They're nuts. That stuff you've been doing with progressive DNA mutation has tremendous clinical potential."

"Maybe," Dave said, his voice drifting off. "Maybe so."

"You'll find a way."

Subarsky flipped off his computer.

"That I will, my friend," he said. "So, today's the big day, yes?"

Eric shrugged.

"I think so."

"I thought the committee was meeting this afternoon."

"As far as I know, they are, but . . . David, there's something I want to tell you about, but it's got to stay between us."

"No problem."

Eric hesitated, then recounted the eerie call.

"Does any of that mean anything to you?" he asked.

"Aside from suggesting that there's someone running around White Memorial with a screw loose?"

"David, I tell you, the guy who called may be crazy, but he—or she; I really couldn't tell—sounded like he knew exactly what he was doing. Any thoughts at all?"

Subarsky drummed his fingers on his ample gut.

"Only one. That stunt we pulled with the laser hardly went unnoticed."

"Tell me about it. Joe Silver was thinking about reporting us to the Human Experimentation Committee."

"Why didn't he?"

"Well, for one thing, we saved the guy's life."

"Minor detail."

"And for another, I convinced my esteemed boss that the only danger of the procedure was that it might not work, and that my hand was poised with a cardiac needle, ready to drive it home, if that was the case. He made it clear, though, that if we ever felt the urge to try out our toy again, we had better have an okay from the committee and a release from the patient."

"As if that dude was capable of signing a release."

"What's the point you're driving at?" Eric asked.

"The point is that the whole goddam hospital knows what we did. This Caduceus may see you as someone who might be willing to bend the rules a bit in the interest of getting some stuff done around here; something that hasn't been approved by the H.E. Committee. Isn't that what it sounded like?"

"Sort of. But that damn electrolarynx sure gave the whole thing a sinister cast."

"Regardless, we should know whether or not the guy is for real in a few hours."

"What do you mean?"

"Well," he said, "if Marshall gets that job in the E.R., I think you can safely say that Caduceus is a bag of shit."

"What if I get it?"

Subarsky lowered his skateboard-sized feet to the floor.

"In that case, my friend," he said, "I guess you won't really know."

4

The administrative wing of White Memorial, located on the ground floor of the Drexel Building, was designed to impress. Crystal chandeliers overhung Oriental carpeting, and cracked, ornately framed oil portraits lined the walls. Guarding the entry to the corridor, a busty, broad-shouldered receptionist coolly appraised Eric from behind a Louis XIV desk.

"I'm Dr. Najarian," he said. "I'm here for a committee meeting."

After spending several hours with Subarsky, he had returned to his apartment and changed—first into the dark suit he had last worn at his med school graduation, and which he ultimately decided was woefully outdated; next into brown slacks and a tweed sport coat that turned out to have a two-inch tear along one shoulder seam; and finally into gray trousers and his navy-blue blazer. It was fortunate, he acknowledged, that he wasn't any *more* nervous about the meeting, because the search for the right attire had spanned his entire wardrobe. Still, the receptionist seemed to approve of the result.

"Dr. Teagarden's committee?" she asked, smiling and pushing her shoulders back just a bit.

"That's right."

"Well, they're just getting started. She asked me to have you candidates wait down there in the sitting room."

"Um . . . exactly how many of *us candidates* are there?"

"Oh, just two. Dr. Marshall's already there."

"Good."

"He's been here for half an hour."

"Bad."

"Pardon?"

"Nothing. Listen, thanks. Thanks a lot."

"No problem. If you need anything, my name's Susan."

Eric thanked her again and headed down the corridor.

"Anything at all," he heard her say.

"So," Eric said as he entered the plush sitting area, *"you're* the other candidate the receptionist was talking about. What a surprise."

"Just a second," Marshall said, engrossed in a book, which Eric managed to see was something by John Updike. "I just want to finish this page. Updike's some talent, don't you think?"

"I haven't read him." In fact, Eric reflected somewhat wistfully, he hadn't read anything outside of medicine in longer than he could remember.

"Well, then," Marshall said with genuine enthusiasm, "you've got a real treat in store."

With his tortoiseshell glasses and aquiline features, Reed Marshall resembled Clark Kent, and in fact was called that in some quarters of the E.R. Eric settled into a high-backed oxblood leather chair and watched as Marshall finished. The two of them had known each other since internship, and had shared many of the victories and much of the heartache that went with becoming a physician. Two years older than Eric, Reed had a wife, a son, a circle of successful friends, and virtually universal respect around the hospital.

Initially, Eric had been put off by Marshall's patrician roots and Harvard education, and by an aloofness that Eric interpreted as snobbishness. But one night, as they sat sipping coffee after working side by side on the casualties of a multivehicle catastrophe, Reed confessed that he was envious of Eric's coolness under fire.

"That's crazy," Eric had replied. "You're the iceman. Everyone in the E.R. knows it."

"What I am," Reed said, with deadly seriousness, "is scared to death of freezing up or of doing the wrong thing, and even more terrified of having anyone know how I'm feeling. In fact, I can't believe I'm telling you this."

"Hey, don't worry. Nothing you say will ever leave this room. You're just exhausted right now, that's all. Believe me. I'm frightened at crunch time too. How could anyone who's human not be?"

"I didn't say frightened; I said terrified. I want to laugh when someone says I'm as good at this as you are."

"Listen, Reed," Eric had said, "this isn't a contest. We didn't select ourselves for this residency—all those professors did. Our job is just to do our best. And believe me, *your* best is damn good."

Beginning with that night, a mutual respect, almost a tacit friendship had grown between them. And over the years that followed, not once had either of them mentioned the exchange again. As far as Eric knew, Reed had come to grips with his dragons. Eric believed that in terms of knowledge, dedication, and rapid response to life-threatening emergencies, he held a definite edge on Marshall. But there were other intangibles—Marshall's dry wit, poise, and eclectic intellect—that made any choice between the two of them difficult.

"Any idea why they sent for the two of us at once?" Eric asked after Reed had set his book aside.

"Nope. All I've heard is that they've made their decision. Knowing ol' Grendel Teagarden, we'll probably learn that some hard-nosed woman from Stanford has been recruited for the position, and you and I are gonna be out of work."

Sara Teagarden, the tyrannical chief of surgery, was as renowned for her outspoken feminism and undisguised partiality toward female physicians as she was for her skill in the O.R. Her volatile capriciousness had made or broken any number of careers.

"Are you sure you want this job?" Eric asked.

Marshall grinned.

"I'm sure Carolyn wants me to want it. You're not married, so you don't know that that's quite enough." He laughed somewhat wistfully. "Oh, I want it, too, Eric," he said finally. "It'd be foolish to say I don't, although even *I* can't say how much. Put another way, my ulcer may be rooting for you, but my ego is pulling for me. Still, I see the whole question as moot because I have no doubt I didn't get it."

"Nonsense."

"This from the man who not only is a legend at his work, but who just happens to have saved a trustee's life."

"He never even sent me a thank-you note."

"Jesus. Well, that's no surprise, given the holier-than-thou philosophy of this place. Speaking of which, before we get called in there, I want to thank you for doing your best not to make a big deal out of all this."

It was Eric's turn to smile.

"You mean not openly," he said.

"Of course. The whole damn committee has been doing its best to set us at each other's throats, privately and in public."

"The famous WMH pyramid."

"Exactly. Room for one and only one at the top. Survival of the nastiest. We both deserve a pat for not taking their bait. I know how much you want the position, and the real truth is, if it didn't mean so much to Carolyn to stay around here, I might have actually considered pulling out of the running."

"You don't have to say that."

"It's true . . . . Well, at least, it *might* be true."

"I wonder what in the hell they're doing in there," Eric said.

"Two-on-one with Grendel?"

"God, what a prospect! If so, my money's on Teagarden. Say, listen, does the name *Caduceus* mean anything to you?"

"Aside from the obvious?"

"Aside from the obvious."

Reed Marshall shrugged and shook his head. "No bells," he said. "Why?"

"Nothing. Maybe later we can—"

The door to the conference room opened and Dr. Joe Silver stepped out. A ferretlike man in his late forties, Silver stood no more than five foot five in the two-inch lifts that, rumor had it, he wore even to bed. He had been the chief of emergency services for five or six years, and ran his office in an autocratic manner that would have made Napoleon proud. He was knowledgeable enough, but he had no sense of people's needs or how to deal with them straightforwardly. And over their years of association with the man, neither Eric nor Reed Marshall had been able to develop anything approaching a warm relationship with him.

"Gentlemen," Silver said, "we apologize for keeping you waiting. If you'll both come in please. . . ."

Both? Eric wondered why the committee would do something so insensitive. Surely, after three months, and interview upon interview, it would have been more appropriate to speak with the losing candidate alone. He thought back to the eerie call. The caller, whoever he—or she—was, seemed so confident of being able to affect the selection process. *Was Joe Silver Caduceus*? It was so like the man to play control games with people.

The committee was seated at a massive hardwood table, with Sara Teagarden at the head. She was a large, androgynous woman with close-cropped auburn hair and gold-rimmed granny glasses. That day she was dressed in a royal-blue suit with a large pearl-and-diamond brooch on the lapel. It was an outfit that somehow made her appear even more intimidating than usual. As she welcomed them Eric tried unsuccessfully to match the cadence of her voice with that of the caller.

Joining the heads of surgery and emergency medicine on

the search committee was Dr. Haven Darden, the chief of medicine. The highly publicized demise of Craig Worrell, the former associate director of emergency services, had bathed White Memorial in an intensely unfavorable light, and the high-powered makeup of the search committee underscored the hospital's determination to put the whole matter to rest. Silver, Teagarden, Darden—Eric had not faced a panel such as this one since his internship application days. He wondered if the triumvirate was about to take the WMH pyramid philosophy to the limit by grilling the two of them in a medical quiz-down.

As if reading Eric's mind, Haven Darden said, "Now don't get worried, you two. We're not about to start firing clinical problems at you."

Of the three committee members, Darden, a tropical medi-cine specialist, was the one Eric felt was least in his corner. Like Reed Marshall, he had come straight up through the Harvard system. Unlike Marshall, though, he had risen from abject poverty. His life, from his illegimate birth in a ghetto in Port-au-Prince, Haiti, through his escape to the United States and his subsequent adoption by a wealthy black physician, had been chronicled in various Harvard publications. There was a rumor that somewhere not far down the line, Darden was slated to become the first black dean in the history of the university. His detractors, and there were a number, pointed to his inability to make any major research contributions to his field. But his reputation for clinical brilliance kept all but the most vociferous enemies at bay, and residents often jockeyed their schedules to be on the wards when Darden visited.

Darden's English was clipped and precise, with just the hint of an accent. And unless he could change his speech radically, Eric decided, there was no way he could have been the caller. He struggled to force thoughts of Caduceus from his mind and to concentrate on the business at hand. In a minute or two the committee's decision would be known, and the whole bizarre affair would most likely be exposed as a hoax.

"Gentlemen," Sara Teagarden began, "we don't wish to drag this business out any more than you do. However, I am sure you know that we are trying to recoup some pretty heavy losses in the public's confidence in our hospital, and in particular in our emergency service. I would like Dr. Silver to explain how and why we have arrived at our decision. But first, I would like to be certain that both of you are still interested in becoming his associate. Dr. Marshall?"

"I'm still in."

"And Dr. Najarian?"

"Yes."

"Very well. Dr. Silver, will you please explain our current position."

Eric gripped the edge of his chair as Joe Silver straightened his notes and adjusted his reading glasses.

"Reed, Eric," he began, "I first want to congratulate each of you for the impression you've made on this committee, and also to thank you on behalf of President Mortensen, the trustees, and all of White Memorial for the marvelous years of service you've rendered here. As you know, the previous associate E.R. director brought us more ill will and bad ink than any hundred other doctors who have ever worked here combined. . . ."

Despite the tension of the moment, Eric and Reed exchanged amused glances. Craig Worrell had gone to the well of his perversion once too often, and had been videotaped soliciting sex from a young woman emergency-room patient in exchange for a hefty narcotics prescription. He was arrested soon after in his BMW in the hospital garage as he urged the undercover policewoman to hurry up and get on with her part of the deal so that he could return to duty. The entire Boston press and TV corps seemed to have been present for the bust. A month later, while free on bail, Worrell vanished. Since then there had been rumored sightings of the man, but nothing more.

". . . Well," Silver continued, "we three are—understandably, I think you'll agree—reluctant to make a final choice if there is the slightest uncertainty. We know that you expected a decision today, and we appreciate that this may seem cruel, but we have voted to, ah, put off making our selection for perhaps another two or three weeks. If this decision puts either of you in a position where you need to withdraw your application, please tell us at this time."

Silver's pronouncement hit Eric like an uppercut. *No decision*—the one option he hadn't considered. But the committee *had* made a definite choice. At least, that was what Silver himself had intimated not two days before. *What in the hell is going on?*

Eric stared at his chief and then, one at a time, at the others on the committee. Their faces seemed plastic, unreal.

". . . Eric? Excuse me, Eric?"

"Huh? Oh, sorry."

Silver looked at him oddly.

"Eric, Reed here has indicated that he is willing to put matters on hold for two or three more weeks. We're waiting to hear whether or not you can do the same."

Eric battled to bring his thoughts together.

"Of course," he heard himself say. "It's fine with me to wait."

The plastic faces grinned approvingly.

"Excellent," Sara Teagarden said. "Dr. Darden, have you any comments?"

The internist looked first at Reed, and then at Eric.

"I would only beg you gentlemen's forgiveness and understanding in this matter. If it were possible, I believe we would choose to keep both of you. However, things being as they are, and with the trustees and press watching our every move, there are a few more avenues we wish to explore, a few more inquiries to make. If either of you has problems or questions, I am sure any of us would be happy to meet with you."

Without further comment, Sara Teagarden hoisted herself to her feet, shook hands with the candidates, and adjourned the meeting.

"You okay, Eric?" Marshall asked after the others had left. "You look green."

This is bullshit. Absolute, insane bullshit, Eric wanted to holler. Instead he just shrugged.

"Sure, I'm fine," he said. "I . . . I had just prepared myself for a decision today one way or the other."

"Me too. I ran into Teagarden just yesterday, and she made it sound as if it was all over. I even had the feeling from things she said that you had gotten the job. I didn't want to say so out there, but it's the truth. Well, listen, I'm due back at the E.R., so I'll see you later. It's only another couple of weeks." He punched Eric lightly on the arm. "You keep your nose clean now, ya hear?"

"You too," Eric said. "You never know when big brother—or big, big sister—may be watching."

Eric stood motionless as Marshall hurried off. The two of them had never spent any real time together outside of the hospital. Now, as their time at WMH was nearing an end, he wished they had.

Susan, the receptionist, was watching Eric as he approached.

"How'd it go?" she asked.

"It didn't. Nothing happened."

"Well, committees are like that. I've taken minutes at some meetings, and you wouldn't believe how little a group of M.D.'s can get done."

"You said it. Well, see you in a couple of weeks."

"Wait," she said. "I have something for you."

She handed him a plain envelope. DR. ERIC NAJARIAN was printed on it in a meticulous hand. Eric's knee-jerk reaction was that the envelope was a note from her, but he quickly realized from her expression that it was not.

"A candy striper dropped this off for you a little while ago," Susan said. "She was real cute, but a little too young for you, I think."

Eric was too distracted to pick up the woman's cue. He fingered the envelope for a moment.

"Thanks," he mumbled, and headed off.

"I'm here all day," Susan said.

Eric turned into the main corridor of the hospital, and then leaned against a wall and tore the envelope open. The note inside was printed in the same hand as was his name.

WEAR THIS, AND WE WILL KNOW was all it said.

Wedged in one corner of the envelope was something metallic.

His fingers stiff and cold, Eric pulled out the object and held it so that no passerby could see. It was a stickpin bearing a black oval stone, possibly obsidian. Inlaid in the stone was a finely tooled gold caduceus.

5

Name?"

"Laura Enders. I already told you that."

"No, ma'am. I have *your* name. I need the name of the guy who's missing."

"Oh. It's Scott Enders. But he's also called himself Scott Shollander."

"A.k.a. Shollander," the desk sergeant mumbled as he pecked out the name on his typewriter.

Laura was just a few minutes into her session with the Boston policeman, but already she wished she could leave. Although he hadn't introduced himself, his name tag read SGT. THOS. CAMPBELL. He was a red-faced, potbellied man, probably in his late fifties, obviously burnt out and totally unenthusiastic about his job. And the more she listened to her own answers to his questions, the more she knew there was no chance he would be of any help.

"Last seen?"

"Well, actually, I haven't seen him for five months."

"Five . . . months . . ." the officer said as he typed. For all the inflection in his voice, he might have just written *five days*. His manner made it clear that over his years on the force, he had seen and heard everything—which was to say, he had seen and heard enough. "I guess it doesn't make much difference what he was wearing when last seen," he said.

"No," Laura said, her sarcasm ill-disguised. "I think you can leave that line blank."

Boston Police Headquarters was about as far from the clear, crisp beauty of Little Cayman as she could ever have imagined a place could be. The floor in the old building was filthy, and the dim lighting succeeded only in keeping the stains on the walls from being definable. But most unpleasant of all was the smell. Odors of people—hundreds of them, it seemed—hung in the air like a miasma.

It was just half past four in the afternoon of a somber, drizzly day. A day before, almost to the minute, Laura had left Communigistics and taken her cab to the D.C. address Neil Harten had given her. She'd been unable to find anyone in the small apartment complex who had ever seen or heard of Scott. She'd then checked into a downtown hotel and called Neil Harten at home to find out if he, or anyone he knew, had ever visited Scott at the apartment. Not surprisingly, his answer was no.

Finally, after toying with the idea of trying to track down the landlord of the building, she had decided she would get a good night's sleep and then stop by the closest police station to file a missing-person report. After that, she would head to Boston to begin her search in earnest.

"Recent photo?"

"Pardon?"

"Do you have a recent photo?"

"Oh. Only this one."

She handed over the photograph of herself and Scott. After barely a glance, the officer set it on his desk.

"No, wait. I need that."

Wearily, Sgt. Thomas Campbell handed it back.

"I . . . I'll have a blowup made of just Scott's face, and bring a copy to you, okay?"

"Whatever you say."

"Sergeant, are you going to be able to help me find my brother or not?"

The aging policeman looked at her. For the first time, Laura saw response in his eyes.

"Realistically now, Miss Enders," he said, "if you were me, how would you answer that question?"

"I . . . I understand," Laura said, gathering her things together.

"I'm sorry. The information you've given me is enough for us to put your brother in our computer, but not enough to assign a detective to the case."

"Sergeant Campbell, I said I understood. I'll drop the enlargement of this photo over as soon as I get it. Thank you for listening to me."

She stood.

"Wait a second," Campbell said. "I really can't do much on what you've given me, but I will at least check your description against, um . . ."

"Against unknown corpses. It's okay to say it."

"Against them." He scribbled the name Bernard Nelson and a phone number on his note pad, tore off the sheet, and handed it to her. "This is the name of a decent private detective," he said. "He works for himself, not one of them big companies, so his rates might be a little better. Maybe he can help you out. And if I learn anything, I promise I'll call you. Where're you staying?"

"The Carlisle. It's downtown on—"

"Stiles. I know the place. In fact, everyone on the force knows that place. Miss, I don't know exactly how to say this, but, um, the Carlisle isn't exactly the best place for . . . What I mean is, a lot of their trade is daytime, for-the-hour stuff. Pros."

"Prostitutes?"

"There *are* a few here."

"But . . . but I'm paying ninety-five dollars a night for my room."

"Welcome to Boston," Sergeant Thomas Campbell said.

Bernard Nelson's office was a ten-minute walk from the police station. On the way there Laura stopped by a photo store and, after sliding two twenties across the counter, received the guarantee that her enlargement would be ready by morning, rather than the "seven to ten days" the proprietor had initially promised.

"Welcome to Boston," Laura muttered as she headed back onto the street.

Over the phone Nelson had sounded as if he would be in his thirties or forties. In fact he was well beyond that—sixty at least, and by no means a young sixty. His office, on the second floor of a tawdry four-story brownstone, consisted of a small reception area, which was empty, and a larger, cluttered inner office. Nelson was standing in the doorway of that room as Laura entered. He was five foot nine or ten, but must have weighed over two hundred pounds, most of which was packed into a gut that made Thomas Campbell's look trim. He wore a ragged green sweater that barely reached his belt, and had an unlit inch-and-a-half cigar butt clenched in his teeth. Laura immediately pictured the man in a smoky tavern, seated elbow to elbow at the bar with Sergeant Campbell. She fought the urge to turn and leave.

Unlike Campbell, though, Bernard Nelson listened to her story with some interest. When she finished, he pulled a sinister-looking long-barreled revolver from his desk drawer, hefted it expertly in his hand for a moment, and then used it to light his cigar.

"That was very cute," Laura said.

"Birthday present from my daughter. Actually, I have a real one locked up. I'm afraid to keep it in my desk like they do on TV, though, for fear that one day I'll mix the two of them up and blow my head—or worse, my cigar—to bits. After my coronary, I promised my wife I'd only smoke one a day."

"It *would* be a shame to waste one that way."

"Exactly." He took a single puff, tilted his head back, and sent a cumulus cloud of smoke swirling toward the ceiling. Then he set the butt in an ashtray shaped like a putting green. "So tell me, Miss Enders, why do you know so little of a man you feel so close to?"

"I never thought about how little I know, really," she said. "At least not until the last few weeks. Scott is, I don't know, sort of private about some things, I guess." She felt a pang of guilt at using Neil Harten's assessment, but by now it seemed appropriate.

"You mean things like where he lived, where he worked, what name he was using . . ."

Laura drew in a deep breath and then exhaled slowly.

"Mr. Nelson, do you have any older siblings?" she asked.

"A brother," he answered, his expression suggesting that he already understood the point she was about to make. "Five years older."

"Still alive?"

"And kicking."

"Did he have much to do with you when you were growing up?"

"No. Most of the time he acted as if I didn't exist."

"And how did you feel toward him?"

"I idolized him," Bernard Nelson said. "Still do, I guess."

"Well, Scott is to me what your brother was to you. That and more. He's my only family, and has been since I was fourteen." She looked across at the detective for a moment. "I couldn't begin to tell you all the things Scott's done for me over the years. And I've never had a chance to do much of anything for him."

"Point made and understood," Nelson said. He glanced at the cigar butt, but apparently decided to save it. "Miss Enders, do you think there's a possibility your brother could have been involved in something shady?"

"Shady?"

"Forgive the TV talk, but it was the best word I could come

up with. You must know what I mean, though. Gambling, white-collar crime of some sort, drugs?"

"Impossible," Laura said.

"Why? Even John Dillinger had family."

"Not funny. What makes you think such a thing, anyway?"

"What makes me *not* think it would be a better question. Miss Enders, people don't go around using false names and keeping their lives so private from their own family unless they have a damn good reason."

"Perhaps in most cases. But I know— What I mean is, I *feel* that I have a good sense of Scott. And that sort of thing just doesn't fit. Now, will you help me look for him?"

"I charge seventy-five dollars plus expenses."

"Sounds reasonable enough, as long as your expenses aren't too high."

Bernard Nelson stared across at her for a moment, and then he smiled.

"Miss Enders," he said, "that's seventy-five dollars *an hour*."

"An hour?!"

"And starting from scratch, not even knowing if your brother's in Boston or not, looking for him's gonna take a hell of a lot of them. It roughs out to about—"

"I just did the arithmetic. Tell me, are you working on anything now?"

"It may not look it, but the answer is yes. Several things."

"At seventy-five dollars an hour?"

"Or more."

"And how many hours do you think it might take to know whether or not you can find Scott?"

"Maybe fifty. Maybe a hundred. Finding someone is fifty percent legwork and fifty percent blind luck. It's impossible to say."

"I . . . I have some money, but not that kind."

"I didn't think you did. Miss Enders, I'd like to help you. Really I would. Jim Rockford always gets cases from beautiful, interesting women, and I'd love to do the same. But I've got two kids in college and a mortgage the size of Nevada. You need someone who's very good at this business, who can do your job full time, and who charges considerably less than the going rate. That person doesn't exist. And if you make too many compromises in who you hire, believe me, you'll just end up losing what money you do have, all for nothing."

"I appreciate your candor," Laura said, making no attempt to mask her discouragement. "What do you think I should do?"

"You could give up and wait."

"Not a possibility."

"Well, then, I suppose I could get you started in the right direction. If you get anything like a lead, come on back and we'll talk."

"That would be a very kind thing for you to do."

"Maybe. But I feel like helping you. Probably it's because you didn't complain about my cigar."

"I wanted to."

"I know. But listen now, and listen good. Before I tell you anything, I want to be sure you know that this ain't Missouri, and it ain't some paradise island in the Caribbean. It's a city. And in cities, more people are out to use you than to help you."

"That's reassuring."

"That's the way it is. You have a nice way about you. A nice, trusting way."

"Thanks."

"Don't thank me. In this business, that's a criticism, not a compliment. Do you get the point?"

"Yes," Laura said firmly. "I get the point."

"Okay, then. To begin, I think you should have a poster made up. Include the photo you told me about, plus any information you can think of about your brother. Offer a reward for information that leads to finding him, but don't say how much. And don't go meetin' anyone in a nonpublic place to hear what they have to say. Take the photo to this guy, and tell him you're a friend of mine." He wrote the name and address down. "Get, oh, a thousand printed. Offer him a hundred less than anything he asks for, and then give him what he asked for in the first place if he'll deliver the poster in a day."

"I've already figured that maneuver out," Laura said. "Where do you think I should distribute them?"

"Start with hotels and motels. And don't rely too heavily on the desk clerks or executives. Get to the housekeeping staff and to the hotel restaurants. Talk to people. Don't just shove the poster at them and leave. Next I'd hit the police precinct stations. Make sure they put it up on the wall someplace. Then stop by the papers. Take special pains to look real good when you go there. If you can interest some reporter, maybe they'll do a story and a picture. If nothing pans out, maybe it'll be worth shelling out some of that cash of yours for an ad. Your brother drink?"

"Some, I guess."

"Then try some of the downtown bars. Scott sounds like a downtown kind of guy. Also, hit the computer stores, just in case he's still in that line of work. Oh, and the hospitals. Especially the emergency rooms. Go to every one of them, even in the suburbs. Again, do whatever you have to, to ensure that your poster ends up on the wall and not in the trash."

Laura felt dizzy as she scribbled down Nelson's suggestions.

"This is going to be some job," she said.

"It could be worse."

"Really?"

"Yeah. You could be paying seventy-five dollars an hour to get it done. Get a good map of the city, and keep track not only of where you've been, but where you're going. If you want to bring your map up here, I'll mark off the parts of town you're to stay away from. It's okay to take cabs around, but I want you to keep the doors locked. A few cabbies—not many, but some—have a scam going where they stop at a corner and some pals jump in and steal women's purses."

"Yes, sir."

"Lock your doors."

"You know, I'm beginning to see why you might actually be worth seventy-five dollars an hour."

"Just remember to send me a deck of Havanas when you get back to that island of yours."

Laura stood and took his hand.

"I'll send them to your wife," she said. "She can ration them out."

A cool, damp evening had settled over the city by the time Laura left Bernard Nelson's office and headed back toward her hotel. The streets were already illuminated, some by quaint gaslights. The sidewalks were crowded with all manner of people, many of them business folk, hurrying home. And by and large, Laura liked the feeling of the place—its oldness and understated sense of purpose. She had been to New York twice, and never felt as comfortable there as she did after just a few hours in Boston.

She stopped at a small newsstand, bought a good street map of the city and a copy of *Skin Diver* magazine, and decided to take Boylston Street down to the Public Gardens. She had just crossed Dartmouth when, in a slow motion nightmare, two youths—one black and one white—began racing up the sidewalk toward her. It wasn't until she noticed the older woman walking just ahead of her that she realized what was about to happen.

With what seemed practiced precision, one of the youths jostled the woman, sending her off balance. The other boy, a step behind, snatched the woman's purse as she was falling to the pavement, and then accelerated. Laura's reaction was pure reflex. As he neared her, she pulled her shoulder bag free and swung it as hard as she could, catching the boy in the arm and sending the woman's purse spinning across the sidewalk. The youth stumbled and whirled about.

"Don't!" Laura barked, stepping between him and the purse.

The boy stopped short. His eyes locked with hers.

"Don't do it," she rasped, hoping that the determination in her own eyes held even a fraction of the fury in his. Behind him, she saw the other youth hesitate, and then turn and run. In continued slow motion, several male passersby began to close in on the confrontation. She saw a flicker of confusion replace the anger in the remaining youth's eyes.

"Fuck you," he spat. Then he bolted off, shoving his way between two startled businessmen.

Several people were mumbling praise and patting her on the shoulder as Laura, her pulse pounding in her ears, retrieved the purse. The old woman was being helped to her feet.

"Are you okay?" Laura asked.

"I . . . I think so," she said, apparently unaware that she was talking to the woman who had helped her.

"Good. Here's your bag."

"Th-thank you, dear."

The woman still seemed dazed. Laura stepped closer to hand her the purse. Not ten feet away, a tall man dressed in a windbreaker and jeans ducked quickly into a doorway, out of her sight. Laura checked to be certain the old woman could walk. Then, barely aware of the smattering of applause, she headed off down Boylston.

A beat later, the man in jeans stepped out from the doorway and followed.

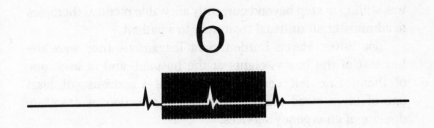

6

The pin was no bigger than Eric's fingernail, but in its remarkable detail and craftsmanship it was a work of art. Set in black stone, the caduceus was hand-sculpted in gold, with fine enamel accents at the head of the staff and along the wings flaring out from just beneath it. The intertwining serpents below the wings were etched so meticulously that under a microscope, Eric could discern their scales, and even the facets in the flecks of ruby that highlighted their eyes.

We are Caduceus, your brothers and sisters in medicine. We care about the things you care about. We care about you.

The words had echoed in Eric's mind since the unexpected decision by the search committee to hold off for several weeks in making their selection. And although he had been unable to recall with exactitude all the phrases spoken by that eerie electronic voice, the sense of the message was clear. Some kind of secret work was going on at White Memorial, something arcane but important; something that he could be a part of if he was willing to step beyond currently allowable medical therapies to administer an unusual treatment to a patient.

Joe Silver, Haven Darden, Sara Teagarden—they were the heaviest of the heavyweights at the hospital, and at least one of them, Eric felt certain, was part of Caduceus. At least one of them stood ready to assure his selection as associate director of emergency services.

Over the four days that had followed the search committee meeting, Eric had kept the caduceus pin in his desk. And although he had tried to ignore it, to approach his job in a business-as-usual fashion, rationalizations for pinning it on his clinic coat reverberated in his mind like distant ocean waves. He reflected on the physicians who made major breakthroughs by flying in the face of medical convention. He reasoned that in point of fact, by using the pericardial laser, he had already demonstrated to others, and to himself, his potential for similar vision and action. He argued that once he learned what Caduceus had in mind, he could always refuse to get involved.

But in the end, neither the promise of the promotion nor any amount of rationalization was persuasive enough. This was not the laser he had developed himself and knew so intimately. It was someone else's work—someone else's priorities. The struggle within him was constant, but again and again his inner voice kept at bay the urge to find out what Caduceus was up to. More than five years of study and total dedication to his work had proved, as far as he was concerned, that he was the better man for the E.R. job. And he continued to cling to the hope and the belief that ultimately that would be enough.

It was early evening. The emergency room, which had enjoyed a few hours of atypical quiet, had suddenly begun to pulse again. Eric had signed out to Reed Marshall, but an accident on the expressway had brought in two major casualties. Until things leveled off, Eric had volunteered to man the minor medical desk, working with the triage nurse to screen walk-ins and treat those who did not need extensive evaluation. He had three examining rooms going at once, and several more patients waiting for laboratory results. Still, the pile of charts in the to-be-seen box on his desk continued to grow.

"Kristen, would you give me a quick moon check?" he asked, dashing off prescriptions and clinic referral forms for several patients at once.

"Full moon tomorrow," the nurse said. "Can't you tell?"

Eric glanced up at the waiting room, which was nearly packed.

"I can tell," he said. "Señora Martinez," he called out, "*Traiga a su padre aquí, por favor.*"

The woman, cradling an infant in one arm, helped her father limp over to the desk. Of all the courses Eric had ever taken—including all the biochemistry, biology, physics, and calculus—the one that seemed the most valuable to him as a physician was his four years of high-school Spanish.

"*Es* gout, *Señora. La gota,*" he said, handing over two prescriptions and a referral slip. "*Es muy dolorosa, pero no es grave.*"

The woman thanked him twice in Spanish, hesitated, and then squeezed his hand and kissed him on the cheek.

"That was very nice. Or should I say, *Fue muy simpático.*"

Eric turned to find Dr. Haven Darden standing just to his right.

"Thanks," Eric said. "I just wish I'd had enough foresight not to drop the language when I entered college. It sounds as if you didn't make that mistake."

The internist's round face crinkled in a smile.

"We speak French in Haiti, remember?" he said. "Starting from there, the other romance languages aren't too difficult to master."

Eric remembered reading in some magazine that the White Memorial chief of medicine had fluency in seven languages. He chose not to comment on the fact. Over his years at the hospital, he had spent some time training with Darden, but had never developed the closeness that he had with many other professors. In fact, Eric had been a bit uncomfortable around the man since the time when he and Reed Marshall were both rotating

on Darden's service. Marshall had, quite in passing, mentioned
the Harvard connection, and had let slip that Darden had invited
him and his wife over for dinner.

If a strong preference was held by anyone on the search
committee for one candidate over the other, Eric believed, it had
to be Darden's partiality to Reed.

"Do you have a patient coming in?" Eric asked.

Darden, meticulously dressed beneath his knee-length
clinic coat, nodded.

"A physician friend is bringing his fifteen-year-old daughter
in with a high fever and a stiff neck."

"Possible meningitis. I don't blame him for being worried."

"Exactly."

"Well, if I can help, just let me know."

Darden glanced out at the waiting room.

"At the moment, Eric, I would say that you are more the
one in need of assistance. I'll tell you what. Give me two or three
minutes in private, and then I shall do what I can to help you
wade through that crowd out there."

"WMH rule number one," Eric said. "Never refuse help.
Just let me explain to the triage nurse, and have her do something to pacify that mob out there. We can go to my office."

Haven Darden followed Eric back to the small chief resident's office that he shared with Reed Marshall.

"Thank you for taking the time," Darden said, closing the
door. "I won't keep you long. Eric, have you spoken with any of
the other committee members since the meeting last Monday?"

"Well, Joe Silver's always around here, so we've spoken
several times. Yesterday I ate lunch at the same table as Sara
Teagarden. Why?"

"I'm curious if either of them said anything about what
happened—why we told you both that we had made a decision,
then announced that we needed more time?"

"Not a word. Typical of the hospital grapevine, though—
everyone around here seems to know what transpired. I think
the nurses have a betting pool going. From what I can tell, they

seem to be split about fifty-fifty, so both Reed and I get encouragement, depending on which of them we're working with."

"Well," Darden said. "This may be an impropriety, but I want you to know that had the committee made its decision, Dr. Marshall would have been chosen." Eric felt a knot in his chest at the news. "Dr. Silver has seemed committed to him all along, and Dr. Teagarden had indicated she was leaning in his direction. Your use of that laser of yours did not sit well with them. You, however, are my choice. And that is why I am telling you this."

"Thank you," Eric muttered, as surprised that Darden would turn out to be a supporter of his as he was shaken by the news of how close he had already come to losing out. He tried to factor in the information with what he already knew. There was no way Darden could have been the caller—no way, even electronically, that he could have masked his clipped, distinctive English. That meant that one of the other two . . .

"I have no strong sentiment against Dr. Marshall," Darden went on, "but I believe he lacks your commitment and dedication to medicine. I like the feel you have for your work—the flare, if you will. You have demonstrated a clinical aggressiveness—a willingness to take chances, to do whatever it takes to get a patient through a crisis—that appeals to me."

"Thank you again," Eric said. "Can you say why Reed didn't get chosen?"

"Not really. Joe Silver's the one who suddenly pushed for an extension. You might not know it, but it was Joe who railroaded Craig Worrell into that post a few years ago, past a lot of strong objections around the hospital, and he took a fair amount of flak when the choice went sour. Maybe he got cold feet about backing another loser."

"Maybe . . ." Eric said distantly.

"If we can sway either of those votes, you're in. We've decided that a two-to-one vote will do it."

"I appreciate your telling me all this," Eric said. "Needless to say, Reed and I were both wondering what had gone on."

"I wish I knew," Darden said. "Eric, I don't think White

Memorial can easily afford to lose a physician with your skill and commitment. And speaking for myself, I would love to have another faculty member with a philosophy so much like my own. The votes at staff meetings are always perilously close between the conservatives and those of us who believe this hospital must move ahead to stay ahead. Do you remember that AIDS outreach program I proposed a year or so ago?"

"I heard about it, sure. I had planned to volunteer to help man the clinic when it was set up. In fact, I signed up on that list you sent around."

"I know. It might not surprise you to learn that Reed Marshall did not. Well, regardless, what you may not know is that my proposal to the medical staff was defeated by just two votes."

"That must have hurt, to come so close," Eric said.

"No idea is ever dead until those who believe in it say it's dead," Darden replied. "Craig Worrell was one of the negative votes."

"I see."

"If I were you, and I wanted that position as much as you seem to, I would do whatever I could to sway the vote of either Dr. Silver or Dame Teagarden in my favor. Can you think of any way you might do that?"

"No," Eric lied, glancing inadvertently at the drawer of his desk. "No, I can't."

"Well, then . . . I, um, I hope you understand that while I have great respect for Reed Marshall, if there is anything you know about him that would help influence either of my comrades on the committee . . ."

"No," Eric said, unable to conceal how startled he was. "No I don't." He hesitated, and then added, "Dr. Darden, I think you should know that over our years of working together, Reed and I have developed a pretty deep respect for each other. Even if I did know something damaging about him, which truthfully I don't, it's doubtful I would be able to share that information with anyone—even if it meant losing out on the job."

"Well said!" the chief exclaimed. "That's precisely the response I wanted from you. And you have my apology for even bringing the subject up. Call it a final test if you want to, and consider yourself to have passed with flying colors. Just keep up your good work, Eric. I'll do what politicking I can. Then we'll cast our chips on the table and let them fall where they may."

Before Eric could respond, there was an insistent knock on the office door.

"Eric, it's Kristen."

"Time to get to work," Haven Darden said, opening the door. "We'll talk again."

The nurse was breathless.

"Eric, Reed wants to see you in Trauma Two right away."

"Go," Darden said. "I'll help Miss"—he read the nurse's name tag—"Baker plow through that waiting room."

Eric hurried past the medical chief and down the hall to Trauma Two. He could smell the blood and feel the chaos and desperation in the room the moment he cleared the door. Reed, an intern named Stuart Spear, and two nurses were clustered about a litter bearing a woman who appeared to be *in extremis*. She was propped bolt upright and was gasping for breath through the blood cascading from her mouth.

"What gives?" Eric asked, noting Reed Marshall's pale, wide-eyed face.

Reed motioned the intern over to the head of the bed and handed him the rigid suction catheter.

"Just keep sucking her out," he ordered. "Jill, get me three units. I don't care if they're cross-matched yet or not. I'll sign. Also, tell the respiratory therapist to get in here."

He hurried over to where Eric stood.

"She took the steering wheel in her neck," he whispered. "At first there was just a trickle, but all of a sudden she erupted."

"She's drowning," Eric murmured. "Her larynx has probably been fractured."

"I tried calling ENT down to trach her, but they're in the O.R."

"I don't think it's wise to put her head back and cut on her neck. Just paralyze her and put a tube in."

"But . . . but what if I paralyze her and then can't see past the blood to get the tube in?"

"Of course you can get it in. I'll work the suction."

"I . . . I'm not so sure that's the right thing to do," Reed said.

Eric glanced over at the patient and the two who were working on her. The respiratory therapist entered the room and began preparing his Ambu breathing bag.

"Reed," Eric said softly, "it doesn't look like you have much time. A trach will be dangerous, messy as hell, and probably take too long. The balloon on the tube you put in will tamponade the bleeding. Call for the succinylcholine. You can do it. *I* know you can. I've seen you tube a hundred people."

"Not like her. You do it."

"You can do it, Reed," Eric whispered. "I'll be right there with you. Just order the sux."

Marshall turned to the nurse.

"Give her sixty of succinylcholine IV, please, and have respiratory set me up with a seven-point-five tube." He looked back at Eric, who shook his head a fraction. "Make that a six-point-five," Reed said. He crossed to the woman, whose respirations were growing less and less effective. "Mrs. Garber, we're going to put a tube in to help you breathe. In order to do that, we're giving you medicine that will make it impossible for you to move. Try not to be too frightened. You'll be breathing better in just a minute."

Moments after the rapidly acting paralytic was injected, its effects began. The woman's muscles, including those that were enabling her to breathe, began to twitch, writhing without coordination or pattern. Then, in seconds, they all went slack. Eric set the litter back flat. Instantly, blood welled up in the woman's mouth. He took the suction and moved to Reed's right hand. The monitor pattern remained rapid and steady.

"Go for it," he said, hunching next to Marshall's ear. "Just think of the anatomy. Look for your landmarks, and concentrate."

Reed slid the broad blade of the laryngoscope along the

edge of the woman's tongue as Eric stabilized her head with one hand and sucked the blood clear with the catheter in his other.

"Take your time," Eric whispered, craning to see what Reed was looking at.

"I . . . I can't see."

"Wipe off the laryngoscope light and do it again. It's only been ten seconds."

Out of the corner of his eye, Eric saw the monitor rate begin to drop. Reed wiped the blood off the light at the tip of the blade and inserted it again. His left hand, clenched about the laryngoscope handle, was beginning to shake.

Eric reached up and depressed the woman's larynx a bit.

"There, look," he said. "That's her epiglottis right there. Just come up underneath it. Easy does it. That's it, that's it."

Marshall began to nod excitedly.

"I've got it. . . . I've got it," he said, slipping the polystyrene tube into place. "Sweet Jesus, I've got it."

Quickly, the respiratory therapist blew up the balloon on the tube, attached the breathing bag, and began a series of rapid ventilations. Eric checked the woman's chest with his stethoscope to ensure the proper placement of the apparatus. Then he looked up at Reed and smiled.

"Hell of a good shot, old boy," he said.

Almost immediately the flow of blood began to abate. The woman's color improved. The relief and elation in the room were nearly palpable.

"Yes, sir," Eric said, patting Reed on the shoulder, "one hell of a shot."

"What gives?"

The team turned toward the doorway, where Dr. Joe Silver stood appraising the scene.

Unable to contain her enthusiasm, the nurse rushed over to him.

"Dr. Silver," she gushed, "you just missed it. Reed just intubated this woman through a massive hemorrhage. One minute she was dying; the next . . ."

She gestured at the patient, who now was being ventilated quite easily.

"Nice going, Reed," Silver said, striding to the bedside.

"Actually, I don't think I could have done it without—"

"What was it? Steering wheel to the neck?"

"Exactly."

"Gutsy move."

"Eric here was the one who—"

"Does she have any other injuries?"

"We've only had time for C-spines and a chest film, but they were normal."

"Excellent, Reed. Really fine work. Well then, why don't you get on with your secondary survey of her." He turned to Eric. "It's a madhouse out there. Your stand-in, Dr. Darden, has apparently forgotten how frantic our kind of work is. He left to examine his patient after seeing about three people in the time we see ten."

"I'll get on it now," Eric said.

"It doesn't look as if you ever had to leave."

Eric started to respond, then just nodded and left the room.

The flow of patients into the E.R. slowed, then virtually stopped. With Joe Silver pitching in, Eric was caught up in less than two hours. The E.R. chief gave no indication that he knew of Eric's role in the Garber woman's resuscitation. Instead, he told almost anyone who would listen about Reed Marshall's heroics. Eric was sure that Reed had spoken up for him, but it was clear that Silver had heard only what he wanted to hear.

With a few final words to the triage nurse, Eric headed down the hall to his office, his back and legs aching from the long day. He glanced back at the front desk, where Joe Silver was orchestrating the care of what patients remained, and tried to imagine what life would be like for him should he be forced to leave White Memorial.

He entered the office and shut the door. In almost a fugue state, he pulled the envelope from the lower drawer of his desk and held the fine caduceus pin in his hand.

From beyond the door he heard the sounds of the hospital. He deserved the promotion. The events in Trauma Two merely underscored that truth. He deserved it, and yet it seemed more than likely that in a matter of days, he would be looking for work.

He ran his finger over the pin. Putting it on would obligate him to nothing. If the work Caduceus was doing was unacceptable, he could simply refuse to participate.

Eric's pulse was raging in his ears as he ignored persistent pangs of uncertainty and fastened the caduceus to the lapel of his clinic coat.

7

Between diving once or twice a day and running five miles several times a week, Laura Enders was in the best shape of her life. Even so, every muscle in her legs ached as she left the subway and climbed the stairs from the Charles Street station to the White Memorial overpass.

She had spent her first full day in the city—two days ago—making countless lists of the places she would go, and locating those places on her map. Then, late that evening, she had picked up the fliers at the printer and begun her search in earnest, planning to work her way, one at a time, through the grids she had drawn on her map. By eleven the next night she had walked at least twenty miles and had left posters with two hundred bartenders, policemen, hotel workers, hospital clerks, and receptionists.

The fliers, standard 8½ by 11, black-on-white, had come out reasonably well, although the blowup of Scott's face was grainy, and flatter than she would have liked. She had stopped by Bernard Nelson's office and left half a dozen with his frowzy receptionist, who accepted them while barely missing a stroke in filing her nails.

It was nearing nine in the morning, and for the first time since her arrival in Boston three days before, the sun was shining. Charles Circle was alive with traffic, ambulances, joggers, and streams of pedestrians headed from several directions toward the hospital. On a whim, Laura stopped in at the Charles Street jail and left off a flier. Then she fell in with the crowd and followed a stretcher through the emergency doors into White Memorial.

She had been to the emergency rooms of two hospitals the previous day and was impressed by how busy each had been. But compared to White Memorial, they were serene. Everything and everyone in the broad, fluorescently lit receiving area seemed to be in motion. The scene reminded her of the teeming life above a coral reef.

Three stretchers, each with a patient and two ambulance attendants, were lined up along one wall. A group of what looked like medical students were clustered in a doorway, listening intently to an older physician. Nurses and doctors in scrub suits crisscrossed to and from the broad semicircular reception counter, dropping off charts, picking up laboratory slips, or just pausing to talk. Behind the counter two women and two men jockeyed past one another, answering phones, responding to questions, and logging patients in and out of rooms diagrammed on a huge white acrylic tote board.

Laura took a minute to gauge which of the four seemed the least harried. She settled on a slight, pale man with graying sideburns and an easy manner that suggested he was a veteran at his job. Then she timed her approach to coincide with his rotation from the tote board to the counter.

"Help you?" he asked.

"I hope so." Laura pulled two fliers from her shoulder bag and set them in front of the man. "My name is Laura Enders. I'm trying to find my brother, Scott. I was hoping there might be a place where I could put up one or two of these."

"Have you checked to see if he's been a patient here?" the man said, scanning the sheet with no sign of recognition.

"No. No, I haven't."

Laura cursed herself for neglecting to do that at the two previous hospitals she had visited. At the same time, she pictured the posters she had left off crumpled in wastebaskets beneath counters similar to this one.

"Well, why don't you let me call the record room and see if they have anything. Have a seat over there and take in the show."

Relieved, Laura settled in a blue molded-plastic chair off to one side. At first she focused on the patients, some clutching wounded or aching parts, some strapped to wheelchairs, and some, it seemed, just hanging around. Gradually, though, her attention shifted to the doctors. Most of them, especially those in scrubs, were her age or younger. And all of them, men and women alike, looked exhausted and harried. Still, many paused for brief gestures of caring toward the patients—a touch or a word. And within the shadows surrounding their eyes was a snap and intelligence that made Laura feel she would enjoy working with these people. Several of the letters of inquiry she had sent out were to programs in physical therapy and rehabilitation. At that moment, heading her life in that direction felt right. Perhaps after she had found Scott . . .

"No luck."

"Huh?" The emergency ward clerk was standing beside her. "Oh, I'm sorry. I guess my mind was wandering."

"I understand," the man said. "I've been working here almost twenty years now, and sometimes I still find myself hypnotized by the whole thing. But I'm afraid there's no record of your brother ever having been here—inpatient or out. I checked both names on that poster of yours."

Laura stood.

"I really appreciate your help," she said. "Do you think you could put up the posters anyhow? I'm pretty desperate to find him."

"I can show the picture around. But posting things out here

is against hospital regs unless they're approved by— Wait a minute. The place you *really* want to put this up is in the residents' lounge. If anyone would remember seeing him, it would probably be one of the residents." He turned and called across to one of the doctors. "Eric. Hey, Eric. Got a second?"

The doctor seated at a desk near the triage nurse turned and looked over at them. Of all those Laura had been watching, he was perhaps the most interesting, and, she acknowledged as he rose and came toward them, the handsomest as well. He was tall—six feet or a bit more. His face was dark and sharp-featured, reminding her a bit of Omar Sharif. And although Laura usually disliked moustaches, his seemed right. But what had impressed her most about the man were the little things she had watched him do with the patients—the warm smiles and reassuring touches.

"Eric," the clerk said. "I think you might be able to help this woman here. Miss . . ."

"Enders," Laura spoke up. "Laura Enders."

"This here's Dr. Najarian. He's our chief resident, and the best doc I've seen come through this place. I'll leave you with him."

"Thank you," Laura said.

The clerk looked from one to the other of them. Then his mouth turned up in a quick, knowing smile before he headed back to his post.

Eric Najarian reached out and shook her hand.

"Pleased to meet you," he said.

Laura was staring at his face, and actually missed a beat in her response. His eyes were wide and dark and held a special attraction for her. And in the moments that followed, she realized why. They were like Scott's eyes, at once sensitive and intense; eyes that spoke of caring and of wanting to know.

"I . . . um . . . I'm looking for my brother," she managed to say.

"Is he lost?" Eric asked.

"No. I mean yes. I mean he's missing." Sensing her cheeks

beginning to redden, she quickly thrust a poster at him. "I flew up here three days ago to try and find him."

"From where?"

Eric continued studying the photo of Scott. For a moment Laura thought she saw something in his eyes—a flicker of recognition. Then, just as quickly, the look disappeared.

"Little Cayman Island," she said. "It's in the Caribbean."

"I know. Just south of Cuba. The best diving in the world, I hear. You dive?"

"As a matter of fact, I'm an instructor. That's what I do there. Do you dive?"

"I wish. In fact there are a whole bunch of things I wish I had time to do—or at least try."

"I was watching you with the patients a while ago. Believe me, you do plenty."

"Thanks."

"For a second there, I thought you recognized Scott's picture. Did you?"

Eric shook his head. "Something about his face is familiar, but nothing really clicks. I'll be happy to post this in the residents' lounge, though."

"I'd appreciate that."

"Where are you staying?"

Before Laura could answer, a young resident came racing up to them.

"Eric," he said breathlessly, "that GI bleeder in Four has really opened up. The stuff's pouring out of him, and his pressure's beginning to drop."

Instantly, the softness in Eric's eyes vanished.

"Is blood off?" he asked.

"Off, but not cross-matched for another twenty minutes."

"What is he?"

"B-negative."

"Jesus. Okay. Have them continue the cross-match and send up three units of type-specific. Use O-negative if they're short. I'll sign for them."

"You coming back there?"

"Right away."

The resident hurried off.

"Look," Eric said, "I've got to go. Let me leave you with someone who can help. Come on."

Before Laura could tell him not to bother, he had led her to a nurse who was standing across the receiving area.

"I've got trouble in Four," he said. "Do me a favor and see what you can do to help this woman out. Nice to have met you, Laura. Good luck with your brother."

"Thank you," she said. But he had already hurried off.

The nurse, a woman in her early fifties, watched him go, and then turned to Laura.

"Now then," she said. "I'm the shift supervisor here. My name's Norma Cullinet. How can I help you?"

It was all Norma Cullinet could do to maintain a façade of detachment and to concentrate on what Laura Enders was saying. Her hands were shaking so, that at one point the fliers she held in them actually began to rustle.

"What did you say your brother did for a living?" she asked.

"Computers. Scott's a computer genius. He works—I should say worked—for an international communications company. He traveled a lot in his work. The last time I heard from him was in February. The last card he sent me and the few before it were mailed from Boston. I'm leaving these all around the city, including the police stations and hospitals."

"I see. . . . Well, I'll be happy to put one of them up for you in our nurses' lounge."

"That would be great. Dr. Najarian also suggested the residents' lounge. Do you think you could tack one up there as well?"

"Of course." *Najarian. He was on that day. He handled the Code 99!*

"Thanks a lot. You've all been great."

"No problem," Norma Cullinet said. "No problem at all."

"Well, I'm off to canvass some computer stores," Laura said. "I wish you luck."

* * *

Norma turned away as Laura was leaving, and then turned back to be sure she had gone. She stared at the face on the flier. *Computer genius? With a sister?* How could that be? The man with this face was a bum with no family. A wino. Perhaps she was wrong, though. It had been several months, and the snapshot wasn't all that clear. Perhaps it was coincidence—a marked similarity but nothing more. Two years, and dozens of cases without a hitch. Now this.

Did Najarian make any connection? He'd given no indication that he had, but he was distracted by the GI bleeder. *Is there anything to do? Anyone to tell?* Craig Worrell would have known what to do. He always knew. *Why in the hell did he have to screw everything up so badly?*

Once again Norma studied the photo. There was, to be sure, a strong likeness to the man who had called himself Phillip Trainor. But from what she remembered, there were differences as well. She was blowing things out of proportion— the way she always did.

Blowing things out of proportion. That was it. Pure and simple. Still, she decided, until someone had been found to take over Worrell's role, she would refuse any further requests from Caduceus.

Her neck and underarms damp with sweat, Norma Cullinet folded the fliers and thrust them into her uniform pocket.

8

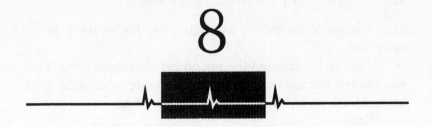

Fourth unit's up and running, Eric. Two more are on the way from the blood bank. What do you think?"

Eric watched the steady spatter of blood from their patient's nasogastric tube into the suction bottle on the wall. They had tried medication, fresh clotting factors, and direct examination through a gastroscope, but nothing had slowed the bleeding, which was almost certainly from an ulcer, and possibly from an ulcer within a cancer.

"I think we punt," he said to the resident. "Go ahead and get the surgical team that's up for the next case. This guy's reasonably stable right now, and I know they'd rather take over while he is. I'm going to take a break and get some coffee. Call me when the surgeons get here."

Eric entered the reception area rubbing at a nagging stiffness along the base of his neck. He couldn't remember how many days it had been since he had last worked out. As with almost everything else in his life, there simply wasn't enough time. Perhaps if he got the associate's job, life would begin to normalize.

Absently he fingered the pin on his clinic-coat lapel. This was his first full day in the E.R. since pinning it on. From what he could tell, no one had even taken notice of it.

"You sore?"

Charge nurse Terri Dillard, five foot one if that, looked up at him with concern. She was a crack E.R. nurse who spent her off-hours instructing at a school of holistic healing. Eric had no real feeling for the things she knew and taught, but it was common knowledge around the E.R. that her massage and therapeutic touch often had patients diagnosed or actually cured before a physician had even entered the room.

"Accelerated aging," he said.

She reached up and dug her thumbs into the muscles at the base of his neck.

"Spasm," she said. "Everything's all knotted up. It's tension."

"Me? What do I have to be tense about?"

"Well, let's see." She continued to dig. "You're waiting to hear if you got a big promotion, you've got an active GI bleeder in Room Four, and a drop-dead-gorgeous brunette with an off-season tan just left before you could get her phone number. How's that for starters?"

"Drop-dead-gorgeous? How could I have missed that?"

"You didn't. That's what these muscles are telling you."

"Are you a witch?"

Terri stopped her massage. "Maybe," she said. "What'd the lady want?"

"She was looking for her brother. She had a bunch of posters with his picture on them, and she wanted us to— Wait a second." He noticed Norma Cullinet crossing from the waiting room, and motioned her over. "Hey, Norma," he said, "did you put up those posters from that woman, Laura?"

"Laura, huh?" Terri Dillard murmured.

Beneath the rouge on her cheeks, Norma Cullinet paled.

"I . . . I didn't want to post anything without getting Dr. Silver's approval," she said.

"That rule doesn't apply to the lounges," Eric countered. "Do you still have one?"

Norma hesitated and then quickly pulled the folded fliers from her pocket and opened one up.

"See," Terri said, "you're in luck. Laura Enders. There's her phone number. Right there."

She and Eric continued to examine the photograph, unaware of Norma, anxiously watching their reactions.

"Looks like he's wearing a wet suit," Terri noted.

"It's possible. His sister's a diving instructor in the Caribbean," Eric said.

Terri glanced up at him and smiled. "I can see that you took no notice whatsoever of how good-looking she was."

"Witch."

"So, any bells?" Norma asked.

"It's a lousy photo."

"Yeah," said Terri, "but I've seen that guy. I swear I have."

"Norma," Eric asked, "why don't you stick one up on our bulletin board and one in the nurses' lounge? Maybe Terri'll think of where she saw him. Who knows, Ter, maybe you'll get the reward."

Terri Dillard pointed to the telephone number.

"Maybe you will, too," she said, "if you can get your head out of medicine long enough to make a call."

"Fat chance."

"Well," Norma said cheerily, "let me know if you figure out who this fellow is."

"Sure," Terri said. "But why?"

"No reason. I'm just interested. There was something about his sister that . . . that reminded me of one of my favorite students."

At that moment the corridor doors flew open, and a large group of surgical residents and medical students entered the E.R. Leading the entourage, erect as a post, was Dr. Sara Teagarden.

"So, where's this bleeder of yours, Dr. Najarian?" she asked.

She was wearing a knee-length clinic coat over her scrubs, and paper booties over her O.R. shoes. And as usual when she entered a room, the idle chattering and random movement of people lessened dramatically. Although he didn't particularly like her, Eric had to acknowledge that Grendel was a force—one hell of a presence.

"He's in Four, Dr. Teagarden," he said.

Teagarden motioned her team toward the room with a shake of her head.

"How many units so far?" she asked, nudging her gold-rims back onto the bridge of her nose.

"Probably six by now."

"We would have preferred being called at three."

"I understand."

In spite of himself, Eric felt intimidated by the woman. Five units before a surgical referral was pretty much standard practice, but he made no comment.

"You called the GI fellow down to scope him?"

"We thought he might be able to get at the bleeding point," Eric responded, already sensing the next volley.

He had, under the stress of a life-threatening emergency, made certain decisions. And now, even though the patient had been skillfully stabilized, those decisions were being challenged by one of the three people in the hospital he least wanted to confront.

"We'd rather scope our own patients," Teagarden said. "I thought I'd made that clear at the last residents' meeting."

"What can I say?"

Teagarden looked at him coolly.

"What you can say, Dr. Najarian, is that when a system is in place with established guidelines, and you have contracted to be part of that system, you are willing to follow those guidelines."

Eric felt himself flush at the surgical chief's rebuke. To either side of him, Terri Dillard and Norma Cullinet were statues. He swallowed the urge to defend his actions and to point out how effective they had been. Teagarden knew as well as he did that he had given the patient good care.

Then, without warning, the surgical chief reached out a fleshy finger and flicked the pin on Eric's lapel.

"That's a most attractive pin, Dr. Najarian," she said. "The caduceus—symbol of everything that is noble about our profession. I would suggest that if you are going to continue wearing it, you commit yourself to conformity with the rules. Now, if you'd care to accompany me, we shall see what needs to be done for that patient of yours."

Darden . . . Silver . . . Teagarden . . . Seated alone in the residents' lounge, Eric doodled the three names over and over again on a blank patient-history form, circling each one. Then he crumpled the sheet up and angrily threw it into the wastebasket.

It was nearing three in the afternoon. The E.R. was in a rare lull. Ordinarily he could take advantage of such a spell by stretching his legs out on a folding chair and napping. This day he couldn't come close. For years the hospital had been a constant refuge for him. For years, problems outside of work— money, family, women—were all but banished the moment he entered the place. But now, thoughts of Caduceus were making it hard to concentrate fully on anything else.

After the confrontation with Sara Teagarden he had followed her into Room Four and had watched as she guided her surgical team through the evaluation and treatment of the GI bleeder. Eventually, as he knew she would, the surgical chief abandoned attempts at medical therapy and called the O.R. In just minutes an operating room had been readied.

As the patient was being wheeled from the room Teagarden had turned and looked at him in a most peculiar way.

"I know the choices we must make on this job aren't always easy, Eric," she said, with a mellowness in her voice that he had never heard before. Then, before he could respond, she turned quickly and left.

"Thinking about that brunette?"

Eric stopped rubbing at his eyes and looked up. Terri Dillard was standing in the doorway.

"No. As a matter of fact I was wondering whom I might call to take out a contract on a certain gargantuan surgical chief."

"You might have to wait in line. . . . I don't know why she needs to behave like that. There was no excuse for talking to you the way she did. None at all."

Eric shrugged.

"I've been able to brush it off by imagining how hard it must be for her to stand in front of a mirror after she showers," he said.

"Ouch."

"Hey, forget I said that. I long ago vowed that when it came to nasty remarks, a person's family of origin and body habitus were off limits."

"Forgotten. Although I have to admit, the image is sort of . . . amusing."

"That's not exactly the word I would have picked."

"Well, guess what. I've been looking at that poster, and I think I remember where I saw that woman's brother."

Terri poured herself half a cup of coffee, sat down beside him, and smoothed the flier out on the table.

Eric stared at the photo for a time, then shook his head.

"Think back," she said. "Remember that day you and your friend used your laser?"

"Sure."

"Remember the Code Ninety-nine in the other room?"

Eric's eyes narrowed. "This guy?"

"Or a twin," Terri said.

"I don't see it."

"Of course you don't. You were only in there for a few minutes, and—don't take this wrong, now—you had other things on your mind."

"Terri, that guy was beyond saving," he said, with more defensiveness in his voice than he had intended. "He was dead before he hit the door."

"Hey, easy, Eric. You know that's not what I was saying."

"Sorry. That scene with goddam Teagarden still has me on edge. Besides, the man in this photo is a computer trouble-shooter. That guy was a drunk. He had a bottle of T-bird in his pocket."

"I'm real good on faces," Terri Dillard said. She stood. "And I think that's the guy."

"Maybe," Eric muttered. "Maybe so."

Terri headed for the door.

"Just in case," she said over her shoulder, "I sent for his chart. It should be up in a few minutes. For that woman's sake, I hope I'm wrong."

Eric's mind's eye flashed on the scene by the derelict's bedside, and on the slow EKG complexes he had chosen to disregard.

"I hope so too."

"Carlisle Hotel."

"I'd like to speak to Miss Laura Enders, please."

"One moment."

Eric cradled the phone against his ear and stared down at the notes he had made describing the unsuccessful resuscitation of a patient known to White Memorial only as John Doe. Despite Terri Dillard's confidence, he had been unable to match the face in the poster with the unshaven derelict he had briefly worked on that day. Even if it was the wrong man, he rationalized, he might be of some help to Laura Enders. Terri had, as usual, been right. He had noticed.

"Hello?" She sounded a bit breathless.

"Laura Enders?"

"Yes."

"It's Eric Najarian. We met earlier today at—"

"White Memorial. I remember. How did your patient do?"

"My patient? Oh, the GI bleeder. He's in the recovery room right now."

"Do you always refer to your patients by their diagnoses?"

Eric smiled at the woman's perceptiveness.

"The leg in Seven, the stroke in Ten—I caution the medical students not to do it; then, when I'm not paying attention to what I'm saying, I do it too. Please don't hold it against me."

"Don't worry. I watched you work, remember?"

"Thank you."

"Sorry if I sound out of breath. I just ran in to change before hitting the street for my evening rounds. Boston's only supposed to have half a million or so people, but right now it seems like ten times that. I guess I should be grateful Scott didn't disappear in New York."

For a few moments there was silence. Eric was looking down at John Doe's hospital record, wondering if it would be cruel to hand the woman even an ort of information, given the doubts he had.

"So," she said finally, "did someone at White Memorial recognize my brother's picture?"

"I, um, no. Not that I know of."

"Oh." There was disappointment in her voice.

"But we put them up in the lounges."

"That's great. Thank you."

"I'll see to it that some copies get posted in other parts of the hospital as well."

"That would be good of you."

For a few interminable seconds there was only silence.

"Laura," he said finally. "I . . . I was wondering if you might be free for dinner."

"Tonight?"

"No, I'm working, and I don't ever know when I'm going to get out. How about tomorrow?"

"Well . . ." She drew the word out, as if trying to find the most tactful way to turn him down. "Well, sure," she said suddenly. "I'd like that very much. I could be ready by seven."

"That's great. I'll pick you up at your hotel. Any special kind of food?"

"My choice, huh. Okay, let's see . . . Do you know of a good Armenian restaurant?"

"Armenian?"

"You are Armenian, yes?"

"Yes, but—"

"I grew up with a girl named Suzy Rupinian. One of my favorite things about having her for a friend was eating over at her house."

"The woman wants Armenian, the woman gets Armenian," Eric said. "Tomorrow night, we eat at Pariegam. It's in the neighborhood where I grew up, so I'm not exactly invisible there. Can you handle that?"

"Sounds perfect. Is it dress up?"

"Dress down," Eric said. "The food at Pariegam is of the gods, but we're talking sawdust on the floor, not linen on the table."

"I can do sawdust. Is Pariegam someone's name?"

"No, it's the Armenian word for friendship."

"Good start," Laura said.

. . . Initial assessment found patient with no pulse, respiration, or blood pressure. Pupils midposition and non-reactive. Standard CPR with endotracheal intubation begun at 10:17 A.M. by Dr. Gary Kaiser, later relieved by Dr. Eric Najarian. Treatment consisted of intravenous epinephrine, atropine, and Isuprel per American Heart Assn. protocol. See nurse's flow sheet for times and dosages. Throughout the resuscitation attempt, patient's cardiac rhythm remained agonal end-stage beats at 8/minute (see rhythm strips). Patient pronounced dead by Dr. Eric Najarian at 10:40 A.M. Transferred to morgue pending identification and notification of next of kin.

The cardiac rhythm tracing was as Eric had remembered: broad, slow complexes that could not possibly have been electrically capable of generating contractions of the heart muscle. Certainly there was more he could have tried: a pacemaker, another series of drugs, more aggressive attempts to measure and balance blood pH. But even if, by some miracle, he had succeeded in restoring a pulse, John Doe was brain-dead. The signs were all there. And for that, there was no therapy.

. . . the choices we must make on this job are not always easy. . . .

"You said it, lady," Eric muttered, reflecting on Sara Teagarden's uncharacteristically sensitive remark. "You said it."

In twenty-four hours he was going to have to sit across from a woman he wanted very much to get to know, and tell her that a nurse who was seldom wrong about such things had identified her brother as the derelict he had failed to resuscitate.

He put his notes and the EKG tracing aside and turned to the nurse's notes. At the bottom of them was a notation, signed by Norma Cullinet: DR. T. BUSHNELL, MEDICAL EXAMINER, NOTIFIED. REQUESTS TRANSPORT OF BODY TO GATES OF HEAVEN FUNERAL HOME FOR HIS EXAMINATION. HE WILL MAKE OUT DEATH CERTIFICATE THERE, AND ATTEMPT TO LOCATE NEXT OF KIN.

Eric checked the receiving area to ensure that the triage nurse was keeping up with the crush of patients. Then he went back to his office and pulled out the Boston Yellow Pages. The Gates of Heaven Funeral Home, Donald Devine, director, was located not far from White Memorial. He had opened this can of worms by calling Laura Enders. Now there wasn't much choice but to try to put the lid back on.

Reluctantly, he picked up the phone.

9

It was nearly nine before the E.R. was quiet enough for Eric to sign out to the senior on duty. He undressed in the on-call room, and then wrapped a towel around his waist and forced himself through a few minutes of stretching exercises. It had been a long and draining fourteen-hour shift, and every muscle in his body seemed to be in some phase of contraction.

The exclamation point on the trying day had been a prolonged but unsuccessful attempt at resuscitating a fifty-seven-year-old coronary victim, brought in by ambulance in full cardiac arrest. From a purely technical standpoint the Code 99 had been handled well enough. But far more often than not, efforts in such cases were doomed. From the loss of blood pressure to the onset of effective CPR, the window to prevent irreversible brain damage was only four to six minutes, if that. And at some point during most resuscitations, physicians went from hoping they would get an effective heartbeat back to praying that they wouldn't. Intellectually Eric had never had a problem with that reality. Emotionally, though, he still tended to take every failure personally.

How had he reacted to the death of the drift diver? he wondered now.

As he showered and dressed he tried to reconnect with his actions and emotions that snowy February day. He had been completely immersed in Russell Cowley's emergency and in the use of the new laser. That much he remembered clearly. But had he reacted at all to the death of the derelict in the next room?

Distracted by the question, he made a final brief check of the E.R., then headed across the largely deserted lobby toward the library. He had an hour before he was due at the Gates of Heaven Funeral Home, and he wanted to review some data on the complications of using less-than-fully-cross-matched blood for emergency transfusions.

His call to the home earlier that day had been answered by a tape in which Donald Devine, to the accompaniment of strings, had introduced himself and promised to be back by ten. The music and the man's unctuous telephone voice bordered on parody, and Eric had formed an image of him that included an elongated face, sloping shoulders, and a waxed moustache. He had left a message outlining his interest in John Doe and stating that, unless he heard otherwise, he would stop by the Gates of Heaven between ten and eleven.

He was entering the long corridor from the lobby to the Bigelow Building when Dave Subarsky fell in step beside him. Subarsky was dressed in jeans, sneakers, and an MIT sweat-shirt. He had an armload of bound journals and textbooks wedged between his forearm and his beard.

"Library?" he asked.

"Where else?"

Subarsky shrugged. "At this hour? How about home?"

"You mean this isn't my home? Damn, now he tells me."

"You look a little more tired than usual, old buddy."

Subarsky used his key-card to open the library door.

"I am, I guess," Eric said. "There's just been a lot going on. Tonight they brought in this fifty-seven-year-old guy with four kids. He was up and walking around one moment, collapsed and dead the next. I explained to his wife that we were working on him, but that he was essentially brain-dead. She begged me not to call off the resuscitation. So we tried. For more than an hour we tried just about everything, but there wasn't a damn thing we could do."

"That's just the way it is," Subarsky said, setting his pile of journals on a reading table. "God shoots . . . He scores!"

"Touchingly put, David. You are a true nonclinician. But fortunately, every so often, if we do things right He hits the post."

"Mayhap," Subarsky said. "Listen, how about a beer after we finish here?"

"Can't. I'm going over to see a guy at the Gates of Heaven Funeral Home."

"Always planning ahead. I like that in you, Eric."

"I'm trying to track down a John Doe we worked on back in February. In fact, it was that day we used the laser."

"God, I hope he's not still there." Subarsky held his nose.

"He might be actually. The M.E. won't release a body until they have a signed authorization from a next of kin. Sometimes they hang on to them for six or seven months before they give up and have the Commonwealth spring for a burial. And unless foul play is suspected, they won't ever do an autopsy. They're as terrified of lawyers as the rest of us."

"I can see the headlines now: PATHOLOGIST BOTCHES AUTOPSY, GETS SUED FOR MALPRACTICE."

"Believe it or not, it happens."

"I've never been to a funeral home. Want company?"

"Actually, I could do with a little moral support. On tape at least, the proprietor of the place sounded *mondo bizarro*. Digger O'Dell, the friendly undertaker."

"Sounds like my kinda guy."

"In that case, you're on. Between the resuscitation we just called off and the Gates of Heaven Funeral Home, I have a feeling I'm going to need a beer or two tonight."

"My treat," Subarsky said.

* * *

The Gates of Heaven Funeral Home was hardly a place to inspire poetic thoughts about the eternal. It occupied a shabby building on a dingy side street six blocks from White Memorial. The windowless façade was painted black, and the ornately lettered sign above the entryway was peeling. Beside the door was a small wooden plaque, hand-painted with the ambiguous motto:

ENTER HERE IN COMFORT: GO IN PEACE.

D. DEVINE, DIRECTOR

Several windows in what seemed to be an apartment on the second story were lit.

"Nice place," Eric said.

"Positively inspirational," Subarsky added. "Makes one want to rush right out and die."

Eric gestured at the doorbell. "Want to do the honors?"

"Be my guest. But first check around your feet for any signs of a trapdoor."

Eric depressed the small lacquered button, setting off a series of six or seven chimes which were loud enough to echo down the empty street. They were playing a melody he recognized, but could not identify.

"Dr. Najarian, I presume?"

Donald Devine's voice flowed forth from a speaker built in over the doorway. Eric swore he could hear violin music playing in the background.

"That's right," Eric said. "I hope this isn't too late."

"Hardly. Hardly. I'll be right down."

"Perry Como," Subarsky whispered. "And a damn good Perry at that."

A pair of lights recessed beside the speaker flicked on, and moments later Donald Devine opened the Gates of Heaven. Had there been a contest to design a mortician, Devine might well have been the winning entry. Thin, almost cadaverous build; sallow complexion; round, wire-rimmed glasses; coal-black three-piece suit; thinning hair, pomaded to his scalp; he was at once prototype and caricature, a man in his forties trying diligently to look sixty.

Eric introduced himself and David. Devine led them inside. The decor of the Gates of Heaven was baroque and musty, and generic string music played through speakers in every room. The air was heavily perfumed, but through the bouquet Eric could still detect the familiar, unmistakable odor of formaldehyde.

"Can I get you gentlemen anything?" Devine asked, escorting them past a small chapel to a reception area. "Some wine? A little tea?"

Both declined. Devine poured himself a goblet of burgundy and then turned down the music from a panel on the wall.

"Pardon me for asking," Eric said, "but is Devine your real name?"

Devine turned to him, his fingertips touching to form a steeple.

"Donald Devine is, in fact, my real name now. I had it legally changed a number of years ago."

"Well, it does go nicely with the job."

"Yes, I think it makes a statement of sorts. It helps put my clients' loved ones at ease."

Devine. Eric wondered if the misspelling was intentional.

Donald Devine motioned them to a pair of heavily brocaded love seats. Then he withdrew a file from the drawer of a small writing desk with glass-ball feet.

"Now then," he said, "you mentioned in your message that you were interested in the ultimate fate of Mr. Thomas Jordan."

"Thomas Jordan?"

"You did say the death of your patient occurred on February twenty-seventh, did you not?"

"That's right."

"Well then, this must be your man." Devine flipped through the file but did not hand it over. "John Doe; Caucasian male; late thirties; acute and chronic alcoholism; probable cardiac arrest due to arterios . . . art-er-i—"

"Arteriosclerosis," Eric said, glancing over at Subarsky.

"Exactly."

"How did you find out his name was Thomas Jordan?"

"Fingerprints, I believe. The M.E. does all that stuff."

"Dr. Bushnell?"

Donald Devine looked up from the file and seemed momentarily startled. Then he smiled.

"Precisely," he said. "Dr. Bushnell. Getting along in years but still as sharp as any of them. He made the ID and located the man's sister in"—he consulted the file again—"Chicago. The woman gave him authorization to release the body. We did the rest."

"Doesn't she have to come in and view it in person?" Eric asked.

"Not with a positive fingerprint ID. All she needs to do is get a notarized statement that she is who she says she is, and she can do the whole thing long distance. I think when she found out what her brother did for a living, which apparently was to drink, she lost her enthusiasm for a trip east."

Eric felt a growing sense of relief. For once, Terri Dillard had been mistaken. John Doe was not Laura Enders's brother. He was not a scuba-diving computer wizard. He was Thomas Jordan, a down-and-out alcoholic with a sister who scarcely cared that he had died.

"So what happened to the body?" Subarsky asked.

Donald Devine flipped to another page in his file.

"Ashes to ashes," he said reverently. "The body was taken to the crematorium in West Roxbury on . . . March 11. I would assume that the urn was sent to the deceased's sister."

"Well then, I guess that's it," Eric said.

"I hope I've been of some help to you gentlemen," Donald Devine said, extending a hand that felt as if it had been kept in a meat locker.

"You've been a great help," Eric said. He was thinking of how pleasant dinner with Laura Enders was going to be, now that he had no bad news for her.

Devine again formed his phalangeal steeple.

"Think nothing of it," he crooned. "At the Gates of Heaven, service is our middle name."

"Nice slogan," Subarsky muttered thoughtfully. " 'Service is our middle name.' I like that."

They thanked the mortician. Then, to the strains of muted string music, they departed.

10

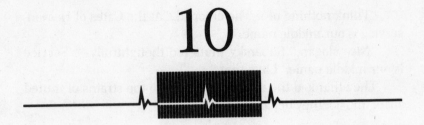

Although the lobby of the Hotel Carlisle was badly in need of refurbishing, the lighting was so subdued that Eric actually had an impression of opulence as he crossed the frayed Oriental carpet in the lobby and settled into a cracked blue leather easy chair near the elevators. He was ten minutes early, and Laura had asked him to wait. The prospect of spending time with her was appealing for reasons even beyond his initial attraction. She would be the first woman unassociated with medicine he had dated in longer than he could remember.

Buoyed by thoughts of the evening, he had enjoyed a day as peaceful, productive, and close to normal as any he had had in some time. The morning, which Verdi had ushered in with an aria that might have been from *Madama Butterfly*, had been spent paying bills and writing some long-overdue letters. In the afternoon he had played racquetball with a friend and attended grand rounds at the hospital.

Normal. After thirteen years of study and training, of ungodly hours and one sacrifice after another in his personal life, he wasn't even sure he knew what the word meant. What he did know, however, was that change was in the wind for him, with or without the appointment as associate director of the E.R.

It had been a full week since the search committee meeting. For three of those days he had worn the caduceus pin, but so far no one had made contact with him. Still, all three members of the committee had seen the pin on his clinic coat, and he sensed that before much longer Caduceus would make its requirements known to him.

A pretty blonde in spike heels and a skintight red dress caught his eye and sashayed over to him.

"Hi. My name's Wendy. You lookin' for a date?" she asked.

"Huh? Oh, no. That's a really nice invitation, Wendy, but no thanks. I'm waiting for someone."

"She this hot?" The woman gestured to her body. Beneath her excessive makeup, Eric saw, was a girl still in her mid-teens.

"Maybe not," he said, stifling the urge to ask her the what's-a-nice-girl-like-you question, or to lecture her on the importance of safe sex. "But tonight I think she's all I can handle."

The prostitute struck a pose and folded down her lower lip in an exaggerated pout.

"Your loss," she said. "You're real cute. I could give you a hell of a time at a hell of price."

"Thanks, Wendy, but no thanks."

"Suit yourself."

She scanned the lobby and set her sights on a man who was buried behind a newspaper.

"Hi, friend," Eric heard her say. She pushed down the top of the paper with one finger and peeked over. "Lookin' for a date?"

"Beat it."

The man, wearing sneakers and a tan windbreaker, snapped the paper back over his face.

"Suit yourself," Wendy said.

The prostitute retreated to her post just as the elevators opened and Laura stepped out. She had on a long gray sweater over jeans, and carried a trenchcoat over one arm. Her sable hair was tied back with a clip, and she moved with the ease and grace of a natural athlete. She was even lovelier than Eric had remembered.

"Sorry to keep you waiting," she said.

"No problem." He stumbled getting up from his chair. "You look great."

"Thanks. It's amazing what twenty miles a day of fruitless walking can do."

"No success?"

"Not unless you count a hundred or so 'hey, baby's,' ten requests for dates, and two proposals of marriage."

"Don't get discouraged."

"I'm not. At least not yet."

"Good. You still up for a slice of Armenia?"

"You bet. The thought got me through half a dozen hotels, two hospitals, a few computer stores, and a sleazy reporter who suggested that there might be a way to run a story about Scott in his paper if I was willing to come by his place tonight for an interview."

"Never underestimate the power of the press. Tell me something, Laura. With all these people coming on to you, what made you say yes to me?"

She thought for a moment.

"Actually, I was quite surprised to hear myself doing that," she said. "And to tell you the truth, I really haven't tried to figure out why I did. But it's better that way, yes?"

Eric helped her on with her coat and they started across the lobby. As they passed the reception desk Wendy winked at him, gave him a thumbs-up sign, and mouthed the words, "Not bad." Laura caught the exchange.

"Friend of yours?" she asked.

"Her name's Wendy."

"She's been here every night. She's so pretty, it makes me sad to think of what she has to do."

They waved to Wendy and then pushed through the glass doors into an evening that smelled and felt like spring. Behind them, the man in the tan windbreaker quickly folded up his paper and followed.

Pariegam was a gritty little place on a back street just off Watertown Square. Every month or two Eric managed to stop by for dinner, and invariably a significant proportion of the other patrons were relatives of his. His parents each had three married siblings, all still living in Watertown; each of those couples had children who, in turn, had in-laws and another set of aunts and uncles.

Only once before had he taken a date to Pariegam, and that night had been a disaster. The woman, a social worker at the hospital, had been so intimidated by the crush of relatives fussing over him and unabashedly sizing her up that she had spilled a glass of wine in her lap. Bringing Laura here was a calculated risk, but he loved the place, and suspected she would too.

"There's still time to change your mind about this," Eric said at the door.

"Is it going to be that bad?"

"That's hard to predict. At best, I think you can hope that only half the patrons in there are related to me. It's highly doubtful we'll be able to slip in and out unnoticed."

"I'm sure they're proud of what you've done with your life, and they have a right to be."

"I'm glad you understand. Armenians have been persecuted as much as any people in the history of the world. Life is very precious to us, and success in life means all the more because of what we've had to overcome to attain it."

"And for the ultimate in success read: *physician.*"

"That's the way a fair number of Armenians feel—especially those my parents' age."

"Well, I promise I won't embarrass you," she said.

"Shit, I'm sorry. I didn't mean to sound so pompous."

"Nonsense. All you're saying is that being a doctor is important to you. I hope someday I find a career that makes me feel that way. Now, if I don't get some dolma and yalanchee in me soon, I could get mighty testy."

Eric stared at her, genuinely impressed.

"You know, I think I like you," he said.

The restaurant, which was always crowded and noisy, was more so than usual this night. The small bar was packed three deep, and every table was filled. At one end of the place, on a small raised stage, a second or third cousin of Eric's was playing the oud, accompanied by a percussionist who was snapping out remarkable rhythms on dumbeg.

"I think you chose well," Laura said.

"I hope so, because from the look of things, we may not get a table for a while."

"Hey, Doctor Eric!"

A short, portly man with a checked apron pushed his way to them through the crowd.

"Hello, Arem," Eric said. *"Ench bes es?"*

"Not bad. I hear you're going to be the director of your hospital. Congratulations."

"God. Arem, it's just the emergency service, not the hospital. And it's only the associate director's job, and I haven't gotten it yet. Otherwise, your information is perfect."

"Hey, that's exciting," Laura said.

"If it comes through it will be. Laura, this is Arem Bozian. Pariegam is his place. Arem, this is Laura."

The proprietor took Laura's hand and kissed it.

"This is quite a guy you have here, young lady," he said. "Quite a guy. The best doctor in the city of Boston."

"Yesterday a man at the hospital told me the very same thing," she said.

"You a doctor too?"

"No, I'm a diver."

A shadow of confusion crossed Bozian's round face.

"She leads scuba-diving trips in the islands," Eric explained. "It's a good job, Arem, believe me. A very good job. How long a wait is there for a table?"

"For you? None." Bozian turned to a small table in the corner where two old men were sipping raki and talking. "Hey, Tomas, Peter, up!" he called out. "You two have been chattering long enough. The doctor here is hungry, and so is his beautiful friend the diver."

The old men exchanged a few sentences in Armenian and then drained their glasses and stood up. In minutes the table had been cleaned and reset for two.

"That's some service," Laura said as they settled into their seats.

"It was you who got them to get up, not Arem or me."

"Me?"

"They talked it over, and decided that even though you were an *odar,* you were pretty enough to make way for."

"An *odar*?"

"That's any woman who isn't Armenian," Eric said.

They ordered dolma and yalanchee—stuffed grape leaves and stuffed cabbage—and chicken with pilaf. By the time their first course arrived, two couples of cousins had stopped by the table for introductions. Laura heard the word *odar* several times as they spoke to Eric in Armenian.

"You're a celebrity," she said when they finally had some time alone.

"*Novelty* might be a better word."

"I understand. This isn't anything I'm too proud of, but when I was in college I entered and won a beauty pageant. Miss Ham Hocks or something like that. For a time I was a celebrity. Everyone made a fuss over me. I didn't like it very much."

"Well, by now I'm used to it here in Watertown," Eric said. "But all the attention I get has been really hard on my younger brother."

"There's just the two of you?"

"Uh-huh. George dropped out of high school He's been in trouble with drugs and alcohol ever since."

"That's terrible. Is he okay now?"

Eric shook his head.

"Are you two close?"

He thought for a time.

"No. Not really," he said. "We're just too different, I guess. Our parents always held me up to him as an example of how he should be, and eventually he came to resent everything about me."

"Things can always change, you know."

"Maybe they will someday. I don't think about it much anymore, but hearing you talk about the relationship you have with your brother made me sad that George and I don't get along better."

"I owe a lot to Scott," Laura said.

"Do you want to tell me about him?"

Two glasses of raki arrived at their table as Laura recounted some of the background of her life, and the events leading to her decision to leave Little Cayman. She took a sip of the clear, oily liqueur, and sputtered.

"You actually drink this?" Her eyes began to water.

"Unless we can put it to better use, like lubricating tractors. Tell me something. Do you have any evidence, besides the postcards, that indicates your brother's in Boston?"

Laura shook her head.

"Nothing, except . . . You're probably going to think this is stupid, but several times since I left Cayman, I've felt this really intense closeness to him. Once was in Virginia at the company he used to work for; once was two nights ago, while I was walking across Boston Common; and once was when you and I met in the emergency room. That time was the strongest of all."

"Are you prone to that kind of experience?"

"Psychic, you mean? Not really. Never that I know of. The feelings are so hard to describe, and they never last long—a minute, two or three at the most. But they're very real, and they help me know I'm doing the right thing."

"I'd like to help you search for him," Eric said. "I could take over canvassing the hospitals."

"That would be wonderful."

"You know, when I called you yesterday I actually thought

I might have some information. The picture of Scott on your poster got a rise from one of our nurses."

Laura stiffened. "What kind of a rise?" she asked.

Eric motioned calm with his hands.

"It didn't pan out," he said. "Back in February, I tried but failed to resuscitate a derelict who was found face down in the snow in an alley. One of the nurses who worked with me that night—her name's Terri Dillard—thought Scott's picture reminded her of the guy."

"A derelict? That doesn't make any sense. Scott earned a really good salary. Besides, I don't ever remember seeing him drink more than a beer or two."

"I told you, the guy wasn't him."

"How do you know?"

"I know because I went to the funeral home where the body was taken, and saw the identification papers drawn up by the medical examiner, the death certificate, and the order for cremation. He turned out to be a guy from Illinois named Thomas Jordan."

Only then did Laura sink back in her chair.

"Thanks for going to all that trouble," she said. "I . . . I'm relieved it wasn't him."

"Me too. Believe me." Eric flashed on Thomas Jordan's EKG tracing, and on the heart rhythm he had chosen to discount. *You don't know how relieved,* he thought. "Listen, Laura, if your brother's in Boston, we'll find him. You said the police weren't any help. Have you considered a private detective?"

Laura told him about her session with Bernard Nelson.

"Did he tell you what to put on your flier?" Eric asked when she had finished.

"As a matter of fact, he did. Why?"

"Well, I think the poster is okay, but I wish you had put a few more things on it."

"Like what?"

"Like special interests—sports he played, distinctive hobbies or habits he might have had."

"I . . . I told you, he didn't share that much of his life with me—especially over the past few years."

"Was he gay?"

"No. I mean, I don't really know."

"I understand. How about any distinguishing marks—scars or tattoos?"

"No scars that I remember, but he did have a tattoo."

"Well, that's the sort of thing you might add to the poster if you do a second printing. A tattoo, huh. Somehow that doesn't exactly jibe with the image you've given me of your brother."

Laura smiled wistfully.

"He got it when he was fifteen," she said. "Our parents were very strict, and Scott was sort of . . . not really wild, but independent—very independent. Once, after a big blowup, he ran away and hitchhiked to St. Louis for three days. They were absolutely frantic while he was gone. Anyhow, when he came back, he had a tattoo. He had it done way up on his hip so our parents wouldn't see it when he had a bathing suit on. The one time he showed it to me, he threatened to cut off all my hair if I ever said anything to them. It was seven or eight more years before they died, and I don't think they ever found out. Isn't that funny? . . . Eric?"

Eric had propped his forehead on the heel of his hand, and was staring down at his plate. Slowly, he looked up at her. His eyes were cold and hollow.

"The tattoo," he said hoarsely. "What was it of?"

"Roses. Why?"

"Three roses."

"That's right." She looked at him strangely.

"With writing underneath each one."

Now Laura paled.

"Mom, Dad, and Laurie," she said. "Eric, what's going on?"

Eric ran his fingers through his hair.

"It doesn't make sense," he said.

"What? Please, Eric, what?"

"That derelict, Thomas Jordan. He had that tattoo. I'm sure of it."

* * *

They left the restaurant without finishing dinner, and walked in numb silence through Watertown Square and down along the Charles River. Overhead, through the hazy reflected glow of the city, flecks of stars dotted the spring sky. Laura slipped her hand into the crook of Eric's arm and pulled him close to her.

"You're really certain?" she asked finally.

"I see a lot of tattoos, many on people I would never have expected to have one. They interest me, so I remember a fair number of them anyhow. And that one was unique because of where it was, and also because it was beautifully done. It struck me at the time because, frankly, there wasn't anything else the least bit appealing about the man who had it."

"Scott was—is—one of the most appealing men I've ever known," she said. "He has a wonderful face, and the most expressive eyes. Couldn't the tattoo just be a coincidence?"

"Of course it could."

"You don't believe that. I can tell."

Eric shrugged helplessly.

"Terri Dillard, the nurse who felt she recognized Jordan as Scott, is a pretty sharp person. The scientist side of me is prepared to consider one coincidence, but now this would be two."

"But the funeral director . . . the fingerprints . . . the death certificate. It doesn't make sense. How could the medical examiner have misidentified the body?"

"I don't think he could have," Eric said grimly.

"He lied?"

"Either he did, or Donald Devine."

"But why?"

"I don't know. I've heard that medical schools pay a hell of a lot for bodies. Maybe they've got some sort of scam going."

"How can we find out?"

"Well, for a start, I think we should have a talk with Dr. Bushnell, the M.E."

They walked away from the river and found a diner with a

pay phone. T. Bushnell, M.D., was listed with a Beacon Hill address.

"It's only eight-thirty," Laura said. "Do you think it's worth trying to call him?"

"I'd rather try it in person. If there's something weird going on, I don't want this guy to have time to think about it."

"Should we go now?" she asked.

Eric took both her hands and held them.

"Can you think of a better time?" he said.

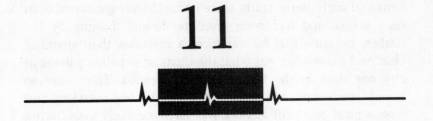

11

There were two observation huts in Charity, Utah: one at the west end of the main street, built atop what was once the Miner's Bank and Trust building and was now the laundry; and one by the clinic in the east end, set beside the water tower, which still functioned quite nicely, storing water pumped up from the spring deep beneath the town. This evening Garrett Pike sat on a three-legged stool in the east end hut, gazing out across miles of rolling desert at the sun, now a huge copper plate dropping close to the horizon.

He was nearing the end of one of his three-month stints at the hospital and was getting antsy to return to L.A. for a three-week break. The setup, which Dr. Barber had suggested to him at his hiring nearly two years before, was perfect. Three straight months of relative solitude in the desert was about all he could handle, and three weeks of the smog and bullshit in L.A. was just about enough as well.

Pike's title was mental health worker, and in fact he did speak to the patients from time to time—ask them their problems and such. But in truth, since he had barely graduated from high school and had been given no formal training by Dr. Barber, he knew that he was more a caretaker than anything else. And a caretaker was what the thirty or so patients living at any one time in the Charity Project needed. They were so heavily medicated, so sluggish, that having one oversleep and miss a meal or a shift at work was far more likely than having one slip off into the desert or commit an act of violence.

Initially, when he had answered Dr. Barber's ad in the *L.A. Times,* Pike had been reluctant to consider working at a hospital for the criminally insane, especially one stuck out in the middle of nowhere. But the pay was great—several times what he was making as a security guard—and Barber had assured him that the project had proven completely successful at keeping patients docile. The key was a long-acting tranquilizer, which was itself being evaluated for more general use.

Whenever the boredom began to get to him, Pike liked to think back to how it was before he took the job, back to the days when he didn't have a pot to piss in, and owed money to everyone and his brother. Now he had a car, a decent little apartment in the city, and even some money in the bank. The secrecy bothered him a little—he was barred from entering the clinic building, and promised immediate termination should he speak of the Charity Project to anyone. But he enjoyed feeling that he was doing something of value to society. And as long as he could go hunting in the desert, and drive into town every few weeks to get his rocks off with one of the girls at Cathie's Place, the bennies of the job far outweighted the drawbacks.

Pike checked the hour and then took his clipboard and pushed himself to his feet. It was time for evening rounds. On the street below, he could see the last of the patients shuffling their way from the dining hall to the barracks. All in all, he mused, the government must consider the Charity Project to be a huge success. Besides himself, there was John Fairweather doing maintenance; the old Indian woman, Jane, in the kitchen; and Dr. Barber. The rest of the jobs at the hospital—all menial and repetitive tasks—were done by the patients themselves.

Three workers and one doctor for thirty or forty patients. Talk about cost-effectiveness!

Pike clipped the two-way radio over his left hip and hung his night stick from a leather thong over his right. There were shotguns locked on the wall in each hut, but the only time he had needed one on the job was a year or so ago, when a young couple from L.A. had stumbled into the town by accident. Pike smiled at the memory of how tough he had acted, and how frightened the psychologist and his pushy wife had looked facing the business end of the Remington. Dr. Barber had given him a decent bonus for handling things so well.

Pike started his rounds by checking through the fields and greenhouses. It had been a while since he had last thought about the couple, and he wondered, as he usually did when that affair crossed his mind, what sort of deal Dr. Barber had struck with them to keep the existence of the Charity Project a secret. A day or two after the pair had left Charity, he had asked John Fairweather about them. But the tight-lipped Navajo had just shrugged.

The store, the laundry, the gymnasium, the showers, the vitamin shop, the women's barracks, the maintenance shed. Pike worked his way down Main Street, one building at a time. As usual, everything and everybody were in place. Except for the arrival of a new patient every two weeks or so, or the departure or death of an old one at about the same rate, there was never a change in the place. Pike assumed that those who left were transferred to a medical hospital, or back to a regular prison, but neither Barber nor John Fairweather had ever actually told him.

The men's barracks occupied the building that had once been Charity's hotel. Twenty-two patients were currently housed there, four or five to a room. Each patient was identified by a single, simple name—almost certainly not his real one. The names were sewn onto every article of clothing, and were recycled when a patient left the hospital for whatever reason.

Tonight, as always, the men were all accounted for. Some sat silently on their beds, staring off at nothing; a few were flipping absently through old, frayed magazines; and two were coloring clumsily with crayons on blank paper. Seeing them like this, it was hard to hang on to the notion that each had been judged criminally insane. Pike studied the bland and expressionless faces as he ticked off the names on his list, and he wondered about what horrible things each of them had done.

Pike started each day at Charity by picking up the roster from Dr. Barber. There were always asterisks beside three or four of the names, indicating which patients were scheduled for examinations or tests. This night, Dan, Charlie, and Bob were starred. Pike motioned the men to their feet and led them in silence from the barracks, down the dark and chilly street to the clinic.

The clinic building, a large new one-story cinder-block structure, was surrounded by a high fence topped with barbed wire. Pike was buzzed through the outside gate and then deposited the three men in the sparsely appointed waiting area. In almost two years he had never been any farther into the building than that room. Fairweather had the run of the place, as did the doctor who, from time to time, came to help Dr. Barber or check on the program. But the clinic was off limits to everyone else.

Pike handed his daily roster over to Barber and left to wait in the east end observation hut. In half an hour or so Barber would notify him by two-way that the patients were ready to return to their beds.

If there was a problem of any kind, Barber would signal him by radio or by a "panic button," which would sound an outside alarm. But in almost two years there had been no such emergency. Nor, Garrett Pike knew, would there be one tonight.

As far as he could tell, the Charity Project was functioning as close to perfection as any program—government or otherwise—that he had ever heard of.

Dr. James Barber sat on the edge of the waiting room desk, studying the records of the three men seated placidly before him. He was wearing a white clinic coat, dress shirt, string tie

with turquoise clasp, and highly polished western boots. In the
pockets of his clinic coat were a stethoscope, a reflex hammer,
an ophthalmoscope, and a .45 caliber semiautomatic Colt pistol.

"Well, Bob," he said, "it looks like just a once-over and an
injection for you tonight. No blood tests. Charlie, Dan—you two
just stay put while I check over your friend here and give him
his medicine."

The two patients with patches reading CHARLIE and DAN
sewn on above their breast pockets, sat dutifully as the third
man was led into a small examining room just off the waiting
area. After donning rubber gloves, Barber checked the man's
blood pressure and temperature, listened to his heart and lungs,
and then checked his eyes, abdominal organs, reflexes, balance,
and response to light pain and vibration.

"You're doing fine, Bob, just fine," he said. "Your memory
seems to be shot, but otherwise there's not a hint of that viral
encephalitis. I think we can consider you a cure. How does it
feel to be part of medical history?"

Barber paused a beat for a response, but knew there would
be none. If he had chosen to start the man's treatment earlier,
there was every reason to believe that not nearly so much
mentation would have been lost. He made a note to confirm that
theory on the next patient with equine encephalitis virus. But
for now, the best he could do was to continue observation on
the man and with time, perhaps, reduce his tranquilizers.

He stepped back, admiring his patient as if he were a hard-
won tennis trophy. Another cure. Carditis, fulminant hepatitis,
and now encephalitis; and promising results with two leukemias
and one of the AIDS patients. Caduceus would be pleased, he
thought. The Charity Project was well ahead of the timetable
they had set. And of course, that also meant that one Dr. James
Barber was closer than ever to the good things—the really good
things—in life.

Barber took a filled syringe from the drawer beneath the
examining table.

"Okay now, Bobby," he sang, "just lower your trousers for
your shot."

"I . . . don't . . . want . . . to," the man said. Each word was forced.

"My, but you are a feisty one," Barber said. "Maybe you still have some more recovery in you after all. But understand this, my friend: What you want or don't want doesn't matter here. We've told you that. It's what you *need* that counts. And what you need right now is this shot. Now, just do as I say."

"I . . . don't . . . want . . . to," Bob mumbled again, shaking his head as if trying to clear it.

"Right now!" Barber commanded.

Still mumbling, Bob undid his trousers and let them fall to his ankles. He was wearing no underwear.

Barber clucked his tongue reprovingly.

"Bob, Bob, Bob. How many times do we have to tell you: We don't want our patients running around without their underwear. Nasty germs can get into places where they shouldn't and raise all kinds of havoc. Is that clear, Bob? . . . I asked, *is that clear?*"

He slammed his fist on the desk.

Slowly, Bob nodded.

"Good," Barber said. He opened an alcohol swab. "Now turn around, Bob. This goes in the behind."

Bob hesitated, then mechanically did as he was asked.

"Oh, yes," Barber exclaimed, "I remember you now—the one with the rose tattoo. Anna Magnani, Marlon Brando—I loved that movie. Well, Bob, whoever Mom, Dad, and Laurie are, I'm sure they'd be very proud of the sacrifice you're making. So here you go. Bend over and let's take another step toward your place in history—and mine on the Riviera."

Barber swabbed a spot just to the side of the tattoo, buried the needle to the hilt, and depressed the plunger.

The man named Bob reacted not at all.

12

Beacon Hill, largely pared
down in the nineteenth century to fill in the Back Bay, was
overbuilt with brownstones and low apartment buildings set
along a tangle of narrow streets and alleys. Its varied blocks
were home to many of Boston's elite, but also to transients and
virtually every class in between. Even though Eric had a Beacon
Hill resident's sticker on his Celica, the drive there from Watertown took considerably less time than it did to find a place to
park.

"Do you go through this every time you bring your car
home?" Laura asked.

"Parking is only half the fun," Eric said. "The other half is
the excitement of wondering whether your car will still be there
when you want to use it again."

"Theft isn't much of a problem on Little Cayman. There
are only six cars and three pickups on the whole island."

"The lines to get resident parking stickers must be very
short."

They found Thaddeus Bushnell's home with no difficulty. It was a run-down structure on the lower portion of the hill, the side farthest away from Eric's apartment. There were three floors in the old brownstone, but only one window on the first was lit.

"How're you holding up?" Eric asked, as he scanned the place.

"I'm upset, and bewildered as hell."

"You're certainly not the only one. I promise we're going to figure this madness out, though."

"I know. It really helps to feel I'm not in this alone anymore. Eric, I'm sorry if I keep harping back to this question, but are you sure about the tattoo?"

"Believe me, I wish I weren't. I'm not sure why, even, but the memory of it is very clear to me. Much clearer than Scott's— I mean, the patient's face."

"You don't have to watch your words with me. Remember, I lived through my parents' death. I just can't believe this, that's all. When I left Cayman to begin looking for Scott, I purposely began preparing myself for the worst. But not something like this."

"Just hang in there a little longer."

For the briefest moment an EKG pattern flashed in Eric's thoughts—wide electrical complexes, spaced at eight-second intervals, gliding across an endless monitor screen.

The man was clinically dead, he told himself. *There was nothing more that should have been done.*

He chased the pattern from his mind and rang the buzzer. They waited, and then he rang again.

"No one's home," Laura said.

Eric rang a third time, more persistently. They heard the sound of someone moving inside.

"What do you want?" The voice was thick and raspy.

"Dr. Bushnell?"

"What do you want?"

"Dr. Bushnell, my name is Dr. Eric Najarian. I'm a resident at White Memorial. We need to speak with you."

"Go away," the voice said.

"Dr. Bushnell, please. It's very important."

"Nothing involving me is very important. Go away."

They sensed the man beginning to retreat from the door. Eric pressed the buzzer again.

"It involves the Gates of Heaven Funeral Home," Laura called out.

A few seconds of silence, and then the door opened a crack. An old man peered out over the safety chain. He was in his seventies at least, and was dressed in a robe and slippers. His silver hair was a disheveled mop. And even from several feet away, Eric could smell alcohol.

"Please, sir," he said. "Please let us in. We won't take much of your time."

Thaddeus Bushnell checked them both up and down, and then pushed the door closed and fumbled the chain free.

"Thank God," Laura muttered as the door swung open. They stepped inside and immediately exchanged bewildered looks.

The foyer of the place was dark. Back-lit by a dim lamp, Thaddeus Bushnell looked even older than they had first thought. He stood several feet away, leaning heavily on a metal walker, glaring at them.

"Now, what is it?" he growled.

Laura stepped forward to him, and instantly Eric saw the man soften.

"My name's Laura," she said gently. "Laura Enders. May we come in and sit down for a bit?"

The old man hesitated, and then turned and led them into a living room that was as depressing as a mausoleum. The furniture, which had probably been elegant at one time, was frayed and dusty. On the cluttered coffee table were several vials of pills and a half-filled bottle of vodka. There were empty bottles on the floor. If Thaddeus Bushnell was conscious of them, he gave no sign. He maneuvered his walker to a worn, floral-printed easy chair, and sank down into an indentation that seemed permanently molded to his thin frame.

Eric introduced himself again.

"Thank you for seeing us, Dr. Bushnell," Laura said, taking a seat near him.

Bushnell tapped a nonfiltered cigarette from a crumpled pack and lit it on the second try.

"Place needs a woman," he said. "It's gone all to hell since Evie died."

"Your wife?" Laura asked.

"Cleaning lady. My wife died nearly ten years ago. Ol' Evie went a month or two after that. I don't suppose you two want a drink?"

"No, but go right ahead," Eric said.

The old man nodded, and then nodded again. Eric realized that he was drifting off. He leaned over, poured Bushnell a small drink, and held it beneath his face, shaking him gently with his other hand.

"The nights get real lonely," Bushnell said, taking the glass. "This stuff helps pass the time."

"Are you a pathologist?" Eric asked.

"Hell, no. I'm a GP. At least I was until I retired."

"But you're still a medical examiner?"

"As far as I know I am," he said. "For a time I kept trying to get my name taken off the goddam county's list, but they kept telling me to wait until they found someone else who was willing to take over. I tell you, there are so many incompetents in the government, it's a wonder goddam Khrushchev hasn't walked right in and taken this whole place over long ago."

Laura gave Eric a sad look that said she hadn't missed the reference.

"So you still do work for the county?" she asked.

"White Memorial, that where you said you worked?"

"I do. Yes, sir," Eric said, glancing again at Laura. "I work in the emergency room." Once more he could see Bushnell beginning to nod off. "Were you on the staff there?"

The man's bloodshot eyes opened again.

"Thirty years or more," he said. "If I could do it all over again, I'd be a goddam vet."

"But you still work as a medical examiner?"

"You can't believe it, can you," the old man said. "Well, neither can I." He seemed suddenly to perk up. "I keep hearing how this state's got one of the most advanced forensic departments in the country. Well, I'm here to tell you that that is a bunch of hogwash. There's no goddam money. There's incompetence at every step of the line. There's fancy equipment that no one knows how to use. There's tests that get sent off and never get done. And there's old farts like me still on the rolls because the state won't come up with the cash to pay anyone else."

"Do you actually do autopsies?" Eric asked.

"Hell no. If I suspect foul play in a death, I turn the whole thing over to one of the state pathologists. But they're so damned overworked, it's a wonder one of them hasn't cut his thumb off during a post. In fact, for all I know, one of them has."

He snorted a laugh at the notion, and then broke into a fit of coughing. As soon as he had calmed down, he lit another cigarette.

"Do you get called in on a case often?" Eric asked.

"Every few days, maybe. Sometimes I don't bother answering my phone, though. It serves 'em right for not letting me retire."

"Dr. Bushnell," Laura said, "we're trying to learn something about my brother. His name's Scott Enders, but you would have known him as Thomas Jordan. This past February, you went to see his body at the Gates of Heaven Funeral Home. From what we can tell, you used fingerprints to identify the body, and then signed the death certificate. Do you remember that? . . . Dr. Bushnell?"

The old man had nodded off again, his burning cigarette still dangling from his lips.

"I can't believe he hasn't fried himself yet," Eric exclaimed, pulling the cigarette free and dropping it into an already-overflowing ashtray.

"Can you imagine him fingerprinting a case and searching out a next of kin?" Laura asked.

"I can't imagine him leaving this house."

"Is it worth pushing things further?"

Eric studied the man and then shook his head.

"He may have signed a death certificate," he said, "but it's doubtful he did any more extensive research than peeking into a casket."

Laura took a tattered afghan from the couch and wrapped it around the old physician's lap. Then, quietly, the two of them stood and left the house.

"Does this make any sense to you?" she asked as she closed the door behind them.

"No," he said. "But I'll bet it makes sense to one Donald Devine. Something really ugly is going on here."

Hand in hand, they walked to where they had parked.

"Want to come up to my place for a bit?" he asked. "Verdi'd love to serenade you."

"Another night, maybe. From what you've told me, Verdi sounds like my kind of parrot. Tonight I've got to be alone for a while to sort some things out. I *would* love you to walk me to the hotel though, if you want."

They worked their way up Charles Street, then crossed Beacon into the Public Gardens.

"You know, I haven't traveled a great deal," Laura said, "but Boston is the most beautiful city I've been in."

"I haven't traveled at all," Eric replied, "but Boston's the only place I really want to live."

"Does continuing to live here depend on getting that promotion at your hospital?"

"If I want to stay in some area of academic medicine, it probably does."

"And your chances are good?"

"Fifty-fifty," he said.

"Well, I hope you get it. But if you don't, then maybe it's because something better is in store for you. Yes?"

"Maybe."

They walked onto the footbridge over the small swan-boat

lagoon, and leaned on the concrete railing. Below them, the lights of the city reflected off the still water.

"Have you ever wanted something so badly you were willing to risk hurting someone to get it?" Eric asked suddenly.

"Hardly. My problem's been never wanting anything badly enough to risk hurting *myself* to get it. Are you talking about the promotion?"

"It's a hell of a jump right out of residency. Really a once-in-a-lifetime opportunity."

"And you have to hurt someone to get it?"

"Not exactly, but . . . it's a long story."

"Eric, I hope you don't take this wrong, but I believe life is a whole string of once-in-a-lifetime opportunities. Some of them happen for us, some of them don't. The worst thing that will happen if you don't get the promotion is that something else *will* happen for you."

"I guess."

"Don't you see that you've already accomplished something that has eluded most people—including me? You've found the thing you want to do with your life. You've sacrificed and studied and worked like hell, and you've made yourself a doctor. Wherever you go for as long as you live, there are people who are going to need what you can do. There are lives you will help change for the better. The promotion is just a thing. The skills you've mastered are much bigger than that."

"Maybe so," he said.

"No maybe's. You cared enough about it to grind through college and medical school and residency. Two weeks ago I wouldn't have been able to say these things, because until then I hadn't ever experienced that kind of caring and commitment. But now I know what it means to be willing to pay a price for something that's important to you."

"You mean finding your brother."

"Yes! I feel totally committed to that, and I'd be willing to endure just about any amount of pain to see things through. But if it came to hurting someone else in order to accomplish what I want . . . well, I think I'd just find another way."

"I appreciate your saying those things to me. I really do." He thought of the caduceus pin. "Tell me," he asked, "do you sense that the man I pronounced dead was Scott?"

Laura tossed a pebble into the dark water.

"Do you?" she asked.

Once again, the scene at the man's bedside that February morning crystallized in Eric's mind. There was no question that he had been distracted by the work he was doing on Russell Cowley, and quite aware that Cowley was a trustee of the hospital. Had his desire for the associate director's position influenced his decision making? There was so much going on that morning. If he'd had just the derelict to think about, would he have given up as quickly?

"I don't know," he answered. "I just don't know."

"Well, then," she said, "if you don't know for certain, I guess we can still hope."

She moved closer to him and put her arm around his waist.

"Are you working tomorrow?" she asked.

"Actually, no. I was scheduled to, but this afternoon Reed Marshall, the other chief resident, called and asked if I would switch days with him. Some sort of appointment the day after tomorrow that he couldn't get out of."

"Well, good. In that case, how about letting me take you out for breakfast tomorrow? Afterward, you can take me to the Gates of Heaven to meet your friend Donald."

"Sounds divine," he said.

She laughed and turned to him. Before he even realized what was happening, they were kissing—softly at first, then with hunger.

"It's been so long for me," she whispered, her fingertips tracing the lines of his face. "So damn long."

Eric slipped his hands beneath her sweater and explored the silky hollow at the base of her back. The taste of her . . . the smoothness of her skin . . . the subtle scent of her hair . . . one moment each sensation was distinct, isolated in his senses; the next there was only the woman. He felt giddy, intoxicated.

"Don't stop," he begged as she lowered her head to his chest.

She pulled herself tightly against him.

"Please hold me, Eric," she said. "For now, just hold me."

For nearly half an hour they stood there, holding each other as the reflected moon glittered off the water below. Then, without a word, she took his arm and they headed off toward downtown and the Carlisle.

"Eric, tell me something," she said as they approached the hotel. "The man you worked on, the one with the tattoo—what did he die of?"

Eric felt himself tighten.

"I don't know," he said. "Exposure, maybe, in the end. He was found in the snow. The initial event? Maybe a coronary, maybe just too much alcohol. He had a bottle of cheap wine in his coat."

"Was there alcohol in his blood?"

"I . . . I don't know. There wasn't time to get a measurement. To all intents, he was gone before he ever reached the hospital."

"There was nothing that could have saved him," she said. It was a statement to herself, not a question.

"No," Eric said, too weakly. "There wasn't."

He could see tears beginning to shimmer in her eyes.

She reached up and kissed him lightly on the mouth.

"Thank you," she whispered. "Thank you for everything. Call me when you get up."

Before he could respond, she had turned and hurried inside. Eric followed with his eyes until the elevator doors closed behind her. Then he turned away, feeling drained and empty, yet at the same time as full and excited about life as he could ever remember being.

Eric wandered home through the deserted downtown streets, then past the gold-domed Statehouse and onto Beacon Hill. His thoughts were a collage of images of Laura Enders, Donald Devine, Thaddeus Bushnell, and Thomas Jordan. In the morning he and Laura would confront Devine with their suspicion that he was involved in diverting bodies to medical schools, and that he was using the signature of an alcoholic old man to authenticate his perfidy. Whatever it took, they would break him down. They would find the body of the man named Thomas Jordan, and they would learn for certain whether or not he was Scott Enders.

It was well after eleven when he entered the building through the alley. He took the back stairs to his apartment and went straight to his bedroom. His clinic coat, with the caduceus pin on the lapel, hung over the door. Laura was right, absolutely right, he thought. His years of obsession with work, and now the promotion that he felt would authenticate that commitment, had blanketed his perspective like a fog. Suddenly, the mist was burning away.

He undid the pin.

Wherever you go for as long as you live, there are people who are going to need what you can do.

It was such a simple truth. But over the years of his immersion in White Memorial he had lost sight of it completely.

He studied the pin for a few moments. Then he took it to the small balcony off his living room and hurled it out into the night. When he stepped back inside the apartment, his phone was ringing. He hurried to the bedroom.

"Hi," he said, assuming the caller to be Laura.

"Dr. Najarian," the distorted, electrolarynx voice said, "we're glad you made it home. We've been trying to reach you."

13

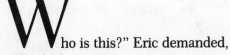

Who is this?" Eric demanded, sinking down on the edge of his bed.

"Who I am—who we are—will be disclosed to you when it is appropriate to do so."

The robotic voice was as chilling as before.

"What do you want?"

"You have been wearing our symbol. In three days the search committee will select you as the new associate director of White Memorial emergency services. But first, tomorrow morning we will have work for you to do."

"Stop right there," Eric said. "I've decided not to participate. In fact, I'm not even on duty tomorrow."

"You are on the schedule. That was checked."

"Reed Marshall switched with me. I'm not on until the day after tomorrow."

"Then you must switch back."

Eric's ear was beginning to throb from the pressure of the receiver.

"I don't think you heard me," he said. "I've decided not to participate."

"You have no choice," the voice responded. "You put on the caduceus. *That* was your choice. Now there is a treatment protocol which must be instituted by you tomorrow morning."

"What kind of treatment protocol?" Eric asked, feeling panic begin to take hold. "To whom?"

"You will be instructed when you report for work tomorrow."

"I'm not going to work."

"Three days, Dr. Najarian. In three days you will get the appointment that you have been hoping for. But only if you complete your part of the bargain. We have that power. Believe me, we do. Is that clear?"

"I want to know who you are."

"You have not yet earned that privilege, Doctor."

"And I . . . I don't intend to."

"Dr. Najarian. We know and you know what is at stake for you."

. . . I hope you get it. But if you don't, then maybe it's because something better is in store for you. . . .The worst thing that will happen if you don't get the promotion is that something else will happen for you. . . .

"Look," Eric said with sudden intensity, "you're right. I *do* want that position. I want it a lot. But I want it based on the work I've done these last five years, not on whether or not I join some club."

"Caduceus is not a club, Dr. Najarian. It is a group of dedicated people on the verge of the most important breakthrough in medicine in modern times. This breakthrough will save millions of lives. We need you."

"I . . ." Eric felt his resolve beginning to falter. Once again he heard Laura's voice. He thought about his decisions at the bedside of Thomas Jordan. Whether he had made the right choices that day or not, his ambition *had* influenced his thinking. Thanks to Laura, at least now he could admit that much to himself.

"Well, Doctor," the eerie voice urged, "what is it going to be?"

"I . . . I can't help you," Eric said.

"You don't understand."

"I know I don't, dammit. You won't tell me enough to understand." Eric sensed growing strength in his voice. "Well, now I don't want to understand. Putting your pin on was a mistake. You have my apology for doing it. But I've taken it off. Just before you called I threw it away. You'll have to find someone else to help do whatever it is you want."

The dispassionate voice grew more menacing.

"Refuse to help us now, and we guarantee that you will be off the staff of White Memorial before the month is out."

"If you have to do that to me, that's your problem," Eric heard himself say. "I'll get by."

"You are making a grave mistake," the voice warned.

"Well, I'm sure it won't be my last."

Eric's hand was shaking mercilessly as he set the receiver down in its cradle.

———ᐧᐧᐧ———

Seated on a doorstep across the street from the Hotel Carlisle, Larry Dexstall angrily stubbed out his cigarette and stared up at the darkened hotel windows. It had been a long day—a long week—and he was desperately in need of a few hours of sleep.

Laura Enders's light had gone on and off several times, suggesting she was having trouble drifting off. Once he had seen her at the window, and twice he had seen the flickering light of her TV. Now it was nearly 2:00 A.M. At 4:00, if the light stayed off, he would go upstairs to the room he had rented and take his chances for an hour or two. It would be a disaster to lose her at this point, but thanks to Neil Harten, starting at sunup he would have to be especially sharp.

From the moment Laura Enders left Communigistics, Dexstall had been following her. He had watched her save an old lady from a mugging. He had followed as she went from store to store, hotel to hospital, refusing to sit down or even slow down for hours at a time. He had watched her interact with people, and had learned her habits and her ways. Tonight, he had seen her meet a man.

Over the week, he had developed a lot of respect for the woman—not a surprising reaction, given that for nearly seven years he had been as close to Scott Enders as anyone in Plan B. He was certain Neil Harten had chosen to use him because of that closeness and his determination to learn what had happened to Scott.

From the beginning Dexstall had been against holding back what little information they had from the woman. But Harten had insisted, maintaining that the less she knew, the more vigorously she would approach her search, and the more likely she would be to stir something up.

Now, suddenly impatient, Harten had decided to up the ante. Instead of being the guide, Laura Enders was to become the bait. It stank, and Dexstall had just hung up from saying as much to the man. But Neil Harten had carte blanche to do whatever the hell he wanted. And over the day just past, he had taken the information his contacts had turned up, and had started sending out the lie that Laura knew where her brother had hidden a certain tape.

He had also ordered Larry Dexstall to be damn sure he was right there when someone responded.

Dexstall waited a few minutes longer, then trudged to an all-night coffee shop to write the note that was part of Harten's new ploy. If only Scott had stuck to the goddam weapons assignment. But Dexstall knew that taking chances and thinking for himself were what made the man so good at what he did.

Dexstall smoothed a piece of paper out on the table and began to write the words Neil Harten had given him. For days he had done a decent job of keeping track of Laura Enders, losing her just once. Beginning at sunup, he would be on her like glue.

14

Although Eric was sure that, like most people, he dreamed almost every night, it was rare for him to wake up with any notion of what the dream had been about. This morning, though, the images were vivid and terrifying. He was in the emergency room, directing a resuscitation, issuing orders to an army of residents and nurses. Then, suddenly, he was dressed in a tattered overcoat, wandering across the Common, a bottle of cheap wine protruding from his pocket. Children passed by, pointing and laughing. A band of teenagers knocked him down and began kicking him. Shielding his face with his arms, he rolled away, trying to escape their blows. All at once he toppled over the edge of a precipice and was plummeting through a heavy blackness, screaming as he fell.

He twisted and turned, hurtling through the void. Then suddenly he became aware of the hideous electronic voice, droning over and over again: ". . . Refuse to help us now, and we guarantee that you will be off the staff of White Memorial before the month is out. . . ."

His alarm clock brought the dream to an abrupt end. Eric lay naked on his bed, drenched in perspiration, his covers and pillow on the floor beside him. Several minutes passed before he was able to sort the nightmare from the actual events of the night just passed. One moment, it seemed, everything was in order in his life. He was counting down the days until his promotion. Then, just a beat later, everything had changed. It was as if a spell had been cast over him.

There was still time, he thought. Time to get to the hospital. Time, somehow, to let Caduceus know that he wanted in, that he was willing to do whatever they asked. He leaped out of bed, toweled off, and was frantically dressing when the phone began ringing.

Thank you, he thought. *Whoever you are, thank you for calling back, for giving me a second chance.*

He snatched up the receiver. "Hello?"

"Good morning," Laura said. "I hope I didn't wake you."

Eric felt instantly deflated.

"No, no," he said, "I've been up for a while."

He sank to the edge of his bed and rubbed at what remained of the sleep in his eyes. He felt dizzy, disoriented.

"I'm sorry I ran away last night," she said. "I really didn't want to leave you, but I was getting so upset thinking about Scott, and I was caught completely off guard by what happened between us."

"I understand."

"But in spite of everything, I did have a wonderful night."

"Me too."

"You sound a little distracted. Are you okay?"

"I'm fine," Eric said, sensing the ungodly tension in his body beginning to lessen. "There's been a lot going on in my life, that's all. I'll explain when I see you."

"Then we're still on for breakfast?"

Eric glanced over at his clinic coat, hanging on his bedroom door. The pin *was* gone, and so, in all likelihood, was the future he had so carefully laid out for himself. But in that moment he sensed relief sweep over him. He had done what he had done, and now, as advertised, his life was already moving on a new, irrevocable path.

"We're still on," he said with sudden enthusiasm.

"Terrific," she said. "They don't have room service in this place, but if you want to come over, I'll pick up some coffee and croissants or something."

"I'll be there," Eric said. "You can count on it."

———⌐⌐⌐———

Najarian not working today. He has revoked his commitment to us, and will be dealt with. Until a suitable replacement can be found, you must handle things just as you did with numbers 105, 106, and 107. The enclosed is our way of thanking you for your continued efforts.

C.

The note was in a sealed envelope on Norma Cullinet's desk when she arrived for work at seven. Included were ten $100 bills. The nursing supervisor read the note once, and then again. Then she shredded it angrily and threw it into her wastebasket. As much as she loved her involvement with Caduceus, as much as she delighted in living on the edge, she detested taking unnecessary chances. And now, for the fourth time since the firing and subsequent disappearance of Craig Worrell, she was being asked to take a fairly big one.

Actually, she acknowledged, two of the three cases she had been forced to handle hadn't really been that risky. The retarded teen on the ward on Merriman 7 had been pronounced dead by his resident and turned over to her without so much as an attempt at resuscitation; and pitiful Gary Kaiser had been so flustered and incompetent in trying to revive the drift diver that he had no inkling the man was receiving ten times the adrenaline dose Kaiser was ordering.

Norma's performance that day had been flawless. Still, the arrival at the hospital of Laura Enders and her posters pointed out that the system devised by Caduceus was not. Although it made little sense, given the description of Scott Enders as a computer expert, Norma was almost certain that the derelict and the woman's brother were one and the same. And if that was so, then clearly the patient had lied in every piece of information he had told her about himself. Given that, surely no one in Caduceus could criticize her for the break in protocol. And now the whole business seemed to have blown over.

Cullinet slipped the bills into her wallet. A thousand dollars for less than an hour's work. She smiled. At least someone was willing to pay her what she was worth. She checked to be sure her office door was locked, and then from her desk withdrew the Xerox copy of an emergency-room admission sheet. The patient, a woman, had been treated at White Memorial forty-eight hours before. Two items on the sheet were marked with a yellow highlighter: AGE—55, and NEXT OF KIN—NONE.

Norma drew a circle around the woman's phone number. Her pulse began to quicken as she dialed and then listened.

"... two ... three ... four ... five ..."

She counted each ring out loud.

"... seven ... eight ... nine ... ten ..."

Four cases, four thousand dollars, she thought. And that was just a token of what was in store for her if the work of Caduceus proved as profitable as she had been assured it would be.

"... fourteen ... fifteen ... sixteen ..."

On the twentieth ring Norma hung up. Loretta Leone was not going to answer her phone ... not now, not ever. She checked the Boston directory, took a deep, calming breath, and dialed the police.

"Hello, police?" she said, affecting the halting, cracked voice of a much older woman. "I've been expecting a call from a friend of mine, Miss Loretta Leone. That's L-e-o-n-e. I was supposed to take her to her doctor's appointment later this morning, but she hasn't called and I can't get an answer at her apartment. She never misses an appointment, but she's not well, you know, and I'm afraid something might have happened to ... No, no I haven't gone over there myself. Her appointment's not until eleven, and I have a terrible back condition that ... Oh, it's Three-fifteen East Harcourt Street, apartment six.

. . . Thank you, young man. You're very nice. Thank you very much."

Norma set the receiver down just as the police officer was asking for her name. She then straightened her desk and carefully destroyed the Xerox. Finally, she unlocked the bottom drawer of the desk and brought out a small metal box, secured by a combination lock. Inside the box were some vials, small jars of powder, and a number of already-loaded syringes. They were labeled NORMAL SALINE, but that was hardly what they contained.

Norma slid one of the syringes into her uniform pocket. If Eric Najarian wasn't on duty in the E.R., then almost certainly Reed Marshall was. And although Najarian was more flamboyant, and probably the better all-around physician of the two, Marshall was damn good, and certainly more meticulous. She would have to be exceedingly careful to keep everything looking smooth and steady for as long as he wanted to continue the resuscitation.

She replaced the strongbox and made a final check to be sure she had put everything away. Then she left the office to begin morning rounds. It would be close to an hour before the police checked on her call, the rescue squad did their thing, and the Priority One was called into the E.R.

Her attention turned to Reed Marshall and the way he handled Code 99 resuscitations. He liked to direct things from near the EKG machine and to leave the actual CPR to the nurses and other residents who were assisting him. She would have to maneuver herself into position to handle the med cart. It would probably be worthwhile checking on the nursing personnel on duty that morning. With luck, the E.R. would be busy, or at least shorthanded.

Lost in thought, studying the staff listing left for her by the night supervisor, Norma wandered past the man from housekeeping and the low sandwich-board sign proclaiming CAUTION: WET FLOOR. She had taken one step onto the glistening surface when her foot slipped from beneath her. She fell heavily, first striking her shoulder against the wall, and then pitching forward over the edge of a flight of stairs. Helplessly, she tumbled down, over and over again. Midway through the fall she heard a horrible snap and felt a searing pain shoot up from her elbow. She landed heavily at the base of the stairs, air exploding from her lungs at the moment her head snapped back against the linoleum floor. Instantly, there was nothing.

The man from housekeeping rushed down the stairs to her. But already, Norma Cullinet was arched and stiffened in the grip of a grand mal seizure.

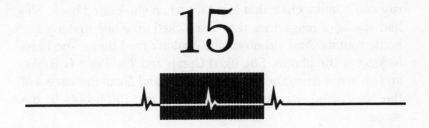

15

Apartment 6 at 315 East Harcourt Street was a cluttered one-room space below street level. Even at midday the narrow, barred windows by the ceiling let in little light, and throughout the winter a damp chill pervaded the place. Still, for nearly twenty years Loretta Leone had been happy to call the room home; happy in large measure because for most of the prior thirty-five years, she had lived in a variety of institutions and often-hostile group houses.

When Loretta first moved into 315 East Harcourt Street, her rent was $50 a month. And despite three changes in ownership of the building, $50 it remained. She paid the rent and bought her food by collecting bottles and cans, many of them saved for her by regular customers. In fact, she had been doing so well of late that she had plastic bags with three weeks' worth of cans stacked against the back wall of her apartment.

She had a telephone, a radio, and a small black-and-white TV. She had a table with four chairs, and the bed that the workers at her last group home had given her. She had a braided rug and a bulky chair that lifted up when she leaned back. She had stacks of magazines that she picked up while making her bottle rounds. And although she couldn't read them, she liked looking at the photos. She liked Oprah and *The Price Is Right*, and on warm days, she liked walking up and down the streets of the North End, waving to the children and the people in the shops.

And every day she loved to call the weather machine and listen to the forecast.

But now, Loretta Leone could do none of those things. She lay face up on her rug, unable to move, totally exhausted from trying to breathe. For a time she could see—trace the cracks in the ceiling with her eyes. But now everything was black. Her arms, especially the one with the new cast, had gone from heavy to numb. And now she couldn't lift them at all. She could feel and hear the fluid gurgling up in her mouth, choking her. For a while she could cough the fluid away, but now she no longer tried. The phone began ringing, again and again. She tried to move to answer it, but nothing happened.

Then, through the darkness, Loretta heard a pounding on her door. She heard men calling out her name.

"I'm here," she wanted to cry out. "I'm here and I'm frightened. Please help me. I can't breathe."

The pounding grew louder. Suddenly there was a loud crash. Loretta knew that her door was being broken down.

Hurry, Loretta thought. *Hurry and help me.*

"Okay, okay. Reach in and open it," she heard a man say.

"There she is. Jesus, look at this place. No wonder the North End's so clean. All the junk's in here."

There were footsteps. Then Loretta sensed a hand touching her on the side of her neck.

"Nothing," one man said. The hand probed again, and then pulled away. "She's gone. See that fluid? Looks like a heart attack."

It took several seconds before Loretta understood.

No, wait, her mind screamed. *I'm alive! I can hear you! I can hear you!*

"Do you want to mouth-to-mouth her?"

"Hell, no. Do you want to put your mouth over that? Just call the rescue squad. Let them do it if they want. Then call the station and report what's going on."

One man made a phone call while the other continued feeling along Loretta's neck. Then he put his ear to her chest.

"You know, every once in a while, I swear I can feel a pulse," he said.

"That's just the pulsing in your own fingers. It happens like that all the time. Jesus, this is some place."

"Billy, check her neck. Tell me what you think."

Loretta sensed the other man kneeling beside her and felt his hand on her neck. His fingers were colder than the first one's.

"*Nada*," he said.

The two men continued to alternate touching her neck, all the while talking about her place. Loretta heard them and felt them through a paralyzing darkness.

Soon there were more voices, other hands.

"Have you done any CPR?" a woman's voice asked.

"A little. Well, not much."

"Dammit, Billy, you know the protocol. Full resuscitation on everyone except in cases of obvious traumatic death."

"You mean like a beheading?"

"That's exactly what I mean. The only one who can pronounce a patient is a doctor. Come on, Ray, Jimmy, let's get moving."

Suddenly Loretta sensed a great deal of commotion around her. Heavy hands began to press on her chest, again and again. Her head was tilted back and something was shoved into her mouth, then deeper and deeper into her throat.

"Tube's in," a man said. "Give me some oh-two."

"Okay, now an IV."

"This cast looks new."

"Get the monitor on her. Here, Billy. You know CPR. Take over this pumping. Sixty a minute. That's it. Steve, ventilate her. Once every few seconds."

"Monitor's on."

"What have you got?"

"Something. Wait a second. Yes, she's in a very slow, regular rhythm. Eight, ten a minute. Complexes very wide."

"Billy, you should have been doing CPR on this woman."

"I'm sorry. I'm sorry. She looked dead."

"She probably is, but that's not your decision to make."

"Check her pupils, will you?"

Loretta felt hands on her eyes. For an instant she experienced a painful flash of bright white light.

"Dilated and fixed."

"I told you she was dead."

"Just keep pumping. Ray, get White Memorial on the radio. Tell them we've got a Priority One."

"Any pressure?"

"None."

"No pressure, no pulse, dilated pupils. Jesus, what in the hell was I supposed to think."

"You weren't. You were just supposed to start CPR and call us."

"I'm sorry. I'm sorry."

"Get some epi in that line."

"White Memorial, this is Boston Rescue, paramedic Driscoll speaking. We have Priority One traffic. Repeat, this is Priority One. . . ."

Voices began to blend with one another in Loretta's mind. And although she understood almost nothing of what they were saying, just the sound of them made her feel better. The hands pumping on her chest hurt her, but they, too, were reassuring.

"Do you want to shock her?"

"What's her rhythm?"

"The same. Eight a minute. Very wide complexes."

"Just end-of-the-line beating. She needs drugs, not current."

"What she needs is a goddam priest."

"Cool it, Billy, will you?"

"The people at White Memorial say just proceed according to protocol and transfer as soon as possible."

"Move the stretcher over here. Over here!"

"Stand back there, ma'am. Someone will be with you to explain everything in just a bit. It looks like heart failure. . . . I don't know if she's going to be all right. Right now it doesn't look good."

"Okay, get set to transfer. You two keep pumping and bagging her. Ready, Ray? Jimmy? Okay. One, two, three, lift!"

Loretta felt herself being lifted and then set down. For a moment the comforting hands stopped pumping on her. Then they started again.

"All right. Move back, everyone. We're coming through. Coming through."

Within the heavy blackness, Loretta Leone sensed more than felt the movement out of her apartment and down the hall to the stairs.

Help me, she thought. *Just help me. I don't want to die.*

———

The bell announcing wake-up in Charity sounded at just after six. Garrett Pike rolled off his cot and dressed. He could tell the day was going to be another scorcher. He studied the playmate on his calendar and decided, as he crossed off April 13, that the photo was a keeper. Once, just once before he died, he would like to spend the night with a woman like that.

He left his room, which was on the floor above the men's barracks, took his clipboard off the wall, and began making his rounds, checking off each patient's name as he roused him and sent him toward the dining hall. One of the men, Dick, was clearly getting ill. He had been bathed in a feverish sweat the previous evening, but Dr. Barber had merely examined him and sent him back to bed. Now, his condition seemed worse.

Pike walked the man to the clinic and turned him over to Dr. Barber. Then he returned to the barracks. He was used to illness among the patients and expected that the man would be shipped out before long. It was not until the last of the male patients had been sent to the dining hall that Pike realized his count was off. In nearly two years, this was the first time.

Feeling the first twinges of panic, he searched the barracks and then hurried to the dining hall. A quick recount told him his survey was correct. The man called Bob was missing.

Dr. Barber at first took the news calmly. But as he, Pike, and John Fairweather began a systematic search, Barber's concern grew. He hurried back to the clinic to ensure that the security system—a network of photoelectric cells and cameras encircling the town—was working properly. The system was— at least so he had told Pike—foolproof. And in fact, following an adjustment made after the Colsons' surprise visit, he had seen animals as small as jackrabbits set it off.

"He's here someplace," Barber exclaimed, ordering a repeat swing through the buildings. "There's no way he's not."

But minutes later John Fairweather called them to a shallow arroyo on the west side of town.

"He left through here," the Indian said, pointing at some gouges in the dry earth.

"That's impossible."

"Not impossible," Fairweather said. "Happened."

To prove his point, he flattened out on the ground and worked his way serpentlike along the narrow gully, just beneath the intersecting photoelectric beams. The alarm, keyed to the loudspeaker system, remained silent.

"Go through again," Barber ordered. "Go higher this time, on your hands and knees."

Fairweather did as he was asked. Instantly the alarm began wailing.

"I don't believe this. I just don't believe this," Barber exclaimed, his composure all but gone.

He raced to the clinic and shut down the siren. Then he brought out a detailed topographical map of the area and set it out for Pike and Fairweather to study.

"Who is he?" Pike asked.

"No one who could have done this on purpose," Barber responded angrily. "It was an accident. A goddam fluke."

John Fairweather shook his head. "No fluke," he said.

"That man was too doped up to find his way out of a paper bag. Someone had to have helped him."

"Hey, don't look at me," Pike said.

"Well, did you watch him swallow his pill like you were supposed to?" Barber demanded. "Did you?"

"I . . . I thought I did," was all Pike could say.

Barber just cursed.

"He has fifteen, sixteen mile of desert to cross before he reach a road," Fairweather said. "Hard desert on days like this."

"Do you think he could make it?" Barber asked.

"Doubtful. Very doubtful."

"Well, I want you to find him, dammit." Barber was nearly screaming now. "I can't believe this. I just can't believe this."

⎯⎠⎞⎯

Two miles southwest of Charity, the man named Bob kicked off a branch of a small saguaro cactus, crushed it with a stone, and rubbed some of the sweet nectar within it over his lips.

16

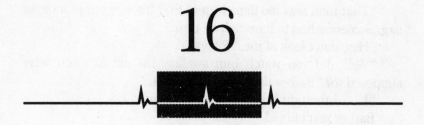

Even when confronted with Eric's near certainty that the tattoo identified Thomas Jordan as Scott, Laura could not shake the hope—and the belief—that her brother was alive. She lay awake for much of the night, creating scenarios that would fit the facts as they knew them. In the end, though, the feasibility of each one of them collapsed beneath the reality that somehow both Eric and the nurse at White Memorial would have to have been mistaken.

Eventually, with the help of a third or fourth trip through the same news on CNN, she managed to slip into a fitful half-sleep. She awoke after just an hour, walked to the window, and gazed out at the night-lit city. Then suddenly, without warning, she was crying; sobbing in the racking, merciless way she hadn't since two days after her parents' funeral—the moment when the reality of their deaths first truly sank in. And she knew, as she braced herself on the window ledge to keep from crumpling down, that she was grieving—not only for Scott and whatever horrible things he had been through, but for herself;

for the connections she had walked away from in her life, or broken before they could grow strong; for the chances she had chosen not to take; for the isolation she had imposed on herself, waiting until . . . until what?

Thirty years of living, and what did she have to show for it? What impact had she made?

She called Eric to invite him over for breakfast, half believing that their evening together had been a dream. She was prepared for rejection, prepared for him to tell her he had business to attend to at the hospital, that she would have to face the day alone. And for a moment as they talked on the phone he seemed about to do just that. She was afraid she had once again given out the keep-your-distance message so many men over the years had accused her of sending. Then, as if a taut cord had snapped, the uncertainty vanished from Eric's voice. Suddenly he sounded anxious to see her.

She put on a pair of jeans and a Shaker-knit sweater, and hurried to a nearby Store 24 for juice, muffins, and two cups of coffee. She was crossing the lobby of the hotel, heading back to her room, when the desk clerk called her over and handed her an envelope with her name and HOTEL CARLISLE carefully printed on the outside. She waited until she was settled on her bed to open it.

Miss Enders—

I saw your poster and the offer of a reward. I know your brother, and I know a lot about him. He was working freight around Warehouse 18 on the East Boston docks. Although I don't know what happened to him, there are people working there who do. Ask around, and be persistent. They will try to lie to you. I will be watching for you, and will make myself known to you when I feel it is right to do so. Your brother is a good man. I hope he's all right.

Laura was preparing to go and question the desk clerk about the note when Eric rang her from the lobby. She took the elevator down, pleased to sense herself so excited to see him again. He greeted her with an uncertain kiss on the cheek. She held him tightly.

Eric glanced back at the empty lobby and then kissed her again, this time with much less inhibition.

"You okay?" he asked.

"I am now. At least I'm better. The things we learned last night about Scott didn't really sink in until about four this morning. The hours since then have been a little rocky."

"I understand. Well, for what it's worth, I couldn't wait to see you again."

"You know, at one point, while we were talking on the phone, I thought you were going to beg off."

"I almost did. I was on the verge of getting myself into a situation at the hospital that probably isn't right. Some of the things you said to me last night helped me decide to get out of it before I drifted in over my head."

"In that case I'm glad I said them."

Eric sighed. "Unfortunately," he said, "a byproduct of my refusal will be that I won't get that promotion."

"What do you mean?"

He hesitated for a time and then briefly recounted his contacts with Caduceus, and his decision first to join their efforts in exchange for the promotion, and then to let the whole business go.

"I think you did the right thing," she said after a time. "The whole idea sounds a little scary."

"Actually, doctors use unauthorized therapies more than you might think—a drug or piece of equipment that's approved for one purpose, but that theory or their own testing has convinced them is effective for another. I did it myself once."

Thoughts of the pericardial laser immediately conjured the scene at the bedside of Thomas Jordan. And in that moment Eric knew that for as long as he practiced medicine, he would never again knowingly risk a patient's life by using an unapproved therapy.

"Well, for what it's worth, I think you've made the right decision—even at the price you might have to pay."

"I hope so. You said last night that the worst thing that can happen if I don't get what I want is that I get something else instead. I just hope that whatever that something turns out to be carries a paycheck."

"That is a definite not-to-worry," she said. "We need doctors badly in the Islands, and I'd love the chance to teach you to dive. How's that for a place to start?"

"You mean I can be a doctor and actually do something else at the same time?"

She smiled and kissed him lightly.

"Lots of other things," she said. "Listen, I've got some coffee that's getting cold up in the room, but I wanted to speak with the desk clerk first. Look what he handed me a few minutes ago."

Eric read the note.

"Where did this come from?" he asked.

"That's what I wanted to find out."

The desk clerk, a thin, wiry Iranian, looked at the envelope, then shrugged and handed it back.

"I couldn't tell you, ma'am," he said. "I came on at six-thirty, and it was right here. Perhaps the night clerk knows something."

"Could you call him?" Laura asked.

"I could, but he's got a day job and I don't have any way to reach him. Why don't you check with him tonight?"

"All right," she said.

Eric stepped forward and placed a ten in view on the counter.

"We'd love it if you could try," he said.

The man hesitated and then took the bill.

"No guarantees," he said.

"You'd think by now I would have learned," Laura said as the man headed to the back room.

"Actually, I never did that before," Eric replied.

Two minutes later the clerk was back.

"Malik says the note was dropped off by a guy with a tan

jacket on. Forty or so, dark hair. He says he's seen him hanging around the hotel lately, but he doesn't know who he is."

They thanked the man and headed for the elevators.

"I saw him, too," Eric said suddenly.

"What?"

"The guy in the tan jacket. I'm sure I saw him last night. He was sitting right over there. My friend Wendy tried to proposition him, but he brushed her off just like that."

"Would you recognize him?"

"Doubtful."

They entered Laura's room and stretched out on her bed.

"What do you make of this latest twist?" she asked, setting the muffins out on a towel between them.

"The note doesn't say anything about when Scott was supposed to have been on the docks, and it doesn't say anything that would prove the guy who wrote it actually knew him."

"So what's your guess?"

"My guess is the guy in the jacket picked up on you, somewhere in your travels, and has been following you around."

"But why didn't he try to set up a meeting? And why the East Boston docks? Surely there are more secluded places he coud lure me to if he wanted to. And why did he write what he did about people lying to me?"

"I don't know."

"So, what should we do next?"

"Well, I think we should go and poke around the East Boston docks, and be persistent because people will be lying to us."

"What about Donald Devine?"

"We can hit the docks this morning. Before we leave, I'll call and arrange for us to enter the Gates of Heaven after lunch."

"What's Devine like?"

"He has Muzak violins playing in his mortuary even when there's no funeral."

"Sounds creepy."

"Let's just say that when I go, he's not the route I want to take."

Laughing, Laura rolled over on top of him. She stroked her lips across his and then kissed him deeply.

"You know," she said, "I really like you."

Eric glanced down beside them.

"Enough to replace that half a muffin of mine you just flattened?"

She pressed her body tightly against his and kissed him with increasing longing.

"Enough to make you forget you were ever hungry," she said.

———✳✳✳———

Reed Marshall glanced out at the crowded waiting room. Then he pressed his fingers against his temples and repeated the word *serene* over and over to himself. He had started in mind-body treatment two years ago, after the stomach pains he had been having were diagnosed as a slowly bleeding ulcer. The abbreviated relaxation exercise, which his therapist had taught him, helped greatly in getting him through times like this in the E.R.

Because of the scheduling change he had made with Eric Najarian, it was his second straight brutally long shift. And of course the volume of patients had been far greater than average. Every room was full. In one of them, still unconscious and awaiting a CT scan, lay Norma Cullinet, the nursing supervisor. She had fallen down a flight of stairs, fracturing her arm and the base of her skull. Now, as if the fates had decreed that he hadn't yet been stressed to the breaking point, there was a Priority One on the way.

From his earliest days at Harvard, Reed had carefully culti-vated his unflappable façade. Besides himself, his wife, his therapist, and perhaps Eric Najarian, no one knew how inaccu-rate that image truly was. Ulcers, migraines, insomnia, periods of profound depression—if not for the mind-body therapy, he might well have come unglued long ago.

Now, though, with the selection of the new associate E.R. director due any day, and Carolyn so desperate for him to get the position, Reed knew he had to maintain. It was ironic that the biggest edge he held over Eric was his perceived coolness under fire. More than once, though, following his "cool" handling of a particularly harrowing case, Reed had gone off to one of the men's rooms and thrown up. In fact, after nearly freezing up with the woman who had ruptured her larynx, he had done just that.

"They're two minutes out, Reed."

The nurse's voice and touch on his shoulder snapped Reed out of his reverie.

"Everything ready?" he asked.

"Ready and waiting."

"Do we have a name?"

"Leone. Loretta Leone. All we have for an old record is an E.R. sheet from two days ago. The orthopedists put a cast on a minimally displaced wrist fracture."

"And she's already intubated?"

"Uh-huh. The rescue squad can't give us a down time, but they think she'd been out for a while when they arrived. Apparently the policemen who found her didn't do much in the way of CPR while they were waiting around."

"What's the latest rhythm?"

"Agonal, idioventricular beats at about eight a minute."

"No response to the epi or Isuprel?"

"None."

The nearby radio crackled to life. "This is Boston Rescue Seventy-Eight, off at White Memorial."

"They're here," the nurse said.

Reed pulled off his glasses and rubbed at the strain in his eyes.

"Is someone still in with Norma?"

"Dr. Teagarden came in about fifteen minutes ago and took over. Apparently she and Norma have been friends for years. She's got the whole neurosurgical service standing by, waiting for the CT results."

"Did she have any complaints about the way we handled the case?" Reed asked.

"None that I heard."

"Okay, then," Reed said, more relieved at that news than the nurse would ever know. "Let's have a look at this Priority One."

The electronic doors to the ambulance bay slid open, and the rescue squad, continuing cardiac compressions and mechanical ventilation, hurried back to the assigned major medical room. Reed met them at the gurney and assisted them in the transfer of Loretta Leone. His initial assessment was not optimistic.

She was the dusky violet color of death. Her pupils were midposition and unresponsive to light.

"Get some EKG leads on her," he said. "We'll run the strip off that. Keep the monitor going as well. It doesn't look good. Not good at all."

This was the moment when Reed had to make a decision as to whether they should proceed with attempts at resuscitation. The rescue team leader, Judy Kelly, was one he had worked with many times. She was perhaps the very best of a group of excellent paramedics.

"Any change?" Reed asked.

Judy shook her head. "This is the rhythm we found her in." She handed over an EKG strip. "It looks the same as the one now."

"Do you have a good IV?"

"Excellent."

Reed listened to the patient's chest to ensure that the endotracheal tube hadn't been pushed so far down the trachea that it was occluding one of the main bronchial tubes.

"She's full of fluid," he said. "Full to the brim. Let's hang in there just a bit, everyone. Give her an amp of bicarb and another amp of epi. And send off a set of blood gases, just in case. I don't think we're going to be at this too long, though."

He glanced up at the monitor screen. The woman's rhythm remained the same—slow, wide complexes at eight or so a minute.

"Call cardiology down here," he said. "We may want to put in a pacemaker. . . . Pupils?"

"Fixed," someone called out.

"Keep pumping. Someone check her femorals to be sure we're generating a decent pulse. Judy, give me your best guess at a down time."

"Twenty minutes minimum before effective CPR was started," the paramedic said.

"What do you think?"

"Honestly?" She glanced over at Loretta Leone and the team that was working on her. "I think it's not fair to this woman to continue."

Reed rubbed at his chin and wondered for a moment how far backed up the waiting room was getting.

"Anybody know if she has any family?" he asked.

"No next of kin," the nurse said. "It's right here on her last E.R. sheet."

"She's like a bag lady, only with a one-room apartment," Judy said. "The place was full of empty bottles waiting to be returned, and junk in every corner."

"Jesus," Reed muttered. "Give her one more amp of epi and call for those gas results. Oh, and you might as well try an amp of calcium as well. I want to keep going until the cardiologist gets here."

The cardiology resident, an overweight, abrasive man named Jason Berger, entered the room with two medical students in tow. One was an attractive young woman.

"Fucking place looks like a war zone out there," Berger said. "What do you have?"

"Fifty-five-year-old woman found pulseless on the floor of her apartment," Reed said. "No medical history except a broken wrist fixed here two days ago. Twenty minutes minimum before CPR was started. There's been no change in anything despite Isuprel, bicarb, and several amps of epinephrine."

Berger looked up at the monitor. "Did you give her calcium?" he asked.

"Yes."

Berger pushed past the resuscitation team and listened briefly to Loretta Leone's heart and lungs. Then he put his arm around the waist of the female medical student. Reed saw her stiffen as Berger led her over to the monitor.

"What do you see?" Berger asked.

The young woman looked flustered and uncomfortable.

"Slow rhythm," she managed. "Very broad complexes. I . . . um . . . I don't know what else."

"What you see," Berger said theatrically, "is a dead heart. We call that an agonal rhythm—the rhythmic flow of sodium, potassium, and calcium in and out of cardiac cells, creating an electrical impulse. It is unresponsive to drugs, it doesn't generate a heartbeat, and it bears absolutely no relationship to life as we know it. What do you want me to do, Reed?"

"I don't know," Reed said. "I just wanted your opinion on a pacemaker before I made a decision."

Berger laughed out loud.

"Have there been any signs of life in this woman?"

He tried once again to work his arm around the medical student's waist, but this time she managed to spin out of his reach.

"Just what you see," Reed said.

"So she's dead. I can slip a wire into her if you really want me to, but I promise you it will be an exercise in futility. What does her family want?"

"She has none."

"None at all?"

"Apparently not," Reed said.

"Reed, I have two caths waiting for me and a full clinic this afternoon. You really want me to put a wire in her?"

"What about that?" Reed gestured to the monitor.

"That?" Berger said disdainfully. "My friend, you know as well as I do that you could just stand here and do no CPR, and watch that rhythm pop along for half the fucking morning. There's no heartbeat under there."

"Thank you," Reed said.

"Then we're free to go?"

Reed hesitated. "You're free to go," he said finally. "That's it, everybody. Thank you very much."

The cardiologist led his small entourage out of the room as the team backed away from the bed. Reed reached up and flicked off the monitor.

On the litter, Loretta Leone's open eyes stared blankly at the ceiling.

"Who's the nursing supervisor?" Reed asked.

"It *was* Norma. Irene Morrissey's taken over for her."

"Get her, please. Have her call the M.E. Thank you once again, everyone. You all did a good job."

Reed Marshall felt the gnawing tightness in his gut begin to abate. Berger was an asshole, but he was also right. There was simply nothing to work with. And even if they did somehow manage to generate a pulse, all they would have created was a vegetable with no next of kin, and nothing to go back to except a bunch of empty bottles.

He glanced at the motionless body. There was a waiting room full of patients needing his attention, and a member of the search committee camped out in the E.R., probably already blaming him for the chaotic backup. With a shrug he turned his back on Loretta Leone and left the room. For as long as he had been in medicine he had hated this part of the job more than any other.

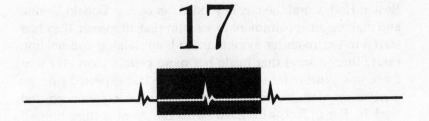

17

The crystal morning had grown overcast by the time Eric eased the Toyota off the Mystic River Bridge and down to the East Boston waterfront. Several times during their drive from downtown Boston he had checked in the rearview mirror for any car that seemed to be following them. But as far as he could tell, none was.

Although he had never been on the docks, the area was one he knew fairly well. At one time he and Reed Marshall had split a weekly moonlighting shift in the East Boston satellite emergency clinic run by White Memorial. Most of the staff at the clinic was hard-nosed Italian, like East Boston itself, and the spirit in the place was the best of any such facility in which he had ever worked. He smiled at the memory of one battle-hardened night nurse named Falano, who had taken to referring to him and Reed as "Dr. Hot" and "Dr. Cool."

Cradling the hundred or so remaining posters on her lap, Laura sat quietly in the passenger seat, gazing out at the panorama of

Boston Harbor and the city beyond. After calling Donald Devine and making an appointment to see him that afternoon, they had stayed in her room for more than an hour, talking and holding each other in ways that made her more certain than ever that there was a future for them together. She had expected Eric, as a never-married doctor in a large city, to be experienced and worldly. But in fact, with most of his life spent getting himself educated and then trained, he was in many ways still very young and tentative.

"It's ironic," he had said as his shyness and uncertainty were becoming clear to her, "that they take a bunch of twenty-four or twenty-five-year-old kids who have spent most of our lives in school or summer camp, present us with diplomas, and pronounce us M.D.'s, and suddenly we're supposed to be qualified to help people with the most difficult and deep-seated problems in intimacy and sex. The most frightening moment I think I've had in medicine wasn't from some traffic accident or shooting. It was two months into my internship, when a bank president with a wife and two kids suddenly started unburdening himself to me about discovering he was homosexual."

In many ways, Laura began to realize, the two of them had led similar lives. Countless people had passed through their worlds, yet both of them remained isolated. White Memorial was no less a haven, no less an escape for Eric than Little Cayman had been for her.

"Whatcha thinking about?" he asked.

"Oh, nothing, everything," she said. "I keep picturing Scott and me as children, working in the field by the house, or running down to swim in the lake. Only all of a sudden, I realize it's not Scott I'm with in my mind at all. It's you."

"Well, just don't go in over your head unless you're sure it's with Scott," he said. "I'm not such a great swimmer."

"We'll have to work on that."

They drove along a high chain-link fence, past a phalanx of huge oil-storage tanks, and parked in a broad dirt lot not far from the main entrance to the dock area. The lot was empty except for several tractor trailers—two of them up on blocks, and all in various stages of rust and disrepair.

"How do you think we should do this?" she asked.

"Well, if that note you got is valid, I think we're going to have to be a little pushy. Why don't we just find out where Warehouse Eighteen is and set about making pests of ourselves? At the very least, we can paste these fliers up all over."

Eric opened the hatch of the Toyota, pulled out a blue woolen watch cap, and put it on.

"This is just so I won't be too threatening to the longshore-men," he said.

Warehouse 18 was a huge corrugated-aluminum Quonset hut, surrounded by stacks of shipping containers, pyramids of oil drums, and loading equipment. There were a few men at work around it, and some equipment operating not far away, but in the main, the whole area seemed fairly quiet.

"Why don't we just wander around for a bit and sort of work up our routine," he said. ". . . Laura?"

She had walked away from him and was staring off down the row of freighters, each tethered to a pier.

"Do you see something, or are you just ignoring me?" he asked, approaching her.

"Just thinking about Scott, that's all," she said.

Eric stood beside her, his arm just touching hers. Over-head, and as far as they could see, gulls were crisscrossing through the cool morning air, their shrill cries punctuating the background rumble of heavy machinery.

"How old were you when he took over for your parents?" Eric asked.

"Fourteen. The accident was two days after my birthday. Eric, I'm going to get to the bottom of all this. I'm going to find out who he was and exactly what's happened to him."

"Well, if he worked here," Eric said, "sooner or later some-one is going to recognize this picture."

And not ten minutes later, in the shipping office, someone did.

The woman, an attractive if overly made-up blonde, paused in her gum-chewing. "Yeah, I seen him around," she said in a heavy Boston accent. "His name wasn't Scott, though. It was

Sandy something. And of course he didn't look quite like he does in that photo. What's that he's wearing?"

"A wet suit," Laura said. "He was scuba-diving."

"Well, here he wasn't any scuba diver," the woman said, tugging at one of her bra straps. "Here he was just a grunt."

"A grunt?"

"Yeah, a manpower guy. You know, a temp. He started coming here, I don't know, a few months ago, maybe more. At some point someone must've hired him full time, though, cause it seemed he was here every day. Then all of a sudden, poof, he was gone."

"When?" Eric asked.

"I dunno. January, February maybe."

Eric and Laura exchanged concerned looks. Both were well aware that Thomas Jordan had died in February.

"Do you remember his last name?" Laura asked.

The woman shook her head. "He bought me coffee once at the truck," she said. "I hardly even got to talk to him."

"You would have liked him," Laura said.

"Hey, wait a minute. Brenda might have something on him in the personnel files."

She called over to the woman who was typing behind her.

"Take a look at this picture. Isn't this that guy Sandy who used to work here?"

The other woman, dark-eyed, slim, and perhaps ten years older than the blonde, studied the poster for a moment and then shook her head.

"No way," she said. "That's not him at all."

"You sure?" the blonde asked. "I could have sworn—"

"You asked, I told you. I know exactly who you mean. Sandy North. This guy doesn't look the least bit like him. Trust me."

The woman turned and went back to her desk.

"Well, I guess I was wrong," the blonde said, somewhat nonplussed.

Eric and Laura could think of nothing to say that wouldn't have been combative. They thanked the woman and left.

"You sure this guy ain't Sandy North?" the blonde asked after the door had closed.

"Debi," Brenda said, "I look at their faces; you look at their jeans. Which one of us is right?"

The brunette waited for a few minutes until Debi started typing. Then she picked up the phone and cupped the receiver.

"A guy and girl just left the shipping office," she whispered. "The woman's got a stack of posters with Sandy North's picture on them. . . ."

"That woman Brenda was lying," Laura said. "I'm almost certain of it."

"She did seem a little too forceful."

"Eric, what would Scott be doing working the docks under *another* false name?"

"I don't know, but I think it's time you faced the possibility that maybe his life took a downward turn after he left that job in Virginia."

"But why would he lie to me?"

Eric shrugged.

"Ashamed, I guess. Maybe he was an alcoholic and it just got the better of him."

"I don't buy it," she said. "There's too much that doesn't hold together."

They headed back toward Warehouse 18, pausing now and again to question one of the longshoremen, or to tack up a poster. At the end of half an hour their enthusiasm was gone. Not only did no one recognize Scott's photo, but many of the men they approached refused even to speak with them. Finally they made their way to the warehouse. The huge metal hangar-like doors of the place were shut. Eric peered through the thick, grimy glass of the smaller entry door. He could make out no movement inside. He twisted the knob and then opened the door a crack, failing to realize that all around the area the work noise had stopped.

"We go in?" he asked.

"If that's being pushy, we do."

Eric inched the door open a bit more.

"Are you two nosy or just stupid?"

The two of them whirled.

Three men, two holding steel crate hooks, stood in a semi-circle around them, trapping them against the wall. Beyond them, Eric realized, the docks were suddenly deserted.

"We're . . . we're trying to get some information about my brother," Laura ventured. "We think he might have worked here."

She offered a poster, but the men didn't move. The center man of the three, a bull whose head seemed to balloon up from between his shoulders, eyed them for a time.

"Go around to the side of the building," he ordered. "Walk slow."

"We're not looking for any troub—"

"Shut the fuck up and move!" the man snapped.

With the three men maintaining the arc around them, Eric and Laura sidestepped around the corner of the building and along the wall until they were screened from the rest of the dock by a mountain of oil drums.

"Okay," the bull said, "that's far enough. Now, where's the tape?"

Laura and Eric looked at him blankly.

"What tape?" Eric asked. "We don't know what you're—"

Before he could finish, the man stepped forward and hit him brutally in the solar plexus. Eric doubled over and dropped first to his knees and then on his side, gasping for breath. A bitter mix of coffee and bile welled in his throat. His eyes were tearing and he tasted blood from where he had bitten the inside of his lip. The bull pulled him to his feet.

"Just keep your mouth shut," he said. "We're talking to her. Now, lady. As you can see, I'm not a very patient person. Your brother killed a friend of mine and maimed another. It's not going to take much for me to do something similar to this jerk here, or to you."

Laura could only stare at him in fear and disbelief.

"Now," he went on, "word has it that you either have a

certain videotape or know where it is. You can save us a lot of time, and both of you a lot of pain, if you'll just tell us where it is."

"I . . . I don't know what you're talking about," Laura managed.

"Suit yourself. Artie, break one of his fingers."

"Wait, please," Laura cried. "I don't know what you want. I don't know anything about a tape. Please don't do this."

"Artie?"

The man, wearing a T-shirt with the sleeves cut away to accommodate his biceps, handed his crate hook to the bull and advanced on Eric, who was still too dazed to react with any force.

"No!" Laura screamed.

Then, from behind the mountain of oil drums, the engine of a forklift rumbled to life.

"Please, no!" she screamed again.

The three men stopped and turned toward the sound. At that moment a drum came hurtling off the top of the pile. It caught the bull-necked leader squarely in the chest, slamming him against the wall. As he crumpled to the tarmac the drum burst open, drenching him with heavy black crude, which also splashed onto Laura and Eric.

"Run!" a voice cried out from behind the barrels. "Get the hell out of here!"

The two men still standing were reaching for guns as Laura grabbed Eric's arm and pulled him through the sticky pool of oil toward the far end of the building. Before they had gone ten yards, there was a shot. Instinctively they dived to the pavement, but behind them, Artie screamed and fell, clutching his thigh.

"He shot me!" he shrieked. "The fucker shot me."

"Run!" the voice shouted again.

As Laura and Eric scrambled to their feet they saw the two men, flattened down in the oil, firing at someone behind the far end of the barrels.

Heads down, they sprinted toward the main gate. Behind them, the shooting stopped. Eric glanced over his shoulder as they neared the gate. Far across the tarmac, he could see groups of workers heading toward the commotion.

"Don't stop," he gasped.

They dashed across the road.

"Thank God," Laura said when they spotted the Toyota, still parked where they had left it.

She held her breath as Eric wiped crude oil off the key and slipped it in the ignition, and didn't exhale until they were speeding toward the bridge and Boston.

———ᴧᴧᴧ———

Irene Morrissey looked down at the peaceful face of Norma Cullinet, and said a silent prayer. Norma's CT scan had disclosed a subdural hemorrhage, and the neurosurgical suite was being readied for her. A White Memorial graduate, Morrissey had stayed active in nursing through six children and, now, eleven grandchildren. At one time she had held Norma's supervisory job, but had given it up several years before to return to part-time work. Now, it appeared, she would be back for a while.

She stayed in the room until an orderly came, and then helped the resident to transfer Norma's IV lines to the gurney.

"God be with you, Norma," she said softly as they wheeled her away. "You're too good a woman to die like this."

She watched until the gurney disappeared around the corner, then picked up her clipboard. There was business to attend to—namely the disposition of the body of a poor soul named Loretta Leone.

She went up to Norma's office—the office that once had been hers—and set Loretta Leone's chart on the desk. When there was no next of kin, her only obligation was to notify a medical examiner and turn the case over to him. It took her a minute to find the M.E. on-call list, which Norma had tacked to a corner of her corkboard. Roderick Corcoran and Thaddeus Bushnell were listed for that day. Irene smiled wistfully. Ted Bushnell and she had known one another for as long as she could remember, and had worked together on any number of his patients over the years. She was surprised to see that his retirement from family practice did not include his position as medical examiner, but pleased at the chance to reconnect with him. She dialed his number. At the seventh ring, just as she was about to hang up, Thaddeus Bushnell answered.

"Hello?" His voice sounded weak and distant.

"Hello, Ted. It's Irene Morrissey."

"Who?"

"Irene Morrissey. I'm the nursing supervisor—well, acting nursing supervisor—at White Memorial. . . . Ted?"

"Yes?"

"Ted, don't you remember me?"

"I don't remember anything," Bushnell said. His words were slurred. "Now what is it?"

"Nothing," Irene said sadly. "Nothing at all."

She set the receiver down, then picked it up again and dialed Dr. Roderick Corcoran.

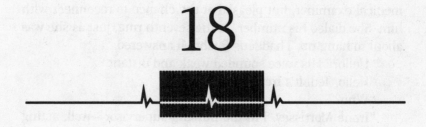

18

They picked up a change of clothes for Laura at the Carlisle, and showered at Eric's apartment. The stench of oil was weaker but still persistent. Equally frustrating was the lack of answers to any of the dozen questions they had been asking of each other. Eric called the East Boston police, then the *Globe* and *Herald*. No one had heard anything about a shooting or any kind of disturbance on the East Boston docks.

"I think we should go to the police," Laura said.

She was sitting on the bed, drying her hair and wondering what kind of an impression she was making on Verdi. From its perch at the foot of the bed, the bird was watching her every move.

"If no one has reported anything," Eric said, "what in the hell are we going to tell them? I have a feeling those guys didn't even work on the docks."

"What are you talking about?"

"I'm talking about drugs."

"What?"

"Well, just look at what happened. Three thugs with guns who seem to know who we are—or at least who *you* are—accuse your brother of killing someone and maiming someone else. Then they demand some sort of videotape. What does it sound like to you?"

He snatched up the phone, dialed the White Memorial E.R., and asked about any gunshot victims or other injuries from the docks. Predictably, nothing had come in. Several calls to other E.R.'s also drew blanks.

"Maybe Artie only *thought* he was shot," he mused.

"Do you think Scott was selling drugs?"

"Laura, I don't know what on earth your brother was into, but it sure wasn't communications networks."

"Who could have saved us out there?"

"Hey, no repeat questions allowed, remember? Especially none with 'beats me' as the answer."

"So where do we go from here?"

Eric glanced over at the clock.

"Well, unless you have another idea, I would think that in half an hour we go to the Gates of Heaven."

"How's your belly feeling?"

"Let's just say that getting sucker-punched like that is not an experience I want to repeat. However, if there's one thing that five years of emergency medicine have taught me, it's how to take a punch. I've been hit at work any number of times by any number of crazies."

She pulled him down and kissed him.

"You know," he said, "believe it or not, there's an up side to all this for me. For the first time in longer than I can remember, I'm immersed in things that have nothing to do with medicine."

"Just with pain and confusion," she said.

"Hey, Pain and Confusion are my middle names. Speaking of which, why don't we head on over to meet with Don Devine. Service is *his* middle name. I'm getting a little antsy for some explanations."

"Just watch your midsection," Laura said.

* * *

Donald Devine was dressed in the same suit and blue tie that he had worn during Eric's previous visit to the mortuary. As before, he ushered the two of them to his office and turned down the background strings. Eric thought he caught a bit of the Muzak version of "Sounds of Silence."

"Now then," Devine said. "What can I do for you this time, Dr. Dadarian?"

"Najarian," Eric corrected, noticing that the man seemed less at ease than he had on their first encounter. "Mr. Devine, we don't want to take up too much of your time, but there are some things we hoped you could clear up."

"Go right ahead," the little man said.

"We have reason, good reason, to believe that the man I spoke to you about the other night—the man you called Thomas Jordan—is Laura's brother."

"That's impossible."

The man's response was nearly knee-jerk.

"Is it?"

"Of course. That body was identified by the medical examiner, signed for by his next of kin, and cremated."

"Mr. Devine," Laura said, "we went to see Dr. Bushnell last night."

"So?"

"So he was drunk and barely able to make it from his chair to the door, let alone do the fingerprinting and research you claim he did."

"What Dr. Bushnell does on his own time is no concern of mine," Devine said, beginning to pace and avoiding any eye contact with her. "He did exactly what I said he did."

Laura crossed to him and forced him to meet her gaze.

"Please help us," she said softly. "We don't want to cause trouble for you, but we are determined to find my brother."

"And I hope you do," Devine said. "But it won't be here, because I have nothing more to tell you."

He tried to hold her gaze but failed. Finally, he forced himself past her and across the room to his desk.

"Mr. Devine," Eric said, taking up the slack, "perhaps you don't understand. We're convinced something's going on here. Something illegal."

"Nonsense."

"Is it?"

"I think I would like the two of you to leave."

"If we go, we'll be back," Eric said, "either with a court order to examine your records, or with a reporter. We promise you that."

"Do what you wish," the mortician said, pausing to mop at his brow with a linen handkerchief. "I have nothing to hide, and nothing more to say to you except that if you continue to harass me, I shall be forced to speak with the police."

"A wonderful idea," Eric said. "Let's do it now."

Arms folded, Devine turned to him.

"I think it's time you left," he said. "You have learned all there is to learn here."

"Mr. Devine, please," Laura said.

"No. I have work to do. Now, would you please go."

Laura and Eric exchanged looks, and silently decided that this was not the time for a major confrontation.

"You know we'll be back, don't you," Laura said. "My brother is all the family I have, and we're going to find him or learn what happened to him."

"I wish you luck," Donald Devine said.

The two of them had started toward the door when Eric turned back.

"Donald, I'd suggest you go right out and get yourself some more handkerchiefs," he said. "Before we're through, you're going to need a bunch of them."

For nearly a minute after the door closed behind his two visitors, Donald Devine stood statuelike by his desk.

"You can come out now," he said finally.

From the back room a tall man with broad shoulders and thick, graying red hair emerged. He wore chinos and a turtle-neck that seemed to be stretched to the limit across his chest.

"Y-you see, Les?" Devine said, shifting uncomfortably. "I told you I could handle them."

"Yeah, Donald," the man said. "You did great. Just great."

Devine, who barely reached the man's chin, backed away.

"You really mean that?" he asked.

"Course I do, Don," the tall man said with a mirthless smile.

"Do you think they'll be back?"

"Now why would I think that, Don?"

"I . . . I don't know."

"You stayed so cool that I'm sure they don't suspect a thing."

"L-look," Devine said. "I've done exactly what you all told me to do."

"And been damn well paid for it."

"I just don't want any trouble. Those people at the hospital told me this wouldn't happen."

The man reached in his pocket, pulled out one of Laura's posters, and handed it to the mortician.

"Are your two visitors right?" he asked. "Is this the man?"

"I . . . I think so."

"Don, that's not good enough. This is the bastard who filmed us that night. Now the question is: Is he the man you brought to Charity or not?"

"Maybe."

The redhead grabbed Devine's tie and twisted it tightly around his fist, nearly lifting the little man off the floor.

"No 'maybe's.' "

"Y-yes. Yes, it's him," Devine croaked.

The man loosened his grip and went to the phone.

"Who are you calling?"

"Who do you think, Don?"

"Dr. Barber?"

"Good guess. If you're right, and this is the guy, then we don't have anything to worry about."

"Listen, I have nearly two hundred dollars in phone bills and another two hundred in gas that no one's paid me for yet."

"Don, just shut up." The man picked up the phone, and then he smiled. "How ironic," he muttered. "Sandy North almost blows our whole operation, takes out two of Gambone's best men, and then ends up shuffling around in pajamas at Charity. I guess there is a God after all."

He stayed on the phone for just two minutes. Then he slammed the receiver down.

"The bastard's gone," he said. "Escaped."

"That's not possible, is it?"

"I just said it happened, didn't I? So I guess it's possible."

His face was crimson.

"I don't like this," Devine said, once again beginning to mop his brow. "I . . . I don't like this at all."

The man appraised him, his lips pulled back in an odd, icy grin.

"I know you don't, Donald," he said. "I know you don't."

———

Dr. Roderick Corcoran held appointments to the pathology staffs of all the medical schools in the city. A medical examiner for nearly thirty years, he was, in the words of one police official, long on experience but short on enthusiasm. In fact, the call that had brought him to the White Memorial autopsy suite had interrupted a session with the architect who was designing his retirement home on Cape Cod.

Now, as he completed his notes on the external examination of the body of Loretta Leone, Corcoran wrestled with the decision of whether or not it was worth adding a set of solar panels to the south roof.

Behind him, the White Memorial autopsy technician, Sang Huang, was preparing to make the huge "Y" incision that would expose the woman's chest and abdominal contents. Sang Huang was nervous. After a four-month apprenticeship in the department, he was doing his first unsupervised case. He was a superstitious man, and not that comfortable around corpses. But the job had nearly doubled his salary, and for that kind of money he was willing to endure a lot.

He paced from one side of the steel autopsy table to the

other, wondering whether he should wait for the pathologist's order, or simply proceed on his own.

This was not the case Huang wanted to start on. The examiner was a man he didn't know. Everything seemed rushed and disorganized. And the corpse was fresher than any he had ever dealt with. He glanced down at the body. The skin was waxen and uniformly pale. There were none of the external signs of death that he was used to—no fatal wounds, no rigor mortis, no dependent lividity. Involuntarily, he shuddered.

"Um, excuse please, Docta," he ventured, "you want I start here now?"

"Whassat?" Corcoran glanced over his shoulder. "Oh, sure, kid, sure. Get me six vials of blood from her heart, then set everything out on the table. I'll be done with this goddam paperwork in a minute."

Huang hesitated, then shrugged and used a scalpel to make incisions from each of the corpse's shoulders to the upper breastbone, then down past the navel to the top of the pelvic bone. At the touch of the blade, the skin beneath it seemed to tighten before falling away. Again, Huang shuddered. There was more bleeding from the incision than he had ever seen before. Much more.

He glanced over at Corcoran, who was still engrossed in his writing. The last thing Huang wanted was to look uncertain or incompetent. He was nervous. That was all. With a resigned sigh he took the huge bone shears, forced them through the thick intercostal muscles, and snipped through the ribs where they intersected with the breastbone. Midway through the procedure, he felt certain the woman had moved. It took every bit of his courage to continue. He worked his hand beneath the left side of the breastbone, and then pulled it up, exposing the heart.

Instantly, bile welled in Huang's throat. He vomited, and collapsed to the floor.

Roderick Corcoran whirled at the commotion and rushed to the autopsy table. Loretta Leone's steadily beating heart gleamed obscenely beneath the bright overhead lights.

"Oh, my God!" Corcoran cried. "Oh, my God!"

At that moment, a dreadful gurgling moan—a cry that seemed to come from the very depths of hell—welled up from the woman's throat. Her body stiffened, then went limp. Her shimmering heart quivered, then stopped.

Reflexively, Corcoran reached down to attempt cardiac massage. But just as quickly he stopped. With the chest cage mutilated, and no help available, there was no sense in it.

He bent down by his prostrate assistant and assured himself that the man's pulse was strong. Then, bathed in a cold sweat, his hands shaking, he skimmed through the woman's chart looking for a name. After a final nervous glance at the corpse on his autopsy table, he snatched up the phone.

"Page operator," he said angrily, "get me Dr. Marshall. Dr. Reed Marshall."

19

E ddie Garcia stretched the stiffness from his neck and shoulders and dropped his rig into fifth for the climb into the Rockies. The night was coal-black, and he was down to one static-filled country/western station, but thanks to a decent night's sleep at his mother's and a few tablets of "Trucker's Friend," he felt keen and alert. It was a good thing, too, because the man he had picked up wandering along a deserted stretch of Highway 163 hadn't spoken ten words in almost as many hours.

An independent trucker, Garcia was hauling beef from Flagstaff to Cleveland under contract to Buckeye Packing. He took the run whenever he could, because he liked the distance and the scenery and because he got the chance to visit his mother and sisters in Mexican Hat. The downside of the detour home was that he was now half a day behind and would have to keep at it, without sleeping, until Ohio.

He glanced over at his passenger, who was propped against the window, drifting in and out of sleep. The man had the hollow, gray, sickly look of someone who had done time, and if Eddie hadn't known that there were no prisons in the area, he might have pegged him as an escapee. Even if he had been, it wouldn't have mattered much to Eddie.

"Hey, Bob, you hungry?" he asked.

"No."

The man sat up a bit but didn't look over.

"You from these parts?"

"What parts?"

"Utah, Colorado. Hey, are you okay?"

"I . . . I'm okay."

"Well, you don't look okay. Mind if I ask what your last name is?"

Bob continued staring out at the blackness ahead.

"I don't know," he said.

"Suit yourself," Garcia said. For a time he just drove and rubbed at the stubble along his jaw. "Look," he said finally, "let's get one thing straight. I picked you up because you were twenty miles from nowhere and looked like you were needin' a ride, and because I was wantin' some company. I'm not the type to pry into other people's lives. I don't give a shit who you're runnin' from or what you're into. I did some time once myself. If I ask you somethin', then it's just for conversation or 'cause I want to help you out if you're sick. You got that?"

"Yes."

The driver looked at him with concern.

"You really don't know your last name, do you?"

North . . . Shollander . . . Trainor . . . Brikowski . . . Enders . . . Pullman . . . Scott Enders's dark eyes narrowed as he tried to sort out the many names that kept swirling through his head.

"No," he heard himself say. "No, I don't."

"Or where you're from?"

Scott shook his head.

"When did you eat last?" Garcia asked.

"I . . . don't . . . know."

Scott pictured a crowded dining hall someplace and remembered now that he hadn't eaten for days, fearing the food was drugged. *But by whom? And why?* He pictured the man named Pike, and he saw himself hiding the last capsule Pike had given him beneath his tongue. *Where did that happen?* There were snatches of other images as well, but none that he could sort out well enough to understand what they represented.

"Well, then," the trucker said cheerfully. "At least you know that you *don't* know when you ate last. Now we're gettin' somewhere. There's a diner about ten miles ahead. Some coffee and a burger will do us both some good. You got any money?"

Scott checked his right-hand pants pocket, but when he tried to reach into his left, the fingers on his left hand, which were bent in a stiff claw, refused to move. *Have they always been that way?*

"I'm watchin' you fumble around and I'm worried about you, Bob," Garcia said. "What happened to your hand?"

Scott merely looked at him and shrugged.

"This is crazy. Absolutely crazy," the driver said. "Are you just puttin' me on, or can you really not remember anything? How did you get to Route One-sixty-three? Someone leave you there?"

"I crawled under the photoelectric cells," Scott said, realizing the fact only as he spoke the words.

"What?"

"I saw the photoelectric cells, and I got down on my belly and crawled under them."

Eddie Garcia shook his head.

"Leave it to ol' Eddie to pick up the craziest bird this side of San Francisco," he muttered.

They pulled into the truck stop, which was nearly deserted. Garcia hopped from the cab and watched as his passenger worked his way to the pavement. It was only then that he noticed the man's limp. It seemed as if he couldn't pick up his left foot properly.

"I know, I know," he said, more to himself than to Bob. "The photoelectric cells paralyzed you."

Garcia ordered coffee regular and cheeseburgers for both

of them, and watched as Bob tried, then gave up trying, to use his left hand. The more he studied the man and the emptiness that seemed to envelop him, the more sadness he felt. He briefly entertained the notion of giving him a twenty and simply taking off. But just as quickly, he discarded the thought. That wasn't his way.

"You really don't remember anything, do you?"

Scott's lower lip tightened. "Not much," he said. "I want to remember something, but I just can't."

A memory flashed of kicking open a cactus and scooping out its moisture, and he wondered how he had known to do that. A succession of disconnected scenes—many of them quite violent—flicked through his mind. None of them brought even a glimmer of recognition or emotion.

Eddie Garcia bought some beef jerky and various other snack foods, paid for their meal, and then eased his semi back onto the interstate. He felt as if somehow he had stopped on Highway 163 and picked up a child in a man's broken body. Now, he had no idea what to do with him.

"Bob, tell me something," he said as they sped through Glenwood Springs and on toward Denver. "Do you have any family? Anyone you want to call? A place you want me to bring you?"

"Mrs. Gideon's horse," Scott said suddenly.

"What?"

"I need to go to East Boston to find Mrs. Gideon's horse."

"East Boston, Mass?"

"Yes."

Scott knew that was true, and important as well, but he had no idea why.

"Bob, who's this Mrs. Gideon? She a relative of yours?"

"I . . . I don't know what I'm talking about." He clenched his good hand in frustration. "Dammit, I just don't know."

"Well, look," Garcia said, "we'll be in Cleveland tomorrow night. You can hitch from there to Boston. Better yet, you can catch a bus. I'll front you the money."

"Mrs. Gideon's horse," Scott said again. "I've got to find it."

Eddie Garcia, relieved to have even the semblance of a plan, shifted into overdrive, and the rig barreled on.

20

Propped on one elbow, Laura lay in Eric's bed watching the gray light of the new day filter over the city. It had been a year or more since she had last spent the night with a man. And even though they had not yet made love, she knew that she wanted to. In a short time they had already shared so much.

She reached over, swept Eric's hair from his brow, and kissed him there. He blinked and squinted up at her. Then, without a word, he drew her over onto him and held her. For nearly half an hour they lay there, her face nestled against his chest.

"Soon?" he asked, reveling in the lines of her body and the smoothness of her skin.

She nodded and kissed him deeply.

"I want it to be perfect, though," she whispered.

He rolled her over and caressed her breasts with his lips. Her nipples hardened to his touch.

"I understand," he said, "and I promise you it will be."

They showered and then shared juice and coffee on the balcony, neither anxious to break the mood by speaking of the day just past. Finally Laura stood and leaned against the railing, gazing across the rooftops at Cambridge.

"Do you have a plan for the day?" Eric asked.

"Not really. I think it's worth going to the police and at least seeing what they're willing to do about Donald Devine."

"I agree. But after yesterday morning I'm not sure I like the idea of your wandering around the city alone. I'm off tomorrow if you can wait."

"I'll see."

"At least wait until noon. I'll call before then."

The phone began ringing. Eric hesitated, not anxious to deal with Caduceus again. Finally he pulled himself up and reentered the apartment. A minute later he was back.

"I've got to go," he said. "Something's happened at the hospital—something pretty bad. Reed Marshall's resigned."

"Resigned?"

"That was my boss, Joe Silver. Apparently, Reed pronounced a woman dead and sent her to the hospital morgue. Late yesterday, they autopsied her and found her heart was still beating."

"No! Is that possible?"

"I really can't imagine it, but according to Silver, it happened. We kid about such things all the time, and there are always stories, but this is the first time I've heard of its actually happening to anybody *I* know. Just the notion of it gives me a sick feeling in my gut. Reed called in this morning and quit. It sounds like he's in a pretty bad way."

Laura followed him into the apartment and sat on the side of the bed as he dressed.

"Eric, how can that be? How could a doctor with all that equipment make such a mistake?"

"I don't know. As I've told you, Reed's about as good as there is."

"Will you call and let me know what happened?"

"I'll call," he said. "But I'm not sure we'll ever know what happened."

From the moment the doors of a hospital open for the first time and the first patient is treated, the facility acquires a pulse and begins to develop a personality as unique as any individual's. It fumbles and grows, learning from its mistakes. It stretches and explores, reaching out more and more to the world around it. Its organs decay and need repair or replacement. Its moods—the collective moods of its patients and employees—grow more distinctive.

Within minutes of arriving at the emergency room that morning, Eric could feel the uneasiness pervading White Memorial. It was the reflection of a great hospital confronting its own fallibility.

The autopsy of Loretta Leone had taken place late the previous afternoon. The hospital grapevine, while by no means always accurate, was as swift as any communications system yet devised. Within hours everyone at every level in the institution had a version of the tragedy.

Joe Silver, looking even more frazzled than usual, met Eric at the triage desk.

"I just got a call from the goddam *Herald*," he said. "This sucks. It really does."

They walked back to Eric's office, where the E.R. chief told him what he knew.

"Marshall blew it," Silver concluded. "He just blew it."

"Nonsense. I refuse to believe that," Eric said. "Reed's damn good at what we do, and you know it." Anger prickled at the base of his neck and then began to burn. "Joe, it doesn't seem to me that you're showing a hell of a lot of loyalty to someone who's worked so hard for you for five years. The least you can do is give him the benefit of the doubt until you know the full story."

Silver glared at him.

"Benefit of the doubt? A medical examiner named Corcoran wants to have my department nailed to the wall, some asshole from the *Herald* is bringing up that Worrell business again and calling me and my staff incompetent, a woman got pronounced dead who wasn't, and *you're* calling me disloyal? You've got some goddam nerve, Najarian." His sallow complexion was nearly scarlet. "You just get out there and do your job and keep your mouth shut to any reporters," he spat. "No wonder people don't want you in a position of authority around here. You're just too damn arrogant. Marshall was overtired from working too many shifts in a row. If you had been on duty yesterday the way you were supposed to be, this would never have happened."

"Now just one minute," Eric started to say.

But Silver had already stalked from the office.

Eric sank to his chair, nearly as furious with himself for not holding his feelings in check as he was with Silver. But what he had said to Silver was true. Reed had his weaknesses, but he was a hell of a doctor. In all likelihood, whatever happened to him could have happened to any of them. Eric snatched up the phone and dialed Reed's home. On the tenth ring Carolyn Marshall answered.

"I'm sorry, Eric," she said. "Reed's in bed. He's not talking to anyone."

"Just tell him it's me and see if he'll speak with me for a minute."

She set the receiver down. In the background Eric could hear a baby crying. He glanced down the corridor at the triage area. The faces of the E.R. staff looked gray and drawn. Not one of them, he guessed, wanted to be at work that day.

"Hey, whaddaya say, pal?"

Marshall's speech was thick and awkward.

"Reed, have you been drinking?"

"Not since I threw up that blood a few hours ago, I haven't. Besides, Valium's so much mellower."

"Jesus. Reed, you've got to stop that shit."

"Why? I'm still conscious."

"Can you tell me what happened?"

"I fucked up. That's what happened."

"We all fuck up, all the time," Eric said. "That's the nature of this job, and you know it as well as I do. If we had all night to sit and debate and hold court, we could do the right thing every time. But the people we deal with are sick, and we have to make decisions. That's just the way things are."

"Well said, *mi amigo*. Well said."

"Dammit, Reed, I mean it. Now please, just tell me what happened."

"The woman had a rhythm and I ignored it. I fucked up. It's as simple as that."

Eric felt a sudden tightness in this throat.

"What kind of a rhythm?" he asked.

"Eight, ten beats a minute. Broad complexes. Looked useless at the time. But I guess they were enough to generate a contraction, 'cause that's what the M.E. said was happenin'. Now, if that isn't fucking up, I don't know—"

"Reed, did you stick the tracings in her chart?" Eric's pulse was beginning to race.

"Course I did. Mr. Thorough, that's me."

"Well, listen. Get rid of that goddam Valium and don't give up on yourself, okay?"

"Whatever you say, Doc. Well, thanks for callin'. See you around, ol' buddy."

"Reed, put Carolyn on for a minute, will you?"

Eric heard him fumble with the phone and then knock something over. Moments later his wife came on.

"Listen," Eric said, "Reed's got Valium someplace."

"He does?"

"Find it and throw it out, okay?"

"O-okay. Eric, do you understand what happened?"

"Nothing that should have caused all this trouble. Carolyn, we pronounce people like this woman all the time—believe me we do. I've done it plenty."

The admission brought a sudden chill. All Eric could think about was the need to review Loretta Leone's chart.

"You're not just saying that, are you?" Carolyn asked.

"No way. Joe Silver nearly fired me just now for sticking up for Reed. I meant what I said to him and I'm not lying to you."

"Thank you," she said. "Will you keep in touch?"

"Of course I will. But for now, just get all the booze and tranquilizers out of the house. Reed once mentioned he was seeing a therapist. Is he still?"

"Um, yes. Yes, he is."

"Well, call him. I think Reed might need to be hospitalized. At least let his doctor decide."

By the time Eric hung up, he was damp with sweat.

It took nearly half an hour to track down Loretta Leone's hospital record. It was in Joe Silver's office, but at first the E.R. chief refused to allow him to see it. Eric persisted. Finally the man relented, extracting the promise that it would go no further than Eric's office and be discussed with no one.

Unable to wait, Eric flipped open the chart in the hallway. From what he remembered, the EKG complexes were identical to those of the derelict he had pronounced dead. Not similar— identical. He spent an hour getting through the mounting backlog of patients, and then sent to the record room for the derelict's chart. He was right. The man's cardiogram and Loretta Leone's were interchangeable.

Was the man who might have been Laura's brother still alive when his monitor was shut off?

Given what evidence he had, Eric knew there was little reason to believe otherwise. The prospect sickened him. Trying desperately to make sense of things, he wandered from the triage area to the deserted residents' lounge and dropped into a battered easy chair.

Could the similarity between the tracings be coincidence?

Once, in medical school, when confronted with a confusing set of findings in a patient, he had suggested to a favorite professor that the explanation might be coincidence. The woman patiently allowed him to braid his own noose before turning to the class.

"Your cohort Mr. Najarian has chosen coincidence as his solution to this problem," she said. "I suggest to you all that while coincidence might from time to time exist in diagnostic medicine, the concept is in the main God's way of placating the intellectually lazy."

Eric managed a thin smile at the memory. Never since that day had he accepted coincidence as an explanation for anything without one hell of a fight. He took the two charts to his office and locked them in his desk. As soon as he could break from the E.R., he would head for the library to begin the process of becoming an expert on metabolic poisons and deathlike states.

Somewhere there existed an explanation for the findings in the derelict and Loretta Leone. And until there was not a source left in Boston he hadn't tapped, Eric vowed that there was no way he would settle for anything even remotely like coincidence.

21

Soon after Eric had left for the hospital, Laura floated back to sleep. She awoke after nine, bewildered and confused to find herself not in her cabana on Little Cayman. Across the room, Verdi was scuffing about beneath his cage cover. Laura set the cover aside and spent a fruitless five minutes endeavoring to coax the bird into a "good morning." Finally, she sat on the edge of the bed, trying to map out some sort of plan for the day ahead. For the first time since leaving the island she felt listless and ill at ease.

Gradually she began to see that meeting Eric—growing to care for him and to have him care for her—seemed somehow to have blunted her sense of urgency in finding Scott.

Was her commitment that fragile?

It frightened and angered her to think that it might not be fear for her brother that had been driving her so, but fear of losing the only real connection she had kept to life beyond the island.

Had her life grown that thin?

She got dressed and walked downtown to the Carlisle. The day, which had dawned cloudless, had grown overcast and unpleasantly damp. The city seemed to be begging for the relief that rain would bring. Several times during her walk she tried without success to spot anyone following her. Just the notion that somone might constantly be watching was sickening.

The Iranian desk clerk had no new messages. Laura went up to her room, turned on some talk show, and lay down. Almost immediately she could feel herself begin to drift off again. The search for Scott was so much easier with Eric along to help, she reasoned. She could catch up on some sleep, do some shopping, and wait until tomorrow to see the police. The thought of another encounter with another bored, condescending officer was not at all appealing. Besides, there was little chance of their helping anyway. Her eyes closed.

". . . and it is our belief as antivivisectionists," one of the program's guests was saying, "that the medical researchers and animal providers have a lobby going in Washington that is as strong and well-funded as any special interest group. . . ."

Laura forced her eyes open, pushed herself up, and stared at the screen. The speaker droned on, castigating the loss of perspective in the medical world.

". . . first mice and hamsters, then dogs, then primates, then so-called volunteer prisoners," she was saying. "And where do you suppose all this is heading?"

Laura snatched up the phone, dialed Information, and got the number of the anatomy department at the medical school. She was connected with a man named Bishoff, the administrator of the department.

"Mr. Bishoff, thanks for speaking with me," Laura said. "My name is Laura Scott. I'm doing some research for a novel, and I need some information on how med-school anatomy departments acquire the bodies they use for students to dissect."

"You a mystery writer?" The man sounded intrigued.

"That's right."

"Published?"

"Well, not yet."

"Oh."

Laura could sense the man's interest begin to wane.

"But I'm under contract," she said eagerly.

"Well, then, in that case congratulations are in order. Your first sold novel. You know, I've been planning a book myself. A medical mystery. I haven't quite gotten to the actual writing yet, but I do have a title: *Take Two Aspirins and Call Me in the Morgue*. Catchy, don't you think?"

Laura wished she had decided on some other ploy.

"It . . . has potential," she said.

"Glad you think so. Now then, author to author, what do you want to know?"

"Well, Mr. Bishoff, where do you get your bodies?"

"Why, they're donated."

"By whom?"

"By the only person authorized to do so—the deceased."

"People sign their bodies over in their wills?"

"That's right. They are required to notify us of their desire when they are sound of mind, and to sign a notarized form in triplicate. A copy goes to their records, a copy goes to us, and a copy goes on their will."

"Do the police ever supply you with bodies?"

"Never."

"And you get enough that way?"

"More than enough, actually. We keep them on ice. Say, wouldn't it be great to have a big chase scene that ends up in a body freezer?"

"It would be, Mr. Bishoff, but I think it may have been done already."

"Oh."

"Tell me," she said, "do you pay for them?"

"The bodies? Hell no. Only burial fees if the family wants to use the county's boot hill up on the North Shore."

"You never pay for a body?"

"Absolutely not. We can't make budget as it is. Does that wreck your plot?"

"It may."

"In that case, I'm sorry."

"One last time, just so I can be sure: There is no way someone can profit from selling bodies to medical schools?"

"Absolutely none."

"Thank you, Mr. Bishoff. You've been very helpful."

"My pleasure. Now I have one question for you."

"Yes?"

"Do you think I should get an agent before or after I write my book?"

Laura smiled. "I think after might be better, Mr. Bishoff," she said.

She hung up and then dialed the number of the medical examiner Thaddeus Bushnell. A recording told her that the line was out of order. Ten minutes later she was in a cab headed toward his lower Beacon Hill town house, hoping that in midday she might find him a bit more sober and easier to talk to.

At the turn onto Bushnell's street, she spotted the wooden barriers on the sidewalk in front of his place. The building itself was gutted—a burned-out shell. The stench of smoke and charred wood hung heavy in the air.

She asked the cabbie to wait and walked to the barriers. A uniformed fire inspector was standing beside what remained of the front doorway.

"What happened?" she asked.

The man stared at her.

"The house burned down," he said, his tone asking: *What do you think happened?*

"What about Dr. Bushnell?"

Laura sensed ominously that she needn't have bothered asking the question.

"You a friend?"

"I . . . I knew him."

The man softened. "I'm sorry," he said. "The old guy never made it out."

"I knew he would do this to himself," Laura said.

"Pardon?"

"Dr. Bushnell. I saw him the other night, and he was drinking too much and smoking. I was frightened that something like this might happen to him."

The inspector looked back at the house, and then at Laura.

"You a reporter?" he asked.

"No, why?"

"Who are you?"

"I'm . . . I'm visiting from the South. Why?"

"Because I'm not supposed to talk to anyone until we've checked on a few more things."

"Please," Laura said, suddenly apprehensive. "Please tell me what happened. It . . . it's very important."

The man sized her up for a few moments and then said simply, "The fire was set. Professional job from the looks of it, but not the best. The old guy was on the second floor. The thing was put together in such a way that he probably couldn't have gotten out even if he wanted to. . . . Miss? You look a little pale."

Laura pictured the frail little man, wrapped in his blanket, speaking of events long past as if they had happened yesterday.

"I'm *feeling* a little pale," she said. "There are some terrible things going on around here."

The man gazed again at the shell that was once Thaddeus Bushnell's home.

"Yes. Yes, I suppose there are." He put his hand out and peered overhead. "Rain's startin'," he said.

———ᴧᴧᴧ———

Except for the elegant Countway Medical Library on Huntington Avenue, the Hoffman Medical Library at White Memorial was the largest in the city. Eric planned to start his research there with a screening of basic textbooks in the areas of toxicology, metabolism, and cardiology. He would pay special attention to the bibliographies at the end of each pertinent chapter, and set up a card file of the journal articles that would form phase two of his project. His operating thesis was that somehow the two patients had encountered the same poison or environmental pollutant—a toxin powerful enough to cause cardiovascular collapse and profound metabolic slowing.

It was just after four in the afternoon. Earlier in the day a light rain had moved in on the city, floating a slick of embedded oil up onto the highways. The result—a series of multi-victim accidents—had kept him at work in the E.R. longer than he had wished. Finally he had signed out to the senior resident Joe Silver had appointed to take Reed's place, and agreed to split shifts with the man each day until a more permanent arrangement could be made.

Earlier in the day, Laura had phoned with a report of her call to the anatomy department and news of the probable murder of Thaddeus Bushnell. Hoping to come up with an explanation for the similarities between the deaths of John Doe and Loretta Leone, Eric had battled back the urge to tell her right then of the horrible error he might have made. Very soon, though, they would have to have that talk.

With a growing sense of urgency, he piled the texts on the corner of a table and began. Within an hour his list of toxins was at forty.

Aconite, curare, botulin, belladonna, sapotoxin, physostigmine, tetrodotoxin, cyanide, arsenic, acetanilide, antimony, barbiturates, bee venom, mandrake root, muscarine, amanita, picrotoxin, reptile neurotoxin, strychnine . . .

One by one on index cards he listed the substances, their toxic doses, routes of administration, sources, and principal symptoms. Each of them was capable of causing death by neurologic or cardiac paralysis, and by inference, specific doses of each might induce a marked metabolic slowdown. The task of sorting them out seemed overwhelming. But so, too, Eric reminded himself, were the hundreds of organic chemistry formulas he was once faced with memorizing.

An hour passed, then another, as he worked his way through his cards. Bit by bit the list grew smaller. For a time, one toxin or another would catch his fancy, only to be discarded by the question *How would both victims have been exposed?* or *Could the effect of the substance possibly stop after metabolic paralysis and before death?* Amanita, a mushroom poison, was one of the leading candidates. So for a time were strychnine and the toad poison bufotoxin. But again and again, as if daring him to refute it, one substance kept cropping up: tetrodotoxin, a product found in certain species of puffer fish, and believed by one researcher at least to be the long-sought-after zombi poison.

In Japan certain chefs were certified by the government in the preparation of fugu, a puffer-fish sashimi dish that straddled the line between food and drug. The chefs, some of whom occasionally died from sampling their wares, sought to preserve just enough tetrodotoxin to cause flushing of the skin, tingling of the lips and extremities, and a mild euphoria. But numerous cases of puffer-fish poisoning had been documented, the effects being, in part, pulmonary edema due to cardiac slowing, respiratory failure, and marked metabolic depression.

Could Loretta Leone and John Doe somehow have inadvertently eaten fugu?

The idea made no sense.

Outside the library the gray evening gave way to ebony night. Inside, the pile of journals on Eric's table grew. Amanita mushrooms, fugu, aconite plant alkaloid. One by one, Eric pared his list until finally only those three remained. Each, in the proper dosage, seemed capable of inducing a state of metabolic slowdown that might be indistinguishable from death.

Behind him the library door opened, then closed. Eric did not look up. Moments later he felt a massive hand on his shoulder.

"Dr. Subarsky, I presume," he said as he eliminated strychnine once and for all from his prospects.

"You are certainly a diligent little beaver," the biochemist said. "Surely you must have something more exotic to do with your free time."

He dropped a load of books on a nearby table, settled in across from Eric, and scanned the books he was using.

"*Journal of Toxicology . . . Poisons of the World . . . Journal of Ethnopharmacology . . .*"

"See, I am doing something exotic," Eric said, realizing only then how much time had elapsed.

"And what, exactly, is that?"

Subarsky leaned back and propped his gunboat sneakers on the table.

"I'm looking into the case of the lady that Reed Marshall pronounced dead yesterday," Eric said.

"Ah, yes, the talk of the town. Nasty mistake the man made. Nasty."

"I'm not so sure it was a mistake."

"*Res ipsa loquitur,*" Subarsky said.

"What does that mean?"

"Roughly, 'the deed speaks for itself.' "

"David, how would you define death?"

Subarsky scratched at his beard. "The usual, I guess. Cessation of cardiac and neurologic activity—that sort of thing."

"What about all these reports I've been reading of people who had those findings for a time and then woke up?"

"I can find you reports of dinosaur sightings in the Grand Canyon," Subarsky said.

"Well, I've been here for hours trying to put together a definition that fits all these reports, and you know what I keep coming up with? Putrefaction. That's what."

"If it doesn't rot, it ain't dead. I like it, Najarian. I like it. Although I can see how it could make for a bit of a space problem from time to time."

"Seriously."

"Seriously? Well, it seems to me that an M.D. degree and thirteen years of higher education qualify you to use '*going* to rot' as your standard."

"But Reed Marshall used that, and Reed Marshall was wrong."

"A fluke," Subarsky said. "One in a billion."

"I don't think so, David. Because you see, I may have made the same mistake."

Eric pulled out the EKG tracings and went over the two cases.

"And where is this John Doe now?" Subarsky asked.

"I don't know. Do you have some time?"

"For you? All the time in the world."

Piece by piece, Eric recounted his meeting with Laura, their visits to the Gates of Heaven and Thaddeus Bushnell, and their close call on the East Boston docks. Subarsky chewed on a pencil as he listened. When Eric finished, his friend whistled softly.

"You have been into some shit, my man. I'll say that."

"David, I have no idea what's going on, but I think the derelict and Loretta Leone were poisoned."

"How?"

"Accident. Product tampering. Psycho. Define *crazy* any way you want, and I'll find you someone who fits the bill."

"And you think you stopped too soon in resuscitating the guy who may have been your new flame's brother?"

"It's possible."

"I don't buy it."

"I don't expect you to, yet. That's what I'm doing here."

"And what have you come up with?"

"Lots of things. But what I keep coming up with is this."

Eric slid his notes on tetrodotoxin across. Subarsky scanned them in a minute.

"So," he said, "once again the zombi poison rears its ugly head."

"You know about it?"

"Some. A few years ago there was a flurry of interest in it. Even a best-selling book. But after a while articles began popping up in the scientific literature refuting most of the methods and claims."

"I know. I've read some of them."

"And you still suspect the drug?"

"Either alone or in some kind of combination. Can a good toxicologist detect it?"

"Probably."

"What about amanita and aconite?"

"Probably."

"Well then, tomorrow I'm going to the pathology department to see if they can screen Loretta Leone's blood. Then I think I'll try to set up an appointment with Dr. Darden."

"Ah, yes, White Memorial's resident Haitian. Good idea."

"If anyone around here would know about the tetrodotoxin myth, he would."

"Agreed. But do you know if he's ever been near Haiti since he came to the States?"

"Actually, I do," Eric said. "There's a clinic in Port-au-Prince that he helped set up. From time to time he takes a resident down with him."

"In that case, he may well be the man who can put you straight."

"What do you mean?"

"Well, I'm no expert in this particular area, but I can't believe any drug could do the things you're concerned about. As an Armenian, you have this overdeveloped, genetically inbred sense of responsibility. That's what makes you such a terrific doctor. But along with it goes your equally inbred Armenian sense of guilt. And right now, that sense is saying that you might have been able to do something to prevent the death of your friend's brother."

"Well?"

"Well, I've known you for a long time, Eric, and I know that if something wasn't right about that case, you would have spotted it."

"Maybe so," Eric said. "But right now, my inbred Armenian intuition is telling me that I'm onto something."

"In that case, if you need my help in any way, just ask." Subarsky scratched at his beard for a few seconds and then added, "However, I am willing to wager a pitcher of Heineken that you are orbiting Mars on this one."

Eric gathered his notes.

"I'll take the bet," he said, "and believe me, I hope you win. Tomorrow I'll hit Darden, the pathology department, and the Countway Library. I'll keep you posted."

"Do that," Subarsky said. "Just let me know if I or my trusty computer can be of any assistance. And in the meantime, I'll keep my telescope trained on Mars."

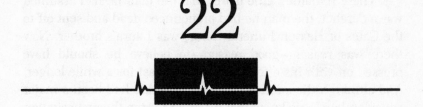

22

I'm at the hotel. Call if you get in before 10. If not, call before you go to work in the a.m. Have not been to the police yet, but plan to do so tomorrow a.m. Hope your library work went well. Thank you for all you've done.

Love,

L.

P.S. Refrigerator and cupboards have been restocked. Hope I didn't disturb any great bacteriology experiment by discarding the milk carton.

The note was on Eric's pillow when he arrived home, along with a volume of exquisite photographs entitled *Diving Off the Caymans.* He flipped through the pages, wondering what it might be like to live in such a place. For so long his life had been on automatic pilot, locked on a single unerring course. Now, there was only uncertainty—uncertainty and a woman.

He set the book aside and spent a few minutes flipping through his notes. He had expected to find Laura waiting in the apartment, and now felt some relief to discover she was not. He had much to work through.

There remained little doubt that the man he had assumed was a derelict, the man he had pronounced dead and sent off to the Gates of Heaven Funeral Home, was Laura's brother. Now there was reason—good reason—to believe he should have pressed on with his efforts that day, at least for a while longer. And although the *quality* of his patient's life had been a major consideration, Eric knew that his order to stop the resuscitation had been based, at least in part, on his judgment of the *value* of that life as well. It was a judgment he, like Reed, would have to live with for the rest of his career.

It was a bit after ten, so Laura's note left him an out—an excuse to delay sharing his conclusions until morning. But the more he thought about it, the more he wanted to get it over with, to tell her everything and to hope for her understanding. Both Scott and Loretta Leone had been somehow poisoned, either by a psycho or an inadvertent exposure to some toxin. Despite Dave Subarsky's doubts, that much seemed clear to him now.

He hoped Laura would see that although he might have made essentially the same mistake as Reed, the deck had been stacked against them both.

He paced the apartment for a time, wondering if other patients in other settings had suffered fates similar to their two cases. Finally, he called the Carlisle. The phone rang half a dozen times before it was picked up. No one spoke.

"Hello?" he said. "Laura?"

Her sigh was audible.

"Oh, thank God," she said. "Eric, I just got a call from some man who threatened me. All he kept saying was 'It's not over. We want the tape.' I screamed at him that I didn't know what he was talking about, but he hung up. I don't know what's going on, but if his aim was to frighten me, he did a very good job."

"I'll be right over."

"You don't have to do that."

"I want to. I was sort of surprised that you weren't here."

"I'm sorry. I thought it might be better if I spent some time alone. I . . . I just started feeling as if I was growing to depend on you too much."

"Laura," he said. "I'm depending on you too. Believe me I am. There're some things I need to tell you about. When I do, I think you'll see that in some ways I have as much at stake in getting to the bottom of all this as you do. I'd really like to come over now."

"What things?"

"Face to face?"

She hesitated.

"I'll be here," she said finally.

Laura sat cross-legged on the bed and listened impassively as Eric recounted in detail his actions and thoughts on the morning the derelict was brought in.

"I knew," she said, when he had finished. "That first night we were together, I could see a shadow cross your face every time you talked about that resuscitation."

"For what it's worth, I'm sorry. We see so many cardiac arrests—so many people brought in essentially dead after a coronary—that unless a case is strikingly different from all the others, we don't have even the slightest suspicion that something other than natural causes might be involved."

"Should you?"

"Well, I guess if we're perfect we should."

"I didn't mean it like that, and you know it," she snapped. "Eric, please. I just want to understand."

He looked at her sheepishly.

"Sorry," he said. "Let me think how to explain this. . . . Okay. There's a concept in diagnostic medicine called index of suspicion. Put in simplest terms, index of suspicion means, if you don't think of it, you'll never find it. The better a physician is, the more diagnostic possibilities he considers and sifts through in a given case. If you think every case of middle-aged cardiac arrest had a coronary occlusion, you'll never diagnose a cocaine overdose in a fifty-five-year-old corporation president."

"I see."

"Believe it or not, the worst physician can usually do the right thing, or at least not do something harmful, ninety or even ninety-five percent of the time. It's that other five or ten percent that separates great from run-of-the-mill in our business."

"Most of us think of doctors so differently from that."

"I know. And the misconceptions—the lofty expectations that the public has of us—are largely our own doing. For years physicians have fostered the notion that things are or aren't, simply because we say so. And the public buys into it—or at least a large segment of it does—because people want the security of knowing that there's someone they can turn to who has all the answers. But please don't think I'm copping out or trying to make excuses for my actions last February. I'm just trying to help you understand what was going on in my head. I . . . I just didn't have a high enough index of suspicion that something way out of the ordinary might be going on."

Without responding, Laura walked to the window and looked out at the city. She could feel Eric's anguish, and the part of her that was growing to love him wanted so much to hold him, to tell him that she understood. But she felt unable to get past the fact that the man whose life had been in his hands that winter morning was, in all likelihood, her brother. . . .

Suddenly she found herself thinking about a situation she had once been in with a diver whose skill and competence she had misjudged. The man had ended up wedged in a narrow tunnel with his air supply all but used up. Luckily, she had sensed trouble and located him just a minute or two from disaster. She was able to buddy-breathe him up to the surface, but the outcome could easily have gone the other way.

She wondered how her life would have changed, how she would have responded had he not made it out of that tunnel alive. The manager of her club, people diving with her day after day—they had no more interest in seeing her as human, as fallible, than she did Eric.

When she finally turned back to him, tears glistened in her eyes.

"I wish you hadn't stopped trying," she said.

"I know. I wish like hell I could have that morning back. Believe me I do. And I know it doesn't help Scott, but I'm determined never to make judgments on the value of anyone's life again."

"And never to ignore the possibility that what seems ordinary may not be at all?"

"That too."

She put her arms around him and touched her lips to his ear.

"Fair enough," she whispered.

———〰〰———

"There it is, pal. Beautiful Cleveland, Ohio."

Eddie Garcia swigged down the last of a thermos of coffee and wiped his mouth with the back of his hand. He was glad to be nearing the end of the run but was anxious about his passenger. Soon, he would have to drop Bob off, point him in the direction of the bus terminal, and go about unloading his rig. The man was no more prepared or equipped to strike out on his own than a kindergartener.

For a time during their journey, Eddie had tried to help him remember something, anything. But beyond recurring references to East Boston, a woman named Gideon, and her horse, he got nowhere. He pressed questions about Bob's limp and about his hand; he asked about his family, his service record. Nothing. Not even a glimmer. It was as if a razor had sliced cleanly through all connections to his past. For a while, Eddie even gave thought to driving him to Boston. But with a perfect turnaround run awaiting him in Cincinnati, that possibility was out of the question.

He guided the semi off the interstate and began working his way through darkened, successively narrowing streets toward Buckeye Packing. It was three in the morning, an hour before he was due in. He didn't know his way around the city at all, but there was a bit of time to look for a diner. If they found one, he would spring for one last meal, give Bob thirty or forty bucks, find out directions to the bus terminal, and send him on his way. That was more than most anyone else would be doing in a similar spot.

Bob himself, after sleeping through most of Indiana and Ohio, had awakened just outside of Lorain, and was once more staring out the window. If there were any thoughts going on in his mind, he showed no sign of them. But Eddie could still sense the aura of sadness and bewilderment enveloping him.

"You feelin' okay?" Eddie asked.

"Uh-huh."

"Good, because you've got some travelin' ahead of you. Boston is still a hell of a ways."

Scott squinted at the passing lights and strained to put together the images swirling through his mind. Nothing connected. Nothing at all.

They turned onto a side street barely wide enough for the rig, and rolled into a broad, deserted flat lined with warehouses and factories.

"Buckeye Packing's just up this road," Eddie said.

"That's good," Scott said with no emotion.

"I thought we might cruise around and see if we can find us some breakfast."

Eddie had slowed to less than ten miles per hour when he saw a man standing in the road ahead, waving a stop sign at them. He was dressed in work clothes and a plaid hunting overshirt. Garcia brought the semi to a stop and rolled down the window.

"Mornin'," he said. "What's up?"

The man, husky, with close-cropped hair, walked to the window, pulled a revolver from his waistband, and held it two feet from Eddie's face.

"Open the door," he growled. "No sudden moves."

A second man, brandishing a shotgun, appeared by the passenger door, and a third stepped just in front of them.

"Hey, wait a minute," Eddie said. "I'm just hauling beef. There's nothing of any—"

"We know what you have," the man said. "Now just get out or you're dead."

Eddie turned to his passenger.

"Bob," he said evenly, "we're being hijacked. Just open your door and do what these fuckers say. Without this rig and this load, I'm busted, but I don't know what the fuck else we can do, goddam it."

Slowly, the two of them opened their doors and dropped to the pavement. The man who had stopped them, clearly the leader of the three, motioned them together and then pointed to an alley between buildings.

"In there," he ordered. "Do as I say and neither of you gets hurt."

"Hey, look," one of the others said. "This guy's a gimp. What are you, some kind of war hero?"

Scott merely looked at him.

"Do what the man says, Bob," Eddie whispered. "Hey guys, please. This rig's all I have."

"In the alley," the man barked.

For Eddie Garcia, the half-minute or so that followed was little more than a blur. It began with Bob bending over, ostensibly to tie his shoe. Suddenly, and with vicious force, he swung his arm backhand, catching one of the hijackers across the throat, and dropping him like a stone. In virtually the same motion, he whipped his good leg around, sweeping the second man to the ground and stunning him with a glancing right, palm up under his chin. The shotgun clattered to the pavement, but the man, not immobilized, lashed out with his feet, knocking Bob over.

The leader of the group, a beat slow to react, was raising his revolver when Eddie kicked him in the groin. The man doubled over as Eddie kicked him again, catching him on the upper arm and sending him sprawling.

To Garcia's left, the first man hit was stumbling to his feet while the second had grabbed Bob by the throat and was beginning to pummel him. In that instant, Eddie saw the look on his passenger's face. It was an expression he would never forget as long as he lived—not one of panic or rage or fear, and certainly not the blank stare he had grown so used to over the miles. Rather, Bob appeared almost serene, removed from what was happening to him, oblivious to the pain. He seemed to be completely ignoring the man on top of him in order to focus in on something else. Before Eddie realized what was happening, Bob had reached out with his good leg and swept the shotgun several feet in his direction.

Eddie dived for it, rolling over and over again as he fumbled to cock it.

One hijacker had already started to run.

The second, realizing what had happened, shoved Bob aside, kicked him hard in the ribs, and was racing toward the alley as Garcia fired. The shot seemed to hit him, but after staggering a step, he barreled on. Moments later, he disappeared into the alley. By the time Eddie brought the shotgun around, the man he had kicked was up and sprinting away. He leveled and fired, but the hijacker was already well out of range. In seconds, the street was quiet again.

Shaken and gasping for breath, Eddie stumbled to his feet. Bob was on his knees, holding his left side.

"You okay, Bob?" Garcia asked.

Scott coughed and felt the searing crunch of broken bone in his chest. He had had fractured ribs before, he knew. But when? And how?

"I'm okay," he managed.

Garcia helped him to his feet.

"You sure?" he asked. "You want to go to a hospital?"

The word brought a barrage of images to Scott's mind, none of them pleasant.

"No," he said hoarsely. "No hospital."

Eddie Garcia stepped back a pace and looked at him.

"I've never seen anyone move like that," he said. "Who are you?"

Scott looked at him sadly and shook his head.

"I don't know, Eddie. I don't know anything. I didn't even plan on attacking those guys. It just happened."

He coughed again, and had to splint the pain to keep from passing out.

"I'm takin' you to a fuckin' hospital," Garcia insisted.

Scott shook his head. "I've got to get to East Boston," he said. "It's important."

"For what?"

"I . . . I don't know."

"Mrs. Gideon's horse?"

"Something. I don't know what."

Garcia opened his wallet and pulled out a hundred dollars— all the money he had but ten.

"Here," he said. "The Buckeye people owe me big bucks for this run. Thanks to you I'm gonna collect. Can you make it back into the cab?"

"I can make it," Scott said, wincing with each step.

"We'll find the bus terminal then." Garcia kept shaking his head in amazement as he started up the rig. "I don't believe what I just saw you do. With your hand and your leg like that. I just don't believe it."

Fifteen minutes later they stood outside the darkened Greyhound terminal.

"You sure you don't want to just stay with me for a while?" Garcia asked. "We can do my Cinci–Phoenix run together, and then maybe get you to a doctor—find out why you can't remember nothin'."

"I'll be okay," Scott said.

"Well, here. This is a number you can call in Utah. It's my mother. She always knows where to find me. If you ever need anything, anything at all, just call."

"Thanks."

"I owe you, Bob. I owe you big-time."

"No, you don't."

Behind them, the lights of the terminal flicked on. Moments later the doors were opened. Eddie Garcia wondered if there was something else—anything else—he could do. Finally, he simply shrugged, held the man's hand for a time, and then walked away. When he reached his rig, he turned back. Bob was still standing there, rail-thin and rumpled, and badly needing both a shave and a bath. Looking at the shape he was in, Garcia simply could not fathom what he had seen him do.

"You sure you know what's what in there, Bob?" he called out.

"Boston bus. I know."

"Well, I hope you find yourself, my friend, and that woman's horse, too. I really do."

The man, in obvious pain, managed something of a smile.

"I hope so, too, Eddie," he said, with no animation whatever. "I hope so too."

Garcia hauled himself up behind the wheel. When he glanced back, his passenger was gone.

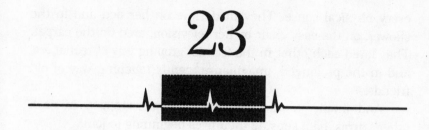

23

The pathology unit at White Memorial was a fluorescently lit, windowless place filling the basement and much of the subbasement of the main building. It had been newly decorated with a mix of Marimekko cloth wall hangings and artificial plants which Eric found not the least appealing.

Although it was not yet eight-thirty in the morning, the day shifts in chemistry, hematology, blood bank, cytology, and histology were in full swing. Wearing scrubs and his clinic coat, Eric passed by each section on his way to the cubicle that housed the hospital's toxicologist. It amazed him that even after five years, there were still so many White Memorial employees whose work he depended on day after day, case after case, yet whom he didn't know.

Although he was operating on precious little sleep, he felt charged and invigorated—excited not only for the discoveries he hoped the day ahead would hold, but by the magic of the night just past. He and Laura had, at last, become lovers in every physical sense. They made love on her bed and in the shower, on the easy chair by her television, even on the carpet. They loved each other in the frantic, groping way of teenagers, and in the prolonged, imaginative, gently touching way of old friends.

And finally, toward dawn, they slept, wrapped in each other's arms, both sensing their lives beginning to join.

The White Memorial toxicologist, a man named Ivor Blunt, could not have been more aptly named. A crusty veteran of nearly thirty years at his craft, Blunt had earned a reputation as much for his eccentricities as for his brilliance. His primary area of research involved the chemical dissection and adaptation of snake venom, and rumor had it that he kept more than one hundred different species of poisonous reptiles in a single huge solarium in his house.

Blunt was still smarting at having "*not* been invited to get involved" in the Loretta Leone case, as he phrased it to Eric. The toxicologist had been reluctant even to see him about the case. Eric persisted, though, and was finally granted a fifteen-minute appointment. It was his plan to break from his E.R. shift long enough to see Blunt and later Haven Darden, and then to leave for the Countway Library as early as possible.

Meanwhile, Laura would file a complaint against Donald Devine and the Gates of Heaven, and also report on the threatening phone call she had received. Whether she told the police about the shooting in East Boston would depend on how much credence they seemed to be giving her story.

Blunt's office was set at the far end of the corridor from the autopsy suite. The door, with IVOR T. L. BLUNT, PH.D. painted in black on opaque glass, was ajar just a crack. As Eric was about to knock, he heard the toxicologist's raspy voice from within.

"Come on, you pig-headed rascal," Blunt was exclaiming. "It's under the chair. Under the chair!"

Uncertain, Eric held back from knocking for a few seconds, and then gently tapped on the wooden margin of the door. The door creaked opened an inch.

"No!" Blunt shouted.

Eric could hear him race for the door at the moment a brown mouse darted out, over Eric's shoes, and down the corridor.

"Damn," Blunt said.

There was a scuffling behind the door. Finally, it was opened. Blunt, looking every bit the mad professor with a frayed tweed sportcoat, disheveled gray hair, and Coke-bottle glasses, stood in the doorway with five or six feet of python draped over his shoulders.

"That was breakfast for Dr. Livingston here," he said, without the faintest trace of humor.

"I'm sorry, sir. I didn't mean—"

From somewhere down the hall came a shriek, then another.

"I know, I know," Blunt growled. "Save your apologies for those women out there. As if I didn't have enough problems around here."

He lowered the snake into a large wire-mesh cage and motioned Eric to a seat. The office had the cluttered, active disarray of an academician's retreat. A huge periodic table of the elements covered one wall, and excellent African safari photos another. The rest of the space was crammed with books and journals. Above Blunt's desk was a sign that read: IF IT LOOKS LIKE A DUCK, AND WALKS LIKE A DUCK, AND QUACKS LIKE A DUCK, COOK IT.

"Thank you for seeing me," Eric said.

"I'm a professor. I'm supposed to see you, so I'm seeing you."

"I wanted to ask your opinion about a problem."

"That Leone woman?"

"Yes, sir."

Eric laid out his sets of EKGs and, as quickly as he could, reviewed the theories he had developed and the research he had done the night before. Ivor Blunt listened quietly, although he continually tapped his fingertips together as if to say, "Get to the end, please, because I already know the question *and* the answer."

"Here," Eric concluded, "are the three toxins I came up with as possible agents in these cases. I wanted to know what you thought of my theories, and also whether you could detect these substances in Loretta Leone's blood."

Blunt studied the list for a bit.

"Amanita, aconite, tetrodotoxin," he murmured. "Nice stuff, nice stuff. Well, sir, the answers to your questions are: no, no, no, and yes, yes, yes."

"Pardon?"

"No, I don't believe any of these three drugs can cause the kind of picture you describe, and yes, I could detect any of them if they were there and I knew what I was looking for."

"But what about those accounts of simulated death in tetrodotoxin poisoning?"

"Scientific Swiss cheese."

"What?"

"Far too anecdotal. No blood sample testing, no levels, that sort of thing. These are big-league toxins, Doctor, I'll grant you that. And nanogram for nanogram, tetrodotoxin may be the nastiest and most fascinating of them all. But I don't see it slowing metabolism enough to fool a competent doctor with modern diagnostic tools."

Two competent doctors with very modern tools were fooled, Eric wanted to say. But the toxicologist seemed impatient and anxious to get on with his day.

"I understand," Eric said. "One last question: If I were to obtain some of the Leone woman's blood, would you test it for me?"

"Completely off the record, I might. As I told you before, the medical examiner has not chosen to involve me in this case. The word I received was that he suspected incompetence on the part of a certain physician, but had absolutely no suspicion of foul play. I think he's dropped the matter altogether."

"Thank you, Dr. Blunt," Eric said, backing from the office. "Thank you so much for doing this for me."

"Just tell those women out there that mouse was your fault," Blunt said.

Eric left the office and went directly to the autopsy suite. He began with the secretary and, over the next half hour, worked his way through the technicians, the residents, and finally the director of anatomic pathology. There was no physical evidence whatever that Loretta Leone had ever been autopsied: no dictation (the medical examiner's office must have the tape, he was told), no body, no blood, and no tissue samples, either in formalin or in wax blocks awaiting sectioning and staining.

He tried calling Dr. Roderick Corcoran, but was told by the medical examiner's office that Corcoran was on vacation for two weeks. The M.E. who was covering him had no information on the case, although she was certain that any tissue or blood samples that had been taken would still be at White Memorial.

Totally dismayed, Eric pressed on, interrupting one person after another to help him search through samples of frozen blood and bottled organs. Everyone he dealt with named someone else as probably responsible for the material he wanted. Finally, as he stood by the department secretary's desk trying to make an appointment to see the chief, he was paged to the E.R. to help deal with a mounting backlog at the triage desk.

As he left the office, a well-groomed man in his twenties who had been sitting in the waiting area stepped into the hallway and called to him.

"Excuse me, Dr. Najarian, but I was waiting to speak with Dr. Pollard, and I couldn't help overhearing your conversation with his secretary. You're interested in Loretta Leone's autopsy?"

"That's right," Eric said, assuming the man was a resident. "Why, can you help me?"

"That depends on what you're looking for."

"What I'm looking for are some tissue or blood samples," he said.

"And you can't find any?"

"Nothing. People at the M.E.'s office think they're here. People here think they're at the M.E.'s office."

"That's strange," the man said.

"Par for the course, I would say." Eric glanced at his watch. "Listen, I've got to get upstairs. Maybe I can check with you on this later. Where will you be in, say, an hour or two?"

"Probably at my paper."

"What?"

"I work for the *Herald*. My name's Cal Loomis."

Loomis reached out his hand but Eric ignored the gesture.

"Why didn't you say who you were in the first place?" he asked.

Loomis smiled.

"You never asked me," he said. "Now, if it's possible, I'd like to talk to you in more detail about these missing specimens."

"Go to hell," Eric said.

He turned and hurried off down the corridor.

It was after nine before Laura forced herself out of bed and into the shower. For years she had listened to men tell her how beautiful she was, but Eric Najarian was the first to make her feel that way. She felt reluctant to dress—to end the night that had brought so much pleasure to both of them. Finally she chose an outfit—slacks and a light pullover—that she felt would not make any particular kind of impression on the police, and headed off.

She was crossing the lobby when the desk clerk motioned her over.

"Excuse me, Miss Enders," he said, "but you have a visitor. He's been waiting quite a while. I told him you probably wouldn't mind his calling upstairs, but he wanted to wait."

He gestured toward the front windows, where a uniformed policeman stood watching the passing scene. His expression gave no indication that such a visitor was anything but common-place at the Carlisle.

The officer turned as Laura approached him. He was a young man—somewhere between twelve and twenty was Laura's initial impression. His hat seemed a size too big, and she smiled at the fleeting thought that his service revolver might be something his parents gave him for Christmas.

"I'm Laura Enders," she said. "You're waiting to see me?"

"Yes, ma'am. I'm Officer Mayer. Captain Wheeler asked me to pick you up and bring you down to headquarters to meet with him. Something about your brother."

"Have they found him?"

"I don't know, ma'am. I was just asked to pick you up."

Laura wished he would stop calling her ma'am. She followed him to the patrol car, which was parked out front.

"Is Captain Wheeler involved with missing persons?"

"Yes and no, ma'am," Mayer said. "He's a captain. He's involved with anything he wants to be."

"Oh."

"But if your brother's missing, and Captain Wheeler's interested, I would think you have a good chance of finding him."

"Wheeler's that good?"

"The best, I'd say. Certainly the toughest."

"That's nice to hear. It's a coincidence your being here. I was just on my way to Station Four to file a complaint against a funeral parlor owner."

"Sure, ma'am."

Laura saw amusement flicker across the young man's face and sensed that she might be in for a long day.

Over the short ride to police headquarters, Laura learned what she could about the man who had sent for her. Wheeler was, according to Officer Mayer, a man who had come up through the ranks and earned his reputation primarily with vice and narcotics. Not too long ago there had been an organized demonstration of protest by a number of uniformed officers when he was passed over for the commissioner's job.

Wheeler's office was located on the third floor of the building Laura had visited on her first day in the city. As the patrolman led her to the elevator, she spotted Sergeant Thomas Campbell taking a statement of some sort from an elderly black woman, and looking every bit as indifferent to her story as he had been to Laura's. As she stepped into the elevator she silently prayed that the encounter with Wheeler would amount to something more than just another set of forms.

"If you'll wait here, please, ma'am," the policeman said, nodding to a bench in the third-floor hallway.

He knocked at and then entered Wheeler's office. Moments later he returned, told Laura to wait, and disappeared down the back stairs. Laura tried, unsuccessfully, to keep her excitement and expectations in check. Her experience with the police, both in D.C. and Boston, had been so uniformly unrewarding that just the thought of meeting with a captain who was interested in Scott had her imagination soaring. Several minutes passed, during which she played through any number of scenarios, testing her reaction to revelations ranging from proof of Scott's death to his involvement in some sort of criminal activity.

At last Wheeler's door opened. A tall, uniformed man, whose shoulders nearly spanned the doorway, smiled at her and motioned her over. He looked about fifty, with thick reddish-gray hair and a confident, weathered face.

"Thank you for coming, Miss Enders," he said, extending a beefy hand. "I'm Captain Lester Wheeler."

Laura followed him into the office and settled in across the desk from him as Wheeler pulled one of her posters from his drawer.

"I've been meaning to get in touch with you about this for a couple of days," he said. "Sorry to have taken so long."

"Do you know something about my brother?"

"Do you?" he asked.

"I'm not sure I understand."

"Miss Enders, do you know your brother's occupation?"

"I've been sensing for a while that what I know is wrong," she said. "He's not in computers, is he?"

The policeman shook his head and smiled at the notion.

"No," he said. "No, he's not—or I should say, wasn't. I . . . don't mean to be too blunt, Miss Enders, but I have good reason to believe your brother is dead."

Despite all her preparation, Laura felt herself sink at the news.

"Go on," she said.

"Your brother was an agent for the government. And a damn good one, I might add. He worked for a group out of Washington that I frankly don't know too much about, except that they supply undercover people to other agencies such as the FBI and DEA."

"Communigistics," Laura said.

"Pardon?"

"Nothing. I just think I know who he worked for."

"Perhaps you do. Well, this past winter your brother was working undercover on loan to us. He was trying to break a drug-smuggling ring operating through the port in East Boston. It's our belief that he filmed a very big deal involving some people we've been trying to nail for a long time."

"A videotape?" Laura could feel puzzle pieces dropping into place.

"Exactly," Wheeler said. "We believe that Scott was taken somehow, and—I'm sorry to say it this way—perhaps even tortured."

"God."

"It's an occupational hazard your brother lived with."

"This is all so hard for me to believe."

"If it was easy for you to believe," Wheeler said, "then your brother wouldn't have been very effective at what he did."

"I understand. Go on."

"Our sources have convinced us that, whatever they put Scott through, he didn't crack. In fact, he nearly escaped."

"Do you know for certain that he's dead?"

"If you mean do we have his body, the answer is no. He probably drowned in Boston Harbor."

"He may not have," Laura said.

She recounted Eric's resuscitative attempts on the derelict, and their subsequent visits to the Gates of Heaven.

"When your man picked me up, I was actually on my way here to file a complaint against Donald Devine," she concluded.

"Interesting," Wheeler said. "Very interesting. Miss Enders, I'm not sure what to make of your story about this Devine, but I can't begin to tell you how badly we want that tape."

"I . . . I'm afraid I can't help you."

"Your brother never communicated with you, however innocently?"

"Never. Except for an occasional phone call, these postcards are all I've ever gotten." She handed him the small stack of cards from Boston. "There's one other thing I haven't told you yet," she said when Wheeler had finished scanning the postcards. "The day before yesterday, Eric and I received a message to check the East Boston docks for news of my brother." She handed him the note and described the events that followed.

"Do you have any idea who saved you?" Wheeler asked.

"I was hoping you might know."

The policeman shook his head.

"Obviously the Feds are playing their own game here," he said. "They probably sent you this as a way of stirring things up. Perhaps they knew that Scott had been working around this warehouse. The man who saved your bacon had probably been following you. Miss Enders, excuse me for pressing, but this is so important. You have no inkling whatsover of where your brother might have hidden the video receiver?"

"Absolutely none."

"Well then," Wheeler said, "suppose we leave things at this: As soon as I have time, I'll see what explanations your friend Mr. Devine has regarding this whole business with that body. You really think it was your brother?"

"I do."

"All right. I'll look into that. Meanwhile, if you're going to stay in Boston, I'd like you to keep me aware of any developments such as that note. But let me say this: If I were you, I'd catch the next plane back to your island. Some very bad people think you know where that tape is. And if they're who I think they are, they don't stop until they have what they want. Things could get real ugly."

Laura did not respond right away. She stared down at the floor, biting her lower lip as an enormous sadness settled in her breast. The confusion and uncertainty had lifted, but in their place was a heavy gloom. She had no remaining doubt that Scott was dead. Nor did she question how he had died. Clearly, the derelict disguise he had adopted was part of his undercover work, and equally clearly, the escape from his captors had led to his death—perhaps from exposure, perhaps from internal injuries.

Eric's theories about a poison no longer made much sense. The similarities between Scott's cardiogram and that of Reed Marshall's patient were, in fact, coincidental. Now, as far as she was concerned, there remained only the side issue of Donald Devine and exactly what he was doing with bodies. And at best, Captain Lester Wheeler seemed only passingly interested in that situation.

She promised her full cooperation, thanked the policeman for his help, and left, vowing that, if nothing else, she would see her battle with the Gates of Heaven through to the end.

24

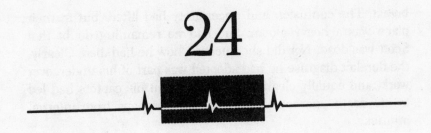

Laura left Police Headquarters and wandered along Tremont Street toward the Common. She had no particular destination in mind, and no particular desire other than to walk until her legs ached too much to continue. She thought about her parents, and actually smiled at the notion of their reaction had they lived to learn what calling their son had finally chosen. At one point they had pushed Scott into the local 4H Club and insisted that he begin grooming himself for farming.

She skirted the Common and wandered past the Combat Zone to Chinatown. On a whim she stopped at a phone booth and tried calling Eric at White Memorial. She hung up when the operator asked for an additional deposit while she was still on hold. There would be plenty of time to fill him in later that night.

She crossed the turnpike on Harrison Avenue and drifted away from the downtown area. She felt drained, deflated. Her search for Scott was, to all intents, over. What remained was no more than the thankless struggle to expose what had been done with his body. It helped her to think naïvely and romantically of what he actually did in his job—of the lives he had saved by intercepting drug shipments; of the assassins he had eliminated.

A group of youths, sitting on an outside stairway, whistled and made a number of lewd requests. Laura was not even aware of them. She glanced over at her reflection in a shop window. Scott had accomplished so much in his life, made such a difference. She had spent years struggling just to connect with herself. Perhaps it was time she explored *her* capabilities, her capacity for helping others. There were a number of excellent physical therapy programs in Massachusetts. If by some miracle Eric managed to stay on at White Memorial, they could continue their relationship while she went to school.

She noticed a cluttered secondhand store across the street and cut diagonally across toward it. The roar of the accelerating car engine was no more than the faintest background noise to her until she caught sight of movement in the corner of her eye. By the time she sensed danger, the chance to react properly had passed.

"Laura, watch out!"

The shout—a man's voice from somewhere behind her—only further confused her and kept her from effective action. She was frozen, dead center in the intersection. The car, a large black domestic model, was bearing down on her with terrifying speed, lining her up for impact with the very center of the grill. She turned to run, but the driver needed only a minuscule adjustment to keep her locked between the headlights. Her last thought was the totally irrational impulse to avoid the impact by jumping up and over the hood. Before she could do anything, though, she was hit—not by the car but from behind. A pair of hands shoved her viciously in the small of her back, sending her sprawling to the pavement, away from the auto's path. She whirled as she fell, landing heavily on her shoulder at the instant the speeding car hit the man who had pushed her. His body careened upward off the hood, hit the roof line just above the windshield, and sailed a dozen or more feet in the air. It landed with a sickening, lifeless thud as the dark sedan screeched off down the street.

Gasping for breath, mindless of the scrapes on her legs and elbows, Laura scrambled across the road on her hands and knees. The man, lying on his back, was shattered. A pool of blood expanded obscenely from beneath his head, which was bent at a grotesque angle to his neck. Bubbling crimson rivulets trickled from each ear.

Laura battled an intense dizziness and nausea as people rushed at her from all directions. It was then that she realized the man lying there—the man who had called her by name before giving up his life for hers—was wearing a tan windbreaker.

"Lie down." "No, leave her be." "Are you all right?" "Did anyone call an ambulance?" "Shit, look at this guy." "Did anyone get a license number?" "Look, man, I know dead, and this guy is dead." "Don't move, dear. Everything's going to be all right." "Hey, look, man, this guy's packin'. See, he's got a piece in his waistband."

"I'm all right," Laura heard herself say. "Please help him if you can. I'm all right. I'm fine."

"Lady, no one's gonna help that dude except a priest."

Laura glanced over at the gun in the dead man's belt, and knew that it was he who had fought off the attackers on the East Boston docks. Over the protests of several people, she forced herself to her feet. Gingerly, she tested her arms and legs.

"Please, leave me alone. Just leave me alone," she begged.

She knelt by the man's body, and after finding no pulse, checked his jeans for a wallet. The thin billfold she withdrew from his right front pocket identified him as Roger Ansell of Ocala, Florida. Laura knew the identification was false. She studied his pallid face.

"You knew Scott, didn't you?" she whispered. "You've been trying to help me find him all along."

Gently she reached up and closed his eyes. In the distance

she could hear the wailing of sirens. She stood and walked slowly through the crowd, which was now a circle at least ten deep. Far down the street she could see the flashing lights of an approaching patrol car. The last thing she wanted was any kind of publicity. Unobtrusively, she worked her way around the mob; no one seemed to realize that she was the one involved in the accident. Then she slipped away down a side street, through an alley, and hailed a cab.

She ordered the cabbie just to drive, and leaned back in the seat, trying desperately to sort out what had happened and why. She wanted so to believe that the hit-and-run driver was some sort of madman, someone insane on alcohol or pills. But no amount of reasoning could convince her of that. Someone wanted her dead—someone who had been following her at the same time as had Roger Ansell. Surely whoever it was knew where she was staying. Did they know about Eric as well?

She stopped at a phone and once again called White Memorial. This time she was told that Eric had signed out and could not be reached for the rest of the day. She had the cabbie drive for another twenty-five minutes, then ordered him back down Harrison Avenue. A patrol car, parked on one corner near the accident scene, suggested there was still perhaps some questioning going on. But otherwise the street seemed as normal to her as the horrible events that had occurred there seemed dreamlike.

After considering and then rejecting several possibilities, Laura paid the driver off on Boylston Street and mounted the grimy stairs to Bernard Nelson's office. Thirty minutes later she was seated beside the detective in his Volvo wagon, on the way to his South Shore home. Nelson chewed on his cigar stub as she brought him day by day through her stay in Boston.

"You've come far, child," Nelson said, "and in a very short time. I don't impress easily, but you have impressed me. Say, listen, I've been considering taking on an apprentice. Perhaps you'd be interested in applying for the position?"

"I'll consider it," Laura said, uncertain of the seriousness of the offer.

"So," Nelson said, "what do you want to do about all this?"

"I'm not sure. I don't see that there's much to be gained from going back to Captain Wheeler."

"Neither do I. At least there's no big rush."

"I guess it's worth calling that man Harten in Virginia."

"Maybe. But I wouldn't expect him to admit anything. That's the way those people operate. My guess is he's the one responsible for sending that note to you. I would bet he was using you as bait to flush out whoever had killed your brother. The man who died back there was probably assigned to make sure you weren't hurt."

"That's terrible."

"Expediency is the name of their game—especially when one of their people is missing or dead."

"So what's left?"

"Well, I don't know about you, but I certainly find this Devine character intriguing. I'd like a chance to visit his establishment."

"What makes you think he'd talk to you?"

"Who said anything about talking to him?"

"You mean break in?"

"Hey, easy with those terms. We call it searching for the truth." He nodded modestly. "It's sort of my specialty."

"May I come?"

"I'd prefer you didn't. But considering that you might sign on as my apprentice, I suppose I could work you in."

"When?"

"As soon as I'm certain he's not home. Maggie will clean up those scrapes of yours and fatten you up with some of her lasagna. Then, after dinner, we'll give Devine a call. If necessary, we'll send him off to pick up a body somewhere in the suburbs."

"Your usual fee?"

"Actually," Nelson said, swinging off Route 3 onto the exit ramp, "searching for the truth runs a bit higher."

⊣⋏⋏⎯

Haven Darden's office and laboratory filled most of the fifth floor
of the Proctor Research Building. Eric found the medical chief
hunched over a microscope. A white-coated technician was at
work nearby, but otherwise the huge space was deserted.

Darden glanced up at him, nodded a greeting, and then
returned his attention to the scope.

"This is pig work," he said. "I could train a high-schooler to
do it. . . . Unfortunately, I couldn't pay him. So here I sit."

"Money's tight."

"I should say." Darden made a few final notes and then
pushed himself away. "So, it would appear that Dr. Marshall has
placed himself into some sort of treatment facility, and out of
the running for the E.R. position. I would say things look very
good for you."

"I'm not counting on anything. I have reason to believe that
certain people in this hospital will do whatever they must, to see
that I'm out of this place as quickly as possible."

"Would you like to expand on that?"

"Soon. Soon I would very much like to do just that. But
right now I have more pressing matters on my mind."

"Such as?"

"Such as getting Reed Marshall well and back at his job."

"You mean that?"

"I do."

"Well, from what I understand, Dr. Marshall has made one
hell of an error."

"I'm not so sure."

"Explain."

Eric leaned against the slate edge of the laboratory bench.

"Dr. Darden, I've come up here because I was hoping you
might be able to tell me something about tetrodotoxin."

Darden's dark eyes smiled. "So, it's zombies you're after, is
it?" he said.

Eric set the EKGs on the counter.

"This one is from the woman Reed pronounced dead, and
this is from a man I pronounced dead in February."

"I assume *he* did not subsequently awaken?"

"Actually, I can't tell you for sure. His body's disappeared."

"Excuse me?"

"I've been able to trace the man's body to a funeral home near here, but I have reason to believe the mortician is into some sort of illegal diversion of bodies."

"Fascinating," Darden said. He folded his notebook. "So, would you like to discuss this rogue mortician, or would you like to accompany me to my office for a crash course in voodoo?"

"I'll take the lesson for now," Eric said, "but I hope I can discuss this other business with you soon."

"Of course you may. I'm a bit cramped for time right now, so I shall have to give you a pared-down course."

"That's fine."

"But let me say in advance that what you shall learn is not what you want to hear."

They walked down a row of slate benches covered with thousands of dollars' worth of idle equipment and incubators, and entered Darden's spacious office overlooking the Charles.

"I prefer this space to my office in the department of medicine," he explained.

"I can see why."

"Looking down on the passing scene has such a calming effect, don't you think?" He gazed out at the river for a moment, then turned back to Eric. "So, now we must talk some voodoo."

"Do you know it well?"

Darden smiled enigmatically.

"Does anybody? I suppose there are those who would consider me something of an expert. Although I left Haiti as a child, I have a small clinic in Port-au-Prince, and much family in the city of Cap-Haïtien on the north coast. My wife and daughter and I return there frequently."

"And do you believe there are zombies?"

"In Haiti, I do. I have no doubt whatsoever. Certain people, usually those who have committed some sort of offense against their fellows, are found guilty by a people's court, usually presided over by a *houngan*—a priest. The offenders learn that they have been condemned to a living death. So strong are their beliefs in the Haitian way and in the powers of the *houngan* that they are quite literally powerless to stem their fate. They are caused, in some way, to come in contact with a *coup poudre*—a mystical powder. Soon after, they fall into a helpless trancelike state, are buried for a time, and then are brought back to this world, usually in a state of diminished mental and physical capacity."

"And the zombi poison, this *coup poudre*?"

Darden shook his head.

"I believe in hypnosis and the power of the mind," he said. "I believe that those who believe, in the very fiber of their being, that they are cursed to die can make themselves do so; and those who believe they are to lie in the state of the undead can also do so. I have seen men told under hypnotic trance that they are to be touched with a hot poker, and then raise a blister at the site where they are grazed by a pencil eraser. I have seen yogis sealed in caskets for many hours without apparent adverse effects. But as for a poison that can accomplish the transformation from living being to zombi, I'm afraid not."

"So you see all this as psychologically based—a cultural phenomenon, and not something biochemical?"

"Tetrodotoxin is an awesomely toxic substance. Highly trained Japanese chefs can prepare fugu dishes with a far from lethal dose. But there is no way a *houngan,* grinding fish in an earthen bowl or tin can, then applying the substance to a victim's skin, can approach the line of death without consistently going over it. Perhaps he might augment the strength of his hypnotic suggestion with a bit of biochemical tingle, but not with anything like what you are suggesting. There is no *controllable* metabolic toxin, so there is no true zombi poison. It is as simple as that."

"Are there any studies you know of reviewing the cardiovascular effects of tetrodotoxin poisoning?"

"Ah, your EKGs. I would suggest that if you sit down with one of our cardiology friends, you will learn that this pattern is not at all uncommon in terminal hearts. We just don't bother to take the tracing all that often."

"Perhaps," Eric said.

"You don't sound convinced."

"There's a lot at stake. Beginning with Reed Marshall's career."

"Well, I can only tell you what I can tell you. A few years ago a Harvard ethnobotanist created a stir surrounding tetrodotoxin and zombies. Since then there has been a flood of letters and articles refuting his claims."

"That's what Dr. Blunt said."

"You spoke with him, then?"

"Yes."

"And he concurred with what I have told you?"

"Yes, he did."

"Then when will enough be enough for you?"

Eric stood and gathered his notes.

"Not just yet," he said.

"I assure you, Eric, in this area there is a sharp drop-off around here after Dr. Blunt and myself."

"Well, sir, I have a free evening and my Countway Library card. If nothing else, maybe I can close that drop-off a bit."

"Maybe you can at that," Haven Darden said, looking at him thoughtfully. "Maybe you can."

25

From the day Eric first set foot in the Countway Medical Library, the airy, regal structure with its wide circular stairways and glassed study carrels had been a special retreat for him. Whether he was working deep in the stacks, or in the silent coccoon of a carrel, hours often passed like minutes. At one stretch, while researching a particularly interesting case, he had been the last to leave the place so many nights that one librarian had called him an "academic barfly."

It was early evening. Eric spread his notes on a reading table near the card catalogue and began to work his way through the file cards containing the extensive bibliography he had drawn up. The approach, which would save time and trips into the stacks, was one he had worked out over his years of study in the place. He noted down the library number and location of the volumes he would need, while organizing his cards by stack section.

The Indian Journal of Medical Research . . . Toxicon . . . Caribbean Quarterly . . . Many of the references were so obscure that only a facility like the Countway in a city the size of Boston could house or quickly borrow them. Eric started with aconite and then amanita. The filtered light of day yielded to the fluorescence of the library as he worked his way through various sections of the stacks, lugging armloads of musty volumes back to his worktable. Within two hours he had read enough to eliminate both toxins as likely possibilities. Only the reference cards pertaining to tetrodotoxin remained.

Pharmacologic Reviews . . . *Kyusha University Medical News* . . . *Ethnopharmacology* . . . Stretching the stiffness from his neck, Eric began the final phase of his search. Within half an hour he was sitting on the edge of his table, bewildered. Many of the volumes in his bibliography—far more than half—were missing from the stacks. With memories of the missing specimens of Loretta Leone still fresh in his mind, he checked with a librarian and assured himself that none of the volumes could be taken out of the library. They had either been stolen, misplaced in the stacks, or were in use somewhere in the library.

Theft, Eric was told, while certainly a problem, was less of one in the Countway than at many other libraries. So together, he and the librarian rechecked the stacks and then began working their way toward each other from opposite sides of the building, checking each table and study carrel. In just a few minutes the young librarian, much relieved, hurried over to him. The volumes, every one of them, were in use. She pointed across the library to a worktable that was set apart from the others. Along the edge of the table, stacks of bound journals formed a wall, obscuring the person using them from view.

Eric thanked the librarian, made his way past the card catalogues and tables, and peered over the wall of books. A black woman, her jet hair pulled back in a tight bun, was taking notes on an article in the *Journal of Tropical Diseases*. Eric waited a few seconds to be noticed, then cleared his throat. The woman finished writing a sentence before she looked up.

She was in her early or mid-twenties, and was absolutely stunning. Her wide dark eyes graced a face that was as smooth, as perfectly shaped and sensual, as any he had ever seen; and her ornate gold earrings and agate necklace, quite possibly picked off a vendor's tray on Boylston Street or Harvard Square, looked priceless on her.

"Hi," Eric managed. "I've been searching for you."

"For me?"

Her expression was less open than it might have been, and beneath her remarkable beauty Eric sensed an intensity that made him a bit uneasy. She pushed back from the table. Her jeans and loose beige sweater failed to hide a figure that was at once slender and full-breasted.

"Actually, what I've been searching for are these," he said, gesturing to the volumes and wondering if the sudden dryness in his mouth and thickness in his lips and tongue were noticeable in his speech.

The woman eyed him curiously for a moment and then said simply, "Take whichever ones you want. Just bring them back when you're done."

"Thanks, I appreciate that." Eric tucked several of the books in one arm and the woman returned to her notes. "Are you a med student?" he asked, reluctant to leave.

"Ph.D.," she said without looking up.

"Oh."

He waited for more, then shrugged and turned away.

"I'm sorry," he heard her say. "I didn't mean to be rude. I'm just under a lot of pressure to get this work done."

"I understand," he said, turning back. "Is your thesis in toxicology?"

"Sort of." She ran her finger absently down one pile of volumes. "I'm in the department of anthropology at B.U. My work is on the use of pharmacoactive substances in the religious rites of certain Third World countries."

Well, you're incredibly beautiful. Eric stopped himself at the last instant from saying the words. He would hardly have been the first to say them—the urge to do so was almost knee-jerk.

"Well, thanks for sharing these," he said instead. "I'll bring them back for an exchange when I'm done. Are you going to be here long?"

"Probably until closing."

"See you later then."

Once again Eric had to force himself to turn away from her. He was very happily in the process of falling in love with Laura Enders, but he suspected that no man, however committed, would have reacted differently.

Over the hour that followed he made two more trips to the woman's table to exchange books. With each visit he learned a bit more about her. Her name was Anna Delacroix. She had finished her required course work at Boston University, and was just beginning the writing phase of a thesis probing the connection between certain African and New World cultures as manifest through their ritual use of psychoactive drugs. She had traveled extensively, first through Europe and Asia as a high-fashion model, and later, on her own, through Africa and the Caribbean basin.

Eric's initial impression of her intensity was, it seemed, quite on the mark.

"The life you've led sounds exciting," he remarked as he made his third exchange of journals.

"I have seen many things on my travels that you simply would not believe," she said, with no particular emphasis.

"Such as?"

Fascinated now, Eric circled to her side of the table.

Anna Delacroix stopped what she was doing and eyed him as she had when they first met, perhaps deciding whether he was someone worth sharing such stories with. Then she said simply, "I have seen a man fly."

By this time Eric knew far better than to be flip with her. And there was nothing in her manner, her voice, or the almost mystical glow in her eyes to encourage him otherwise.

"Tell me about it, please," he said.

"Are you really interested?"

"Yes. Yes, I am."

"Sit then. Do you know of the country Gabon?" she asked.

Her focus was now locked on his face, and whether unsettled by her beauty or the deep commitment in her eyes, Eric had trouble holding her gaze.

"I know it's in Africa," he said.

"West Africa, actually. On the coast. I heard of a priest in the central highlands of that country who could levitate himself, and I sought him out."

"You traveled alone to these places?"

"When necessary. I assure you, Dr. Eric, I can take very good care of myself. I found the village, and grew to know the man. We spoke for hours each night. Still, it was nearly two weeks before he would show me what he could do. One evening, just after sunset, while there was still much light in the sky, he climbed to the top of a tower made of bamboo. The topmost platform of the tower was, I was told, nearly thirty meters—ninety feet—high. For several minutes the priest stood right on the edge of the platform, his arms stretched straight out like wings. From where I sat he was a black crucifix against the deepest blue sky you could imagine. It was an incredible, incredible sight. Then he simply leaned forward and floated free of the platform."

Eric tried to remain expressionless, but he knew she could read the incredulity in his eyes.

"In answer to the questions you are too polite to ask," she went on, "no, I did not take anything at all, and yes, he did, although he wouldn't tell me what. It took perhaps ten minutes for him to drift to the ground. It could have been much longer. I was so mesmerized by what I was witnessing that I lost all track of time."

"No tricks?"

She shook her head. "No tricks," she said. "At least not the kind you mean."

"Photos?"

"He wouldn't allow it. And frankly, I had no desire to take them. It was neither his wish nor mine that I go out and convince the world of what he could do. He knew, his people knew, and I knew, and that was quite enough."

"Well, now *I* know," Eric said.

"Yes, but you don't believe it. It's written all over your face."

"Not that long ago, you would have been right. I wouldn't—*couldn't*—have believed your account. But what you see in me now is astonishment, mixed perhaps with skepticism, not disbelief. I'm a good doctor, Anna, and yet, I'm here plowing through these volumes because of a growing belief that both I and a friend of mine, who is also a fine physician, have each recently pronounced patients dead in our hospital who were, in fact, very much alive."

The woman glanced at the volumes. Then she nodded and smiled knowingly, as if the pieces of a puzzle had fallen in place.

"Tetrodotoxin," she said, almost reverently.

"Exactly. Do you know much about it?"

"I do. For one thing, it will most likely be a full chapter in my thesis, if not more. And for another, some of my roots are Haitian—my father, I have been told, though I never knew him, was born there."

"Do you believe the drug has the power to slow metabolism without stopping it? To take a body to the line of death without crossing over?"

"Do you?"

"I . . . I don't know what to believe."

Once again Anna Delacroix's eyes held fire.

"The drug can do what you ask . . . and more," she said.

Eric felt her energy, her heat. He ran the edge of his hand across the sweat on his forehead.

"How do you know?" he asked hoarsely. "Is there proof? Proof a scientist could not refute?"

For more than a minute she said nothing. Eric studied her exquisite face, her perfect mouth, and silently prayed that she would at least share with him what she knew.

Finally she took one of her file cards, carefully printed an address on it, and passed it to him.

"This place is in Allston," she said. "Can you find it?"

He glanced at the card. "I can find it."

"Ten o'clock tonight, then. Come alone and meet me there, Dr. Eric, and you shall have your proof." She stood. "Perhaps when this night is over, you will know in your heart that there are those who can fly . . . and those who can die without dying."

She turned quickly, picked up her notes and her jacket, and moments later was gone.

26

Shielded by a new-moon darkness, Laura and Bernard Nelson made their way from the alley where he had parked, down several more alleys, and finally across the street to the entrance of the Gates of Heaven Funeral Home. For two hours they had placed periodic calls to the mortuary, each time reaching only Donald Devine's answering machine. Finally, Nelson had shrugged and said simply, "I guess we go."

The detective carried with him a small black medical bag, containing what he called his "tools of truth"—two powerful penlights, various Exacto knives, screwdrivers, tape, a crowbar, pliers, a voltage meter and battery-powered soldering iron, wire, suction cups, a ring of keys and other oddly cut pieces of metal . . . and one Littman Cardiosonic stethoscope.

"If we're stopped by the police," he said as they set off, "you had better do a damn good job of convincing them that I'm your family doctor making a house call on your ailing aunt. If they ever open this little kit of mine, we're cooked."

The wooden shutters on the upstairs windows were pulled closed. Nelson checked the windows on the alley side of the structure and reported that they, too, were shuttered. They rang the doorbell several times, listening each time to the melodic chimes echoing from within.

"What tune are those playing?" Laura whispered.

The detective smiled.

"It would appear our Mr. Devine has a sense of humor," he said. "They're playing Tchaikovsky. A snippet of the death of Odette from *Swan Lake*."

"You could tell that from seven or eight notes?"

"Maggie's a ballet nut. After six or seven years of being dragged, I finally gave up and got interested."

"You're amazing."

"Tell me that after we're inside," Nelson said, tossing his cigar stub aside as he scanned first the edge of the door jamb, and then the windows.

"You're sure you want to do this?" she asked.

"That's still up to you. How committed are you to finding out what this mysterious mortician is up to?"

"Very committed."

"In that case, stay in close to the building, in the shadows, and keep your eyes on the street. I'm going back into the alley and around to the rear. Listen for a tap from the inside of the door. If it's clear for me to open it, tap back twice. If not, tap once and then head back to the car. I'll meet you there."

Nelson reached in his medical bag and withdrew a nip of Jack Daniel's.

"To the truth," he said.

"To the truth," Laura echoed.

She took a small sip, and in a single quick gulp, Bernard Nelson disposed of the remainder. He then slid along the side of the Gates of Heaven and disappeared down the alley.

Over the long minutes that followed, only one car drove past the darkened mortuary. Laura zipped up the thin black leather jacket Bernard had given her, and pressed herself tightly against the building. She had tried calling Eric any number of times since the nightmare on Harrison Avenue, but without success. In a way, she was grateful. He almost certainly would have insisted on coming along, and if for any reason they were caught in their illegal entry, the negative publicity would doubtless kill whatever chance he still had for the White Memorial promotion.

A couple, holding hands, crossed the narrow street just two doors away. Laura froze, easily holding her breath for more than a minute until they had let themselves into their building. She glanced down at the doorknob. *What is taking so long?* She thought about the man who had called himself Roger Ansell. He had probably once stood somewhere right on this street, watching as she and Eric paid their visit to Donald Devine. *Did he have a wife? Children?* First Scott, now him. Regardless of the reasons, it seemed stupid and senseless and sad.

The taps—two of them from inside the mortuary—were barely audible. Laura responded with two of her own. Bernard Nelson opened the door, and she stepped into a darkness that was so complete, so palpably dense, that she instantly relived the moment when her flash failed during a night dive in a massive undersea grotto called the Sultan's Cave.

"Wait a minute," she whispered. "I've got to let my eyes adjust."

"There's no light for them to adjust to," Nelson said. "Here." He passed her a pair of surgical gloves and then a slim penlight, which cast a narrow but surprisingly potent beam. "Just keep it low, away from our faces."

"Hey, I dive for a living, remember? There's no verbalizing eighty feet down, so we live and die by using our lights the right way."

"Sorry. Sorry I took so long too. The security system in this place turned out to be rather sophisticated."

"Are you sure it's deactivated?"

"That's the weird thing. The system wasn't on in the first place. We could have used one of the keys on my Ring of Truth and been safely inside in two seconds. God, there's enough formalin in the air here to grant eternal pickling."

"It really does smell like death."

They moved carefully from the foyer to Devine's parlor, Laura keeping her flash fixed on the floor while Nelson swept his beam along the walls.

"What are we looking for?" Laura asked.

"Oh, shelves, bookcases, drawers, a wall safe—that sort of thing. If this Devine is the meticulous little mouse you describe, I'd be amazed if he doesn't have records of whatever he's into. I wish I felt comfortable turning on a light, but frankly, that's a risk I'm not willing to take except as a last resort. If our divine friend happens to return, even a sliver of light through those shutters could warn him and cost us escape time."

Bernard pulled a tool from his kit, popped open the drawer of Devine's imitation Chippendale desk, and rifled quickly through its contents, scanning sheets, then carefully replacing them.

"Pull every book off those shelves, Laura—carefully," he said, motioning to one wall. "Check to be sure each is what the binding says it is, and then set it right back where it was."

It took twenty minutes to finish with the room, and another ten to search the small chapel adjacent to it.

"This is tougher than I thought it was going to be," Laura said as they picked their way through the rear door of the chapel into the casket room.

"It gets even more difficult if the proprietor of the establishment walks in on us."

Laura squinted, trying to adjust her vision to the new room, which was smaller and if possible even darker than the others. There seemed to be four or five caskets displayed on stands of various heights. The walls were overhung with maroon velvet drapes, which emitted a mustiness competitive in intensity with the formalin.

Laura attempted to ignore the odors by breathing through her mouth. As she scanned the floor, trying to get some sense of the space, she stepped forward, bumping against one of the caskets. She put her hand out to steady herself, and set it down on the waxen face of a man. Laura gasped, recoiling against another casket as her penlight clattered to the floor. Immediately, Nelson's flash sought her out.

"That casket." She struggled to clear the sudden hoarseness from her throat. "There's a body in there."

Bernard played his light down her arm, past her pointing finger, into an ornate, velvet-lined coffin, and finally onto the face of a man.

Laura gasped. "That's Donald Devine!"

The mortician, his hands resting peacefully on his vest, stared sightlessly upward. In the center of his forehead, just above his wire-rimmed spectacles and just below his pomaded hairline, was a single small bullet hole, surrounded by a halo of dried blood.

"Less than a day, I'd guess," Bernard murmured, touching the back of his hand to Devine's pallid cheek and then hefting the corpse's arm, which seemed stiff and plastic. "But I'm really not very good at that sort of stuff. I *can* tell you for certain that he didn't do this to himself."

"This is horrible."

"Maybe. But it tells me that you were right. Your friend here was into something shady. And whatever it was, he was obviously in over his head."

"Should we keep searching?"

"I doubt we'll find anything that whoever made this little hole didn't find, but you never can tell. Besides, with the danger of Mr. Devine walking in on us lessened considerably, I think we might even risk turning lights on as we go."

"If you think it's all right. Do you mind if we skip this room though?"

"Not at all."

"You know, I think he lived upstairs. Maybe it would be worth looking there."

"Maybe it would at that," Bernard Nelson said.

The staircase to Devine's apartment was off the back hallway. The apartment itself consisted of an eat-in kitchen, a TV room, and two bedrooms, one of which was a small museum, overfilled with a startling collection of medieval weapons and armor, including mace-and-chains, broadswords, crossbows, lances, daggers, and several helmets.

"The mouse that roared," Nelson mused.

"This place is truly creepy," Laura said. "How about I do the bedroom and you do Camelot?"

"Just be sure there are no unshuttered windows before you turn on any lights," Nelson cautioned. "Check behind the drapes and pictures, and under any throw rugs. Mark my words. This guy kept detailed records of whatever he was into, and he kept them in a safe. Say, you wouldn't have an extra cigar on you by any chance?"

"Sorry. But listen, if we find the safe you predict, I'll buy you one—whatever kind you want."

"What a sport."

"Only one, though, and only if we find that safe."

Just ten minutes later, they did. Laura was trying to move a large oil painting—some sort of rural scene—when she backed against a black spoke-backed chair, set on a small Oriental rug. The chair did not budge. Laura dropped to her knees and lifted the edge of the rug. The legs of the chair were bolted through it to the floor. Between the bolts she felt a small recessed latch. Releasing the latch, she tipped the chair backward. The rug and a hinged portion of the oak flooring tilted upward with it. The strongbox, a foot or so square with a dial lock and heavy metal handle, was concealed in the space below.

"Bingo!" she cried. "Mr. Nelson, you are truly a prince of your profession."

"I hope you're still considering that apprenticeship offer of mine," he said, first examining the lock, then rummaging through his medical bag for his stethoscope.

He spent the next fifteen minutes pressed against the floor, listening to the tumblers of Donald Devine's safe.

"There's a gizmo that does this electronically," he muttered, "but I'm just too damn cheap to invest in it. Besides, half this business is the challenge, right?"

Laura sat on the dead man's bed, trying to draw some sort of connection between Devine and the drug dealers who had killed not only her brother, but almost certainly Roger Ansell as well. Ansell and Devine: two men violently dead on the same day, and both of them connected in some way to her. She shuddered at the thought.

"Easy," Nelson was urging. "Easy . . . easy . . . and . . . *voilà!*"

He grasped the handle and slowly swung it down ninety degrees. At the moment he pulled the small door open, they heard the sound of voices beneath the window.

"Quick, the lights!"

Bernard gathered up what he could from the safe as Laura shut off first the bedroom light, and then the others upstairs. Stygian darkness returned to the apartment as the front door was unlocked and opened.

"To the stairs," Nelson whispered. "Up here we're trapped."

They felt their way to the stairs and tiptoed down, reaching the first-floor rear hallway just as the light snapped on in the front parlor. Reflexively, Nelson opened what appeared to be the basement door. The two of them stepped onto the staircase beyond it and pulled the door closed. Save for a sliver of light beneath the base of the door, they were once again enveloped in blackness. They huddled on the staircase, Laura midway down and Bernard near the door, listening as what sounded like two men moved toward them.

"Can you hear what they're saying?" she whispered.

"One of them's furious because the other didn't get Devine's records before he killed him. The other one's whining some sort of apology."

"Do you have your gun?"

"What do you think?"

"Well, what are they saying now?"

"I think one of them's headed upstairs. The other one may be coming here. You'd better move down a few more stairs; in fact, go all the way to the bottom. If he opens this door, I'm going to need some room to help him make a rapid descent."

"Just be careful. It's pitch-black down here. I can't see a thing."

"Shhhh."

From upstairs they heard one of the men shout something.

"I'll be right up," the second voice called back from just outside the basement door. "I'm sorry, boss," they heard him say. "I didn't understand what you wanted me to do. Honest I didn't."

Several minutes passed. Laura remained motionless in the darkness on the bottom basement step. Above her, she could faintly discern the bulky silhouette of Bernard Nelson, pressed against the door.

"What's happening?" she whispered.

"They may be leaving or looking for us. I can't tell. Not another sound until I'm certain they're gone—"

His voice dropped off suddenly. Laura could hear muffled footsteps and voices. Then she saw shadows moving in the thin slit of light beneath the door. Her heart skipped as a shoe scuffed against the wood. Bernard Nelson remained still. Finally, after what seemed an eternity, the footsteps began to recede to another part of the house. Fifteen silent minutes went by. The light beyond the door was turned off. Another fifteen minutes passed, then still another. Finally, Laura could stand the tension no longer.

"What's going on?" she asked.

"Beats me. I think they're gone."

She worked her way up several steps.

"Do you want to risk opening the door?"

"I think so. First see if you can find a light down there. Maybe there's a way we can get out of here without going through the house."

Laura backed down the stairs and felt along the wall until she found a switch. After an hour of near total darkness, the bright overhead fluorescent lights were blinding. Bernard Nelson made his way down to her as Laura blinked and rubbed her eyes into focus.

Then the two of them stood side by side, staring incredulously at the space in which they had been hiding. The room was perhaps fifteen feet square, painted gleaming white, and equipped with a stretcher, a cardiac monitor, and other sophisticated-looking medical equipment. One wall was lined with shelves of linens, bandages, medications, and solutions. Against the wall opposite the stretcher were a small desk and chair, and hanging just over the desk, a set of metal and leather limb restraints.

"Well, I'll be damned," Nelson muttered.

"It's like an intensive care unit."

"Not *like* one, child. It *is* one."

They walked about the room, looking over the equipment and checking in the wastebasket and desk drawer.

"I'm no doctor," Nelson said, "but this stuff looks like state-of-the-art to me."

"I agree. Look at this medication. There must be fifty different drugs here. This place frightens me."

"I'd be worried if it didn't." Nelson held up the folders and ledger he had taken from Devine's safe. "Maybe these will give us a clue. From what I could tell, our friendly visitors found the safe, so there's no sense going back up there. Whether they're upstairs or outside watching the house, I don't know, but I vote we try to get these out of here. Are you game?"

"The sooner we get out of here, the better."

They turned out the lights, tiptoed back up the stairs, and then, ever so slowly, opened the door.

27

Are you sure there're no messages for me? Najarian, Eric Najarian . . . No, you don't understand. *I'm* not registered at the hotel; Laura Enders is. But she might have left a—Look, forget it. When she does get in, just leave her a message that Eric called, and that I'll call back later. . . . That's Eric Na—"

The desk clerk had hung up.

Eric snapped the receiver back in place and wandered across the virtually deserted street. He was in one of the seedier areas of Allston, just half a block from the Sproul Court address that Anna Delacroix had written down for him.

For nearly two hours he had been calling Laura, both at her hotel and at his apartment. From what he could determine, she had phoned him at the hospital at least twice during the day, but had left no message other than that she had called. He was beginning to worry, but not unduly so. It was only a quarter of ten. He would finish his business with Anna Delacroix and then go straight to the Carlisle.

A city within the city, Allston's crowded tenements and triplexes were home to many college students, as well as to ethnic pockets of Vietnamese, Thais, Hispanics, Haitians, Pakistanis, and first-generation immigrants from various Eastern European countries.

Sproul Court itself was a dingy, poorly lit, dead-end side street, lined with wooden three-story structures, most of which had porches off the second- and third-story flats. All of the buildings, it seemed, had a shop or store of some sort on the street level. The posters in the windows of the businesses suggested that the main clientele in the area was black.

With some time to spare, Eric wandered the length of the street, past the "grocerette" and the package store, Craissou's Tailor Shop, and the Treasure Island Used Clothing Boutique. There was little that was quaint about the decaying buildings, sooty windows, and trash-cluttered alleyways, and he found it difficult to connect the street in any way with the enigmatic, exquisitely beautiful woman he was to meet there.

Still, he felt tense and excited. If she was true to her word, Anna Delacroix would provide the proof he could use, along with the fruits of his library investigation, to convince some of the powers at the hospital—and even more importantly, to convince Reed Marshall—of the validity of his tetrodotoxin theory. He would then gain some allies, and his efforts could shift from determining whether such poisoning was possible to why it had happened . . . and *how*.

Although he had not yet found a specific description of the cardiographic pattern in tetrodotoxin poisoning, he had catalogued a number of accounts of the clinical presentation, all of which included the classic signs of rapidly progressive heart failure: shortness of breath; intractable coughing; cyanosis, first of the lips and fingertips, then later of the face, hands, and feet; frothy fluid building in the chest and welling into the throat; air hunger leading to panic, leading to even worse air hunger; and finally somnolence, loss of consciousness, and death.

"Dr. Eric, over here."

Anna Delacroix was standing in the shadow of a storefront,

not far from one of the few lampposts on the street. She was wearing a wide floppy-brimmed hat, and had a bandanna of some sort tied loosely about her neck.

"Did you believe I'd come?" he asked.

"Of course I did. You have doubts, and you are desperate to have those doubts assuaged."

"Can you assuage them?"

"Not I, but there is a man inside this store who has some things to say that you will find most interesting." She gestured at the window behind her, which was filled with the trappings of a hardware or dry goods store. The uneven hand-painted letters on the glass said simply: BENET'S. Beyond the display, a dark shade was drawn. "I had to convince him that you would never divulge his name to anyone," she went on. "You will honor that pledge?"

"Of course."

"Good. Because as you will see, any indiscretion could cost either him or me our lives." She looked at Eric gravely.

Anna led him into the alley, knocked once on a side door to the shop, and entered. Inside, seated on a stool, was a gaunt, willowy man with silvering hair and a face that spoke of illness or perhaps merely of a life of too much pain. He shook Eric's hand with no firmness. Anna introduced him as Titus Memmilard, her mother's brother and once the proprietor of Benet's, which was now run by his family.

Titus mumbled a greeting. His speech was slow and thick, and his accent, which Eric assumed was Haitian, was so dense that Eric had to concentrate to understand the man's words.

Benet's was a cluttered melange of tools, fabric, electrical supplies, canned goods, and grain. It was illuminated by a single low-wattage bulb, suspended beneath a metal reflector. Whether intended or not, the effect of the subdued lighting, the drawn shade, and the hushed tones was dramatic and mysterious.

"You wanted proof of your suspicions," Anna said. "Well, my uncle here is that proof. Look into his eyes as you listen to us, and you will know that what we share with you is the truth.

Once, he was the most vigorous and vibrant of men—a musician and a poet, a leader in our community. Now he is a shell. Our troubles began several years ago when word began spreading around our community of the arrival here from Haiti of a most powerful *houngan*—a priest with the power and knowledge of *vodoun*. The *houngan*, we were told, was to be known only as Mr. Dunn."

At the mention of the name, Titus Memmilard seemed to stiffen.

"Evil and pain," he said. "The *houngan* brought evil and pain."

Anna patted the man's hand.

"What he brought," she said, "was the *coup poudre*."

"The magical powder," Eric said.

"Exactly." Anna looked impressed with his knowledge. "Death powder, mystical powder; take your pick. In Haiti, the *coup poudre* is the sword of the *houngans*. There are government courts and officials, but the *houngans* are the real judges, and a living death is their only punishment."

"Go on."

"This rogue priest, this Mr. Dunn, is known only to the group of thugs with whom he has surrounded himself. He is a criminal in every sense of the word—a mobster. It is rumored that in Haiti he was one of the Tonton Macoutes, François Duvalier's secret police. He preys on people's weaknesses and superstitions. He extorts money from our businesses and sells narcotics to our children. Two years ago, after several attempts to enlist the aid of the police, my uncle attempted to organize the merchants to fight back. One of Dunn's collection men was beaten up. Another was robbed of his stash of drugs before he could sell them. Word came from Mr. Dunn that my uncle was to be made an example—that he had been marked for living death. His family tried to protect him, but several of Dunn's men came with guns and took him away. Uncle, are you able to tell this doctor what happened next?"

Eric turned to the old man. "Please try," he urged.

"I received the *coup poudre* from the Evil One himself,"

Titus said, weakly clearing phlegm from his throat. "Across my mouth and under my arms." He demonstrated by drawing his hand across the areas.

Eric remembered reading in several sources that absorption of tetrodotoxin was nearly as rapid and complete through the skin as through the gastrointestinal system.

"Did you see the man's face?" he asked.

"It was the face of hell."

Eric looked to Anna, who shrugged and shook her head.

"Perhaps a mask," she said. "Go on, Uncle."

"They tied me down, but soon they cut me free. There was no need to bind me, for I could no longer move."

"You remember all of this?"

"Some things he remembers clearly. Some not at all," Anna explained. "What we do know is that two days later, this man who now sits before you was found lying on a cot in this very room, cold and quite dead. His eyes were taped shut. A note by his body warned against moving him or calling for medical help. Over the following two days, though he was watched constantly, not once did anyone see him take so much as a single breath."

"My wife mourned over me," Titus said hoarsely. "I could hear her and feel her hand when she brushed it over my face."

"You were awake?" Eric asked.

"I was."

Eric saw himself staring down at Laura's brother as he pronounced the man dead, and felt a painful queasiness churn in his gut.

"After those two days, Dunn's men came again," Anna said. "And once again they dragged my uncle away. A day later he was found wandering down an alleyway near here, retarded in mind and body and quite incapable of caring for himself. When he could tell us, he claimed that his captors had forced some sort of powder into his mouth, and then injected something into his arm. Finally they beat him with their fists and set him free. His senses have returned somewhat over these years, but he remains a man without a soul, and no one outside his family will have anything to do with him."

"That's very sad," Eric murmured, "and very terrifying." He had not the least doubt that what he was hearing was true. He gazed across at the broken old man, and then reached out and held one bony hand in his. "I am very sorry for what has befallen you, sir," he said. "And I am very grateful that you would share your story with me."

"As you might guess," Anna said, "my uncle served the *houngan*'s purpose well. The beast has met little resistance since then. The merchants pay, and the children buy his drugs. And we have no more idea who he is now than we did when he first appeared on the scene."

At once fascinated and fearful, Eric tried to create a scenario whereby Scott Enders and Loretta Leone would have been intentionally poisoned. Both were street people. Perhaps they had seen something, or learned of something, that threatened the priest and his operation.

"Anna, is there anything I can do?" he asked. "Anything at all?"

"Perhaps," she said, after thinking over his request. "Perhaps there is. Dunn's payment demands have been increasing steadily. Once again there is a small group who is willing to stand up to him, if they can. I am part of that group, Eric. We have begun meeting secretly to try and form a plan, but we are still frightened—very frightened. Dunn is as ruthless and sadistic as a man can be. He has many spies and informants, and may already know us. But we do not know him. We have no one to strike at, and no support from outside our community. And worst of all, he has the terror of the *coup poudre*.

"Talk to people, Eric. See if you can get some of your doctor friends or, better still, someone in the Police Department interested in this." She wrote a number down and handed it to him. "Please be careful, and do not return to this store without calling me."

Eric glanced at his watch. It was twenty of eleven.

"I need to think about all this, Anna," he said. "Then I'll call you."

"Whatever you decide to do or not do will be understood," she promised. "Uncle, you can go upstairs now."

They waited until Titus Memmilard had shuffled off, and then they left his shop. Sproul Court was deserted and totally silent, save for the faint rumble of traffic from the thoroughfare several blocks away.

"Do you need a ride anywhere?" Eric asked.

"No, thanks. I don't live too far from here, and I need the air."

"That was a terrifying story your uncle just told."

"I hope you believe it."

"How could I not?"

"And I hope you will find a way to help us. I sensed in the library that you were the sort of man who might. That is the real reason I chose to share this with you."

Anna looked at him in a way that made his mouth go dry.

"I'll call you," he managed. "At least I can promise you—"

Eric's words were cut short by a hand clasped tightly over his mouth from behind. His head was pulled back and a long, razorlike stiletto was set against his throat. At virtually the same instant, a tall black man pulled Anna back by the hair and slipped the broad blade of a hunting knife beneath her chin.

"Not a word," he ordered. "Not a fucking word or you're both dead."

Eric's heart, driven by a sudden flood of adrenaline, began pounding mercilessly. The powerful hand across his mouth pulled even more tightly. Eric felt his lip split. Then he felt the dagger break skin.

"Please," he rasped.

"Shut up!"

Eric sensed blood beginning to trickle down his chest. He tried to look over at Anna, but the hand held him too tightly. Then, without lowering their knives, the two men half-dragged, half-shoved them several doors down the street to the only storefront on the block that was boarded up.

"So," the man holding Anna said in a rich Island accent, "word has it that you are interested in challenging the power of the spirits and their priest, and the *coup poudre*. Well, my beautiful friend, perhaps you are about to get that chance."

In response to a tap from the man's boot, the solid wooden door opened, and Eric and Anna Delacroix were shoved rudely onto the floor inside.

28

Not in his worst nightmares had Eric conjured a situation more terrifying than the hell he was living through this night. He and Anna Delacroix were gagged, their arms and ankles lashed to their chairs in a room heavy with incense and glowing with the flickering light of several dozen candles. Two decapitated chickens, hanging from a rafter, dripped blood onto the floor between their feet, forcing them to keep their knees spread apart to avoid being soiled. Around the dingy room hung bones—some of them human-sized—fluid-filled glass jars containing the bodies of toads and snakes, and carelessly tied bunches of what appeared to be dried weeds and wild flowers. On two sides of the room, surrounded by candles, were bizarre altars, each featuring a cluster of a dozen or more cheap plastic or ceramic figurines—statuettes of women and cowboys, clowns and madonnas, cupids and dogs. Resting on a dish at the center of each cluster was the head of a recently slaughtered chicken.

The two men who had captured them at knife-point had

changed into loose blood-red robes, smeared white greasepaint around their eyes, and now knelt across from each other, hammering out rhythms on broad hand-hewn drums. Every two minutes or so, they paused to smoke what smelled like hashish from a dual-throated hookah.

With the gag pulled tightly between his teeth, Eric had to struggle just to breathe. His torn lower lip was throbbing, as was his right elbow, which had slammed against the floor when he was thrown down. Beside him, Anna Delacroix stared stoically ahead, unwilling to give the men the pleasure of seeing her fear. Initially, after the two of them had been secured to their chairs, the men had teased her—touching her face and breasts and making lewd remarks. After a time, though, her silent, contemptuous glare seemed to spoil their sport.

Ten minutes had elapsed since they were tied down. The two men, for all their gestures and threats, had done little else, and seemed to be biding their time—waiting for something or someone. Suddenly, without any obvious signal, they stopped pounding on their drums. The taller one stood before them.

"The Holy One, the Voice of the Spirits, approaches," he said. "I shall remove the bonds around your mouths, but only if you promise that not a word will be spoken by either of you unless asked for by the Holy One. Do I have that promise?"

Eric nodded, but Anna continued to stare straight ahead.

"Do I?" the man yelled at her.

Still she would not respond. Eric's gag was removed, hers left in place. He ran his tongue over the slice in his lip. He tested the tightness of the clothesline that was pinning his arms to the chair. Without help, he knew there was not a chance of freeing himself, not in a thousand years. He began calming himself, forcing himself to concentrate on the situation. It was a process he had used hundreds of times in the E.R. over the years, but there he was always in control. The pounding in his ears and the spasms in his belly refused to abate.

He glanced over at Anna. She remained quiet, but below the fetters on her wrists, her fists were tight and bloodless. Despite his promise of silence, Eric could not contain his fear.

"Please," he said. "Please listen to me."

The tall man stood, poised to replace Eric's gag. Then he stopped as the door to the back room opened and a man stepped out. Actually, Eric realized, it was impossible to know for certain the new arrival's gender or, for that matter, his race. He wore a flowing, hooded white robe, gloves, and an intensely frightening full-faced mask with a death's-head painted on it.

But even more terrifying than the priest's appearance was the large ceramic bowl cradled in his left arm. Using a heavy wooden pestle, he continued to grind down something in the bowl as he glided to a chair facing them and sat. Eric knew what that bowl contained.

"Please," Eric said rapidly. "You've got this all wrong. Please listen to me."

The tall man looked to the priest for guidance as to whether he should replace the gag. Almost imperceptibly, the death's-head turned once each way. The priest continued grinding.

"L-look," Eric said, "I'm a doctor. She's a student, a college student. We're just trying to learn, not to harm anyone. You must believe that."

The tall man glanced at the priest. Then he faced the two captives and said with unsettling pleasantness, "And learn you shall."

He crouched by his drum, and the pounding began once again, the counterpoint building in loudness and tempo. Candlelight shimmered off the smiling white-and-black death mask as the priest stood, still working the pestle through the powder in the bowl.

"Please!" Eric screamed, trying to be heard over the crescendo of the drums. "Please don't do this!"

He looked over at Anna. The angry scorn in her eyes had now given way to undisguised terror.

"No!" he screamed as the priest approached her.

Eric watched as a gloved hand dipped into the bowl and withdrew a mound of moistened chalky-gray powder. Anna began to squirm in her chair, her eyes widening. Then, as the hand neared her cheek, she began thrashing her head wildly about. The drums intensified until it seemed as if the room were exploding.

"Nooo!" Eric shrieked as the hand laid a broad swatch of powder across one of Anna's cheeks. "Please, no!"

The moment the *coup poudre* touched her cheek, the drums abruptly ceased. Anna stopped moving. The room was silent and still. It was as if with the brush of the first grain, she had resigned herself to having been poisoned. Eric wondered if perhaps she knew, as he did, that struggling now would only speed the absorption of the tetrodotoxin. Once again the hand dipped, this time slowly painting Anna's other cheek.

The priest turned away, and for the briefest moment, Eric thought he was to be spared. Then, like the rumble of distant thunder, the drums began to build once again. The leering death's-head turned back to him. The gloved hand extended slowly, three fingers coated with powder. Eric snapped his head from one side to the other, screaming at the priest to stop, to understand. He hurled his chair over backward, then twisted onto his side. And when he could move in no other way, he slammed his head against the floor. Mindless of his struggling, the priest bent over and swabbed the gritty poison across first one cheek and then the other.

"Please don't do this," Eric moaned again and again as his chair was pulled upright. "Please don't . . ."

The priest knelt and ceremoniously dipped one finger into the pool of blood by Eric's feet.

"There . . . will . . . be . . . no . . . return . . . for . . . you . . . from . . . this . . . trip," the tall man said, punctuating each word with a drumbeat.

The death's-head priest pressed a disk of blood onto the center of Eric's forehead, and then Anna's. Then, without ever having said a word, he shuffled from the room.

Totally helpless and drained, Eric tried once again to regain his composure. This time he focused on what he had learned of tetrodotoxin and the ways of reducing or reversing its toxicity. Depending on the dose they absorbed, they still had an hour or two before the effects of the drug began, and as much as a day before they would be helpless. If they could get free, they might have a chance.

Get calm, he begged himself. *If you ever needed to be alert and focus in, you need to now. If you don't, you're going to die.*

He turned to Anna, but before he could speak, a broad band of adhesive tape was pulled tightly across his mouth. Then the cloth that had been used as his gag was pulled over his eyes and tied firmly. For perhaps twenty minutes or half an hour he sat that way. The only sound he heard was Anna's labored breathing. *Are we alone? Have we been left to die?*

Carefully, he began once again to test the bonds on his arms.

"Don't bother, man," the tall man said from nearby. "You're out of here now."

With that, Eric's hands were cut free and retied behind his back. Then his ankle ropes were severed and he was pulled roughly to his feet.

"Nod goodbye to your foxy friend, Mr. Doctor. We're not too interested in what happens to you anymore. But we've got some high ol' times in store for her. Yes, sir, some high ol' times."

The two men dragged him out the back way, tied his ankles together again, checked to be sure his pockets were empty, and then shoved him onto the metal floor of a van that smelled as if it had been used for hauling rotten fish. For the next half-hour or more, they drove. Initially, Eric tried to make some sense of the turns and straightaways, but he quickly gave up.

At last the truck jounced onto what seemed to be a dirt road and stopped, its engine still running. Eric was pulled from the back and thrown to the ground. The bonds on his ankles were cut, but his gag and blindfold were left on, and his hands left tied behind his back.

"Just stand right there, man. Listen carefully, and don't move. There's a nice sharp knife lying on the ground about four feet away from you. I won't tell you where. Wait until you can't hear this truck engine no more, and then go for it. We could use that knife to cut your throat, Mr. Bigshot Doctor, but we're not going to. You know why? Because, man, we really don't give a shit about you. We've got the one we want. She's business. You're sport. And whether you make it or you don't, the disbelievers will get the message we want to send."

Eric heard the two men laughing as they jumped into the van. It sprayed sand and gravel on him as it roared away. Moments later, the night was silent as a tomb.

29

orking blind, Eric spent what seemed an eternity finding the small folding knife, and longer still positioning it to saw through the clothesline binding his wrists. During the process he cut himself at least half a dozen times. Finally he shook his arms free. He ripped the blindfold from his eyes and the tape from his mouth, and used them to stem some of the bleeding from his hands and wrists. He was on a dark, wooded dirt road, with no sign of a house in any direction. The cool early-morning air smelled and tasted like country.

Eric felt himself still on the edge of panic, but he was steadied a bit by the realization that at least he was no longer helpless. If the only drug on his face was tetrodotoxin, someone somewhere had to know of a way to blunt or negate its effect. The key for him now was clear thinking and aggressive action.

He knew that a paved road was not far off, and he was fairly sure of the direction the van had taken. Unwilling to increase his circulation too much by running, he strode quickly that way.

In less than five minutes he was walking down a deserted, two-lane country highway. He sensed that he was north of the city, but it was only a guess.

Through some trees, around a curve in the road, he could make out a dim light and a structure of some sort. He cut across the woods and found himself standing beside a small Mobil station, which was darkened for the night but obviously in current use. There was no sign on the building that gave even a clue as to where he was. Eric scanned the narrow highway but saw no other buildings. He peered through the large plate-glass window, looking for a phone. There, on the cluttered metal desk, he spied something he needed even more at that moment—an envelope.

Above the desk, an STP wall clock told him that it was 2:15. Perhaps two hours had passed since he and Anna were poisoned. He felt desperate to get the death powder off his face.

In the weeds alongside the building he found a brick. As he stood poised before the window, he noticed the thin, metallic strip of a security system. It was just as well, he thought. With any luck he could get at the envelope and summon the police with the same maneuver. He stepped back a pace and hurled the brick with all his strength. The spectacular implosion of glass was accompanied instantly by the wailing of a siren. Eric kicked away a few large shards and stepped into the office.

He grabbed the envelope and hurried to the restroom. Trying to ignore the bloody apparition in the mirror, he carefully used the small knife to scrape as much of the powder as possible from his cheek into the envelope. When he felt certain that Ivor Blunt could make an identification from a fraction of what he had saved, he scrubbed his face with soap, rinsed it, and then scrubbed it again. Still, with his eyes lost in dark hollows and his lower lip split and stiff with clotted blood, he looked very much like precisely what he was at that moment—a man who was dying.

The pay phone behind the desk required a quarter even to get a dial tone. If the wailing alarm wasn't somehow connected to the police, Eric knew there was no telling how much time he would lose waiting for someone to respond. He searched the top of the desk for a coin, but succeeded only in learning from several bills that he was in Bob Kuyper's Country Mobil in Wayland—a rural community twenty miles or so west of Boston. He huddled over the desk, using his knife to work on the lock.

"Okay, asshole, get on the floor!"

The harsh voice, from not ten feet away, drove Eric's heart into his throat. His service revolver leveled, a rugged young officer stepped through the shattered window and motioned Eric away from the desk. Behind the policeman Eric could see a second officer, undoubtedly this man's backup.

"Wait, officer, please. I'm not a thief, I'm a doctor and—"

"Shut the fuck up and get facedown!"

The man, younger than Eric, seemed quite tough but also a bit nervous. Eric knelt in a spot away from the broken glass and then prostrated himself on the oily floor. The policeman circled him warily, finally positioning himself against a wall, safe from any attack from behind.

"Please listen to me," Eric begged. "It's a matter of life and death, believe me it is."

"Put your hands behind you!"

"You've got to—"

"Do it!"

Eric did as he was ordered. The policeman knelt roughly against the small of his back and expertly snapped a pair of handcuffs into place. Pain from the knife cuts seared up Eric's arms.

"He's cuffed, Sarge," the man called out.

"Keep him there," the other man responded. "I'm going to check around out here."

The policeman stood up.

"Okay, then," he said. "I'm Officer Carney. That's Sergeant Clarkson out there. You're under arrest. You have the right to remain silent—"

"Please, please," Eric begged. "I know all that. I waive all my rights. You've got to listen to me."

"Sit up. Slowly."

Eric did as he was told.

"Will you listen to me now?" he asked.

The young policeman nodded. For the next three minutes he listened without saying a word. Then he helped Eric to his feet and crunched across the shattered glass to what was once the plate-glass window.

"Hey, Sarge," he called out. "I think you'd better get on in here."

West Valley Regional Hospital was a tiny, fairly new facility located about five miles from the station house where Eric had been taken and booked for breaking and entering, plus malicious mischief. It was 3:30 A.M. With Officer Carney keeping watch, a nurse was bandaging the lacerations on Eric's wrists, two of which had required suturing.

The bleary-eyed physician on duty was a moonlighter, a senior surgical resident from Worcester named Jennifer Farrell. Trying mentally to place himself in her position, Eric had dropped a few names from her training program, and then cautiously and calmly recounted the events of the evening, using enough jargon to convince her that he was, in fact, a physician. Finally he showed her the envelope of powder and begged her to contact White Memorial for verification of his identity, and to get the home phone number of Dr. Ivor Blunt.

The nurse had just finished her work when Sergeant Clarkson and Jennifer Farrell reentered the room.

"Well, apparently you are who you say you are," Clarkson said.

"That's a relief."

"Tell us again what you want us to do now."

"Well, first of all I want someone to get over to Allston and see if they can find Anna Delacroix."

"That's already being done. We called the Metropolitan Police from the station."

"Thank you. Now I'd like to call Dr. Blunt and have him meet us at White Memorial."

"Who is he again?"

"He's a toxicologist, and probably the only one in the city who has the equipment and know-how to identify this poison."

"Do you agree with that, Doc?" Clarkson asked the resident.

Dr. Farrell shrugged. "I know of Dr. Blunt," she said. "And I know that we can't do a thing with this powder here."

"How does our friend here seem to you right now?"

Jennifer Farrell rechecked Eric's eyes, heart, lungs, and blood pressure.

"No problem," she said. "Dr. Najarian, are you sure you don't want me to sew that lip of yours?"

"I'm sure," Eric said, unable to keep impatience from his voice.

"Okay," Clarkson said after some thought. "Dr. Farrell, do you have a phone with a second extension?" She nodded. "Dr. Najarian, I'm going to listen while you talk to this Dr. Blunt. If it sounds on the up-and-up, I'll drive you in to White Memorial. Just remember, you're still under arrest. Any crazy stuff and you'll be back on the floor."

"I understand."

Ivor Blunt was outraged at the early morning call. Eric quickly found himself squirming in his seat as the crusty toxicologist questioned his every statement.

"Let me get this straight," Blunt said. "You want me to get up, shlep into the hospital, turn on my equipment, and analyze some dust that was put on your cheek during a voodoo ceremony in downtown Allston?"

"Correct."

"Dr. Najarian, are you crazy?"

"What I am is poisoned, Dr. Blunt," Eric said evenly. "Please, you've got to help me."

"Doctor, try to see it my way. You come into my office asking if I can analyze a woman's blood for this toxin that's never been found in Massachusetts. Then, not twenty-four hours later, you're calling me from some podunk hospital, claiming to have been poisoned with the stuff."

"That's right, sir."

"You sick now?"

"Not yet, no."

"If these men wanted you dead, why didn't they just put a bullet between your eyes?"

"I believe they wanted to make a point to the people they've been terrorizing," Eric said.

"Terrorizing with tetrodotoxin."

"That's right."

There was a prolonged silence, during which Eric rattled off what prayers he knew.

"I think you're crazy," Ivor Blunt said finally, "but since you've already got me wide awake, and since I'll never get back to sleep over my wife's snoring, I'm going to do what you want."

"Thank you," Eric sighed. "Thank you, sir. We can be at your lab in forty-five minutes."

"Take your time. Bring me your powder and four red-top and one green-top tubes of blood."

"I'll have them drawn here."

"Fine. Do you have a personal psychiatrist on the staff?"

"No. No, I don't."

"That's too bad," Ivor Blunt said.

30

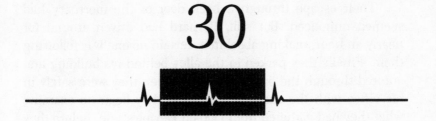

I don't like this, Bernard,"
Laura said, listening as Eric's apartment phone rang a ninth,
then a tenth time. "I don't like this at all."

For nearly three hours they had sat in Bernard Nelson's
office, drinking coffee, sorting through the material they had
brought with them from the Gates of Heaven, and trying to
locate Eric. There was a message from him at the Carlisle which
had come in some time around ten, but since then, nothing.
Five calls to his apartment and one to the hospital had gotten
them nowhere.

The nervous energy generated by their break-in at the
funeral home and their grisly discoveries was wearing off, and
Laura was beginning to feel desperate for some sleep. Bernard
Nelson was bearing up even less well, and had already taken a
prolonged nap on his couch. They had decided, at least for the
night, that she should steer clear of her hotel. If someone had
tried to run her down, there was good reason to avoid anyplace
she might be expected to be.

Their escape through a back door of the mortuary had seemed unnoticed. But still, Bernard had driven around for nearly an hour, making absolutely certain no one was following them. Finally they parked in the alley behind his building and entered through the basement. Only when they were safely in his office with the curtains drawn did they begin to examine what they had gathered from Donald Devine's safe. Before they did, however, Bernard placed a brief, anonymous call to the Boston police, suggesting that someone stop by the Gates of Heaven.

"Where could he be?" Laura asked, concern shadowing her face as she set the receiver down.

"Where did you say his parents lived?"

"Watertown."

"Maybe he went home and stayed over."

"Why wouldn't he have left the number at my hotel, or at least have called back?"

"I don't know, Laura." Nelson rubbed at his eyes. "Listen, I hope you don't misunderstand what I'm about to say. I know you think a great deal of Eric. And I suspect from what you've told me that those feelings are not ill placed. But people are not always what they seem to be. You haven't known him that long. There are any number of things he could be into that he hasn't let you in on."

"Maybe." Laura thought for a moment and then added, "But I don't think so. I think we should go over to his apartment."

Bernard Nelson massaged the back of his neck and once again stretched out on the couch.

"Laura, a couple of days ago in East Boston, some heavies nearly tore the two of you apart. Yesterday afternoon someone probably tried to kill you. There's every reason to believe that whoever they are, they're watching his place as well as yours. If they've already got him, the best thing we could do is wait until they contact us. It's you, and your brother's tape, they're after, not him. If they haven't got him, well, then the best thing we can do is wait anyhow." He forced a smile. "Besides, one break-in a night is my limit."

"I have a key."

Bernard looked up at her and softened.

"Are you sure his phone's working?"

"The operator says it is."

"Well, I still think we're better off getting a couple of hours sleep and at least waiting until it's light. It's just too dangerous, really it is. Trust me on that."

"I'm very worried about him."

"I know you are. Listen, the couch in my waiting room's a fold-out. Give me just a couple of hours."

"Oh, okay. What about all of this?" she asked, gesturing to the piles of notes, receipts, and ledgers.

"Laura, our late friend generated and squirreled away more paperwork than the Department of Defense. If we couldn't make any sense of this stuff at two A.M., our chances are even less at three. There's something buried in there that's going to shed some light on the man and his basement, I'm certain of that. But frankly, at this point I can barely remember my own name."

"I understand," Laura said.

"Good. In that case you remain the leading candidate to become my apprentice."

"Bernard, before you sleep I want to tell you again how grateful I am for what you've done."

"Cigars, woman. Talk in terms I can relate to."

She smiled. "I haven't forgotten. Listen, why don't you use the fold-out. I'll stay up for a while longer going through this stuff. Then I'll try Eric one more time. If we haven't connected with him by, say, six or seven, we can try his place."

"Good enough."

Groaning with the effort, Bernard Nelson pushed himself up, grabbed a pair of old army blankets from his closet, tossed one on the couch, and then lumbered into the waiting room with the other. In minutes, Laura heard the sonorous breathing of exhausted sleep. Then, with a sip of cold stale coffee, she settled in behind the desk.

Bernard had estimated that in their haste to get out of Donald Devine's bedroom he had gotten perhaps half the contents of the safe. Before they left the mortuary, he had slipped back to the upstairs apartment and verified that, as they suspected, whatever they had left behind had been taken, and the apartment ransacked. Undoubtedly the police would put robbery at the head of their list of motives. Of course there was still the intensive-care room to explain away.

Laura set aside the folder of correspondence and contracts, and concentrated on two ledgers. One of them, dating back six years and replete with names, addresses, payments, and various abbreviations, seemed to be a record of the considerable number of clients Devine had tended to. The other, held closed with a heavy rubber band, was also a list of names and abbreviations. However, between the last page and cover, this one was stuffed with receipts from various gas stations—at least a hundred of them, and possibly many more than that. Laura set the pile in front of her, made some room, and one at a time smoothed each one out, arranging them by date.

At 5:20, with the first light of day filtering through the curtains, Laura could no longer keep her eyes open. Without even trying to make sense of what she had found, she shuffled to the couch and was asleep almost as her head touched the pillow. Resting on the desk was a calculator, a pad scribbled with figures, and the Rand McNally atlas she had extracted from Bernard Nelson's eclectic collection of novels and reference volumes. The atlas was open to a map of the mountain states. Tucked in the cleft between pages was the pencil she had used to circle a small, sparsely populated area in southeast Utah.

———ᚃᚃᚃ———

Barred from the spectrophotometry lab by Ivor Blunt, Eric paced about the pathology department's waiting room. From time to time he swore his heart had skipped beats; at other times a breath or two seemed to be heavier than normal. He flexed his fingers and rubbed his hands, wondering if the tingling in them was the first sign of progressive neurotoxicity, or merely the result of his lacerations.

The sergeant from Wayland had turned out to be something of a godsend. After driving Eric to White Memorial and getting a positive recommendation on him from the head of hospital security, Clarkson had decided to void the criminal charges against him. In exchange, Eric gladly promised to pay the Mobil station owner for repairs to his window and security system.

After Clarkson left for Wayland, Eric had stopped by the emergency room for a confidential talk with the senior resident assigned to Reed Marshall's shifts. As he rechecked Eric's vital signs and physical exam, the bewildered resident did his best to appear to understand what had happened, but Eric knew he was being patronized. Nor was that reaction surprising. Until Ivor Blunt confirmed the identity of the tetrodotoxin, Eric was resigned to being very much on his own.

He sat on the arm of a chair and thumbed through a dog-eared copy of *People*. Like grotesque neon, the leering death's-head face glowed in his mind. Extortion, murder, narcotics, preying on the weak and superstitious—the man or woman behind that mask was a monster. He wondered where Anna Delacroix was, what horrors she was enduring—if in fact she was still alive.

His thoughts were interrupted by voices and a commotion of some sort in the hallway outside the waiting room.

"No, dammit," he heard a man say. "You all stay out here. We'll handle this. When we have something to say to you, we'll say it."

"You have no right," a woman's shrill voice cried.

"We have every right. Now just stay back here before I bust you for interfering."

The glass door to the waiting room was pulled open, and two Metropolitan District policemen entered.

"Dr. Najarian?" one of them asked. He was a thin, aging black man with a heavily creased forehead and kind eyes.

"That's right. Have you found out anything about Anna?"

The policeman, whose name tag identified him as Patrolman Medeiros, flipped a note pad open. Behind him, the other officer, younger and huskier than Medeiros, turned as several people pressed against the door.

"The natives are restless, Tony," he said.

"Goddam cannibals," Medeiros muttered. "Brian, just don't let 'em in here."

"Who are they?" Eric asked.

Medeiros looked up at him.

"Reporters," he said. "A couple of them were at the station when the call came in about this Delacroix woman and your voodoo ceremony. One of them recognized your name."

"Mine?"

"That's right. Apparently the *Herald* is about to hit the streets with an article about you and a missing body of some sort."

"Oh, Jesus," Eric said, remembering the stern faces of the selection committee as they discussed the hospital's campaign against negative publicity. "What about Anna?"

"Twelve Sproul Court in Allston. That the address of the store you went to?"

"That's right. Benet's. It's like a hardware store."

"You sure this man—this Titus Memmilard—was the owner?"

"Of course I'm sure. He said it, and his niece said it."

Eric felt confusion and a terrifying emptiness beginning to set in.

"Well, Doctor, number Twelve Sproul Court is a hardware store named Benet's all right. But the Benets, who live upstairs, and who we woke up and scared half to death, have owned that store for more than five years. And they've never even heard of anyone named Titus Memmilard—or, for that matter, Anna Delacroix either."

"That's . . . that's impossible."

But even as he said the words, Eric knew he was hearing the truth.

"And that other place," Medeiros went on wearily, glancing at his notes, "the place three doors down where you claim you and this Delacroix woman were taken at knife point and alleg-edly poisoned."

"Yes?" Eric felt ill.

"You said it was a boarded-up empty store that had been turned into some sort of voodoo temple."

"That's right."

"Well, Doctor, I don't know how to tell you this, but there're no boarded-up stores on that whole street. On the first floor of the building three doors down is a candle shop."

"Are you sure you were on Sproul Court?"

Eric could tell now by the way the two officers were looking at him that they felt certain he was quite mad.

"Oh, we were on Sproul all right," Medeiros said. "Were you?"

"Of course I was. Officer, contrary to what you're thinking, I'm not crazy. Everything happened exactly the way I said it did. Did you go inside the candle shop?"

"No. After what we encountered down the street, we wer-en't too excited about trying to get someone to let us in. But there's a whole window filled with candles and a bunch of other little knickknacks, and we could see inside perfectly well. Not a headless chicken in sight, Doc. Not one."

Eric sank back in his chair, desperately trying to sort out what he was hearing.

"This is insane," he said.

"Now there we're in agreement."

"What about the woman?"

"What about her?"

"Officer Medeiros, you've got to believe me. I met Anna Delacroix in the Countway Medical Library. She's a grad student at B.U. She asked me to meet her on Sproul Court, and we were abducted by two men at knife point and poisoned in a very frightening ritual."

"You know what we think, Doc? We think you were pledg-ing some sort of fraternity or club and the whole thing got carried away."

"That's ridiculous."

"You take any drugs tonight?"

"Only the one that was put on my skin. There's a toxicologist in there right now. After you hear what he has to say, maybe you'll believe me."

As if on cue, the door to the laboratory slammed open, and Ivor Blunt stalked into the room, his expression a strange mix of anger and bemusement.

"Talcum powder," he said.

The two officers exchanged smiles. Eric could not even speak.

"Plus a little dirt, a little lint, and a smidgen of oil of some sort," Blunt went on. "Maybe olive oil. Dr. Najarian, you are one crazy son of a bitch, and at this moment I wish you nothing but ill."

"Don't you see," Eric pleaded, looking from one of the men to the next, "the whole thing was a setup to discredit me—to make you all think exactly what you're thinking. I'm telling you, it all happened just like I said it did."

"I'm going home," Blunt said. "If you get poisoned again, please don't call."

He stormed back into his lab.

"I don't think he believes you," Officer Medeiros said in pointed understatement. "Dr. Najarian, you've caused a lot of people a lot of trouble tonight."

Eric couldn't remember the last time he had broken down and cried, but he knew that if he tried to speak, that was precisely what would happen. He had been *had*—maneuvered step by step by Anna Delacroix into an abyss of humiliation and discreditation from which he would never recover. He bit at his swollen lower lip and slowed his breathing until it seemed safe to stand and confront the policemen.

"Listen," he said, "my lip, these cuts on my wrist—I'm not making these up."

"Hey, split lips and slashed wrists we see all the time. We don't doubt for a moment that you've gotten yourself messed up in something tonight. But we're just as certain that something isn't what you've been telling us."

"Then what?"

Medeiros shrugged. "Drugs, women, some other kind of sex. Doc, look, we're really not bad guys, and we *do* have feelings. But we're also cops. We listened to you, we checked your story out, and we found nothing. Nothing. Believe me, you are far from the first M.D. we've dealt with who got himself into a jam. Shit, just a few months ago there was that guy from your emergency room who got arrested for—"

"I know, I know. But this is not like that. Believe me it isn't."

"Doc, the people upstairs in the E.R. tell me you're a damn good doctor—one of the best, they say. But they also tell me you've been pushing yourself real hard lately. Now, I don't know you, but until something comes along to convince me otherwise, I have to think you got big problems, and that maybe you ought to get some help before you get hurt any worse than you already are."

"I don't need any help except to find someone who can recognize the truth when he hears it."

"Hey, suit yourself. You want a ride home?"

"No, thank you. I can manage—oh, shit."

"What?"

"Whoever did this to me took my keys, my wallet, everything. I can't even get into my own place."

"Anyone else got a set?"

"No. Well, yes, but I don't know where she is. In fact, if you want to know the truth, with everything that's happened to me, I'm getting damn concerned about her. I may need your help in finding her, but I can't do a thing until I get into my apartment."

Medeiros looked at his partner. "Do you think we should help him out?"

The other man shrugged and then nodded.

"We don't like people to know this, but we got ways of getting into places," Medeiros said. "Come on. And as for your girl," he added, "unless you have evidence of foul play, we'd suggest you wait forty-eight hours before filing a report. In your case, better make that seventy-two hours."

He put his hand on Eric's shoulder and guided him through the door. In the hallway five reporters crowded up to them. One of them, begging Eric to wait until her camera crew arrived, shoved the microphone of a portable recorder in his face. All of them were firing questions.

"Doc, tell us about the voodoo priest." "Are you dying?" "How does it feel?" "Who is this mystery woman? Why isn't she registered as a student at B.U.?" "What did the analysis of the poison show?" "Are you going to be hospitalized?"

"Do you want to talk to them?" Medeiros whispered.

Eric shook his head.

"Out of the way," the policeman ordered. "Brian, run interference."

"Hey, be fair," someone yelled. "Doc, tell us about the missing body—the one who got autopsied alive."

"What is it with this hospital anyhow?" another reporter asked. "First that weirdo doc dealing drugs for sex, now this."

With Eric between them, the two officers pushed past the pack and hurried down the corridor. A minute later Eric was in the back seat of their cruiser.

"I can get into the building," he said. "My downstairs neighbor keeps a set of keys hidden in back for his various women to use."

"We love hearing that sort of thing," the officer named Brian said.

"Listen, thanks for doing this for me."

"It seemed like you were having a bad night," Medeiros responded.

Eric almost managed a smile. He knew that his career—at least at White Memorial—was, to all intents and purposes, over. And if, as he suspected, his near-arrest was reported to the Board of Registration and Discipline in Medicine, his career as a physician might be in jeopardy as well. Anna Delacroix had certainly served her masters—whoever they were—with distinction.

They entered Eric's building from the alley and went up

the back stairs. Officer Tony Medeiros knelt by the door, examining the lock.

"This should be nothing more than a credit card job," he said.

He tested the knob, which turned easily.

"It appears you forgot to lock up, Doc," he said, pushing the door open. "McGruff the crime dog would be very upset with—"

Instantly, the three of them tensed. Through the doorway they could see that the apartment was in shambles. Medeiros and his partner loosened the holster guards of their service revolvers as they stepped inside. Drawers had been pulled out and thrown on the floor; book cartons were spilled open, papers strewn about; a lamp was smashed. They made their way through the place, checking Eric's closets, which had been treated as rudely as the rest of the apartment.

Then, in the kitchen sink, they found Verdi. The parrot was dead, its neck apparently snapped. At the sight of the bird, Eric moaned and sank onto a chair, his face buried in his hands. He was now beyond tears.

"Any idea who might have done this?" Medeiros asked. "Or why? Or, for that matter, how they got in? There's no sign of a break-in anyplace."

"They took my keys. I told you that," Eric said without lifting his face.

"Hey, Tony," the other officer called out just then, "I'm down here in the bathroom. You ought to come down here. I think I may have just found an explanation for everything."

With Eric close behind, the policeman hurried down the hall.

Brian stood to one side of the bathroom, his arms folded. Covering the sink was Eric's oval bedroom wall mirror. On top of it were a razor blade, straw, and tiny spoon. Several thin lines of white powder were laid out in a row, and there was the suggestion that several more in the row had been already used. On the toilet seat was a plastic bag containing what Eric suspected was at least a thousand dollars' worth of cocaine.

If he felt any shock at that moment, it was at the realization that he was not the least surprised. Whoever had pulled Anna Delacroix's strings did not want him dead—they wanted him publicly and personally destroyed.

"Drugs can make people do some pretty bad, pretty weird things," Tony Medeiros mused, as if he were speaking to a nine-year-old. "Even if those people happen to be doctors. Believe me, you shoulda just said no."

He reached back and pulled his handcuffs from his belt.

Without a word, Eric turned and put his hands behind his back.

"Do you really think I trashed my apartment, killed my own pet, and left this stuff here? Then came back with two cops?" he asked when the manacles were in place. There was a numb calm in his voice.

"Doc," Tony Medeiros said, "the minute we see something like this, all we get to do is act. Someone else gets to do the thinkin'. Brian, call this in, will you? The doc and I will wait in what's left of the living room."

As he sat on his couch, surveying the wreckage of what had once been the simplest, most focused of lives, Eric felt a strange, surreal peacefulness settle in. Whoever had done this to him was frightened and threatened—either by something Eric was about to discover or something he already knew. Well, they had beaten him and broken him down; they had terrorized and discredited him. But they hadn't killed him. And that, they were going to find, was their mistake.

From far in the back of his mind, a melody began to sound. At first Eric could tell only that it was there, but soon he was nodding the tempo to himself and softly humming along. He was still immersed in the tune when they led him down the stairs and into the squad car.

It was the chorus from Kris Kristofferson's "Me and Bobby McGee."

Freedom's just another word for nothin' left to lose. . . .

31

You know, Mr. Najarian, the two of you are needing to be getting your acts together. First you call and leave a message that you called and that you are all right; then she calls and leaves a message that *she* called, and that *she's* all right. Then you both do the same thing all over again. But neither of you leaves a number. Get it what I am saying?"

"Yeah," Eric said, picturing the Iranian desk clerk slithering along behind the Hotel Carlisle desk. "I get it."

"So, you would like to leave a number, yes?"

Eric looked across the corridor of the Station Four jail at the officer who was waiting to take him to court for his arraignment on charges of possession of a Class B controlled substance, and possession with intent to sell.

"No," he said. "Just tell her I called, and that I'm all right. I'll call later."

He hung up and then allowed his hands, which had been cuffed in front of him, once again to be secured behind his back. He winced at the now-familiar electric pain that shot up from his wrists, and wondered how Jennifer Farrell's suture lines were holding up. He also wondered for perhaps the hundreth time where Laura was, and why she hadn't stayed in her room that night.

According to the Carlisle desk clerk, the last call from her had come in about 6:00 A.M. Now, it was nearly eleven. Eric gave silent thanks that at least she had not chosen to sleep at his place, and hoped that wherever she was, she had spent the intervening hours more pleasantly than he had.

Still, the more he thought about things, the more certain he became that something had happened to frighten her, or at least alert her to potential danger. She had made a point of leaving the message at the Carlisle that she was all right, but still, she would not leave a phone number. Possibly she recognized the desk clerk as one who would, at any given moment, be the devoted servant of the highest bidder. As it was, the man had sounded pretty damn eager to put together some information.

Perhaps, Eric speculated, somebody had gotten to him already. Perhaps Laura had seen one of the men from the docks watching the Carlisle, or been accosted by someone and escaped. Now, she was probably registered in another hotel, wondering where *he* was. Eric cursed himself for not being available to her.

"You got a jacket?" Eric's guard asked as they approached the front doors of the station.

"No. But it looks pretty nice out. I don't think I'll need one."

"Suit yourself. I just asked because some of 'em like to have jackets to pull over their heads."

"Pull over their—?"

Eric never had the chance or the necessity to finish his question. Two more officers joined them as they pushed through the doors into a mass of bodies, microphones, and clicking cameras—a group at least five times larger than the one at the hospital, and many times more rude. Eric shielded his eyes from the flashbulb assault and tried to ignore the barrage of questions, the kindest of which were in thoughtless bad taste. Suddenly, over the din, a hoarse, high-pitched voice called out rapidly to the crowd.

"Move aside. Move aside. We have no statement whatsoever to make at this time other than to affirm that this man is innocent of any wrongdoing and will be found so when all of the facts become clear. Now, please give us room and let us pass."

Eric stared over at the source of the voice, a rumpled man in an ill-fitting suit, carrying a scuffed briefcase.

"Who are you?" one of the reporters called out.

"Who the hell do I look like, Gandhi?" the man said. "I'm Dr. Yossarian's lawyer."

"Najarian," Eric whispered.

"Connolly," the man said. "Felix Connolly. You okay?"

"I'm okay. Why are you doing this?"

"I owe a certain private detective a favor," Connolly whispered.

"I understand," Eric said, remembering Laura's account of her meeting with Bernard Nelson, and knowing now where she was. Considering her description of the detective and his office, the appearance of the lawyer who owed him a favor was not that surprising. He could only hope the man knew what he was doing. "Laura's all right?" he asked.

The attorney nodded. "Let's keep names to a minimum just in case," he said. "She had some problems yesterday, but she's okay now. Our mutual friend has her keeping a low profile. I'll tell you what I know when we're alone. You'll have to go over to the courthouse in the cruiser. I'll take my car and meet you there."

He nodded at the battered Volkswagen beetle parked directly behind the police car.

"A Mercedes might inspire a bit more confidence," Eric said.

"Don't worry," Felix Connolly said. "Looks can be deceiving. Believe it or not, from time to time I've gotten even bigger baddies than you off."

* * *

With a surprising mix of charm, bombast, candor, and legal
acumen, Felix Connolly cut a swath for Eric through the brier
patch of a district court criminal arraignment. Along the way he
succeeded in persuading the assistant district attorney to drop
the charge of possession with intent to distribute, and the judge
to lower, by 400 percent, the $10,000 bail recommended by the
prosecution. Finally, after the date was set for a hearing to
determine probable cause, and the case was remanded to the
Suffolk County Superior Court, Connolly rushed Eric out of the
building, past the screeching gaggle of reporters, and into his
VW.

"Nice going," Eric said as Connolly inched through the
crowd and into the flow of traffic. "You're very good at what you
do."

Connolly acknowledged the compliment with a nod.

"In case you don't know it," he said, "Bernard Nelson is too.
Your friend is lucky she found him."

"I still can't believe what she's been through."

"You haven't done too badly in that department yourself."

"I guess. Well, I think we're past the last of the damn
reporters."

"Don't bank on it," the lawyer said, reaching behind Eric's
seat for a newspaper and handing it to him. "I suspect some of
them are following us right now. You're big stuff. This is the
early edition of the *Herald*. Take a look at it, and then I'll show
you the extra they came out with a few hours ago."

The early edition contained a four-inch, double-column,
bylined story on page 3, dealing essentially with the crusade of
one brave doctor to locate the body and tissue specimens of a
woman rumored to have been autopsied alive. Except for a brief
bit of biographical material about Eric, the story consisted
entirely of *No comment*s and *Absolutely untrue*s from hospital
officials and the medical examiner's office. A quote from Joe
Silver denied the rumors about the living autopsy, and added:
"Dr. Najarian has been at this hospital for five years, and knows

better than to speak to the press about any hospital business, especially when he has none of the facts."

As damaging as the early edition was to Eric's hope of a continued career at White Memorial, when compared to the extra it was a ringing endorsement.

ZOMBI DOC CHASES THE UNDEAD

The front-page article, complete with a picture of a dazed Eric being led from the pathology office by two policemen, would have been at least a nine on any ten-point scale of sensationalist journalism. Wherever the truth had eluded the reporter, or in certain spots where the facts had not jibed with the rest of the article, fabricated pieces had simply been thrown in. Interviews with Ivor Blunt, the Wayland police, and several staff members of the hospital painted the picture of a high-strung, overworked young man who had recently been turned down for a promotion to associate E.R. director and had turned to cocaine to keep himself going. His obsession with the poison tetrodotoxin, it was suggested by Blunt and others, was clearly the result of a cocaine-induced paranoia.

"Charles Manson, move over," Eric muttered, as he scanned the article.

A sidebar replacing the original article on page 3 resurrected the arrest and subsequent disappearance of Craig Worrell, whom the *Herald* had dubbed "Sex Doc." The reporter, who, Eric mused, was probably a department chief after this piece of work, had not missed the fact that the position "Zombi Doc" had once been the leading candidate for was the one "Sex Doc" had vacated. Eric wondered if even hoary White Memorial would be able to survive this latest assault on its reputation.

"It'll pass," Connolly said.

"At this point I almost don't care. I just really want to see Laura, that's all. Are we headed there?"

"We most definitely are not. Like I said, there are probably a few reporters and who knows what other manner of vermin following us. Bernard Nelson is worried about your friend's safety. And take it from someone who's known him for a long time, Bernard Nelson doesn't worry without cause."

"So what do we do?"

"Well, and please don't take this too personally, the first thing we ought to do is find someplace for you to shower."

Eric smiled ruefully and buried his face in his hands.

"No offense taken," he said. "I don't know what shape my place is in, but I picked up my spare key before they arrested me, so at least I can get in there."

"I'll go up with you," Connolly said. "My IOU to Bernard isn't paid off until I deliver you to your friend with no one following us."

"How're you going to be sure of that?"

Connolly smiled enigmatically.

"For right now, let's leave that one between me and the bug," he said.

Mindless of the chaos in his apartment, Eric hurried to the bedroom and called Bernard Nelson's office. Laura had learned of his arrest from one of the all-news radio stations.

"You made the TV news as well," she said. "I couldn't believe what I was hearing."

"That makes us even. I couldn't believe how close you came to getting killed."

"Eric, did Connolly tell you about Donald Devine?"

"He did, yes. I think you were crazy to take such a chance."

"You don't really."

"No," he said. "No, I don't really. I just wish I had been in the crazy place you were instead of the crazy place I was."

"I want to hear all about it. Has the lawyer told you to be careful coming here?"

"He has. He's figured out a way, but he won't tell me what it is."

"Great, because, Eric, something very weird is going on, and Donald Devine is—I mean *was*—right in the middle of it."

"What do you mean?"

"Well, I'd rather tell you all the details when I see you, but one of the ledgers we took from his safe has a long list of clients, listed only by initials and dates. After each set of initials there are several other abbreviations and names."

"Yes?"

"We've been able to piece together that shortly after each date, Devine—or someone else driving his hearse—drove from Boston to somewhere in southern Utah. Dozens of trips."

"I really want to see that book."

"You will. And, Eric, there's more. The last entry in the book was never completed. It's just a date and the initials L.L."

"L.L.?"

"Eric, it's the date when Reed Marshall pronounced that woman dead."

"Loretta Leone! Devine already had her initials in his book?"

"It appears so."

"Laura, did you check the date in February when—"

"There's an entry for that date too," she cut in. "The initials are P.T."

"We'll figure out what that means," Eric said excitedly. "Hold tight. I'll be there soon."

"I'm glad you're okay."

Eric said goodbye and gently replaced the receiver.

"Sounds like some things are beginning to happen," the lawyer observed.

"They are that," Eric said. "Hopefully, Mr. Connolly, by the time we're done, there are going to be some people at White Memorial who will be in need of your services at least as much as I was. I don't know what's going on yet, but what they did to Laura yesterday and to me last night suggests that we're jabbing at an exposed nerve. Between what I've learned and what Laura and your friend Bernard have got, I think we may already have a lot of the pieces. And somewhere out there is the glue that will help us put those pieces together."

Felix Connolly pulled a small silver flask from his suit-coat pocket and unscrewed the top.

"In that case, my man," he said, "I drink to glue."

Rocky DiNucci slipped his hand into the pocket of his tattered, oil-stained chinos and assured himself that nothing had happened to the sixteen dollars he had been paid for sweeping out two warehouses and emptying barrels along the East Boston docks. He was headed for Stella's Package Store, where he planned to treat himself to some decent zinfandel, a couple of hard-boiled eggs, and maybe even his favorite, a prosciutto and genoa sub with the works. Rocky was being especially careful, knowing that as often as not his money seemed to find a way to disappear before he could spend it.

Once a promising middleweight, DiNucci had absorbed far too many punches over the years, and had done further damage to his nervous system with cheap wine. Still, he prided himself on being a "good Joe who never done nobody no harm," and he delighted in showing anyone who would look the cracked photographic proof that he had once been a sparring partner of middleweight champ Carmen Basilio.

Rocky spent the cold months in any of a number of shelters around the city, but for most of the year he lived in a makeshift shanty of wood, cardboard, and sheet metal, tucked beneath an elevated stretch of Route 1A, half a mile from the waterfront.

He could read decently and even write some, and he still knew the fight game well enough to help out at Cardarello's Gym when they asked him to. And from time to time over the years, he had tried to pull his life together—to get detoxed and put together enough money to get a year-round place. But always, within a short time, he was back at the bottle and back under Route 1A.

Rocky left Stella's with two packs of Camels, half a dozen boiled eggs, two half-gallons of Cribrari zinfandel, and nearly six dollars in cash. He gave all of his change—seventy-eight cents—to two boys who asked to see his photograph. Then he headed home, thinking about how he would spend what remained of his pay, and where he could safely hide it until he did.

The afternoon had gone from sunny to gray, and Rocky was sure a storm was on the way. He stopped at a vacant lot near the crossover to the highway and poked around until he had picked up several pieces of scrap metal to patch his roof. Then he crossed the road to his hut. That the plywood door was partly open didn't bother him too much. Older kids were always playing war and using his place for a fort. And since he kept the things that mattered to him in the canvas shoulder sack he carried everywhere, getting robbed was never a worry.

"Hello," Rocky called out as he approached. "Anybody in there?"

There was no response.

He set his package aside and inched open the door with his foot. There, lying face-up on the pile of old blankets he used as a bed, was the body of a man. It wasn't until Rocky knelt beside the motionless form that he realized it wasn't a corpse. The man was merely asleep.

Rocky poured himself a glass of wine, settled down on a wooden carton, and studied his guest. Through the dim light he could just make out the details of the man's face. It was a face he felt certain he had seen before—a face he knew. But from where?

After nearly an hour and two more glasses of zinfandel, Rocky cleared his throat. Then he cleared it more loudly. Finally he reached out with his foot and nudged the intruder on the thigh. The man stirred, then woke. With great effort he pushed himself to a sitting position.

With the first good look at the man's pale, thin face—his cracked lips caked with dry blood; his glazed, empty eyes—the name of a fighter flashed into Rocky's mind. It wasn't that this man and Jesse Kidd looked alike, but that they had the same look. It was the look of death—the look on Jesse Kidd's face as he struggled to get up from the canvas during a six-round prelim against Rocky one Friday night in a smoky Newark arena. Kidd never did make it to his feet, and ten minutes after the knockdown he was dead.

"Hi, pal, don't be afraid. My name's Rocky. This here's my place. You okay?"

Scott Enders stared at him for a time and then shook his head.

"I think I have some broken ribs," he said. "It hurts to breathe."

"You from around here?"

"No, from Cleveland."

"Cleveland, huh? I could swear I seen you before. What's your name?" Scott pointed at the tag sewn on his shirt. "Bob, huh?" Rocky sniffed. "Whassat, some kind of prison shirt or something?"

"I don't know," Scott said.

"You want a drink?"

"Yes."

Rocky started to hand him the bottle, but then changed his mind and passed over the half-filled glass, keeping the bottle for himself.

"You got any money?" he asked.

"Some."

Scott pulled out what remained of the bills Eddie Garcia had given him, crying out softly at the pain that exploded from where the hijacker had kicked him in the chest. Several times during the trip from Ohio he had coughed up blood in the bathroom of the bus. Now, every breath was an agonizing effort. After he arrived at the terminal in Boston, a cab driver had taken twenty dollars of his money and had dropped him off somewhere in East Boston. The next thing Scott remembered was being nudged awake.

Rocky DiNucci eyed the money.

"Well, Bob," he said, "if you want to pay me a few bucks rent, I'll be happy to share this place with you."

"I've got to find Mrs. Gideon's horse."

"Right, sure you do."

Scott knew he was making no sense to the man. He wanted very much just to head off—to try to find whatever it was Mrs. Gideon's horse represented; to try to find himself. But the long journey and the unremitting pain in his chest had sapped him dry. He felt at once hot and terribly cold, and all he could think about was sleep. He handed the bills over and then lay back on the blankets.

"Hey, thirty-five bucks is too much," he heard Rocky say. "Here, I'll keep ten and you keep the rest. You sure you're okay? Maybe you should go to the hospital. . . . Well, suit yourself. Maybe you'll feel better after a little sleep. . . . You sure you haven't been in these parts before? I could swear I seen you. . . . Well, no matter. If I seen you before, I'll figure out where. . . . People make fun of me sometimes, but they don't know that ol' Rocky DiNucci has the memory of an elephant. If I seen you before I'll figure out where. Yessir, Bob, ol' Rocky the elephant'll figure out where."

32

The odometer on Felix Connolly's lime-green Beetle had been frozen at 99,000 miles when he bought the car in 1980, and at 99,000 it remained. Still, during their drive through the chaotic late afternoon traffic, Eric was impressed with the bug's élan. He was also relieved that the attorney had returned his flask to his suit-coat pocket after a single draught, and had shown no inclination toward another toast. There was too much at stake at this point to have to question the man's judgment.

If Connolly was concerned about being followed, he showed no sign of it, staying essentially in one lane and seldom, if ever, checking the rearview mirror. Nor did he offer Eric any explanation as to why they were headed into the Roxbury section of the city, directly away from Bernard Nelson's Boylston Street office.

"Trust the bug," was all he would say.

Before leaving his apartment, Eric had called Joe Silver at White Memorial. The E.R. director coolly suggested that it would be in everyone's best interest if Eric voluntarily removed himself from the staff until the whole matter of his arrest on drug charges was resolved.

Eric intimated, without giving any details, that there were some illegal and dangerous practices going on at White Memorial which he would be in a much better position to ferret out on the active staff. If Silver was part of Caduceus, he hoped that his tacit threat might provoke some telltale reaction or remark.

The E.R. director seemed not the least influenced by any of Eric's concerns. He tersely gave him until the following afternoon to remove himself voluntarily or be summarily suspended.

After hanging up, Eric carefully wrapped Verdi's body in newspaper and set it on the balcony, hoping that before long he would be in a position to do something more appropriate. Connolly had set 3:30 as the time they would leave. Over the few minutes remaining, Eric propped himself against the balcony railing. Gazing out across the rooftops, he took stock of himself in the light of Joe Silver's demand for his suspension. He was apprehensive about his future and angry at Silver's lack of confidence, but most of all, he ached for the shame his parents would be feeling.

Earlier in the day, during a lull at court, he had called them and tried to impress on them his innocence. Not unexpectedly, they took his difficulties quite personally and were unable to see far enough beyond their own bewilderment and humiliation to find the words that would have indicated they truly believed him. The very worst things he had ever done in his life were far too mild to prepare them for dealing with events like these. His being forced out of White Memorial would hurt them even more than his brother's arrests had.

Silently, he renewed his vow to see things through—to find those who had decimated his world and Laura's, and to absorb whatever punishment was necessary to bring them down. Afterward, assuming he was still alive, he would pick up what pieces were left and make some sort of new life for himself—with Laura a part of it, he hoped.

"Gray Cougar and blue Volvo," Felix Connolly said.

"What?"

"Don't look back, but there are at least two cars working a tail on us. They've been at it since we left your apartment."

"Reporters?"

"That depends on how lucky you're feeling."

"Not very," Eric said.

"Then I don't think they're reporters. Tighten that seat belt and feel free to close your eyes any time you want."

Connolly pulled out his flask and took a small gulp. Then, before Eric could comment, he shifted down a gear and floored the accelerator. The VW shot forward past two startled drivers, into a tight, skidding right-angle turn, and down a side street. Eric glanced behind just as the Cougar screeched around the corner, followed a second or two later by the Volvo.

The side street was typical of many in this most run-down part of the city, with trash and broken glass lining the gutters. Dilapidated red brick buildings were separated from the curb by three-foot sidewalks, and from one another by narrow alleyways. The pursuers, whoever they were, had made up considerable ground by the time the VW was halfway down the street. It was unlikely they would reach the next cross street without being overtaken. Then, suddenly, even that concern was meaningless. Ahead of them, hood up, a disabled old Chevy was parked at an angle that completely blocked the street.

"Shit," Eric said, glancing back once again. "What do we do now?"

At that instant, Connolly slammed on the brakes and spun left into a cluttered alley that was so narrow, Eric had not even noticed it. The VW cleared the buildings on either side by barely two inches.

"Bernard insists on calling this Nelson's alley," Connolly explained as they crept along, "even though I'm certain I told him about it. He and I bought this little chartreuse beastie just for days like this, so it doesn't get driven much. Although actually it's sort of a pleasant change from my Mercedes. That junker back there with its hood up belongs to a friend of ours who's probably in some bar down the street right now. It weighs a goddam ton. If our pals can't get past it—and they can't— there's no way they can reach the street we're heading to."

Eric turned just as two men entered the alley on foot and began sprinting after them, but he knew they were too late. After just a few yards they stopped, apparently realizing the same thing. Clearly enjoying the whole scenario, Felix Connolly eased the bug onto the roadway and accelerated back toward Boston.

"Any questions?" he asked.

"Only one," Eric said. "Do you have anything left in that flask?"

———∿∿∿———

Felix Connolly drove Eric to the Back Bay and pulled up in front of an old, elegant brownstone on the river side of Beacon.

"Your friend is in apartment Three-B," he said. "If you need anything, here's my card. That number'll reach me day or night." He leaned over and shook Eric's hand. "You're a class act, Doc," he said. "You've handled yourself well through all this."

"Thanks for saying that. You're something of a piece of work yourself, Felix. Hang on to that flask."

The name slot next to the bell for apartment 3B read simply: RING ONCE AND WAIT. Eric's finger had barely left the doorbell when Laura spoke to him through the intercom and buzzed him in. She checked over the safety chain, and then pulled him inside the apartment and held him tightly. He could feel the tension in her body and in her kiss.

"I'm okay," he whispered, stroking her hair. "Everything's going to be all right."

He waited until some of the tightness in her muscles had lessened and her breathing had slowed, and then stepped back and surveyed the small apartment. The space was beautifully apportioned, with Scandinavian furniture and Oriental area rugs set on a polished hardwood floor. On a loft eight feet above, a double futon abutted a half-moon window overlooking the Charles.

"This place is beautiful," he said. "Whose is it?"

"He didn't say so outright, but I have to assume it's Bernard's—or maybe someone he knows very well. He dropped me off here a while ago, gave me a set of keys for each of us, and told me we should make ourselves at home here for as long as we need to."

"Where is he now?"

"His wife drove up here with some clothes for him, and then took him to the airport. Assuming the plane left on time, he took off about an hour ago for Salt Lake City."

"Business?"

"*Our* business, Eric."

"But Utah? With all that's going on, shouldn't he be—"

"Hey, slow down. I want to lay all this out for you in order. Are you sure you're okay?"

"Thanks to that lawyer, I am," he said. "I'm really exhausted, that's all. And I'm desperate as hell to get back at someone—anyone—for what we've been through. You know, I wasn't even able to bury Verdi. I left his body on the balcony."

She kissed him once again and then led him to the oak table in the dining alcove.

"You'll get the chance," she said. "For what it's worth, Bernard and I believe that whoever killed Verdi broke into your place looking for what we have right here." She motioned to the pile of ledgers and papers on the table. "This is some stuff, Eric. Wait till you see it. A lot of it didn't make sense to us, but we have a feeling it will to you. Are you up to looking at it now?"

"I'm exhausted, but I'm not dead," he said. "Let's do it."

They began by scanning Donald Devine's two ledgers, but quickly discarded the larger of them as being pure mortuary business. The other book was much more of an enigma. There were, in all, seventy entries, spanning more than two years. The first entry read:

P.F. — 3/19 — Rx by W., transf. by C. — arr. GOH 3/21; dpt. 3/24. Cost to GOH $200; transp. costs $511; Tot. $711; Dep. $150; bal. due, $561. Pd. 4/2.

"You have gasoline receipts that correspond to this P.F.?" Eric asked.

Laura retrieved a small stack and placed them in front of him.

"There are some I can't find, but fifty-nine of the seventy entries match a set of these," she said. "They're all round trips from Boston to somewhere around here." She pointed to the circled area in the atlas.

"What in hell was he into?"

Laura turned his face to hers.

"Eric, don't you see? The man had an intensive-care unit in his basement. Why would he have that if he only dealt with corpses? He was transporting bodies, all right, but I don't think they were dead ones."

"Let's see if we can break one of these entries down," he said.

When they had finished, they rewrote the item, filling in as much information as they could.

P.F. March 19
Treated by W.
Transferred by C.
Arrived Gates of Heaven March 21
Departed March 24
Cost to Gates of Heaven $200
Transportation costs (Gas receipts plus meals)—$511
Total $711 ($200 + $511)
Balance due, $561 ($150 advance payment)
Paid April 2

The initials heading each entry were different, but the abbreviations W. and C. were present in every item, except for the last four. Three of those four, including P.T., were treated by C. and transferred by C. The fourth, coded L.L., was incomplete.

As they studied each item, other patterns began to emerge as well. Each case spanned four or five days, from the initial date through transfer to the Gates of Heaven two days later, and ending with transport, presumably to southeastern Utah, two or three days after that.

"This is incredible," Eric muttered over and over. "This is absolutely incredible."

"These people listed here weren't dead, were they?"

"I don't think so."

"What could Devine have been up to?"

"I'm not sure *he* was up to anything—at least not on his own. He was a strange little duck, but unless he was an absolute Jekyll and Hyde, it's hard to imagine him doing anything but taking orders from someone and getting paid."

"I agree." She walked across the room and back. "Eric," she asked finally, "do you think Devine could have had anything to do with Caduceus?"

He pushed away from the table and looked up at her. Since their earlier conversation, and her description of Devine's macabre basement chamber, that notion had been drifting in and out of his thoughts as well.

"If all of these initials correspond to WMH patients, I think you may have something," he said. "With these dates, it shouldn't be too hard to check out—especially if I can get into the record room, or at least tap into the record room computers. Wouldn't that be something." He pounded his fist into his hand. "Goddam but wouldn't that just beat all."

Laura's face was glowing.

"Eric," she said, "I think he was part of them. I really do."

At eight-thirty they packed up Donald Devine's material and opened the bottle of Chardonnay that Laura had picked up for them.

"Tell me something," Eric asked. "Why do you think someone tried to kill you yesterday?"

"I don't really know," she said. "Bernard thinks the people Scott was after still believe I'm a threat because I can locate that tape. If they thought I already had it, they'd have tried to capture me, then kill me later. Now he says I shouldn't leave this place until he gets back from Utah. But, Eric, I won't last a day cloistered in here."

"You've got to do what he says."

"I don't. Listen, I'm the one who started this by coming here. It's *my* brother we're after. I need to do *something*."

"Look, just give me till tomorrow morning. I'm going to find a way to screen the files in the record room. Afterward, depending on what I find, we'll make some sort of move . . . and we'll do it together."

"What if the people at the hospital know you've been suspended and don't let you have access to the records?"

"It wouldn't surprise me if Caduceus has already seen to that," he said. "But I'm not planning on going anywhere near the record room. If I'm correct, the whole system's computerized."

"Explain."

"Give me a minute," he said, picking up the phone.

Laura listened as he called the White Memorial emergency room and spoke to a nurse who was obviously a good friend. In just the minute he had promised, he hung up, having obtained the access password to the WMH records.

"It's FILE-RITE," he said. "Cute, huh? The password's all over the hospital, because every floor and nurses' station needs access to the records."

"You mean anyone from anywhere can call in and get anyone else's medical record?"

"It's not *that* easy. There's probably a call-back built into the security system to prevent unauthorized outside callers from getting in. It requires the caller to type in his phone number, and then checks it against an approved file and either hangs up or returns the call."

"So you've got to use a computer inside the hospital?"

"Exactly."

"For how long?"

"Dunno. It depends on how complete the user menu for the records department is. If it's real complete—and I think it is—I may need only a couple of hours to do what I have to."

"But where in the hospital can you work that long without somebody seeing you?"

He pulled her to him.

"Remember my friend Subarsky—the one I built the laser with?"

"The one you grew up with in Watertown."

"Exactly. He has an IBM that's connected to the hospital system, and he's probably good enough with computers to fill in the million or so blanks in my knowledge."

"Well, I promise to stay put if you promise to be careful."

He traced the lines of her perfect mouth with his fingertip.

"And I promise to be careful if you promise to let me at that smooth little place just below . . ."

She cupped her hand to his lips as she undid the top few buttons of his shirt. Then suddenly she pulled away and raced up the ladder to the loft. Before Eric could react, her sweater floated down onto his lap. Seconds later her jeans followed.

"Can you make it up here with your injuries?" she called out.

"I can," he said. "In fact, if this meteor shower continues, I may not need the ladder."

He left his clothes at the foot of the ladder and climbed up to the loft. Laura lay naked on the futon, her chin resting on her hands as she stared out the half-moon window at the river. Beneath the soft glow of light reflected off the ceiling, her slim, long body was like a sculptor's masterpiece.

She turned to him. "Does it frighten you that I'm falling in love with you?" she whispered.

"The only thing that frightens me is realizing I've never let myself feel anything until now," he said.

For an hour they made love—desperately at first, then with such slow, exquisite tenderness that before long it seemed neither of them could survive another touch. Finally, locked in each other's arms, they slept, their breathing and their bodies working in gentle, perfect harmony.

♪♪♪

Six miles away, in East Boston, Rocky DiNucci shuffled into a phone booth, laughing to himself. Crumpled in his hands was a poster he had torn off the side of a warehouse on the docks.

"Rocky the elephant," he cackled. "They call me punchy, but what do they know? Yessiree, yessiree. Ol' Rocky the elephant. That's me."

He dropped a coin into the phone, smoothed the poster out, and dialed.

33

At five thirty Eric was up, alternately pacing about the apartment and poring over the ledger taken from Donald Devine. After a peaceful hour in Laura's arms, visions of Anna Delacroix, the death's-head mask, and Verdi lying dead in his sink began intruding on his sleep. Surviving as an emergency physician had meant becoming somewhat inured to the ugliness and brutality in the world, to the sad results of man's capability for violence, self-destruction, and a myriad of unfeeling acts. But nothing had prepared him for the evil he and Laura were confronting.

He shuffled to the bathroom and studied himself in the mirror—the bruises, the tension in his jaw, the strange metallic anger in his eyes. It was like looking at a total stranger. He had been battered and pushed beyond the limits of his tolerance by faceless men and women who seemed ready to kill and maim without hesitation. And now he knew that if he was to survive, if he was to spend his life in the profession he had chosen and with the woman he was growing to love, he had to be ready to fight by their rules.

Laura and Bernard Nelson had taken the first steps toward reprisal. Now it was his turn. And waiting for him in Dave Subarsky's lab was the weapon he would use to begin his counterattack against the faceless ones—a computer. Leaving a note in case Laura awoke, he slipped from the apartment and made copies of the ledger pages at an all-night convenience store on Berkeley.

He returned to find her up and cooking breakfast. She was wearing only a man's dress shirt, and the sight of the full length of her wonderful legs immediately began diverting Eric's thoughts from the task at hand.

"Bernard said to make full use of the place," she said. "You don't think he'll mind that I borrowed one of his shirts, do you?"

"If he learns where it's been, I don't think he'll ever wash it again."

"You got the copies?"

"Uh-huh. I'm going to wait another fifteen minutes and then call Dave. With luck, we'll be able to screen the E.R. visits on the days listed here, looking for people with these initials."

"I want to come."

Eric shook his head.

"I know waiting here's going to be harder than what I have to do," he said, "but you can't take the chance of someone's recognizing you."

"But what if they recognize *you*?" she asked.

"If they wanted me dead, they could have done it. No, they want people thinking I'm crazy so no one will pay any attention to what I have to say. There's no way they could know how many people I've spoken to about my tetrodotoxin theories, so their best approach is simply to discredit me altogether. Killing me would only add weight to the possibility that I was onto something."

"I hope you're right. I just keep wondering how that woman knew to be at the medical library."

He looked at her, startled.

"You know," he said, "with all that's happened, I hadn't thought about that at all."

"Well, do. And please be careful."

He kissed her on the back of the neck.

"I will. I have too much to live for to cash out now."

"Okay, then," she said reluctantly. "I'll stay here and catch up on the soaps. It's only been two or three years, so I shouldn't have much trouble. Damn! I don't like being made helpless."

"I know. But after what happened yesterday, we should try at least to pick and choose when we take chances."

"Just do me one favor, then. Start with that P.T. person."

"You think that was Scott?"

"The dates match."

"Okay, I will. But, Laura, please don't hold out too much hope."

"When I see his body, I'll stop hoping," she said, setting Spanish omelets and a dish of hash-browns on the table. "And when I see you back in this apartment in one piece, I'll stop worrying."

Eric broke from their meal to call Dave Subarsky. Five minutes later he was back.

"We're in luck," he said excitedly, helping himself to seconds. "Dave feels there's a good chance we can get into the record-room system."

"Just be careful," she said again.

He flexed his muscle.

"Does a man with these biceps need to worry?"

"Eric, I'm serious."

Eric pulled her to her feet, slipped his hands beneath her shirttail, and held her tightly.

"Damn right," he said.

Eric took the river walk to the hospital. The flat gray morning was chilled by a steady wind that whipped at him from behind and sent a heavy chop across the dark water. An occasional bundled jogger chugged past, but otherwise he was alone. He tried to focus on the computer search he was about to attempt, but his thoughts were continually sidetracked by the question Laura had raised. *Just how did Anna Delacroix come to find me at the Countway?*

He had assumed that her interest in him had been triggered by his interest in tetrodotoxin, and that her perception of him as a threat to her cult had subsequently arisen as a result of the information he had shared with her about the White Memorial cases. But what if she had been at the Countway *because* of him? What if her people had already known of his growing suspicion of the arcane poison? *How would they have found that out when I didn't really speak to anyone outside the hospital?*

He turned the questions over and over in his mind, considering first the likelihood that Anna or someone connected with her had been following him all along, and then the possibility of whether the death's-head priest could have purposely sent her to make contact with him while they were arranging the whole Sproul Court nightmare.

The questions were still gnawing at him as Eric entered the hospital through the outpatient department and quickly took the stairway down to the tunnel connecting all the WMH buildings. He passed no one who showed any particular notice of him along the way. Dave Subarsky was waiting in his office with coffee and doughnuts.

"So," he said, "public enemy number one surfaces. Man who kill our women, rape our buffalo." He set his beefy hands on Eric's shoulders. "You holding up okay?" There was no mistaking the concern in his eyes.

"I've been better."

"I should hope so. Here, have a chocolate-covered. I understand they're a special favorite of the criminal element."

"I'm about as much of a criminal as you are."

"Careful what company you put yourself in. I've been known to pull a few labels off mattresses in my day."

Subarsky hoisted his size thirteens onto the corner of the desk and tugged absently at his beard.

"I take it, then, that every phantasmagoric thing you've been telling the press and the police is true."

"Everything."

"And the cocaine?"

"Do you know a straighter arrow about that stuff than I am?" Eric asked.

"But why would someone set you up like that?"

"That, my furry friend, is what I was hoping you might help me figure out."

"Well, then, that being the case, my computer is at your disposal, along with my somewhat limited knowledge of its applications. But first, how about telling me what we're looking for?"

Eric set the copies of Donald Devine's ledger on the desk.

"Settle back, big fella," he said. "This ain't gonna be pretty."

Starting from the day in February when he failed to resuscitate the man named John Doe, Eric took the biochemist step-by-step through his initial meeting with Laura, their encounters with Thaddeus Bushnell and Donald Devine, and finally to the tie-in with the horrible events surrounding the death of Loretta Leone. Subarsky listened thoughtfully and without comment. When Eric finished describing Laura's break-in at the Gates of Heaven, and the conclusions suggested by Devine's notes and the basement intensive-care room, Dave whistled softly through his teeth.

"You have gotten yourself into *some* shit, my man," he said. "I will say that."

"Laura's in even deeper than I am. Some organized-crime types think she's a threat to unearth this video showing them in a drug deal. Apparently her brother did the filming while he was undercover. Yesterday the bastards tried to run her down. They actually killed a guy in the process."

"She doesn't know anything about the video?"

"Nothing."

"Like I said, you are really into some shit. . . ." Subarsky crumpled a sheet of paper and lofted it into the wastebasket ten feet away. "So," he said, "where do you want to start?"

"Look at this list, Dave. If we can find WMH patients whose

names correspond to these initials, we'll have at least forged the link from Devine to the hospital."

"And you think one of the three bigwigs on that search committee is part of this Caduceus thing, and whoever that is tried to recruit you and may be at the bottom of this whole business?"

Eric shrugged. "Maybe. At this point I'm only guessing."

"Well, then, Don Quixote," Subarsky said, booting up his terminal, "let's have at it."

Using the FILE-RITE password, Dave quickly worked his way into the main menu of the record-room computerized data system. As Eric had suspected, White Memorial had gone into electronic data in the most comprehensive way. The menu of available functions and maneuvers was exhaustive. Subarsky retrieved from his desk a manual describing in detail the hospital's computer capabilities and codes.

"Here," he said, handing the manual over, "you do the brain work; I'll do the grunt work."

Eric studied the screen, and then the book. "Type RE-TRIEVE," he said.

With Eric issuing the commands, they moved like mice in a maze from one menu to the next, into dead-end alleys and then back out again. Their goal, the reward waiting at the far side of the maze, was a list—a compilation of those patients seen in the emergency room on February 25, the first date noted beside the initials P.T. Twenty minutes passed.

"We could always just call the record room and ask them what we're doing wrong," Subarsky said.

"Not unless we absolutely have to. I don't know for sure if Caduceus is behind this, but if they are, there's no telling who's with them. And if someone from the record room just happens to be, and we alert them, we've lost everything."

"Pardon me for saying so, laddie, but you're startin' to sound just a wee bit paranoid."

Eric held up his bandaged wrists.

"Make that a whole bunch paranoid," he said. "Please, Dave, just bear with me a little longer."

"It's your dime," Subarsky said, polishing off a custard-filled doughnut in three bites. "It's a good thing we spent all those late nights together locking horns over the laser, 'cause I can always fall back on those one or two times when you were actually right."

"Try SYNTHESIZE again," Eric offered.

"We're just gonna end up the same place as last time."

"No, I don't think so, Dave. The command's coming *after* the date this time. Just try it."

Subarsky typed in the word and then hit the return key.

ALPHABETIZED OR SEQUENTIAL? the screen asked.

"We've got it," Eric cried. "We're in!" He hunched over the biochemist's broad shoulders. "Tell the beast to alphabetize our list."

Seconds after the command was typed in, a list appeared, headed by the date 25 *February*, and set in computer-perfect alphabetical order. The name *Trainor, Phillip* was on the list, along with his birthdate and hospital number. *Was he Scott Enders?*

They scanned 27 February, the day of the actual resuscitation, but could not find a Phillip Trainor.

"Don't worry," Eric said. "He probably was entered as John Doe."

He wrote the name *Phillip Trainor* next to the initials P.T., and then had Dave call up an image of Trainor's E.R. sheet.

"Near drowning, hypothermia, contusions . . . David, this was Laura's brother. I just know it was. He was here two days before I pronounced him dead. Can you print that sheet?"

"Given half an hour, maybe."

"Never mind," Eric said excitedly. "I'll take notes. We're onto something, Dave. Just watch."

Eric noted down all the information he could, and then began searching for the other initials on Devine's list. In minutes, the pattern began to come clear. Over the past two-plus years, certain patients were seen in the White Memorial emergency room for problems varying from colds to broken bones.

Within forty-eight hours those same patients were brought back to the hospital essentially dead on arrival.

Every one of them was signed out as acute heart failure secondary to myocardial infarction, and every one of them was transferred to the Gates of Heaven Funeral Home pending examination by the medical examiner. And in every case, that medical examiner was Thaddeus Bushnell.

"Why didn't someone ever pick up on this?" Eric asked. "Sooner or later, a nurse or doctor—" He stopped in midsentence and began flipping rapidly through his notes.

"What is it, pal?" Subarsky asked.

"What it is, David," Eric said grimly, "is the answer to my question. Look, look here. Except for the last three cases, Craig Worrell and Norma Cullinet were involved with every one. That's Worrell as in W., and Cullinet as in C.—the abbreviations in Donald Devine's record book. The reason Worrell wasn't part of the last three cases is that he got arrested and then disappeared."

"I'm impressed," Subarsky said. "I really am. But we still don't have the answer to the sixty-four-dollar question. Why? What would anybody want with a bunch of corpses?"

"That's the point. They weren't corpses. They looked dead enough to get pronounced dead with no one raising an eyebrow, but—Dave, don't you see? That's the tie-in! That's the goddam tie-in with everything!"

"What?"

Eric paced across the room and back.

"Can I take over there for a second?" he asked. "The EKG department records are totally computerized. We call up tracings all the time."

"Help yourself," Subarsky said, pushing himself up. "Listen, I've got a little experiment going on in the lab next door that I need to rerun with some new reagents. Give a holler if you need me. Otherwise, I'll be back in ten or fifteen minutes. By then, I expect you to have all the answers for me."

"David, keep all this between us, okay?"

"That goes without saying, my friend. Congratulations on unearthing all this."

"Nice choice of words, Subarsky," Eric said, summoning up an EKG. "Real nice."

Subarsky lumbered off as the first tracing appeared on the screen. It was the EKG taken during the resuscitation of patient P.F.—a forty-eight-year-old woman Eric now felt certain was named Pamela Fitzgerald. The pattern was one Eric knew all too well: broad, slow complexes at the rate of six to eight per minute. Checks of two other cases showed the same.

Eric set the keyboard aside. On a sheet of paper he wrote the questions:

> How?
> Who?
> Why?

Beside the first, he wrote:

E.R. or inpatients with no next of kin. Tetrodotoxin administered by C. Resuscitation attempted by W. or by unsuspecting resident. Transfer to G. of H. for further treatment in basement by ?. Possible antidote given. Death certificates presigned by T. Bushnell. Mortuary records forged. Transportation of drugged? subject to Utah by D. Devine.

Beside the second:

Craig Worrell. Norma Cullinet. Donald Devine. Sara Teagarden? Joe Silver? Best Bet: Haven Darden. Death's-head priest. Anna Delacroix.

And finally, by the third, he could write only a large question mark.

Sickened and frightened by what he was discovering, Eric wandered out into the corridor. Through the high plate-glass windows, he could see the ambulance parking area far below and the entrance to the emergency room. Everywhere, it seemed, business was as usual. Patients and nurses, uniformed EMTs, and white-coated physicians bustled in and out of the buildings, proud or relieved to be associated with the hospital considered by many to be the world's best.

And no place was there even a hint of the terror their august institution had spawned.

Eric felt unsettled and anxious about what lay ahead—about the possibility of making a mistake that would alert the wrong people too soon. Timing was everything—timing and an airtight case. His credibility, for the moment, was all but destroyed in everyone's eyes except, he hoped, Dave Subarsky's. If Caduceus realized how far he had come, there was no telling what countermeasures they would take.

Already they had seen to the removal of Loretta Leone's body and tissue samples. That move in itself spoke of resourcefulness and power, just as surely as the deaths of Thaddeus Bushnell and Donald Devine spoke of the lack of moral boundaries. The worst thing he could do would be to tip his hand too soon. Records could be removed as easily as had Leone's specimens. People could be bought off or silenced altogether. Incriminating evidence could be planted. And of course, he and Laura could simply disappear.

"Give up?"

Dave Subarsky moved in beside Eric and stared down at the E.R. lot.

"Hardly. I'm just deciding where to head next."

"And?"

"The nurse I kept mentioning, Norma Cullinet?"

"Uh-huh."

"She's a patient on the neurosurgical service. She fell and fractured her skull."

"So?"

"So, I don't know what shape she's in, but I think I'm going to try and talk with her."

"Neurosurgery, huh? Well, I hope she's better off than most of the neurosurgical patients I've seen. Most of those you couldn't communicate with at all unless you had an English-Vegetable dictionary."

"Not true and not funny," Eric said.

"Sorry. You know me—nothing's sacred."

"I know. Sorry for snapping. It's just that this stuff is so damn ugly, I can't handle any sicko humor right now, even yours."

"I understand," Subarsky said. "Sometimes my mouth just has a mind of its own. Well, listen, pal, I've got a slew of errands to run in town. Let me shut off my terminal and I'll walk you down."

The two of them were headed down the stairway toward the tunnels when Eric looked back at Subarsky.

"I appreciate your help this morning, David," he said. "Now I want you as far away from all this as possible, okay?"

"Sure."

"I mean it. I don't want to be the cause of anyone's getting hurt, especially a friend."

"Okay, but you know I'm here if you need me."

Eric hesitated, and then stopped and handed over the Xerox ledger sheets and his notes.

"David, if anything happens to me, I hope you'll try to break this thing open," he said.

"Nothing's gonna happen, but if it does, you can count on me doing just that."

"Thanks," Eric said. "Thanks for everything."

Once in the basement, the two men shook hands and headed in opposite directions.

Five floors above, in Dave Subarsky's office, the telephone was ringing. It rang more than a dozen times before it stopped.

———

"Dammit, Eric, where are you? Where the hell are you?"

Laura Enders listened as the phone in the office where Eric was supposed to be continued to ring. Finally she set the receiver down and finished dressing. Her hands were shaking and she could barely focus on what she was doing. Five minutes, she decided. She would try once more in five minutes. Then she had to do something.

It was only boredom, really, that had led her to check in with the desk at the Carlisle. Now she wondered if the force at work was something much stronger than that. The message, which she had copied down verbatim after three repetitions by the Iranian desk clerk, had come in during the early morning.

> *Your brother Scott is with me. To find out where to get*
> *him and where to bring reward, call 236-4356 every hour on*
> *the hour until you reach me. Rocky.*

It was nearing nine o'clock. Laura struggled to keep her hopes in check. More likely than not, the call was a hoax—or worse, a trap. Under no circumstances would she give anyone the number at Bernard's apartment; nor would she go anywhere alone. At two minutes before the hour, she tried Dave Subarsky's office once more. Once more there was no answer. She watched the seconds march off on her watch until another minute had passed, and then dialed. A man answered on the first ring.

"This is Rocky," he said.

"Rocky, this is Laura Enders."

She held the receiver with both hands to keep it steady.

"I got yer brother at my place. You still offerin' a reward?"

Laura's immediate sense was of an older man with not much education. In the background she could hear traffic noises.

"Yes, Rocky," she said. "If you really have him, I'll pay."

"How much?"

"First tell me, is he all right?"

"He's not so good, no."

"What's the matter?"

"How should I know? I ain't no doctor. Now, how much are we talkin' here?"

His voice had the deliberation and thickness of a drinker's.

"Five hundred dollars," Laura heard herself say.

"Six."

"Okay, okay, six. But no deal until you tell me something. My brother has a tattoo on his left hip. Describe it."

"If I have to go back and check, it'll cost you another fifty."

"That's fine. I'll call this number in five minutes."

"Better make it ten," Rocky said.

He hung up without waiting for a reply.

During the minutes that followed, Laura remained by the phone, moving only twice to try the number at the hospital. At nine-fifteen she called once again.

"Mom, Dad, Laurie, three flowers," Rocky said immediately.

Laura felt the muscles in her body go lax. She struggled to keep from dropping the phone.

"Where are you?" she demanded.

"Do we got a deal?"

"Yes, we have a deal. Now where are you?"

"Six-fifty?"

"Yes, yes. Now please, just tell me where to go."

"East Boston. There's a big vacant lot that starts on Bow Street. You'll see a couple a rusty barrels in one corner. Be there in an hour with the money, and come alone."

"I'll have to have a driver."

"Just keep him the hell away from me. Once I get the money, I'll tell you where you can find yer brother. Don't fool with me neither, lady. I ain't no dummy."

"I won't. I promise."

It could still be a trap. Laura tried desperately to think through the possibilities of how the man could have learned of Scott's tattoo. Finally, she knew there was no choice but to go and see. She opened the Yellow Pages to TAXIS, then just as quickly she stopped and put the book aside. There was a better, safer way. After writing a lengthy note explaining to Eric everything that was happening, she picked up the phone and dialed 911.

"My name is Laura Enders," she said. "I must speak with Captain Wheeler, Captain Lester Wheeler. It's an emergency."

34

The neurosurgical service occupied the eighth and ninth floors of the Fox Building, the newest—and in Eric's opinion the most appealing—of White Memorial's twelve buildings. The broad, well-lit corridors, pastel decor, and airy rooms seemed as perfect a setting for recovery as a hospital could offer. Eric had done two rotations on neurosurgery, and knew the floors well. Norma Cullinet's room, 814 according to patient information, was quite far from the nurses' station—down a separate corridor, in fact. The location suggested that she was quite stable, at least as post-op neurosurgical patients were measured.

Still wary of his uncertain status in the hospital, Eric stopped by the laundry in the subbasement, signed out a knee-length clinic coat, and made his way up the staircase he remembered as opening almost across the hall from 814. As he climbed, he tried to sort out what he had come to know of the woman over the five years of their professional association. She had always impressed him as being conscientious enough, but now that he thought about it, there had always been a hard edge to her, a distance that kept many of the nurses and residents from calling her by her first name.

Still, a hard edge was one thing, murder quite another. And the evidence Eric had amassed left little doubt in his mind that Norma Cullinet had administered a powerful metabolic poison to nearly a hundred unsuspecting patients, and then had calmly waited for them to be brought back to White Memorial clinically dead. Hard edge or not, it was difficult to imagine her doing the things he suspected. But then again, it was difficult to imagine *anyone* in the healing arts doing them.

As Eric neared the eighth floor, a plan began to take shape. If, in fact, Caduceus was behind the pseudo-deaths, and if in fact Norma was one of them, it was reasonable to assume that she knew he had been approached to join their cabal. If he could now convince her that over the days since her accident, he had undergone a change of heart and signed on, there was every reason to believe she might slip up.

What he wanted most from her was confirmation of his theories about Caduceus and its makeup, and some kind of affirmation that one of the search committee members was the powerful central figure in the secret society. And of course, what he also wanted desperately to learn were the reasons why—why a group so totally empowered by society would callously destroy the lives entrusted to them.

Once on the eighth-floor landing, Eric paused to catch his breath and compose himself. If, as was possible, Norma Cullinet was unwilling or unable to provide the information he needed, so be it. There would be other ways. The important thing was, he was finally on the offensive.

He opened the heavy door a crack and peered out. Except for an aide engrossed in her linen cart, the corridor was deserted. A final deep breath, and he crossed the hall. There was a sign in red on Norma's door: NO VISITORS. PLEASE CHECK AT NURSES' STATION. Eric hestitated a beat, and then slipped inside and closed the door behind him. The room was in near darkness, the only light leaking through a small gap in the drapes. Norma Cullinet, her head swathed in bandages, lay on her back, asleep.

Eric cleared his throat loudly and then took two steps toward the bed.

"Norma?" he said softly. "Norma, it's Eric Najarian."

In that instant, as his eyes adjusted to the darkness he noted the unnatural tilt of her head and the wide, static opening of her mouth.

"Oh, Jesus!" he cried, racing to the bedside. "Norma! Norma, wake up!" He simultaneously pulled the light and nurse's call cords as he checked her neck for a pulse. "Oh, damn!" he heard himself murmur.

He checked her airway with his finger, shoved her pillow down between her shoulders to throw her head back, and gave her chest a quick thump. Then he gave her two mouth-to-mouth breaths.

"Help! Code Ninety-nine in Eight-fourteen!" he screamed as he began cardiac compressions. "Code Ninety-nine in Eight-fourteen."

He did a cycle of compressions and another pair of breaths, and then reached for the phone with one hand as he continued closed-chest compressions with the other. The operator answered on the fifth ring.

"This is Dr. Najarian," he rasped. "Code Ninety-nine, Fox Building, room Eight-fourteen. Call it!"

He slammed the receiver down and once again screamed for help. He heard the commotion and footsteps in the hall at the moment the operator's droning voice began sounding through the overhead page: Code Ninety-nine, Fox Eight-fourteen . . . Code Ninety-nine, Fox Eight-fourteen.

A nurse rushed in, followed moments later by another with the crash cart. The overhead lights were turned on.

"Dr. Najarian," the nurse exclaimed, "what are you—?"

"She coded," Eric cut her off. "Get a line in her. You, give me an Ambu bag please."

A third nurse arrived. Now Eric had all the hands he

needed. In less than a minute, an IV line and breathing tube were in, and the defibrillator was charged.

"Three-sixty," Eric said, ordering the voltage he wanted. "Everybody clear!"

A breathless resident raced into the room as Eric, holding electrode paddles on the side of Norma's breastbone and beneath her left breast, depressed the red button on the paddle in his right hand. Norma's body arched off the bed and her limp arms shot upward like a puppet's.

"Resume compressions, please," he ordered.

"This woman's my patient," the resident said. "Could you please tell me what's going on?"

"I came here and found her dead in bed," Eric said. "Could someone please get the EKG hooked up. I need an amp of epi now. Everyone get back—we're going to shock her again."

"What were you doing in here?" the bewildered resident asked.

Eric ignored the question, and twice more administered high-voltage shocks.

"Keep pumping, please," he ordered. "Give the epi. Have we got a tracing yet?"

Several medical students, the respiratory therapist, and a medical technologist added to the crowd that was building in the room. Seconds later Joe Silver raced through the door.

"Najarian, what the hell?"

Eric raised his hand, trying to calm his chief while at the same time scanning the EKG tracing. There was no cardiac activity whatever.

"Give her an amp of bicarb, please," he said. There was an edge of panic in his voice.

Joe Silver's eyes were blazing as he pushed through the crowd to the bedside. Eric felt a suffocating tightness building in his own chest.

"What in the hell are you up to?" Silver demanded.

"I came here to see Norma, found her dead in bed, and called a code."

"She was checked less than an hour ago and she was fine," a nurse offered.

"What are you doing in that?" Silver said, gesturing at Eric's white coat.

Around the bedside there was a mounting air of confusion. The nurse kneeling on the bed continued her compressions, and the respiratory therapist continued manual ventilation. But both of them, as well as the nurse drawing meds, were staring at the two emergency physicians, awaiting instructions.

To Eric the entire scene seemed like a grotesque tableau. Then Joe Silver inserted himself between Eric and the bed.

"Dr. Gordon," he said to the neurosurgical resident, "take over the resuscitation at the bedside. I'll handle the EKG. Dr. Najarian, please wait outside. I'll deal with you when we're through." He checked Norma's pupils, then turned his back to Eric and checked the EKG. "She's fixed and dilated and straight-line, everyone. Could I have a milligram of atropine IV. Keep pumping there, but switch if you're tired. You're doing a nice job, but things don't look good . . . not good at all. Has anyone notified her family? If she's Catholic, better call a priest too."

Eric stared at his chief. At another time, just a few short days ago, he would have felt totally lost and humiliated. Now, he felt only anger. Heedless of the many eyes still fixed on him, he turned away from the bedside and stalked from the room.

The resuscitative effort lasted another twenty minutes, although Eric had correctly sensed the futility of it from the moment his fingers touched the side of Norma Cullinet's neck. He stood in the hallway, listening to the fruitless battle within room 814 and wondering whether Norma's death was a post-operative complication or in some way the result of her connection with Caduceus. He also began debating whether it was worth waiting to face the almost-certain onslaught against him by Joe Silver, or whether he should simply march across the hall to the stairway and leave.

He was on the verge of selecting option two when room 814 began to empty. Most of those leaving pointedly avoided looking in his direction. Those who inadvertently made eye contact with him either shook their heads or quickly looked away. The upshot of this latest chapter in his nightmare was going to be bad—very bad.

"That woman was one hell of a nurse."

Joe Silver, his eyes about level with Eric's chin, stood hands on hips, glaring up at him.

She was a murderer, Eric wanted desperately to say. *Are you one, too?* But he knew that until he held proof far more irrefutable than the notes that were folded in his hip pocket, any attempt at attacking Norma Cullinet would merely be adding Joe Silver's shovel to those already trying to bury him.

"I'm sorry she didn't make it," he managed.

"Yeah, you seem all broken up," Silver said. "You gonna tell me what you were doing in there, or do you want to wait until after the pathologists tell us why she died?"

"It happened just as I said it did," Eric responded, holding on to his rage by only the finest of threads. "I came up here to talk to Norma about some things and found her dead; and I did my best to resuscitate her. I don't think I did anything to deserve the kind of treatment I just received from you in there."

Silver looked as if he were about to spit in Eric's face.

"Your indignation doesn't even deserve a response," he said acidly, "but let me lay it out for you. First, you're involved in a series of very bizarre, disruptive events, all of which suggest that you are drug-addicted, crazy, or most likely both. Next, you are told by me to stay away from this hospital until this whole business is straightened out. Yet here you are, dressed up like a goddam professor, in the room of a woman whose door says NO VISITORS, and she's dead."

"You've got it wrong," Eric said simply.

Joe Silver glared at him.

"Damn, but you're an arrogant son of a bitch. Well, you just listen up, Najarian. I don't want to see your face in this hospital again until the pathologist's report on this woman is in. If her death is on the up and up, you'll get your chance to explain all the other madness you're into. But if she was murdered, I plan to be at the head of the line of those who will want to see you hung up by your goddam crazy Armenian heels and stoned."

Without waiting for a reply, he whirled and stormed down the eighth-floor corridor.

"Well, fuck you very much, Dr. Silver," Eric said courteously. "I'll try to be worthy of your understanding and confidence."

Furious, he ran down eight flights of stairs to the basement, threw his lab coat in a corner, and then took the tunnel to one of the side exits. A chilly mist was swirling down from the heavy late-morning sky. And although it was twenty minutes by foot to Bernard Nelson's apartment, Eric had no inclination to do anything but walk. He crossed over Cambridge Street and wandered up Charles—the same route he and Laura had taken on their first night together. It was a night that seemed several lifetimes ago.

He had come so close, so damn close. Now, rather than putting an end to their nightmare, he had only intensified it. If, as seemed quite possible, Norma Cullinet's autopsy showed her death to be murder, his unauthorized presence in her room, coupled with the other suspicions surrounding his sanity and drug use, would quickly vault him to the head of any list of suspects. One step forward, two steps back. Perhaps the Najarian could become a new dance craze.

He picked up a copy of the *Herald,* wondering what new absurdities they had chosen to print about "Zombi Doc." What he found instead was a front-page teaser and page 3 spread on the robbery/murder at the Gates of Heaven. According to the write-up, there were no signs of forced entry, leading police to suspect the murderer was known to the victim. Investigators were currently focusing on names in an appointment book recovered from Donald Devine's desk. Nowhere in the article was there mention of the macabre treatment room in the mortuary basement. *Did the police choose to withhold that find, or had the room been dismantled before they even arrived on the scene?* Those questions were troubling, but not nearly as much

so as the possiblity that among the names in Devine's appointment book would be one Dr. Eric Najarian.

One step forward, two steps back.

Eric folded the paper, slipped it into his jacket pocket, and
leaned against the corner of a building, physically and emotionally spent. Across the street, three stories above a chic Italian
bistro, two workmen undaunted by the rain were washing
windows from a suspended platform. Eric was musing on the
possibility of his one day earning a living in such a manner
when the door to the café opened and Anna Delacroix stepped
out, arm in arm with a man.

She wore a rich knee-length leather coat, and her hair,
unpinned, billowed to her shoulders. But there was not a whit
of doubt in Eric's mind that it was Anna. Nor, he suddenly
realized, was there any doubt as to her companion. He concealed himself behind the corner of the building and watched
as Haven Darden walked the spectacular woman around to the
driver's side of a smart gray Alfa convertible, embraced her
fondly, and blew her a kiss as she drove off. Then the White
Memorial chief of medicine straightened his tie, checked himself in the mirror of a store window, and strode off toward the
hospital.

Eric moved to follow, but then quickly halted. Haven Darden was not going anyplace where he couldn't be found. At last,
there was no need to make any move until he was absolutely
ready, absolutely in control. So much made sense now—so
many disconnected pieces had suddenly converged and
meshed. He had reached the center of Caduceus. Now, all that
remained was finding a way to break Dr. Haven Darden down.

And this time, there would be no steps back.

35

To Laura Enders, the drive to East Boston through the Callahan Tunnel seemed interminable. In point of fact, something—an accident or breakdown—had stopped traffic in one of the two tunnel lanes, locking her and Captain Lester Wheeler in a snarl that already spilled well back onto the expressway on the Boston side.

"Last time we went, Eric and I took this beautiful, very high bridge over to East Boston," she said.

Wheeler, wearing jeans and a blue Irish-knit fisherman's sweater beneath his windbreaker, nodded.

"The Mystic River Bridge. We could have taken that, but I thought we'd go this way so we can come up behind that Bow Street lot, not on the side your man Rocky wants us to."

"Why?"

"Just in case it's a trap. The first thing we teach our detectives is: where possible, never play anyone else's game."

"I understand. That man's voice sounded honest to me,

though. I don't think we're headed for any trap, and I think Scott is somewhere just on the other side of this tunnel."

"I hope you're right," Wheeler said, inching toward the East Boston side of the harbor. They were in an unmarked police car, which had a blue light on the dash and a metal-mesh screen separating the front and back seats. "I'm sure you read in the papers where we found that funeral parlor owner, Donald Devine, in permanent repose in one of his caskets."

"Yes. Yes, I did read that. I'm not surprised. I told you the last time we spoke that he was into something shady."

"You did in fact. The question is what?"

Laura just shrugged. She and Bernard Nelson had decided to tell no one, not even the police, of her role in the hit-and-run death on Harrison Avenue, or of their break-in at the Gates of Heaven—at least not until the nature of Devine's business dealings became clear, or someone was arrested for his murder. In addition, the policeman had already asked her pointedly about Eric and his well-publicized misadventures. It seemed unwise to say anything just yet that might raise further questions of her reliability.

"Beats me," was all she said. "Listen, Captain Wheeler, in case I forget to say so later, I really appreciate your coming with me today. I don't think I would have felt completely comfortable taking a cab."

"It was pure luck you caught me in," Wheeler replied. "Technically I have the week off. I was just in the office catching up on paperwork when you called. Now, do you want to go over our strategy again?"

"You're going to hang back but keep me in sight. If there's no sign of trouble, I should just pay up and bring Scott back to the car. If there *is* any problem, I'll raise one of my hands over my head, and you'll fly to my rescue."

"Perfect. I also want to caution you not to get your hopes up too high. There are a lot of nut cases around this town, along with some pretty resourceful folks who would like to ensure that you never lay your lands on that tape your brother made."

"Well, as I told you, I can't produce something I know

nothing about. And as for my hopes being too high, the only thing that will snuff them out is seeing Scott's body. Do you have family?"

"Me? Well, yes and no. My wife took off years ago with the guy who taught her painting class. She took my two boys with her. They're grown men now, but I haven't heard from either of them for eight or ten years."

"That's too bad."

"I manage okay," Wheeler said.

They broke free of the tunnel, and Wheeler maneuvered the sedan through traffic to a side street.

"You sure know your way around," Laura said.

"I should. Twenty-five years on the force."

He turned on the windshield wipers.

"I hope Scott's not standing outside in this," she said. "Rocky made it sound as if he was sick."

Wheeler turned down another narrow street and then pulled to a stop by what appeared to be several abandoned building lots. Behind the lots was a low hillock that extended for most of the block. The steep slope, composed of shrub-covered sandy soil, was an eyesore. It was littered with rusting pieces of automobile, discarded bottles, flattened milk cartons, and the like. The faded, peeling three-deckers bordering the lot on each side seemed to sag under the weight of neglect.

"Nice place," Laura said.

Wheeler glanced around nervously.

"Bow Street is down the other side of this rise. See those two trees right at the top there?"

"Uh-huh."

"I'll be right between them watching. You head up over there. Take a second once you reach the top to size things up. If this Rocky character is for real, he'll be down on the other side, waiting for you to come in on Bow Street. At the first sign of trouble, I want that hand in the air. Got it?"

"Got it," Laura said. "Now we've just got to cross our fingers and hope."

"You cross them for both of us," Wheeler said. "I want to keep my hands free."

They exited the patrol car together and then split up. Laura walked to the far side of the lot before starting up the slope, while Lester Wheeler worked his way directly up to the pair of scraggly oak trees on the left side of the crest. Fine sheets of rain swept down the hillside at them.

"Come on, Scotty," Laura prayed as she trudged upward through the wild blackberry bushes and scrub oak, "be here. Please be here."

She checked the pocket of her jacket to ensure the $650 was there. She had tucked another $200 in the back pocket of her jeans, just in case. At the top of the rise she paused and looked across at where Lester Wheeler was kneeling behind the two oaks. When their eyes met, the police captain nodded to direct her attention to the broad, littered field below them. To one side of the field a makeshift lean-to—possibly a play fort for the neighborhood kids—was propped against a rusting chain-link fence. Squatting beside the lean-to, trying to shield himself from the rain and remain hidden from Bow Street, was a man. The street beyond him looked deserted.

Laura's pulse had already skipped several beats before she realized the man was not her brother. He was dressed like a hobo, but even at a fairly good distance Laura could make out enough of his bearing and his weathered face to sense that he was no threat to her. With a final nod to Wheeler, she picked her way over the damp soil, down the gentle slope toward the man she assumed was Rocky.

She was still some fifty yards away when she sensed, beyond a doubt, that her brother was down there as well—almost certainly within the small rickety structure. Only the total of her self-control kept her from bolting down the hill and into the lean-to. Instead, she forced herself once again to stop and survey the field, looking for some sign—any sign—of a trap. Behind her and far to her left, Wheeler gave her a thumbs-up sign and motioned her ahead. She was just twenty yards away when Rocky turned and noticed her.

"Rocky, I'm Laura Enders," she said quickly.

"Yeah? Well, whaddaya tryin' to pull?" he exclaimed. "You're supposed to be comin' up that street."

"Is my brother in there?"

"I'm not telling you where he is," Rocky said, unaware that his expression had already answered her question, "until I see the color of your money. Six hundred and fifty, in case you forgot. Well, I'm here to tell you that ol' Rocky didn't. He's got the memory of—"

"Here," Laura said.

She threw the bills on the sand at his feet as she hurried past him to the lean-to and threw back the oilskin flap.

"Oh, God," she gasped, racing inside.

Scott was there, sitting on a small pile of rags, his back propped against the fence. His breathing was shallow and labored, and his complexion dusty. Laura threw her arms around him, but then just as quickly pulled away when there was no reaction.

Rocky appeared in the doorway.

"He don't seem to know much of anything," he said. "Not his name, not where he's from, nothin'. All he keeps talking about is a horse."

"Rocky, do you have any water?"

"Nope. Not here I don't. Jes' wine. They's some at my place, but it's a walk from here."

"That's okay. The wine will do. We've got to get him to a hospital."

"I told him I'd call him an ambulance, but he wouldn't have no part of it. All he wanted to talk about was that damn horse."

"Get me the wine, please."

Laura took her brother's face in her hands.

"Can you hear me okay?" she asked.

"I can hear you." His voice was grainy and his speech dry and thick, but there was still strength there. Laura could feel it.

"Do you know who I am?"

Scott studied her, then shook his head.

"Do you know who *you* are?"

"I . . . I don't know anything."

"Oh, God," Laura murmured. She willed herself not to break down, and then said calmly, "Your name is Scott. Scott Enders. I'm your sister. My name's Laura. Does that help?"

The man with her brother's face as it might be at age sixty shook his head once again.

"Can you stand?" she asked.

"My legs are okay. Got kicked in the chest, though. Ribs are broken."

"We'll get you help, don't worry."

Rocky entered the lean-to with his wine, and Laura forced a few drops between Scott's lips.

"Help me get him up," she ordered.

"Don't . . . need . . . help," Scott said, crawling from the hut and then painfully pushing himself upright.

Laura immediately noticed his limp and the clumsy way he used his left hand.

"Tell her about the horse, buddy," Rocky DiNucci urged. "Tell her about that damn horse."

Laura duckwalked out of the lean-to and then looked up at the twin oaks on the crest of the hill. Lester Wheeler was either well hidden or gone.

"What horse?" Laura asked.

She supported Scott's arm with one hand, although she was encouraged to see that, as he had promised, he could stand quite well on his own.

"Mrs. Gideon's horse," Scott said with no emotion. "I've got to find Mrs. Gideon's horse."

"*Our* Mrs. Gideon?" Laura asked incredulously.

Marjorie Gideon, a feisty spinster who wore cowboy boots and Wranglers at age seventy-five, had owned the farm nearest to their parents' small spread in Missouri. She was also reputed to be one of the wealthiest people in the county. As far as Laura knew, she had died years before.

"I don't know," Scott said.

"Scott, where did you come here from?"

"I don't know," he answered haltingly. "I was in a town in

the desert. . . . I saw the beams and found the way to get beneath them. . . . Eddie Garcia picked me up and brought me to Cleveland."

"Utah!" Laura said. "Scott, you were in Utah, weren't you?"

"I . . . don't . . . know." He shook his head in frustration, as if trying to clear the mist from his mind. "I've got to find Mrs. Gideon's horse."

Laura struggled to understand. Marjorie Gideon had owned several horses, and had been happy to let Scott and Laura go riding in exchange for mucking out the stalls. But that had been so many years ago.

"Scott, tell me something," Laura asked suddenly, trying to keep Rocky from hearing, "does the horse have anything to do with a tape—a videotape?"

Scott looked at her impassively.

"Maybe," he said. "Maybe it does."

"Think, Scott. You've got to think what it means." She studied her brother's face but knew he was nowhere near putting his thoughts together. "Don't worry about it right now. I have a car and a man to help. We'll get you to a hospital. Everything's going to be all right."

Laura turned toward the top of the hill. There was still no sign of Lester Wheeler. She raised her hand, just in case, but at that instant she realized the gesture was unnecessary. Wheeler had somehow made his way around and was approaching them along the fence from the Bow Street side.

"Captain Wheeler," she called, "come quickly. It *is* Scott, but he's hurt. He's hurt badly."

"Well, then," the policeman said, "we'll just have to get him some help."

He was just ten feet away when Laura sensed a change in her brother. The muscles in his arms tightened, and his body seemed to tense. His hollow eyes were riveted on the policeman.

"Scott, are you all right?" she asked.

The moments that followed were a slow-motion nightmare.

With a guttural cry, Scott pulled free of her and lunged at Wheeler, his arm sweeping down in an awkward karate stroke aimed at the man's neck. The attack was too slow and far too weak. Wheeler, who seemed prepared for the onslaught, parried the blow easily with one hand while he pulled his other hand from beneath his jacket. Laura saw the gun and recognized the long silencer attached to it at the same moment Wheeler slashed the barrel across Scott's face, sending him sprawling to the wet ground.

"Don't!" Laura screamed, charging the man.

Wheeler whipped her across the cheek with the back of his gun hand. The tip of the silencer gashed her skin, and she spun down almost on top of Scott.

"Hey, just one minute there," Rocky DiNucci said, bringing his hands up in a semblance of his boxing stance.

Without hesitation the policeman pointed the ugly silencer at the hobo's mid-chest and fired. There was a soft pop and a puff of smoke from the muzzle. Rocky flew backward as if kicked by a mule, slammed against the lean-to, and collapsed beneath a heap of plywood, scrap metal, and canvas.

Wheeler whirled, and in seconds had handcuffed Laura and Scott together and pulled them to their feet.

"Move!" he growled. "And not a word. Not a fucking word."

Without a glance at the man he had just killed, he shoved his two prisoners down along the chain-link fence to his cruiser.

Heedless of the throbbing wound on her cheek, Laura pressed the sleeve of her jacket against the gash on Scott's face. Their handcuffs still in place, they were in the rear of the unmarked cruiser, heading through the back streets of East Boston toward the harbor. Scott was awake and responsive, but his breathing was even more labored, and twice he had coughed up small amounts of blood.

"Please," Laura begged through the metal mesh. "Can't you see he's dying? We've got to get him some help. . . . Dammit, what kind of monster are you?"

Lester Wheeler did not respond. He eased the cruiser through the narrow streets and onto the road that paralleled the docks.

Laura recognized the area. Just a week before, she and Eric had parked in a spot not far from where they were.

"How are you doing?" she whispered.

Scott's bloodied lips pulled back in something of a smile.

"He's one of them," he rasped. "The men in the tape."

"You remember that?"

"Yes."

"And do you know who I am now?"

Scott looked at her, but shook his head.

"No," he said flatly.

"That's okay, Scott. It's okay."

He let her reach across and squeeze him gently. Suddenly she stopped and leaned forward, staring through the screen and out the windshield. Ahead of them was the lot where she and Eric had parked. She recognized the rusting tractor trailers resting on piles of railroad ties. It was the trailer nearest them that had caught her eye. Painted on its side was the depiction of a Greek goddess, and enclosing the painting, in large red script, were the words APHRODITE MOVING AND STORAGE. *Aphrodite!* Marjorie Gideon's favorite horse.

Laura brought her lips close to her brother's ear.

"Scott, look," she whispered. "That trailer. That's where the tape is, isn't it?"

Almost imperceptibly, Scott Enders nodded.

36

It wasn't supposed to have happened like this, Eric thought as he searched once more through Bernard Nelson's apartment for a note or some sort of explanation as to why Laura had left and where she had gone. He was supposed to have returned to her in triumph, having not only solved much of the mystery of Caduceus, but also quite likely having identified the death's-head priest as well. Then, after toasting their success with what little remained of Laura's wine, they were to formulate a plan for breaking down Haven Darden. And finally, they were to set about doing whatever was necessary to implement that plan.

Desperately, Eric flipped through every magazine he could find, lifted every vase and dish, and even looked in the oven, searching for some sort of clue. Fueling his urgency was the faint but definite odor of cigarette smoke, which had hit him the moment he entered the place. Unless Laura had a smoking habit she had never shared with him—and given her concern with fitness and health, that possibility seemed remote—someone else had been in the apartment.

He checked in with Dave Subarsky, who had returned to his office, but Dave had heard nothing from her either. Subarsky promised to remain at his desk until one of them had word from her. Calls to Eric's apartment and Bernard Nelson's office were no more fruitful. Finally he phoned the Carlisle, but the unctuous desk clerk, who had been on duty only since nine, had nothing at all to offer. Eric left a message with the man for Laura to contact him at the apartment or through Dave Subarsky. Then he climbed to the loft and lay down—to wait, and to think.

Through a thin spatter of rain he gazed across Storrow Drive at the Charles and at Cambridge beyond. Laura was out there somewhere, he reasoned, and she was almost certainly in trouble. What other conclusion could be drawn from the cigarette smoke and the absence of any note from her?

Was it Scott's tape that had gotten her into difficulty? Or perhaps Haven Darden had decided to use her as insurance against Eric's getting any closer to Caduceus. One scenario flowed into another in his mind, each one more disturbing and frightening than the last.

Fueled by anger and helplessness, Eric began to focus on Darden: the one variable he might yet be able to control, the one person he still might be able to take by surprise. The timing was not what he would have chosen, and the idea that began to take shape was rough, but there was no way he could just sit around and wait to hear from her. In minutes, he felt ready to act.

His call to White Memorial was quickly put through to the medical chief. There was trouble, serious trouble at the hospital, he told Darden—trouble involving Sara Teagarden and a clandestine society called Caduceus. Darden coolly responded that the only trouble at White Memorial of which he was aware involved a resident named Najarian.

Eric stressed his innocence and begged for Darden's forbearance. He said enough, just enough, he hoped, to whet the man's interest without making him suspicious. Tetrodotoxin *was* being used at White Memorial, and patients *were* being harmed. He had proof of that now—irrefutable proof. Several people involved with the secret society had already died violently. He had proof of that as well.

Gradually, but oh so skillfully, Darden suspended his façade of cynicism and doubt and expressed a mild curiosity to learn more. His hand clenched on the receiver, Eric suggested meeting at Darden's lab at four, at which time he promised to present proof of every allegation. In response to Eric's concern about being seen in the hospital, Darden gave his assurance that no one else would be around.

"Eric, you have generated a great deal of ill will around this hospital in an amazingly short time," Darden said. "I am trusting that what you have to say to me will be the truth, supported not by your speculation but by hard facts. Please do not give me any reason to join those who have closed ranks against you."

"You have my word on it," Eric said. "By the time I'm done, you will believe me. I promise you that."

Eric waited until Darden had hung up before slamming the receiver down.

"Sleazy, smug bastard," he said.

He paced the apartment, marking time in case Laura called, and trying to sort out his approach now that Haven Darden had taken the hook. Assuming the man honored his promise to have his lab deserted by four—and with that assumption Eric felt reasonably safe—there remained only one more detail to see to: a weapon.

By three, Eric had conceived of a solution to that problem as well.

He left the apartment and walked quickly to where his Celica was parked. He had a full hour left, but with traffic beginning to build, it would be at least a ten- or fifteen-minute drive to and from the Metropolitan Hospital of Boston.

———✛✛✛———

Bernard Nelson tightened his seat belt for the fourth time since take off, and silently prayed that the *huevos rancheros* he had been foolish enough to have for breakfast would find some sort of quiet resting place within his body.

The Cessna 172 was patched in places with duct tape, but its owner and pilot, a man named Chippy, seemed interested enough in his own survival to dispel the most strident of Nelson's misgivings. It would have helped, Bernard acknowledged, if he had a better idea of what they were looking for in the craggy desert west of Moab. But what he *did* know was that the late Donald Devine had made any number of trips to Moab, and had filled up twice in the area almost every time. The man had to have driven somewhere.

He also knew, from an hour's experience, that asking the laconic residents and gas station attendants of the town if they had seen a hearse cruising off into the desert was not the quickest way to make friends or gain confidences.

"How much fuel do we have left, Chippy?" he asked.

"Another hour, m'be," the pilot said. "How far we go on't 'pends on the wind."

Chippy was a dark, weathered man in his fifties—Indian or part Indian, Bernard guessed. He flew with effortless confidence, and spoke in a patois that was, at times, almost unintelligible. It seemed as if he left out almost as many syllables as he pronounced. Bernard checked the detailed map he had bought in town.

"In that case," he said, "let's fly to Hanksville, and then over to St. Joseph. Can we do that?"

"We can. Ain't nothin' t' either place, though."

"That's okay. Try to stay around three hundred feet if you can."

"It'd help if ya knew whachas lookin' for."

"I know it would." Bernard thought for a time, then decided to chance adding one more name to the list of those who thought him crazy. "Chippy, someone's been driving out here at least once a month. From what I can tell, he was driving a hearse. I'm trying to figure out where he was going, and what he was up to."

The pilot, who seemed unsurprised by the revelation,

drummed his fingers on the control wheel. Then he put on his earphones and motioned for Bernard to do the same.

"Moab, this's Cessna Two One Papa Delta," he said into his radio. "D'ya copy? Repeat, this's Two One Papa Delta callin' Moab Air."

"We hear you, Chippy," a voice crackled.

"Morton, put Marianne on, will ya?" He turned to Bernard. "Jes' had me a thought," he said.

"Hi, Chippy, it's Marianne."

"Say, beau'ful, how's it goin'?"

"You coming back soon?"

" 'Nother hour, m'be. We're out here 'bout twenty miles north of Hanksville. Do you 'member a ways back tellin' me 'bout some ghost town near here?"

"That'd be Charity. It ain't no ghost town, though. It's a hospital of some sort now. A mental hospital, if you can believe that. Set up, oh, two or three years ago. But the head doctor there sent a notice around forbiddin' any overflights."

Bernard nodded quickly.

"Jes' wondrin', thassall," Chippy said. "Where 'bouts is't anyway?"

"Twenty or twenty-five miles west of St. Joe's. Don't you cause no trouble, now, Chippy Smith. For all I know they're listening to us right now."

"Hey, do I cause trouble? Well, we'll jes' be swingin' by Hanksville an' back. See you in an hour. Papa Delta out."

"Can you find it, Chippy?" Nelson asked.

"I kin try."

Bernard gazed down at the vast, rugged terrain, rocky and barren of all but the simplest vegetation, yet in its way serenely beautiful. Of primary interest to him, though, were the dirt roads and tire tracks that from time to time skimmed past.

They had flown northwest for twenty minutes when Bernard caught the flash of sunlight off something metal or glass.

"Chippy, there, over there," he said. "Did you see it?"

The pilot nodded and banked to the east. It took another five minutes of circling before they spotted the Jeep, which was largely covered with dust and almost completely hidden from the air by a rocky overhang. Smith dipped down to 120 feet and made a second pass. Beside the vehicle was an elongated mound of dirt. Protruding from the mound were what looked like shoes and pieces of clothing.

"Can you set us down?" Bernard asked.

"If I do, the takeoff's gonna use up our tourin' fuel."

"Can we still get back to Moab?"

"Pro'bly."

"Go for it."

Smith shrugged and pulled back up to 200 feet. Minutes later, he dropped down over what might have been a roadway or dried-up creek bed, and neatly set the Cessna down in a cloud of dust and pebbles.

"You're a hell of a pilot," Bernard said.

Chippy smiled. "I try," he said.

They located the Jeep with little difficulty. Its canvas roof was intact, although covered with half an inch of fine sand. Together, they walked around to the mound they had seen. Two skeletons, locked in each other's arms, lay in the shadow of the vehicle. Their tattered sneakers and the bleached white stalks of their legs protruded obscenely from beneath the covering dust.

"You can wait over there for me if you want," Bernard said. "I'm going to try and figure out who they are."

"Ain't much that upsets me," Chippy Smith said.

They used a rag from the Jeep to brush the dust away from the bodies. The flesh had largely rotted or been eaten away from the two skulls, but from the ragged clothing, jewelry, and what hair and gristle remained, they were able to determine that what they were seeing had once been man and woman.

Bernard knelt beside the two forms and caught a whiff of the fading scent of death. He noticed the bulge of a wallet in the jeans of one of them, and reached for it. The pocket fell open at his touch.

"Richard Colson, Santa Barbara, California," he read, sadly

looking from the smiling face in the driver's license photo to the grotesquely grinning skull.

Chippy found a purse on the floor of the Jeep, and from the wallet inside they learned the name and face of Colson's wife.

"Nice-lookin' couple," he said. "Any idea how they died?"

"None, except I don't think they were shot. How close are we to that Charity place?"

"Ten miles, m'be."

Bernard slipped the wallets into his jacket pocket.

"Think you could keep this a secret for a while?" he asked.

"You police?"

"Private." He fished his ID from his wallet and flashed it, along with a hundred-dollar bill.

"That ain't necessary," Chippy said, pointing at the money. "I'll jes' take whacha owe for the flight an' keep quiet."

Bernard handed the bill over anyway.

"I promise these folks'll get taken care of properly," he said. "I just don't want anybody at the hospital alerted yet until I get a look at what they're up to. These two may not be connected at all with what I'm looking for, but then again, they just might."

The two men stood in silence for a time, gazing down at the ghostly remains. Then they turned and headed back to the plane. As the engine roared to life, a scorpion crept out of the eye socket of Marilyn Colson's skull and scampered across to the safety of a nearby pile of rocks.

37

Except for a single tiny window built at eye level into the steel door, the room at the rear of Warehouse 18 was like a vault—a hollow cube of concrete, perhaps twelve feet on a side. In one corner of the room were a plastic bottle of water and an empty metal bucket, presumably for holding human waste, and along one wall was a stack of four quilted packing blankets.

For more than an hour Laura Enders had been alone in the room with her brother—or rather with what remained of his mind and body.

After whipping the two of them down with his pistol, and coolly murdering the hobo named Rocky, Lester Wheeler had driven through a side gate at the docks and then around to the front of the warehouse. The huge hangarlike doors had opened for them without a signal, allowing Wheeler to drive straight down a long aisle between packing crates to the back room. There, two men—whom Laura recognized from her close call on the docks with Eric—undid the manacles binding her to Scott and shoved her alone into the bleak cell.

Several times over the hour that followed she heard her brother's sickening screeches from somewhere in the warehouse. She pounded at the door, screaming until her hands and voice could do no more. Then she sank down on the foul-smelling blankets and cried. Finally, Scott was thrown in with her, moaning and barely conscious. His breathing was even more labored than before, and his face and hands were bloody. When Laura knelt to tend to him, she realized that several of his fingernails had been torn off.

Now, as she paced from one side of the narrow prison to the other, Scott slept, at times moaning, at times crying out softly like a child. She ached for his pain, for his crippled body and memory, and for the hopelessness of their situation. And she struggled to ignore the gruesome, fleeting wish that his breathing would simply stop.

Outside the small window she could see men working as if nothing were amiss. One of them drove a forklift, transferring crates from one section of the huge warehouse to another. Several others wandered by, laughing or talking or drinking beer. One of them actually looked over at her and smiled.

"Damn you," she muttered. "Damn you all to hell."

She tore off a piece of her shirt, dampened it, and gently wiped Scott's face. His eyelids fluttered and then opened. He focused on her with an ease that surprised her.

"Have they hurt you?" he asked.

"No," she said. "Not yet. Did you tell them what they wanted to know?"

"I . . . I don't think so. Right now that videotape is keeping us alive."

"You *do* remember the tape then?"

"Yes. So much is still missing for me, but I do know that. The receiver's locked in that Aphrodite trailer, just as you said."

"And how much else do you remember?"

Scott winced as he propped himself up on one elbow.

"Some little scenes or details clear as day. Most things not at all. I wish I could say I remember you, but I really don't. Were we close?"

Laura stroked his hair from his forehead.

"Yeah," she said hoarsely. "We were very close."

"I'm glad."

He pushed himself up until he was sitting, and leaned against the wall. His eyes seemed to hold a remarkable power. If anything he seemed stronger than when she had found him in Rocky's lean-to.

"We've got to get out of here," he said.

"What?"

"That cop is either going to use drugs or he's going to do something to you in front of me. Whatever it is, we can't wait around to see."

"Scott, there are a bunch of men out there, and this place is like a fort. There's no chance."

He pushed himself to his feet, grimacing at the pain but refusing to cry out.

"There's always a chance," he said. He tried unsuccessfully to stifle a thick cough.

Laura stood in front of him. "Can you move enough to do anything?"

"I made it this far, didn't I?"

Laura heard the new forcefulness in his voice, and knew that he had summoned it for her. He was still so lost and in such pain; they had taken nearly everything from him. And yet he seemed able to reach within himself for more.

"Scott, you know what you did for a living now, don't you?" she said.

He forced a thin smile and touched the clotted blood on her cheek.

"Maybe," he said. "Maybe I do." He peered out the window at the workmen. "Tell me, those big doors we drove through, did they open upward or to the side?"

"To the side, I think. Yes—yes, I'm sure of it. They folded open in sections on a track."

Scott glanced out the small window and then knelt by the door and studied the keyhole. Laura had to help him up.

"Bring that over," he said, motioning to the bucket. She did as he asked. "Do you have a belt on?"

She pulled off her belt, which was fairly wide and fastened with a metal buckle that had some heft. Scott tried undoing his own, but his clumsy hand and torn fingers made the task impossible. Laura undid it for him.

"What are we going to do?" she asked.

"First we're going to get this door open."

"How?"

"I hope with that," he said, motioning to the metal bulb protector overhead. "There's a forklift out there. We've got to get to it. If we do, I'll drive. Just don't depend on me to turn the key, okay?"

"O-okay. Scott, I don't know if I can do this."

He looked at her for a moment, then shrugged and said, "I think you can. Here, hook these belts to each other and then to the handle of the bucket. Then practice swinging it around in a way that will knock off that metal guard. The bulb'll probably shatter but that's okay. We'll have enough light. When that metal guard falls down, grab it." He peered out the window, following the progress of the forklift. "Start practicing, and I'll tell you when. Spread these blankets out beneath you in case the bucket hits the floor."

Laura set the blankets in place, dangled the bucket for a moment, and then began swinging it in front of her in increasing circles like a lariat. She found that if she held her arm at shoulder level, she could just reach the light without hitting the floor. While she was practicing, Scott coughed and spat some bright-red blood onto the floor. Laura started to protest, but he waved her off.

"Please," he said, "we don't have much time before Wheeler gets back, and in this shape I don't think I can take him, even if he gives me the chance." He checked outside the window again. "Now. Do it now, and try to hit that thing hard. If the bulb breaks without that guard falling down, we may not have enough light to get at it."

Laura started with a few slow arcs. Then she began whirling the bucket around, increasing the speed and the length of the belts each time.

"That's it, that's it," Scott said. The bucket grazed the metal. "Keep going. Keep going."

Laura's upper arms and shoulders began to cramp. Her smooth swings became weaker and more erratic.

"Don't stop," he urged. "Find the strength. Come on, you can do it."

She bit into her lower lip and grasped the belt tightly with both hands, increasing the speed of her swings. Her arms quickly grew numb and heavy. The cramps worsened. Then, at the moment when she felt she had to stop, the bucket slammed against the metal guard, popping it free, and sending it clattering against the wall. The bulb sheared off, spraying small shards of glass across the room. Laura let the bucket drop soundlessly onto the blankets, and then raced over and retrieved the protector.

"That was good," Scott said, pausing between words to breathe. "That was real good." He studied the metal piece by the light of the window. "Stamp on this as hard as you can. I need a piece of it about this long."

Laura set the guard on the concrete floor and stamped it flat. The welds holding the stiff wire broke apart, yielding several pieces of the length Scott had indicated. She snapped one off and passed it over. He studied it briefly and then handed it back. With Scott directing her, she pinned the metal beneath the lip of the bucket and bent two right angles into it, and a loop handle at one end.

"Now put it in the keyhole with this end down and turn it slowly until you feel it catch."

Laura knelt by the door as Scott kept watch.

"I don't feel anything," she said.

"Push it in farther. Use both hands to hold it, and use that little handle you built."

"I can't feel anyth— Wait, wait a second."

The makeshift key turned half an inch.

"Keep going. Keep going. I think you've got it."

There was a muffled click from inside the door. Laura released the wire and sank back on her hands, smiling up at her brother.

"Nice job," he said, opening the door a fraction of inch. "There's a crowbar resting on some cases over there. I need it. You're going to carry that bucket. You may have to hit someone hard with it. Can you do that?"

Laura glanced over at his hands.

"I can do it," she said.

She stood up and moved beside him. Carefully, he eased the door open. The area around them was deserted.

"The lift is somewhere down there," he whispered, gesturing with his head. "We'll go straight across to where that crowbar is and work from there."

Laura's heart was pounding in her ears as they slipped out the door, closing it behind them, and stepped quickly across the narrow aisle. Scott, who had looked fairly solid while leaning against the wall, stumbled and pitched heavily against the crates.

"You okay?" she asked.

He slipped the crowbar free and hefted it gingerly in his one functioning hand.

"Better now," he said.

From somewhere to their right they could hear voices. Staying flat against the cases, they worked their way toward the sound. At one point they passed not ten yards from a pair of workmen without being seen. Scott moved painfully, at times dragging his left leg. Even in the shadows Laura could see the pallor of his face and the flecks of drying blood that dotted his lips and chin.

The voices were close now—very close. Scott peered around the corner of a stack of crates and held up two fingers.

"I'm going for the forklift," he whispered. "Head straight for the man in the cap, and use that bucket." He pointed to a spot just behind his ear. Then he reached up with his crippled hand and gently touched her face. "Ready?"

She put her arm around him and, for a moment, held him close.

"Ready," she said.

They broke around the corner and headed straight for the two men. One, a heavyset black man, was seated on the forklift. The other, wearing a woolen cap, was several feet closer. He turned at the sound of their approach and was fumbling beneath his jacket when Laura swung the galvanized metal bucket with all her strength, connecting solidly with the side of his face. He cried out and fell heavily, pawing futilely at the gush of blood from just beneath his ear.

The man on the forklift had no chance at all. Scott lunged across the seat, thrusting the beveled edge of the crowbar upward through the soft tissue beneath his jaw, and then on through the bone of his palate. The man slumped forward before toppling off the seat and onto the concrete floor. Scott fell back with the effort, but just as quickly Laura had him back on his feet. She helped him onto the seat, took her place beside him, and turned the key. The forklift's electric engine whirred to life at the moment they heard the cries and footsteps of approaching men.

Scott spun the lift to the right, heading at full speed across the aisle by their cell, and then left into the corridor leading straight to the huge front doors. Laura glanced over her shoulder just as several men rounded the corner behind them.

"Stay low!" Scott yelled, crouching behind the wheel.

The forklift sped ahead toward the doors as several shots were fired.

"Not there, asshole!" someone screamed. "Those are the goddam ammo crates!"

His warning was punctuated by a rumbling from within one of the crates. Suddenly the entire wall exploded, showering the forklift with debris. Another explosion followed, and then another. The warehouse instantly filled with hot black smoke. Scott hunched over the wheel, staring intently ahead.

"Well, I'll be damned," Laura heard him say. "They were here. They were here all the time."

She glanced over and saw him actually smiling. They were less than twenty feet from the door. Behind them, the exploding maelstrom continued. Then, directly ahead of them, Lester Wheeler stepped into view, his pistol ready.

"Get down and hang on!" Scott ordered.

The sound of Wheeler's rapid volley of shots was lost in the explosions, but bullets clanged off the forklift. An instant after the last shot, they slammed against the warehouse doors at top speed. The two central panels flew apart, ripped free of their supports, and crashed to the pavement. Black smoke billowed out from the gaping opening, and moments later, Lester Wheeler raced through.

"Stay down!" Scott demanded, looking back over his shoulder at the scene.

At that instant his head snapped oddly to his left, and he pitched forward onto the wheel. The forklift swerved right, then left. Laura steadied the wheel with one hand as she pulled her brother free with the other. His body was limp, although his foot remained pressed on the accelerator. Then Laura saw the hole—a small black rent in his forehead just above his right eye. A trickle of blood had already begun to seep from the margins of the wound. Beneath the hole, Scott's eyes were glazed and unseeing.

"No!" she screamed. "God, no!"

The forklift had skidded past an oil-drum pyramid and out onto the long pier. Scott was totally lifeless except for his hands, which still clutched the wheel, and his foot, which held fast on the accelerator. Behind them, with the rumble of a hundred freight trains, Warehouse 18 blew apart.

Still steadying the wheel, Laura looked back. A fireball of pitch-black smoke was rising from the destruction. Lester Wheeler, who had stumbled during the blast, was scrambling to his feet.

"You bastard!" Laura screamed. "You goddam fucking bastard!"

Wheeler stopped, leveled his gun at her, and fired at the moment the forklift careened off the end of the pier. Scott's body lolled off the seat as the heavy machine yawed in the air and plummeted the fifteen feet to the harbor. It landed on its side, nose first, hurling Laura ahead as if she were shot from a cannon. She skimmed several feet across the surface, then hit the chilly water with dizzying force.

Laura felt herself sinking beneath the weight of her sodden clothes, but the icy chill almost instantly cleared her head and she struggled back to the surface. Scott was nowhere to be seen. Above her, Lester Wheeler appeared at the end of the pier, fixed his weapon on her once again, and fired. She ducked back beneath the surface as first one bullet, then another, skimmed past her face.

She had instinctively taken a decent breath, and now she desperately forced herself to calm down and concentrate. She was about four feet below the surface, and was being maintained in almost perfect buoyancy against the salt water by her clothes. This was her world, she realized, her element. Above her was the man who had just murdered her brother.

When it seemed he had nothing left, Scott had reached inside and found enough to save her. Now she had to do the same for herself. She had to move, then breathe, then move again. If she could just hold out and fight the cold, she could beat him. *She could beat him!*

Ignoring the overwhelming chill and the air hunger burning in her chest, Laura forced herself down another two feet and kicked back toward the pier.

Not yet, she screamed to herself as she pulled ahead. *Not yet, not yet, not yet!*

Water seeped down her nose and into her lungs. Still, eyes closed, she swam.

Finally, with her head pounding and her chest screaming for air, she kicked to the surface.

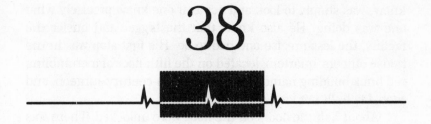

38

The dozen buildings of Metropolitan Hospital of Boston filled most of two blocks between the South End and Roxbury sections of the city. In the days before Medicare and Medicaid, it was the busiest of all the Boston hospitals, at times running as many as five hundred patients a day through its emergency room. Now, with a progressive drain to many newer facilities, its patient load had dropped off, and two of its three medical school affiliations had pulled out. Still, with its location near the poorest section of the city, there were plenty of severe trauma cases and medical crises.

With the E.R. at White Memorial inaccessible to him, Eric had chosen to use the frantic pace of Metro to provide him with a weapon he could use to break down Haven Darden. The ride there took fifteen minutes—precisely the same amount of time it took him to find a place to park. He set the material taken from Donald Devine's safe on the floor of the Celica, and entered the hospital through the main entrance.

The key to moving unnoticed about any hospital, Eric

346 MICHAEL PALMER

knew, was simply to look and act as if one knew precisely what one was doing. He also knew that the bigger and busier the facility, the less precise one had to be. His first stop was in the house officers' quarters, located on the fifth floor of a crumbling red brick building named for a nineteenth-century surgeon, and probably built not long after his death.

About half the doors on the floor were unlocked. There was nothing of use in the first two rooms he checked. Opening another door, he had actually stepped inside before realizing that a nurse and resident were on the narrow bed locked *in flagrante delicto,* their uniforms in a heap on the floor. The couple glimpsed him just as he was slipping back out the door, pulled a sheet over their heads, and giggled.

In the next room he tried, Eric found what he needed. He undressed there and emerged wearing someone's discarded surgical scrubs and a white clinic coat. Next, he headed to the E.R., praying that the place would not be in any sort of lull. A trio of ambulances unloading at the emergency bay told him his luck was holding.

He crossed the waiting room and entered the treatment area. Every room, it seemed, was in action. A nurse hurried past, taking no notice of him. A second nurse smiled at him as she entered the room of a new trauma victim. Purposefully, he continued down the busy corridor and into the med room, which was deserted. In less than a minute he was out. His hand was buried in his clinic coat pocket, concealing a filled 10cc syringe, hooked to a 1½-inch-long, 22-gauge needle. Then, casually, he strolled from the emergency room back to the house officers' building to change.

The game was on.

———

The drive from Moab along unmarked dirt tracks took Bernard Nelson nearly three hours in his Land Rover. Before college, Nelson had spent six years in the marines, most of those with a wilderness survival unit. Once, during his training at Camp Pendleton, he had been flown far out in the Mojave Desert by helicopter, and set loose by himself with enough rations and water for two days. The trip back to civilization had taken five days, but the things he had learned about survival and about himself had proven well worth the danger. He was sure the skills he had stored away were still there.

After finding the bodies of Richard and Marilyn Colson, he and Chippy Smith had flown to within distant sight of Charity. Following their return to Moab, Smith had drawn up a remarkably detailed map, including sketches of various distinctive rock formations and arroyos. Now, according to Bernard's compass and watch, he was close enough to go on foot. His safety net was Chippy, who had promised to fly out with help if twenty-four hours passed without word from him.

In addition to warm clothing, water, fuel, and some food, Bernard had brought along his Smith & Wesson and a new Nikon with a telephoto lens. With luck, he could get close enough to the town to take pictures without ever having to go in.

It was midafternoon by the time he found a large overhang beneath which he parked his Land Rover and prepared his gear. He slid his wallet and those of the Colsons beneath the front seat, and made his way toward the line of hills shielding Charity.

Near the top of the hill he crouched down and moved forward on his hands and knees. He believed he had followed the pilot's map to the letter, but there was always the chance something had gone wrong. Flattening out even more, he held his breath and peered over the crest. Below him, perhaps a quarter of a mile away, was the town.

Using his telephoto, Nelson could make out several people working in a remarkably robust cornfield. The village beyond seemed neat and well maintained. Staying low, he dropped into a dry creek bed, and worked his way down. At the edge of the field he knelt and watched as three men in work clothes trudged in slow silence back and forth from the tall stalks to a wheelbarrow, loading it one ear of corn at a time.

Through his lens Bernard studied the men's faces, each of which bore the expressionless mask of heavy tranquilizing medication. Fearing he was too close to chance the noise of a shutter, he crawled along the dusty margin of the field and crouched down in a gully not twenty feet from the rear of the first structure. The air was still and hot, the town eerily silent. Carefully, Nelson withdrew his revolver and released the safety. At that instant he heard a soft scraping noise behind him. He whirled to see the butt of a shotgun flashing down from the dazzling blue sky. It connected solidly just above his right ear. His teeth snapped together and pain exploded through his head. Then, amidst an overwhelming flood of nausea, he toppled face first onto the dry ground.

By the time his consciousness began to return, Bernard was face up in a wheelbarrow, awash in his own vomit. His head was tilted backward, giving him a view of a man's groin. His fingers scraped along the dirt roadway as they moved ahead.

"Don't move," the man warned.

Nelson choked briefly on some food and stomach acid, and closed his eyes against the overwhelming nausea. His spine, pressed against the metal rim of the wheelbarow, felt as if it were about to snap in two.

"I'm not a threat to anyone," he heard himself say.

"Shut up!"

"Please, listen to me."

The dirt changed to pavement. Nelson opened his eyes a crack. He was being wheeled along a walkway, through a gate in a chain-metal fence, and up to a low cinder-block building.

"Please let me up," he said.

"Get up yourself," the man barked.

He dropped the handles and stepped back. Nelson tried rolling to one side, but the wheelbarrow instantly tipped over, pitching him heavily onto his chest. Waves of dizziness and nausea washed over him once again.

"Can I get up?" he asked.

"Do it slowly."

Nelson propped himself on one elbow.

"I'm not here to hurt anyone," he said.

"I know. That's why you're carrying this."

The man waved Bernard's gun in front of the detective's face. He was tall and angular, probably in his early thirties, and he had on cowboy boots, jeans, and two shirts—a black T and an unbuttoned flannel with the sleeves cut off. Stepping away, he slid his shotgun out from beneath his belt.

"You don't need that," Nelson said, sitting up gingerly.

"I'll decide what I need and don't need. Get in there."

He motioned to the nearby doorway. Bernard stumbled to his feet, went inside, and sank heavily onto a metal folding chair. The place, sparsely furnished and undecorated, smelled like a hospital.

"What is this?" he asked.

"I'll do the askin'," the man said.

The moment his vision had cleared, Nelson had begun sizing up his captor. His first instinct told him the man was not in any position of authority. Now he felt fairly certain of it.

"My name's Nelson, Bernard Nelson," he said, rubbing at the expanding egg behind his ear. "You surely know how to hit a man, Mr. . . . ?"

"Pike. Garrett Pike." He tossed over a towel and let Nelson wipe himself off. "What're you doing here?"

"I want to speak to whoever's in charge."

Pike checked his watch. "You'll get your chance in just a little bit," he said.

"Do you have some ice I can put on this?"

"You don't need no ice. I barely touched you."

"Some touch," Nelson said. "What is this place, anyhow?"

"What does it smell like?"

"A hospital."

"Then that's what it is. Now what are you doin' here?"

Bernard continued sizing up the man and liked what he saw. Garrett Pike was slow, but he wasn't dumb. Nor, Nelson decided, was he any great threat.

"I'm looking for someone, a man," he said. "Can I reach in my pocket?"

"Slowly."

Bernard pulled out the flier with Scott Enders's picture, and handed it over.

"This man."

Garrett Pike did not respond, but Bernard could see recognition spark in his eyes and he knew his search was over.

"Never seen him before," Pike said.

"You're a lousy liar, Mr. Pike, but I like that in a man."

Pike seemed flustered by his candor. He glanced at the door, as if hoping his boss would appear and relieve him of this responsibility. He settled down in a chair across from Nelson.

"Suppose we just wait 'n let you answer to Dr. Barber."

"He's in charge?"

"Uh-huh."

"Tell me, Garrett," Bernard said, anxious to take the offensive before Dr. Barber or anyone else arrived, "do you really think this is a hospital?"

"I know it is."

"Then what are you doing holding this man here, who just happens to be a government agent who disappeared in Boston several months ago?"

"You're out of your mind."

"Am I?"

"This place is for the criminally insane. If he was here— which he ain't—it'd be because he's a danger to society. And your being here with this gun tells me you were trying to bust one of our patients out."

Nelson shook his head sadly.

"Garrett, Garrett," he said. "Have they really taken you in that badly?"

"You just shut up."

Pike checked his watch once again. Nelson felt desperate to win the man over before anyone else showed up. He thought about the gruesome discovery he and Chippy Smith had made. He was grasping at straws, but still . . .

"Listen," he said, "do the names Richard or Marilyn Colson mean anything to you?"

There was a moment of telltale hesitation before Pike said, "No. Why?"

Sensing the man's confusion, Bernard bored in.

"I found their bodies out in the desert, that's why. You kill 'em?"

"I . . . I don't know what you're talking about."

"I think you do. I think they stumbled on this place and you killed them—took them out in the desert and shot 'em both dead."

"I never heard of them."

"Pike, listen to me. My Land Rover's parked just over those hills there. Right behind the cornfield. The Colsons' wallets are under the front seat along with my ID. I'm a private detective from Boston. Tomorrow morning, whether I show up in Moab or not, this place'll be crawling with cops. Believe that. Help me now, and I promise you'll get a break."

"I don't believe a word you've—"

Pike was cut short by the sound of car doors slamming. A minute later two men entered the room. Bernard managed one last furtive look at Pike, but the guard just turned away.

"Dr. Barber," Pike said, "I'm glad you're back. I found this guy spyin' on the town, takin' pictures. He says his name's Bernard Nelson, and he claims to be a private detective from Boston. He had this on him." He handed over Bernard's gun. He hesitated for a beat, and then reached into his pocket. "He says he's here looking for this guy."

Barber scanned the flier, then clucked disapprovingly.

"We've been expecting occasional attempts to break our patients out of here," he said, "but nothing as crude as this. Good job, Garrett. You can expect a double-sized bonus in your next check."

Pike looked as if he were about to say something. Then he simply nodded and walked out.

"Take him to the back, John," Barber ordered. "Use the straitjacket."

The man named John, a full-blooded Indian from his appearance, pulled Nelson to his feet and shoved him rudely down the hallway into a two-bed infirmary. There, Nelson's legs were bound together and his arms forced into the sleeves of a canvas straitjacket that barely fit over his middle. Barber followed them into the room.

"That's good, John," he said. "Don't go too far."

The Indian grunted a reply, and left.

"So then," Barber said, "what have we here? An old fat man who carries a gun and a poster and claims to be a detective. But instead he goes and gets himself caught by a bohunk with the IQ of a rabbit."

"It's over for you, Barber," Nelson said evenly. "I'm not the only one who knows what's going on here."

Barber looked around.

"Then where are they all?" he asked. He paced about the room for a time, then sat down on the bed nearest Bernard's chair. "So then, suppose we start with the basics. Bernard Nelson: that really your name?"

"No," Nelson said. "It's Thumb; first name, Tom."

Nelson's initial read of the man was not encouraging. There was nothing in his eyes but a flat, sadistic coldness. As if verifying the impression, Barber stepped forward and with one pudgy hand squeezed Nelson's cheeks tightly against his teeth.

"Don't fuck with me," he said, pulling Bernard's face up. "I've given a good chunk of my life to this project, and I expect to spend the rest of it enjoying the rewards. So you better believe me when I say that I don't have the least hesitation in causing pain to someone like you who wants to make trouble for us. Now, who are you, and what are you doing here?"

Bernard waited until Barber had released his grip.

"Look, how about we trade?" he said. "You tell me what the hell is going on here, and I'll tell you how many dozens of people will show up here if I haven't returned to Moab by tomorrow."

"You're bluffing, my fat friend. I can see it all over your face. If anyone besides you was interested in this place, they would have been out here with you today. And as for the folks in Moab, they know this place is a hospital for the criminally insane, and they don't care to know anything more."

Nelson searched desperately for a soft spot in the man. All he came up with was the sense that he was confronting a fanatic with an enormous ego. It was not much of a card to play, but unfortunately it was the only one he held.

"Your man Pike called you Doctor," he said. "Is that a sham, too, like the hospital story?"

"M.D., Ph.D., as a matter of fact," Barber said proudly. "There, I did my bit. Now, who are you really? Who sent you?"

"Bernard Nelson *is* my name. I'm from Boston. I'm working for the sister of the man on that flier."

"Scott Enders. Never heard of him."

"I think you have. Maybe not by that name, but I think he's here, and I think he was brought here by Donald Devine."

Barber's attempt to mask his reaction was too slow, and he obviously sensed that.

"Very good," he said. "Good timing, decent delivery. I'm impressed. What else do you know?"

"I know enough to tell you that the best thing you can do is come clean about what's going on here, and hope that I believe enough of your story to help you deal with the authorities."

"*You* help *me*?" Barber began pacing again. "Talk about chutzpah. You sit there trussed up like a goddam Thanksgiving turkey offering to help me. Well, let me tell you something, friend: This is no fly-by-night operation you've stumbled onto. There's more at stake here than you could ever imagine, and minds a hell of a lot sharper than yours have worked out a response for every contingency." He took a small strongbox from a locked metal cabinet, and withdrew a vial of powder and a pair of rubber gloves. "And right here just happens to be our response for this one."

The man's eyes were growing wider and wilder. Bernard had read the account of Eric Najarian's night of horror, and had no trouble making the connection to what he was experiencing.

"It won't wash, Dr. Barber," he said. "Too many people know where I am."

"I don't think so," Barber replied. "I think you came here snooping around because nobody knows anything for sure. If anyone does show up, we have certification for our facility and perfectly documented files on all of our patients. You see, we've been very, very careful about that sort of thing. Now then, what else do you have to tell me?" He slipped on the rubber gloves. "Amazing stuff, this," he went on. "Active if taken orally, active if just rubbed on the skin. Absolutely amazing."

"Is that what you fed to the Colsons?"

Barber stopped momentarily. Then he smiled and shook his head.

"No good. Content decent, delivery poor. You found their remains somewhere out there in the desert, and now you're pissing into the wind and hoping you won't get soaked." He withdrew a small spatulaful of the powder from the vial, moistened three of his gloved fingertips, and carefully spread the powder on them. "Better try something else."

"I'm telling you," Nelson said, desperately clinging to his crumbling façade of control, "too many people know. They know about you, about Donald Devine, about the little room in Devine's basement, everything."

The physician brushed the glove close to Nelson's face. Bernard closed his eyes and instinctively pulled his head away.

"I listen to you, and I still hear bluff," Barber said. "You had better come up with something more pithy, or, I promise you, you're in for a long—or perhaps I should say a short—afternoon." He glanced at his watch. "Time's run out, Mr. Nelson. Either you have shot your wad and you don't know anything more about us, or you're not taking me seriously enough.

"Well, sir, let me tell you how this stuff works. I'm primarily a research Ph.D., but as I said, I *am* an M.D. as well, and a very well trained one at that, so I know what I'm talking about. At this dose, you will have about, oh, one or two hours before the air you're breathing starts to feel like molasses. After that, it's just a matter of time. Your arms and legs will go numb, and your guts will stop moving. You'll start coughing your lungs out. Finally, your heart will slow to the point where your blood's hardly moving at all. The only thing that will be working is your brain, and that will keep working right up until near the very end. At that point, if I want to keep you around for, say, a little work in our cornfield, I can stop the process and start you on the tranquilizers we use—that is, if you even require them. Otherwise, I'll just get you a mirror and let you watch yourself terminate. Sound okay?"

"Give it up, Barber," Nelson said. But he heard the fear in his voice, and could tell that the madman holding him could hear it too. It was all happening too fast. He hadn't expected it to be this way. *There has to be something I can do . . . anything.*

"Suit yourself," Barber said.

"Wait."

"Yes?"

"Okay. Okay, you're right. I don't know what's going on here or who is involved beyond Donald Devine."

"That's better, Mr. Nelson. Much better."

"But people do know where I am."

"As I said, we can deal with that."

"Perhaps you can, but then again, perhaps not. Listen to me, please. If the work you're doing here is as important as you say, I'm sure you don't want to jeopardize it. I've got friends—important friends—in politics and on the police force. Tell me what's going on here and what you're doing. If you can help me understand what's at stake, I'll do everything I can to get the right people to understand."

Barber continued pacing as he thought about the proposal. Then, quite suddenly, he kicked a folding chair close to Bernard and sat down, resting his gloved hand palm up in his lap.

"Mr. Nelson, every day thousands of people are dying unnecessarily from dozens of so-called incurable diseases—diseases like hepatitis, influenza, encephalitis, and many forms of cancer. And of course we both know that the world is on the brink of an epidemic that, in just a few years, will make the horror of the black plague seem like a cartoon. Well, detective, what you've bumbled into here is a project which, at this moment, is this close to having an answer." He held up his thumb and forefinger for emphasis.

"What do you mean?"

"I mean a universal antiviral antibiotic, that's what I mean. The ultimate cure!" He nearly shouted the words, then deflated noticeably when he saw the lack of comprehension on Bernard's face.

"I'm sorry if I look confused," Bernard said, trying not to glance at the man's hand. "I always thought penicillin was a pretty decent antibiotic."

Barber groaned his impatience.

"Pearls before swine," he muttered. "First of all, penicillin is effective only against bacteria, not viruses. And second of all, like the dozens of other antibacterial drugs on the market, it's useless against most organisms because they become resistant about as fast as you can get the stuff home from the pharmacy. Our drug not only kills the little beasties, but changes in the body as fast as they do. *Ergo,* no resistance. It will save millions of lives."

And be worth hundreds of millions to you, Nelson thought. He tried to appear impressed with what he was hearing, but he couldn't shake the sinking feeling that Barber was prolonging this purely out of boredom and the need to assure himself of his own importance. In the end, nothing Bernard could say or do was going to move the man one iota.

"Tell me more," he said.

Barber smiled and stood up, shaking his head.

"I think not, Mr. Nelson," he sang, moistening his lips with his tongue. "I think not."

"Please, wait," Bernard said, squirming in his seat. "I have some questions I'd like to ask you ab—"

"I had hoped you'd be a little more intellectually stimulating, being from Boston and all. I don't mind telling you, you're a great disappointment in that regard. A great disappointment. Well, sir, I suppose you will simply have to find another way to amuse and educate me."

"Don't do it, Barber. Please listen to m—"

"This dose is roughly ten times what your friends the Colsons received. Will it work ten times as fast? Will it work the same way? Will Little Nell find true happiness? Will E continue to equal MC squared?"

Continuing a stream of nonsense questions, Barber reached out, grabbed Bernard's hair viciously with one hand, and meticulously smoothed the damp powder across both his cheeks with the other. At the man's touch, Bernard felt his heart stop, and truly believed it was going to end for him right there. Moments later, it began to beat again.

"Whether or not I'm here to see it, you're through, Barber," he rasped.

"Will the South rise again?" the man went on in his chilling, singsong voice. "Will there be peace in the valley someday?"

He turned, scooped up the strongbox, and left the room.

Gripped by fear unlike any he had ever known, Bernard first tried to rub his cheek against his shoulder. Then he hurled himself to the floor, attempting to scrape the powder off on the linoleum. Some of the poison did come off, but he knew it was not nearly enough.

For a time, he could only lie there, silently praying that Barber's performance was a ruse—his version of the hideous charade that had been played with Eric Najarian. But as minutes passed and he began to feel a heaviness settling into his chest, he knew better.

"I'm sorry, Maggie," he said softly. "I'm sorry for being so damn stupid."

He struggled to his feet, threw himself on the bed, and rubbed what more he could from his cheeks onto the cotton blanket. Finally, totally winded by his efforts, he stopped.

"I'm so damn sorry," he said again.

Helpless now, Bernard closed his eyes, listened to the pounding of his heart in his ears, and waited.

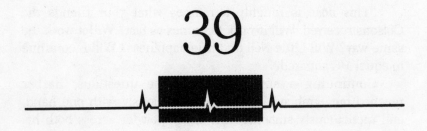

39

Carrying Donald Devine's ledgers, Eric entered White Memorial through a little-used side door, and took the subbasement tunnel and back staircase to Haven Darden's lab. Tucked carefully in the pocket of his jeans was the loaded syringe. As the medical chief had promised, the entire floor was deserted. Through the darkness of the lab Eric could see light spilling from Darden's inner office.

He paused by the outer door, trying to solidify his composure and his resolve. He thought about Scott Enders and Loretta Leone; about Laura's torment and Reed Marshall's shattered career; about all those others who had suffered. And finally, he conjured up the images of the obscene, makeshift voodoo shrine and of the death's-head priest—quite possibly Darden himself—leering down at him through the candlelight. The man was evil—fully deserving of the terror he was about to experience.

"No mercy," Eric whispered as he opened the door. "No mercy at all."

He walked between a row of incubators and then turned

left toward Darden's office. The medical chief, natty as usual in a custom-tailored shirt, silk tie, and black suspenders, met him at the door. Eric was pleased to see that he wore no suit coat.

"Come in, Eric, come in," Darden said. "I was relieved to get your call. I'm sure it comes as no surprise that your friends here at White Memorial have been most concerned about you."

"I didn't really feel I had any of those left," Eric forced himself to say.

"Oh, you do. You do."

Darden sat down behind his desk, but Eric remained standing, his hand cradling the syringe in his pocket. He imagined the man making love to Anna Delacroix, and sensed his anger and disgust grow even stronger. Haven Darden had a family, children. The woman—half his age, if that—was beautiful enough to have any man. How much was he paying her for her services? What did he lay out for her assistance in destroying Eric Najarian?

No mercy.

"Sit down, sit down," Darden said. "I don't mind telling you that the things you alluded to in your call have me most intrigued."

Don't fool around. Don't wait!

"I'd like you to look at this," Eric said, setting Devine's ledger on the desk. "It was taken from a safe in the Gates of Heaven Funeral Home."

As Darden opened the cover Eric stepped behind him and slid the syringe free.

"I'm not sure what I'm supposed to be seeing here," Darden said, suddenly swiveling around to face him.

Eric thrust the syringe back into his pocket.

"It . . . it's the list beginning on the second page."

Darden pulled open his desk drawer and reached inside.

It's a gun! Eric's mind shrieked. *Move, dammit, move!*

Before he could react, the medical chief pulled out a pair of reading glasses and slipped them on.

"Perhaps I'd do better if I could see the words," he said, turning back to the desk.

Once again Eric eased the loaded syringe free. He focused on Darden's left trapezius, the heavy muscle just at the base of his neck. A final, deep breath and . . .

Now!

In synchronized motions, he shoved Darden's chair in, pinning him against the desk, locked his left arm tightly beneath the man's chin, pulled the plastic needle guard off with his teeth, and drove the needle down to the hilt in the spot he had chosen. Darden cried out at the pain and tried to squirm free, but Eric held him fast. He spat the needle guard onto the floor.

"Move again and you're dead!" he said. "I mean it!"

"What are you doing?" Darden rasped.

"This syringe is loaded with succinylcholine," Eric said. "Two hundred milligrams—enough to paralyze you totally in a matter of fifteen or twenty seconds. At the slightest provocation, I'm ready to give you every bit of it, and you had better believe that."

"Y-you're crazy!"

"You bet I am, Doctor. It'll help us both if you remember that. It would also help if you think about what it's like to be paralyzed and unable to breathe while you're still wide awake. Surely you're an expert on that. Now, first you're going to tell me where Laura Enders is, and then you're going to tell me about Caduceus."

"I . . . I don't know what you're talking about."

"Dammit," Eric rasped, forcing the needle down harder. "I don't have time for this. The only person in the world I care about right now is missing, and you know what's happened to her. Now, I know who you are. I know about Donald Devine and Norma Cullinet, and that goddam place in Utah. I even know about Anna Delacroix. My fuse is really short right now, so I'm warning you: Stop playing games with me!"

Eric felt the tension in the man's muscles let up. Still, he continued to hold him fast, his thumb poised on the syringe.

"Eric, listen to me," Darden said with sudden calm. "I know you've been through a lot. You may think that what you believe is right. But I promise you that I know nothing of what you're saying. Nothing!"

"And I suppose it wasn't you who called me the morning of the committee vote and promised me the position if I joined Caduceus."

"Eric, I have been your supporter in that matter all along. I told you that several weeks ago. It was Dr. Silver who changed his mind and asked for an extension of the vote. I swear to you it was."

"I . . . I don't believe you," Eric said, feeling the first sickening doubt begin to take hold. "And I suppose I was just imagining things when I saw you in a tender little clinch with Anna Delacroix."

"I assure you, Eric, I know no one by that name. No one. I am a happily married man. Now, please, pull that needle out of me before you do something you'll regret for the rest of your life."

"No. You're a liar and a goddam monster. There's no telling how many people have died because of you. Anna Delacroix or whoever the hell she is set me up, and I saw you with her on Charles Street just a few hours ago. Now I want the truth, dammit. Where is Laura?"

"She's dead, Doctor. Now don't move. Don't move a muscle."

Eric barely managed to maintain his grip as his head spun toward the voice. The tall man standing just inside the doorway was wearing a police captain's uniform and holding a gun leveled at Eric's chest. Suddenly, his words registered.

"What do you mean she's dead?" he asked, a horrible emptiness swelling in his chest.

"Please, Officer," Haven Darden cried. "This man's crazy. Please get him to pull this needle out. He's trying to kill me."

"Oh, I know what he's doing," Lester Wheeler said. "Why, thanks to the miracle of modern telecommunications, I knew what he had in mind almost as soon as he did. You really should have paid more attention to the two men repairing the phone line outside that apartment you were staying in, Doc."

Eric's eyes narrowed.

"Wheeler?" he asked.

"At your service. Now, if you would be so kind as to administer that drug."

"No, wait! You don't understand," Darden pleaded.

"I understand exactly," Wheeler said. "Unfortunately, the good doctor has already shared far too much with you."

"Darden's not Caduceus?" Eric said, loosening his grip around the man's neck.

Before Darden could respond, Wheeler leaped forward and, with animal quickness, slammed his fist down on the top of the syringe, emptying its contents into him. Darden screamed in pain as the policeman whirled and jammed the muzzle of his pistol up under Eric's chin.

"Not a move!" he ordered.

"Jesus," Eric said. "You just killed this man."

"No, Doctor," Wheeler said smugly. "You did." He glanced at his watch and then looked down at Darden, who sat staring numbly up at the two of them. "Fifteen or twenty seconds. Isn't that what you said?"

"I . . . I don't know," Eric said, now forced to his tiptoes by the gun barrel. "Succinylcholine is the most powerful anesthetic we have, but its onset of action is unpredictable. I . . . I never really intended to use it. Now please, if you'll just let me get to some equipment, I can save him."

Haven Darden tried to rise, but Wheeler reached out and shoved him back into his seat.

"Please," Darden whimpered. "Please help me."

Already his speech was beginning to thicken and slur. In just another ten seconds, his arms and hands began to tremble.

"No!" he cried. "Oh, God, no!"

Wheeler forced Eric several steps back as the medical chief's body jerked spasmodically, his head twitching uncontrollably. Then, suddenly, he pitched from his chair onto the floor, his legs snapping and kicking. In less than half a minute it was over. The hideous contractions in his limbs vanished as quickly as they had appeared. His head lolled to one side and stopped moving, his cheek pressed helplessly against the lino-leum, spittle oozing from the corner of his mouth.

Wheeler quickly manacled Eric's hands behind him. Then he knelt down and peered at Darden for fully half a minute, assuring himself that the drug had done its job.

"Okay. Now, Doc," he said, standing. "You and I are going right out the front door of this hospital to my cruiser. If you want to scream and kick, that's okay with me. I want everyone who will listen to know what you've done, and why I'm taking you in. They all think you're insane anyway."

"What happened to Laura?"

"Oh, yes, sweet Laura. Well, I'm afraid she and her brother discovered that the water in Boston Harbor wasn't to their liking."

"She found Scott?"

"She did. They were even together at the end. Now, let's get out of here."

"You can't possibly get away with this," Eric said.

Wheeler grabbed Eric by the back of the neck and shoved him over Haven Darden's inert body and out the door.

"Wanna bet?" he asked.

40

"ou have the right to remain silent," Lester Wheeler said as he half-shoved, half-dragged Eric into the elevator of the research building. ". . . If you choose to speak, anything you say may be used against you in a court of law or other proceeding. . . ." He pushed Eric out of the elevator and into the bustling main thoroughfare of the hospital.

"What happened to Laura? What did you do to her?"

". . . You have the right to consult with a lawyer before answering any questions and you may have him present with you during questioning. . . ."

"Dammit, Wheeler, give it up. You're not taking me out of this hospital," Eric said, increasing his resistance as they approached the main lobby.

"Do us both a favor and make a break for it," Wheeler whispered. He continued in a voice loud enough for everyone around to hear. ". . . If you cannot afford a lawyer and you want one, a lawyer will be provided for you by the Commonwealth without cost to you. Do you understand what I have told you? Okay, move aside, folks. Please move aside."

The crush of bewildered early-evening visitors parted like the Red Sea to allow the policeman and his prisoner to pass. Eric recognized several of the nurses and residents who were watching.

"Find Dr. Silver for me, please," he called out as Wheeler hurried him past.

"You've got no friends around this place," Wheeler said. "Least of all Dr. Silver. Earlier today he had the hospital attorneys file a restraining order to keep you out. Face it, you're finished." He tightened his grip on Eric's arm and continued loudly: ". . . You may also waive the right to counsel, and your right to remain—"

"God damn it, I'm not going with you!" Eric screamed as they entered the busy main lobby.

Instantly, the huge reception area was silent. A hundred or so people stopped milling about and froze, as one. A security guard, who was standing off to one side, spoke quickly into his radio and began moving toward the two men. Eric stumbled forward and fell to his knees, shouting words of protest. Wheeler grasped the handcuffs and pulled him to his feet by jerking his arms straight up behind his back. Eric hollered out in pain, twisted his body to one side, and fell heavily to the tiled floor. Bystanders tripped over one another, trying to move away. The guard reached them just as two more security men raced into the lobby.

"Can we help?" he asked Wheeler.

The captain flashed his shield.

"I've just arrested this man for the murder of Dr. Haven Darden," he said. "His body is up in his lab."

Several in the crowd gasped. A woman cried out.

"We know Dr. Najarian," the guard said. "He was alone with one of our nurses when she died this morning. There's a restraining order out against him. We've been on the lookout for him all day."

"Please," Eric begged, still on his side on the floor. "You've got to help me. I didn't kill anyone. He did. He did!"

The two other security men arrived and spoke briefly with their colleague. One of them immediately sprinted off for Darden's office. The remaining pair helped Wheeler pull Eric to his feet. At that moment Joe Silver and two residents arrived.

"I'm this man's chief of service," he said. "What on earth is going on now?" He looked stonily at Eric as he spoke.

"Captain Wheeler, BPD," the officer explained calmly. "I've just arrested this man for the murder of Dr. Haven Darden by some sort of lethal injection. Haven is a personal friend of mine. He called me a short while ago and told me Najarian here had phoned and threatened him. I hurried over to escort him home, but when I got there, I was too late. I found this man with an empty syringe in his hand, standing over Haven's body."

"Damn you, Najarian," Joe Silver said.

"I didn't do anything," Eric pleaded. "It was this man. He's crazy. He's working with Dr. Darden. Craig Worrell was involved with them too. They're responsible for everything. For Norma, for Loretta Leone—everything."

"Eric, just shut up and get the hell out of here," Silver said.

"Come along now," Wheeler ordered. "And do it quietly."

Once again Eric began to struggle.

"I didn't kill anyone! They did! Why doesn't anyone believe me?"

"*I believe you*," Haven Darden said loudly.

The crowd fell away, revealing the medical chief standing calmly beside the security guard.

"Now *you* must believe me that I had nothing to do with this Caduceus, or any other plot."

Joe Silver, totally bewildered, stared at the man.

"What in *hell* is going on?" he managed.

"As soon as you called succinylcholine an anesthetic, Eric," Darden went on, "I knew it was water. Captain Wheeler is a criminal. Dr. Najarian meant only to frighten me. This man tried to murder me, and confessed to murdering someone named Laura. Sir, you are an animal."

Before anyone could react, Lester Wheeler drew his pistol and fired. Darden grabbed at his left shoulder as he reeled backwards and dropped to the floor. People screamed, falling over one another as they scrambled to find cover. Wheeler managed to get off another shot, this one wild, before the security guards were on him. Groaning loudly with every step, he dragged the three guards toward the main entrance like a fullback hauling tacklers toward a touchdown. Two muscular young men raced from the crowd and helped wrestle him down. Suddenly, from within the melee, Wheeler's gun sounded again. Immediately the struggling stopped. The guards moved back. The policeman, on his knees, toppled over in slow motion and lay wide-eyed and motionless. Blood was rapidly soaking into his shirt from a dollar-sized hole in his chest.

"Call a code Ninety-nine!" Joe Silver screamed at the receptionists. "Someone get to the E.R. and bring back two stretchers."

He raced over to where Haven Darden lay while the residents hurried to tend to Wheeler.

"The keys to these handcuffs," Eric said, scrambling to where the policeman lay. "They're in his shirt pocket."

The residents were already stripping Wheeler's clothes away. The wound, Eric could see, was almost certainly mortal, even with immediate surgical help.

One of the guards retrieved the keys and freed Eric's hands. A stretcher arrived, and Wheeler's lifeless body was transferred to it and rushed to the E.R.

For a few frozen seconds Eric stood alone, trying desperately to sort out what had happened, what had been said. Laura and Scott both dead. *Was Wheeler telling the truth about that?* And Darden—*how could he* not *be Caduceus?*

Numbly, he crossed to where Haven Darden lay. Joe Silver had already ripped the man's shirt away, exposing a wound that entered and exited through his shoulder. Darden, though in obvious pain, remained completely conscious and surprisingly calm.

"You thought very quickly, Eric," he said. "I always admired that in you."

"I . . . I'm sorry I had to do what I did," Eric said. "I was desperate."

"And do you now believe that I am not part of this Caduceus plot?"

"I don't know what to believe."

A stretcher arrived, and Eric and Joe Silver gently lifted the medical chief onto it.

"Perhaps," Darden said, "it would help if I told you that I know who your mysterious Anna Delacroix is. Dr. Silver, if you could, I'd like a minute alone with Eric."

Joe Silver looked about uncomfortably.

"Perhaps I'd better stay," he said. "I need to hear this too."

The battle to save the life of Lester Wheeler was short-lived. Eric stood by the doorway of the trauma room, watching the monitor and the furious efforts of the thoracic surgical team, and hoping against hope for the miracle that might save the one person who could tell him Laura's fate.

In a room just down the hall, Joe Silver was attending to the father of Rebecca Darden, known to Silver as Ariel Dumonde and to Eric as Anna Delacroix. Haven Darden would, in all likelihood, be Silver's last case at White Memorial. As soon as he was certain the medical chief was stable, Silver had promised Eric he would drive to the private psychiatric facility where Reed Marshall was being treated and offer Marshall what help he could. He would also strongly recommend that the hospital keep him on the emergency staff in some capacity.

Then, in the morning, he would submit his resignation to the hospital administrators, explaining to them how he had been seduced by a beautiful woman, and later blackmailed by her into changing his vote on the search committee. He knew nothing of the reason he had been required to delay the vote, but with his own career, marriage, and children at stake, he had made a choice he would now have to live with for the rest of his own life.

Eric felt his heart sink as the surgeon working on Wheeler shrugged, stepped back from the table, and flicked off the police captain's monitor. The lone spark of hope he had nurtured was gone. At a loss for what he could possibly do next, Eric wandered down the hall to Haven Darden's room. The medical chief, alone save for a nurse, was sitting up on his stretcher, an IV draining into his wrist. Heavy bandages swathed his wounded shoulder.

"Is he dead?" he asked.

"He is."

Darden motioned Eric inside, and then asked the nurse to leave.

"Rebecca was always too beautiful for her own good," he said.

"She is that, sir. I'm sorry for what you're going through."

"And I for what *you* are going through. Obviously, as far as my daughter is concerned, things are going to get much worse. She has a great deal to answer for."

"I hope she can shed some light on what's happened to Laura."

"I hope so too," Darden said. His voice was husky and distant. "You know, my wife and I began worrying about Rebecca when she was still in grade school, when we found she was getting other children—boys mostly—to do things for her or give her things in exchange for kissing her or touching her or just being her friend. We . . . we brought her to Haiti with us any number of times in hopes of breaking through her narcissism, and instilling in her some sort of social conscience. She seemed like a different person there—so interested in everything, so anxious to know the country. There was no way to know that she would just take what we were giving her and . . ."

He began to weep. Eric took his hand and held it.

"You're a good man and a great doctor," he said. "I don't know what to say except that you deserved better."

"Thank you. Is there any more you can tell me about what Rebecca was involved in? What those people were doing?"

"Not precisely. But when I do know, I promise—you and I will sit and talk about it."

"I would be grateful. I'm very sorry about your friend. I hope Captain Wheeler was mistaken about her."

"I hope so, too, Dr. Darden, but I fear he wasn't. Do you think Rebecca might be home now? I'd like to call her."

"She might. She doesn't have a job, you see. Never seemed to need one. I should have asked her about the sports car and the furs and all the other things, but . . ."

"Please, sir, try to get some rest. You've lost a fair amount of blood."

Eric left the emergency room and headed through the crowded corridors to the Proctor Building and Dave Subarsky's lab. Remarkably, the hospital seemed perfectly normal, as if the violence he'd witnessed had never happened.

It was unlikely that Dave had heard anything at all from Laura, but there was always the chance. If there had been no word from her, at least his friend could help him decide whether it was better to call Rebecca Darden immediately or try to confront her at the Cambridge address Haven Darden had given him.

The research floor was largely deserted, and the door to Subarsky's lab locked. Eric found one researcher—a young biochemist named Jessica Marsh—locking up for the evening.

"Excuse me," he asked, "have you seen David?"

"He left a while ago," the woman said.

"Do you have a key to his lab? Dave must have assumed I had mine, but I left them at home."

"I have keys to all the labs on the floor," she said. "But I'm not allowed to—"

"Please, Jessica," Eric implored. "Dave was supposed to meet me here. I'm sure he's left a note for me inside. There's a call that might have come in on his phone that I've got to know about."

The woman hesitated.

"Please, it's very important," Eric urged. "Listen, you've seen me working here alone dozens of nights. You know Dave and I are friends."

Reluctantly, she pulled her keys from her purse and opened the door.

"I shouldn't be doing this," she said.

"Thank you, Jess. You won't regret it."

As she was turning the key, the phone inside began ringing. Eric raced inside, slamming his thigh against the corner of a lab bench as he rounded it to the inner office. He snatched up the receiver.

"Hello?"

"Yes, I'm trying to reach Dr. Dave Subarsky."

Eric felt his pulse leap.

"*Laura?*"

"Eric, yes, it's me! Oh, God, I've been worried about you."

"*You've* been worried—I thought you were dead."

"I almost was. Eric, it's Captain Wheeler, the policeman I told you about. He's behind everything."

"I know. I know. Laura, Wheeler shot himself here in the hospital. He's dead. You don't have anything to worry about anymore. Where are you?"

"I'm at a house in East Boston. Eric, I found Scott. He . . . Wheeler killed him."

"Jesus. Oh, Laura, I'm so sorry. Listen, just tell me where you are. I'll come and get you. You can tell me all about everything then."

"I'm at this couple's place not far from the docks. They picked me up by the road. I spent some time in the water, and I was chilled to the bone, but I'm okay now."

"Tell me the address," he said, feeling through the top desk drawer until he found a pen. "I'll be right over."

"You don't have to. I spoke with your friend Dave an hour or so ago. I thought he would be here by now. I was just calling to make sure he had left."

"Well, he's not here."

"That's strange. Maybe the traffic was—Wait a minute. The doorbell just rang. He might be here now. . . . Yes, yes, it's him. Eric, listen, I know where that tape is. Scott remembered before he— I'll be right down, Mrs. Poletti. Just tell him to wait a minute. You still there?"

"Oh, I'm here. I'm here. I can't believe you're all right."

"I'm fine. Eric, get this. The tape is in an old tractor trailer right in the lot where we parked that day we went to the docks. We were right next to it!"

"Amazing."

"We're going to stop by and get it on the way back to Boston. Where will you be?"

"I don't know. . . . How about Bernard's apartment?"

"Perfect. I'll see you there in an hour or less. And Eric?"

"Yes."

"Eric, I love you."

"I love you, too, kiddo."

Eric hung up and leaned back in his chair, his fists clenched, his arms stretched upward. The nightmare was over.

A few moments of quiet and absolute exultation, and then he pushed back from the desk and stood up. Below him, in the partially open desk drawer, something caught his eye—something that he must have pulled forward in his search for a pen. He picked it up and hefted it in his hand for a moment, his mind unwilling to accept what it was and what it meant.

But he knew.

What seemed a lifetime ago, he had stood beside the occupational therapist as she demonstrated an electrolarynx for him.

His heart pounding, Eric pulled on the other desk drawers. Both were locked. Using a letter opener, he forced the first of them open and spilled its contents onto the desk. Tucked among the computer printouts and lab reports was a five-by-seven color photo, clearly taken in a tropical setting. Dave Subarsky, wearing a baggy surfer's bathing suit, stood leaning against a palm tree. Nearly dwarfed inside his arm, her perfect body glistening in the sun, was Rebecca Darden.

Barely able to breathe, Eric forced open the bottom drawer and withdrew something enclosed in a brown paper bag. His hands were shaking as he set the bag on the desk and ripped it open. Lying there, glowering eerily up at him in the dim light of the desk lamp, was the death's-head mask.

With a cry of pain, Eric snatched up a phone book. *Paolini? Paretti? What in the hell did she say their name was? Did she even say the name of their street?*

He spent half a minute staring at the columns of names before shoving the book aside. Then he grabbed the hideous mask and bolted from the lab.

41

Eric's cab ride through the heavy evening traffic was an agonizing exercise in frustration, beginning with a tie-up on the Mystic River Bridge that stretched back almost to the hospital. To make a bad situation even worse, within minutes of his leaving White Memorial, a furious wind-driven thunderstorm erupted, sending torrents of water cascading down the access ramp and instantly flooding the roadway beneath overpasses. Strobes of lightning flashed through the taxi as the cabbie pawed at the thickening film of condensation on the windshield.

After three fruitless attempts at convincing the man that this was an emergency worth taking risks for, Eric forced himself back into his seat, fidgeting constantly as he stared out through the pounding rain. If, as he suspected, Subarsky and Lester Wheeler had coordinated their efforts, Laura was in a situation as potentially lethal as his had been. Except for the question of *why*, the final pieces of the Caduceus nightmare had fallen into place. And now, through the twenty-twenty vision of hindsight, Eric cursed himself for not seeing his friend's involvement sooner.

The biochemist's insistence on accompanying him to the Gates of Heaven, his appearance in the hospital library at just the right moment, his knowledge that Eric would be at the Countway, and finally, his convenient disappearance just before Norma Cullinet's death—the signposts were all there, clear as fucking day.

It had undoubtedly been Dave's idea to try to enlist him as Craig Worrell's replacement in Caduceus, and Dave's finger that had been on his pulse ever since.

Why hadn't he seen it? Why hadn't he at least considered the possibility?

The cabbie inched along the bridge and then stopped, unable even to change lanes. Eric gauged the distance across to East Boston and knew they had no chance. It was perhaps half a mile to the exit, and another half a mile to the docks. Leaving the death's-head mask on the seat, he shoved a ten-dollar bill into the Plexiglas scoop, raced from the cab, and dodged between cars to the narrow sidewalk.

Before he had sprinted even a dozen yards he was soaked to the skin. Rain lashed at him as he bounded up the steep grade toward the crest of the bridge. Far below, the harbor and city flashed like white gold beneath sharp volleys of lightning. By the time he reached the downward slope of the span, he had slowed to an awkward trot, pulling in the moist, exhaust-filled air with desperate gulps. A stitch of pain became a knife, cutting into the side of his chest. Every stride seemed the last he could take, every breath a hand twisting the blade. Still he ran, down the narrow exit ramp and over the McArdle Bridge across the Chelsea River.

Finally, as he stumbled onto Meridian Street on the East Boston side, he had to stop. Propped against a telephone pole, he gasped for breath, begging the pain in his side to abate. The parking lot was just a few hundred yards away. If Laura and Subarsky were there, he had to be ready. Gradually, the stiff ache in his chest subsided. His breathing grew steadier. He pushed himself away from the pole and walked quickly along the dark side of the street. Cars and trucks sped past, showering him with street water.

As he neared the lot he began casting about for something he could use as a weapon. Subarsky was inches taller than he was, and perhaps seventy-five pounds heavier. Eric's main advantage in any match with the man would be surprise—that and the mounting rage he was feeling for all he and Laura and so many others had been put through. The best his brief search could produce was an empty whiskey bottle. Still, it was something.

The lot was just ahead. It was cut into a tree- and brush-covered slope that paralleled the roadway, and was dimly lit only by a streetlamp diagonally across the road near the dock area. Eric crouched low and made his way to the edge of the trees. Through the persistent, driving rain, he could make out the two decaying trailer hulks, propped up on railroad ties at the far side of the lot. Otherwise, the place appeared deserted.

Cursing the situation, and trying to sort out what his next move should be, Eric slogged through the muddy puddles to the trailers. One had only a faded shield and the letters D & E painted on the side. The other, at least at one time, had been the property of the Aphrodite Moving and Storage Company. Both the trailers were rusted well beyond any practical use other than storage, perhaps.

The rear doors were gone from the D & E trailer, and its wooden floorboards were splintered and decaying. Even from several feet away and through the rain, Eric could smell the odor of stale urine coming from inside. The Aphrodite trailer, which was intact and in much better shape, was secured with a bulky padlock. Eric hefted the surprisingly heavy hardware in his hand as he weighed the possibility that he was in the wrong place against the likelihood that he had somehow beaten Laura and Subarsky to the spot. There was, of course, a third option— that the two of them had already been and gone, but he refused to allow himself to consider that.

He checked beneath the trailer, searching for some sort of

trapdoor, and was walking around to the front end when twin spears of headlight swung into the lot and stopped not twenty feet behind the trailer. Eric flattened himself against the side and inched along to his right until he was concealed from view. Even through the gloom he could discern the distinctive silhouette of a Saab 900 Turbo—Subarsky's car.

Eric had been in the Saab, a year-old convertible, any number of times. Why had he never even wondered what a man constantly scrambling for research grants was doing with such elegant transportation?

He slipped around the railroad tie supports and ducked under the trailer. From that vantage, on his knees and elbows in the mud, he could make out only the lower half of the Saab. He wondered if Laura was inside. Five minutes passed with no movement from the car, and no sound other than the steady rumble of rain on the metal roof. Eric began to shiver from the inactivity. He grasped the neck of the whiskey bottle and was trying to formulate some sort of plan when the car door opened and closed. A man in a knee-length poncho stepped out into the downpour and approached the trailer. From his walk and the size of his boots, Eric could tell it was Dave.

Eric edged to his left, and was nearly out from beneath the trailer when he was transfixed by the beam of a powerful flashlight.

"Hey, amigo," Subarsky called out down the full length of the trailer, "how nice of you to be here to welcome us."

Eric shielded his eyes against the glare.

"Is Laura with you?" he shouted back.

"She is, yes. But when I caught sight of you scampering around as we pulled in, I decided that perhaps I might do well to truss her up a bit. I assume you know by now that you weren't really supposed to be in any condition to get here."

"Wheeler's dead."

"So your beautiful friend here told me. Nice going, buddy. Damn fine work. I told him outthinking you wasn't going to be that easy, but he's always been an arrogant son of a bitch. He was arrogant when he busted me for dealing at MIT. And then he was arrogant enough to suggest he become my business partner. I'll bet dollars to doughnuts he died arrogant too."

"Give it up, Dave," Eric said.

"Now that I don't even have to split the profits with super-cop? You can't be serious. I wish I could consider taking you on in his place. Caduceus and the Charity Project could still use a guy with your panache. But now I fear I just wouldn't ever be able to trust you."

"What's the Charity Project?"

The beam of light went off. In the seconds it took for Eric's eyes to adjust, it was shining on his face once again—this time from just a few feet away.

"It's the key to the kingdom, that's what," Subarsky said. "DS-Nineteen—the drug that time and the fops in Washington forgot."

"The DNA-bound antibiotic? I thought you gave up on that."

"Oh, no, my friend. The shortsighted powers-that-be did. I always knew they were wrong, so I just stepped back and retooled. Put me together a quality team with vision, and set about making DS-Nineteen a reality. Now then, why don't you just wriggle on out here and we'll find someplace a little drier to continue our basic science seminar?"

Without hesitating, Eric swung the bottle as hard as he could. The glass exploded against the flash, shattering its lens and bulb and sending it flying out of Subarsky's hand.

"Hey, nice move!" Subarsky cried. "But I thought you wanted to hear about my antibiotic."

Eric had already spun around and scrambled out from under the trailer on the other side. He splashed back to the Saab. Laura, her mouth sealed beneath a broad piece of adhesive tape, stared out at him helplessly. She was lashed by her wrists to the steering wheel, and a single piece of rope across her throat pinned her back against the headrest. Eric was trying to kick in the passenger window when Subarsky stepped up beside him.

"Please," he said, "don't do that. Don't do that. I have a five-hundred-dollar deductible that doesn't cover—"

Eric took a roundhouse swing at his face. Subarsky blocked it with his forearm, then calmly shoved Eric backward at least ten feet and down into the mud.

"I'm sorry this is happening, old friend," he said. "If I hadn't had to go back to my apartment to get these magic keys to use on that he-man lock over there, you would have missed us, and you wouldn't be nearly so muddy."

Eric pushed himself to his feet. Subarsky circled around and cut him off from the road, but Eric knew he needn't have bothered. As long as Laura Enders remained the man's prisoner, he was never going to run. One way or the other, it was going to end right here.

"Dave," he said, trying to stall until some idea, some flicker of an advantage came to him, "how can you hurt so many people just to develop a goddam drug?"

"Hey, watch your tongue, fella. Use any delaying tactic you want. I like that, and I'd expect nothing less from you. But don't stoop to calling DS-Nineteen names. We're talking about a living antibiotic here—an antibiotic that kills viruses and keeps killing them because it mutates as fast as they do."

"It didn't work. That's why no agency would fund its development."

"Didn't work in a test tube or a culture bottle," Subarsky corrected. "But tinker with it, tighten a nut here, a bolt there, and stick it into a living infected person, and whammo! The field is suddenly bloody with little teeny virus corpses, including—we are about to prove—the one that causes you-know-what. Impressed?"

Eric squinted across at him and, in spite of himself, realized that he *was* impressed. The government grant agencies had clearly underestimated the man's genius. Faced with possibly the most lethal epidemic the world has ever known, they had blithely cast off one of the few scientists equal to the challenge.

"So," Eric said, "the tetrodotoxin was your tool for diverting no-next-of-kin patients to your place in Utah. Get 'em pronounced dead, and then get 'em out of town."

"I wish it were that simple. I tried using that doggone toxin in every way, shape, and form I could, but in the end, only the *houngans* could do it right. Can you believe it? A Ph.D. in biochemistry from MIT, and I've had to import my stuff from a bunch of witch doctors."

"Enter Rebecca Darden."

"Ah, you know about my little island princess too. Eric, you are really quite a guy. If you know, I assume ol' Haven knows as well."

"Not yet, but I plan to tell him."

Subarsky laughed merrily at Eric's bravado.

"I wish you hadn't said that, pal, because now that makes you a *real* threat. You see, I don't think ol' Haven would approve of me."

"He wouldn't be in the minority."

"Oh, stop it! Be witty or be silent."

Eric glanced about for a board or rock, but saw nothing he could use. Behind Subarsky, traffic continued splashing along Meridian, but no one even slowed. A police cruiser was about the best he could hope for. He decided to continue stalling for as long as his adversary would allow.

"So Rebecca Darden uses the contacts her father helped her make in Haiti, and gets the powder for you."

Subarsky slapped a spray of water from his beard.

"She does that, yes," he said. "But mostly she uses her contacts to get cocaine for me and Lester to sell. Cocaine and some of the best poppy this side of Istanbul. How in the hell else was I going to finance my work? Lester and I tried doing it for a time with weapons, but as our operation's grown, we just haven't been able to generate enough business to meet our overhead. So we decided to diversify. We haven't abandoned the weapons business, but cocaine is much easier to handle than Uzi semiautomatics, know what I mean? Damn sight better markup, too."

"Jesus, David, you are sick. How did you make a thug like Wheeler understand something as complex as DS-Nineteen."

"Simple," Subarsky said. "I just told him that the real name of the drug was *Money*. Once it's perfected, we bargain for amnesty if we need to, and then name our price—as in eight zeros; maybe even nine. Ol' Lester understood that kind of science. Believe me he did.

"So we skim enough from our business endeavors to maintain life and limb, and keep sweet Rebecca in shoes, and then we throw the rest into the project. The way things are going out in Charity, another year, maybe two is all it's gonna take."

"I don't believe it."

"Frankly, Eric, I'm very ticked off at you, so I don't really give a damn what you believe. Things were going mighty smoothly until your friend in there showed up and turned your head. Now, with most of my teammates gone, we may have to consider a relocation—some new players, and even a new base hospital." He sighed theatrically. "Still, I have managed to salt enough away to take Rebecca on a sabbatical if I find I must."

"You are really sad, David."

"You're damn right I am," Subarsky shot back, his tone suddenly much harsher. "I'm sad because thanks to you, I may have to retool again. And I'm sad because I'm getting soaked and catching a chill standing here talking to an old pal from Watertown who doomed himself by being too goddam smart for his own good."

He reached his long arms up like an attacking grizzly, and took a step forward.

"Now," he said, "since the lovely Laura over there is absolutely positive that a certain video is locked in that trailer, and since the well-known chap buying poppy and blow from us on that tape is waiting to reward me handsomely for it, suppose you just let me—"

Head down, Eric charged the man, hurling himself through the rain at his chest, flailing with his fists at Subarsky's face. Subarsky stumbled backward. Eric lashed out again, connecting

solidly with his cheek. Then Subarsky reached out and effort-
lessly shoved him back to the ground.

"Happy now?" he said. "Is it out of your system?"

Eric looked up. He had hit the man with everything he had,
yet Subarsky was merely standing there, licking at a small tear
in his lower lip and smiling at him through his beard. Eric tried
another onslaught, but the advantage of surprise was gone.
Subarsky grabbed him by the front of his jacket and slammed
him against the trailer as if he were weightless. Eric's head
snapped against the metal door. His arms and legs instantly
went limp, and he dropped into a muddy puddle. Before he
could fight through the dizziness to react again, Subarsky was
on him. Kneeling on his back, he pulled Eric's arms behind him
and tied them with a short length of clothesline. Then he knelt
heavily on the back of Eric's thighs, and tied his ankles with
similar quickness and skill.

"All right, then," he said, making no effort to roll Eric over
or remove him from the puddle. "There being no further objections, I move we take out the magic key set and find the one
that fits this Bozo lock. Do I hear a second?"

"David, don't hurt us," Eric said, rolling onto his side. "It
won't help anything to hurt us."

"Says you," Subarsky mumbled, peering through the downpour as he sorted through a sophisticated-looking ring of keys
and oddly bent wires. "Why, just wrecking my flashlight the
way you did carries the goddam death penalty."

"David, please . . ."

"Now just shut up, little fella. Sit back in your puddle, enjoy
the last few moments of your earthbound existence, and watch
a master locksman at work. Believe it or not, these beauties were
made by one of the engineering students at MIT. He sold them
for a thousand bucks a set, and was ready to retire by the time
he graduated. There's nothing they can't open."

He selected one of the keys, examined it, and then gently
inserted it into the opening at the base of the padlock. Although
there was a brand name of some sort die-stamped onto the oddly
shaped padlock, it had become known around Plan B as the

Scottlock, out of deference to Scott Enders, who had designed it. The actual keyhole was well concealed beneath a small sliding panel at the *top* of the apparatus. The keyhole at the bottom was another piece of business altogether.

As Dave Subarsky worked the key he had selected in up to its hilt, the metal tip completed an electrical circuit between a tiny lithium battery and a wire-enclosed plastic capsule. In seconds the heat from the wire coil had melted the plastic, releasing a single large drop of concentrated hydrochloric acid.

Subarsky was dramatically humming a fragment of Bach's Concerto No. 2 in E, and gently jiggling the key, when the hydrochloric acid first touched the wad of chemically treated plastique explosive wadded into the base of the lock. He was bending over, peering at the keyhole, when the apparatus exploded.

Eric watched in stunned horror as, in an instant, both of Subarsky's hands and a good portion of his face were blown away. Bellowing insanely, pawing at the remains of his eyes, he stumbled backward. He was still on his feet after absorbing a blast powerful enough to have actually blown a large hole in the metal door.

Eric rolled over in time to see Subarsky, still shrieking incoherently, reel blindly past the Saab and onto Meridian Avenue. The driver of the oncoming sixteen-wheeler, high on cocaine he had bought from a dealer in Cambridge, never saw the figure lurch out of the shadows and onto the road; nor did he feel the impact when the reinforced steel grille-guard of the truck slammed into the man full force.

What remained of the genius biochemist's right arm became entangled in the metal grate as the semi roared on through the rain. The young driver, immersed in a Guns and Roses tape, sang along as he drove, unaware of the huge, grotesque ornament suspended just below the Mack bull dog on his hood.

Fighting the rain and a sudden profound exhaustion, Eric took nearly fifteen minutes to work free of his bonds. Then, using a rock, he smashed in the passenger window of the Saab. A minute later, he and Laura were inside the trailer. The video receiver was on a crate in the front left corner. It was enclosed in an oilskin sack, and its wire antenna had been brought out through a tiny hole drilled in the trailer wall.

"Here," Eric said, handing the tape over. "I think you should be the one to turn this in."

"That lock was the second time today that Scott's saved my life," Laura said.

They huddled together in the trailer as she told him about finding her brother, their subsequent capture and escape, and Scott's death. She had eluded Lester Wheeler and his men by swimming underwater from one pier to the next. Finally, nearly unconscious from the cold, she had stumbled up the bank and onto the roadway. An elderly woman and her husband, on their way home from the market, had picked her up and brought her to their home.

"I've got a bit of a story to tell you, too," Eric said, "but unless I get some dry clothes on soon, I may end up getting pneumonia and being taken to White Memorial Hospital. And we all know what happens to people who are brought there."

"Not any more it doesn't," Laura said. She jumped off the trailer and helped him to follow.

EPILOGUE

The ten-seat Learjet swooped down through the cloudless midmorning sky like a falcon, leveling off sharply at 2,000 feet. Inside the cabin, five passengers pressed their foreheads against the windows and peered through the glare across the stark San Rafael Desert, each one anxious to catch a first glimpse of Charity, Utah.

"We've sighted the town, Mr. Harten," the pilot said over the intercom. "About five miles ahead at ten o'clock. We've been cleared into Moab, so if it's okay with you, I'll make a couple of passes at this altitude and then head over to the airport."

Within three hours of receiving Laura's call at his home in Laurel, Virginia, the head of Communigistics International had the government-owned jet on the ground at Boston's Logan Airport. By 7:30 A.M. the Lear was airborne once again, streaking west. Sharing the cabin with Neil Harten were an associate of his from Plan B named Thorsen, plus Eric, Laura, and Maggie Nelson.

Twenty-five hundred miles away, they knew, Bernard Nelson lay unconscious, hooked to a ventilator in the intensive care unit of the hospital in Moab. And from what Eric had learned from his conversation with the attending physician, the detective's condition was not good.

Their odyssey had begun with an early-morning phone call to Maggie Nelson from a man named Smith in Moab. From what she could tell, her husband had succeeded in finding and penetrating the facility at Charity, Utah, only to be poisoned by the head of the operation there, a physician named Barber. Details of Nelson's subsequent rescue by a Charity employee named Pike were sketchy, but apparently Barber had been shot and wounded in the process, and another employee killed. Although he was conscious when the ambulance arrived at the town, during the ride to Moab, Bernard had slipped into a coma.

Maggie Nelson's first move had been to call Laura at Bernard's Boston apartment.

Now, the travelers stared down in awed silence at the fantastic scene below. The town, barely a smudge on the massive landscape, was surrounded by police cruisers and ambulances. Dozens of people were milling about along the single main street. Others lay on stretchers outside a low cinder-block building.

The pilot made two wide swings overhead, giving those on each side of the aircraft a good look. Then he banked to the east and shot across the rugged desert toward Moab. Seated next to Neil Harten at the rear of the plane, Eric briefed him on what he knew of the poison tetrodotoxin.

With the intervention of Haven Darden, the hospital administration had allowed Eric to search the offices of Dave Subarsky and Norma Cullinet. In a locked box in the nurse's desk, he found a number of ampules of intravenous adrenaline. He also retrieved two of what appeared to be baby-food jars, each about half-filled with a coarse grayish powder. One had a small stick-on label reading simply "T."; and the other, "D."

When confronted with the find, and a brief explanation of his daughter's role in the Charity Project, Haven Darden picked up the phone and asked Eric to wait in the corridor outside his hospital room. After just a few minutes, he called him back inside.

"My daughter says that the powder labeled 'T.' is what we suspected," he said. There was great sadness in his eyes, but also undisguised relief in his voice that Rebecca had agreed to cooperate. "The other is some sort of substance to reverse the effects of the toxin. Rebecca says that the dose of the antidote is between two and five grams, and that her cohorts had been dissolving it in saline and administering it intravenously. They also used large doses of adrenaline, but she has no idea of the amount. Most of the work was done in the monitoring room at the mortuary. Later this morning, she has agreed to go with my wife and our attorney to the police."

"I'm sorry you and your wife have to go through this, sir," Eric said.

Darden shrugged.

"Who knows how much of a child's behavior is the fault of the parents?" he said. "Perhaps in the long run some good will come of all this for her and for us."

The antidote dissolved readily in sterile saline. Working on his tray table in the plane, Eric used a small scale to measure out the dose Haven Darden had suggested, and then carefully drew it up into a large syringe.

"An IV injection of an unknown unsterile powder is not my idea of fun," he said, "but I can always treat any infection that results."

"What's your sense of the doc in Moab?" Harten asked.

"He seemed okay, but he wasn't too excited about administering the dose of adrenaline I've settled on."

Together, Eric and Darden had reviewed Reed Marshall's resuscitation efforts on Loretta Leone, and had determined that his aggressive approach and repeated use of the drug had almost certainly begun reversing her toxicity and increasing the speed and force of her cardiac contractions even while she was awaiting autopsy.

"Belts on, tray tables up, everyone," the pilot broadcast. "We're landing."

"Are you going back up front with Laura?" Harten asked.

Eric shook his head. Throughout the early portion of their flight, Harten had sat with her, candidly answering questions and sharing information about her brother's life of dangerous service. Over the hours that followed, Eric had seen the reality of Scott's death take hold.

"She needs a little time by herself," he said.

"Is she going to stay in Boston?"

"I hope so."

A soft squeak of the Lear's main gear signaled the perfect landing in Moab. A police cruiser and two cars raced out to bring the passengers to the hospital. Hand in hand with Laura and Maggie Nelson, Eric hurried up the walk and straight to the ICU.

The local internist had done a remarkable job of holding Bernard together. Although the detective was still unconscious, his blood pressure had begun responding to the massive adrenaline doses the man had given, and his kidneys had already started working.

Neil Harten and the others waited in the small family room as Eric huddled with the internist. While they were administering the tetrodotoxin antidote and another dose of adrenaline, a stretcher bearing another patient was wheeled into the ICU.

Eric moved to help evaluate the new arrival, and found himself staring down at the man who had once been his boss. Craig Worrell, drawn and filthy, stared blankly up at him with rheumy, jaundiced eyes.

"His temp's one-oh-four," the ambulance attendant offered.

"Looks like fulminant hepatitis," Eric said to the internist. "This man's a doctor from White Memorial in Boston. He was part of that Caduceus group I told you about—at least he was before he got into trouble at the hospital. I guess this is part of the Caduceus early-retirement plan."

"He looks bad."

"Maybe that DS-Nineteen wasn't working as well as Subarsky said it was. You want to work on him?" Eric asked.

"Not really, but I will."

"I'll stay with Nelson."

In just half an hour Bernard Nelson began to show signs of responding to the treatment. Harten and his associate headed off to investigate Charity firsthand, while Laura and Maggie Nelson took up a vigil at Bernard's bedside.

Two hours passed, during which several cardiac crises arose. Laura clutched Maggie's hand tightly as they watched Eric move from one side of the bed to the other, checking Bernard's physical condition, evaluating lab reports and the monitor pattern, and then calmly issuing instructions to the nurse. And she knew that regardless of what lay ahead for the two of them, she would never lose the admiration she was feeling for him at that moment.

Over the next hour, Bernard's condition seemed to stabilize. The need for Eric's intervention grew less frequent. Laura could see the deep lines of tension across his forehead begin to recede. Finally, four hours after their arrival, Bernard's eyes fluttered open. Minutes later, he reached up and pointed to the endotracheal tube, imploring Eric to remove it.

"Has he made it?" Maggie Nelson asked.

Eric took both her hands and helped her up. Then he hugged her.

"You married one tough guy, Mrs. Nelson," he said. "He's a real bear."

"I know," she said.

He stepped back while she bent over, spoke a few words to her husband, and gently kissed him on the cheek. Then he sent the two women out of the room and motioned the nurse in. Laura watched from a distance as Eric whispered in the detective's ear, then quickly pulled out the polyethylene breathing tube. Bernard sputtered and gagged as the nurse suctioned out his mouth and pharynx.

For a minute, there was total silence as Eric stood poised to replace the tube at the first sign of trouble. Then Bernard cleared his throat.

"Anyone got a cigar?" he croaked.

* * *

One by one, those Charity victims needing the most care were brought into Moab. The rest were transferred to other facilities. Eric worked through the night alongside the hospital staff, treating infections and other vestiges of malnutrition and neglect.

Shortly after dawn the next morning, he left Maggie Nelson with her husband and picked up Laura at the motel where she was staying. Together, they walked along the largely deserted streets of the town. To the south, the sunlight of a new day sparkled off the rich red clay of the hills.

"This place is so beautiful," she said. "And the hospital seems very good."

"For a place this size, it is," Eric said.

Laura locked her arm in his.

"Think you'd ever consider working here?" she asked.

"I think my lowest gear may still be about ten times higher than the highest one I'd ever need here."

"Well, maybe that's just what you need."

He held her close.

"Maybe. I'll tell you what: If we ever get tired of Boston and White Memorial, I'll think about it."

"Good. Because I understand real estate around Boston is through the roof, and here there's a whole town for sale, just a little ways down the road."

ABOUT THE AUTHOR

Michael Palmer, M.D., is the author of *The Sisterhood, Side Effects,* and *Flashback.* A graduate of Wesleyan University and Case Western Reserve University School of Medicine, he trained in internal medicine at Boston City Hospital and Massachusetts General Hospital. Dr. Palmer is currently on the emergency-room staff of Falmouth Hospital. He lives with his wife and three sons on Cape Cod.